10, May 2021

For George,
with gratitude!
Your friend in
th garden State

Cannic Hays

NAKED TRUTH

OR EQUALITY, THE FORBIDDEN FRUIT

A NOVEL

CARRIE HAYES

HTPH
PRESS
NEW YORK

For Olivia, you are my very best reader
And for Robert, you are my very best friend
With love and gratitude

DRAMATIS PERSONAE

Reuben Buckman Claflin m. Roxana Hummel Claflin
In addition to their two sons, Maldon and Hebern, Buck and Roxana had five daughters

Margaret b.1827 (Meg)	Mary b.1831 (Polly)	Victoria b.1838	Utica b.1841	Tennessee b.1845
m. Enos Miles div.	m. Ross Burns div.	m. Canning Woodhull div.	m. J. Kelley div.	m. Jack Bartels div.
m. William O'Halloran	m. Benjamin Sparr	m. Colonel James Harvey Blood div.	m. Thomas Brooker div.	

The approximate value of 1 US dollar in 1868 = $17 in 2019

DRAMATIS PERSONAE
continued

New York City
Jesse Grant, *father to Ulysses S. Grant*
Luther Challis, *railroad speculator, stockbroker*
Edmund Clarence Stedman, *poet, journalist, stockbroker*
Col. Jubilee James Fisk, *owner of the Erie Railroad and the Grand Opera House*
Anthony Comstock, *founder of the New York Society for the Suppression of Vice*
Dr. Paschal Beverly Randolph, *Rosicrucian, spiritualist trance medium*
Mrs. Elizabeth Cady Stanton, *suffragist*
Miss Susan B. Anthony, *suffragist*

The Vanderbilts
Commodore Cornelius Vanderbilt, *richest man in America*
William Henry Vanderbilt, *Cornelius's eldest son*
Frances (Frank) Crawford, a *Vanderbilt cousin*

Gentlemen of the Press
James Gordon Bennett Jr., *proprietor of the New York Herald*
James Gordon Bennett Sr., *Bennett's father and founder of the New York Herald*
Whitelaw Reid, editor of the *New-York Tribune*
Horace Greeley, founder of the *New-York Tribune*
Charles Dana, editor of the *New York Sun*
John Green, journalist, the *New York Sun*

The Beecher Family
Harriet Beecher Stowe, *revered author of* Uncle Tom's Cabin
Isabella Beecher Hooker, *the youngest sister*
Catharine Beecher, *educator and eldest sister*
Rev. Henry Ward Beecher, *celebrated pastor of Plymouth Church, Brooklyn*

Brooklyn
Theodore Tilton, *editor, poet, lecturer, member of Plymouth Church*
Henry Bowen, *board member of Plymouth Church*

Woodhull & Claflin's Weekly
Stephen Pearl Andrews, George Blood, Annie Swindell, Dr. Joseph Treat

NAKED TRUTH

OR EQUALITY, THE FORBIDDEN FRUIT

"People in earnest have no time to waste
in patching fig leaves for the naked truth."

-James Russell Lowell

PART ONE

THE BEGINNING OF THE BATTLE

"Mediums! I know that this thought has come to all of you, at some time. It came to me and remained with me until I was brought back to God and gave up the sin of mediumship. It is no wonder, when one considers the character of their occupation, that mediums have trouble, and are among the most unhappy people on earth."

-from *Mediums Unmasked* by Julia E. Garrett

SHOW BUSINESS

From the *Ottawa Free Trader*, April 1864:

MISS TENNESSEE CLAFLIN,
The Great Magnetic Doctress and Clairvoyant Physician,

who has so astonished the people by her wonderful cures and mysterious revelations during her travels in the United States, examining the sick and afflicted, curing them with unparalleled success, and through her magnetic influence and wonderful operations, has caused invalids to walk in a very short time who had not done so for many years. This lady seems to be endowed with the healing art, and supernatural gifts to such a remarkable degree, that she convinces the most skeptical of her wonderful powers and gives information of much importance that people from every walk of life come to consult her. Her skill and powers of mind are so great, there seems to be no disease but will give way to her treatment.

This lady is a physician, indeed. Cancers killed and extracted in from 4 to 24 hours, without pain or the use of instruments. She has established her Infirmary at the Fox River House, in Ottawa, Illinois, where she may be consulted upon all matters pertaining to Life, Health, and Diseases of the Human System.

All who wish to test her skill and powers of mind, should call immediately.

CONSULTATIONS $1.00

May 1868
The Improved Movement Cure Institute
67 West Thirty-Eighth Street

THE DOOR IS ajar, enough to lean forward and peer out. "My God!" Tennessee mutters. She was careful to arrive unseen by all and sundry and has been confined to the water closet a good thirty minutes. She opens her bag next to the commode. "Must I live this life always?"

If she leans toward the left, she can spy her sister closing the drapes while someone else lights candles on a large round table. Tennessee fumbles out of her jacket and unbuttons her skirt. She leans toward the right, and her skirt falls to the ground. She pushes it aside with her foot, then steps out of her boots. She hasn't bothered with undergarments. All she wears is a thin chain round her neck with a pick for the lock she practiced on earlier.

"After tonight," she promises herself, "you'll be your own mistress."

Stock brokerage, Tennessee decides. She unpins her hair. Investment, that's what she'll do. After all, this is New York City. Enough with the séance shenanigans.

She slips on a gossamer sheath and runs her fingers over the fabric. It's transparent, save for the illuminated paint they'd used earlier. Just a bit, here and there, to enhance its otherworldliness. She hears the participants enter, taking their seats around the table. They introduce themselves using their given names only. Tennessee puts a black cloak over her shoulders and angles herself to study the Spirit Box on the far side of the room. The box is tall as a man and made of quartersawn oak.

Earlier, when Victoria confirmed the appointment, Tennessee had protested that they hadn't performed the Spirit Box in ages.

But Victoria had smiled, "It will be fresh then, won't it?" which tickled Tennessee's funny bone. Fresh for crazy, unrehearsed and dangerous. Like it was when they were girls, scrambling, conniving, and doing their damnedest to make it work out.

Then Victoria had added, "Afterall, Tennie, it's not as though you're a blushing virgin."

Which is true enough.

The candles are placed in front of each participant. Tennessee watches Victoria sit down next to a familiar looking woman.

"I thought your sister was in attendance?" the woman whose name is Harriet whispers to Victoria.

"She will join us later, at the reception," Victoria answers, then says to the others, "May I request that we begin with one of my favorites, *Jesus, Lover of My Soul?* I am Mrs. Woodhull. I mean, Victoria," and extends her arms as everyone at the table joins hands. There is a moment's stillness.

"Oh, Lord," Victoria says, looking heavenward. "It is my prayer that Your love may abound, so our hearts are pure and blameless for the day of Christ. Filled with the fruit of righteousness, to the glory and praise of God. Amen."

The participants answer, "Amen."

Victoria gently releases the hands on either side of her and instructs, "After I am secured within the Spirit Box, please, blow out your candles and begin to sing."

A man walks her to the cabinet. He binds her wrists with a silken cord, then closes the door and locks her in. The key safely inside his waistcoat, he returns to his seat.

Everyone there is a devoted believer, each with a passionate reason for attending. They rejoin their hands, their elbows suspended in the air above the table. Harriet blows out her candle and the others follow suit. The darkness is absolute. Someone begins, then everyone joins in.

Jesus, lover of my soul,
Let me to Thy bosom fly,
While the nearer waters roll
While the tempest still is high!

As soon as she can hear Victoria singing from inside the cabinet, Tennessee pads into the room, unnoticed by the participants in the dark. She takes the pick and runs her fingers down the door of the Spirit Box. She finds the lock and opens the door.

Being double-jointed, Victoria has slipped off the cord. The sisters approach the participants on either side of the table. Tennessee stands behind Harriet.

Wilt Thou not regard my call?
Wilt Thou not accept my prayer?

"Mother," Tennessee whispers. "Oh, mother."

Lo! I sink, I faint, I fall—
Lo! On Thee I cast my care:
Reach me out Thy gracious hand!

She touches Harriet's face, almost imperceptibly. "I am blessed in the arms of the Lord and watch over you and my brothers and sisters." Tennessee's kiss is soft on the back of Harriet's neck. "Every moment, Mother."

Harriet sighs, and Tennessee knows the woman's heart is filled with longing.

While I of Thy strength receive,
Hoping against hope I stand

Whispering, touching, the act goes on while everyone continues to sing. Tennessee crosses the room and lets the cloak fall from her shoulders. She lights a stick of flint with her thumbnail and holds it overhead, watching the participants, naked underneath her gossamer shroud. Should anyone open their eyes, they'll be riveted by her tantalizing specter, while Victoria, unseen, sneaks back into the Spirit Box. That done, Tennessee extinguishes the flame and quickly pulls the cloak over herself.

Obscured in the darkness, she re-locks the Spirit Box, and seemingly vanishes into thin air.

The hymn is finished. Everyone is still. Through the crack in the door, Tennessee begins to sing an old, old, version of *Haec Dies*. She starts quietly, increasing the volume as she hears Victoria's harmony through the Spirit Box.

Haec dies quam fecit Dominus! This is the day the Lord Hath made!
Exultemus et laetemur in ea, alleluia! Let us be glad and rejoice therein, Hallelujah!

They sing it three times. Music is the gift and the Lord is the light. What the sisters do with the rest of it is how they feed the family.

———

Afterward, everyone gathers in the parlor. Tennessee is fully dressed, the pick safely put away. "I don't believe we have had the pleasure," the host, Dr. Taylor, presents himself.

"I am Mrs. Woodhull's sister, Tennie C. Claflin, at your service."

"How do you find our humble clinic, Miss Claflin?"

"Indeed!" Tennessee exclaims. "I am fascinated by your invention of the water chair."

"Ah yes, the water chair is a most efficacious remedy for Hysteria." He smiles with pride.

"Its movement provides a continuous tide, releasing those afflicted by life's travails, to crisis. Its success has been," he offers Tennessee a cup of tea, "without limitation."

Tennessee notices the elegant Harriet whom she had called Mother. Harriet has pale grey eyes, like her own. Who is she?

"Praise the Lord," Harriet says. "I have been with my cherished husband more than thirty years and Hysteria has been my cross to bear for just as long now. On advice from our family surgeon, we have invited him to operate on our daughter and to surgically remove the physical source of her Hysteria altogether."

The tea scalds the back of Tennessee's throat when she realizes who Harriet is. She struggles not to sputter.

Harriet adds, "Consequently, she now has dimples above and below."

"But how," Victoria exclaims, "can she then conceive a child in wholeness?"

"Is this lapsang souchong?" Tennessee asks, wondering how Victoria has failed to recognize Mrs. Stowe. "Vicky, it's delicious."

"Is it not in the Bible," Victoria ignores her, "or certainly, praise the Lord, in the Spirits, that both partners must enjoy ecstatic release for a child to be blessed by God?"

There is an uncomfortable silence. No one dares to respond. Finally, Harriet Beecher Stowe replies, "To imply there is a connection between a woman doing *that* and the wholeness of any resulting children is barbaric and disgusting. No Christian woman exposes her husband to such a repugnant loss of self-control." She turns to Dr. Taylor. "I shall take my nourishment in my room. Good night."

"Good night, Mrs. Stowe."

The evening is crisp, the smell of fires in the grate mingle with new leaves and fragrant blossoms as the hansom cab makes its way toward Greenwich Village.

"*Uncle Tom's Cabin*," Tennessee chuckles. "We always loved that book. Fancy that!"

"It's not funny, Tennie," Victoria groans. "Harriet Beecher Stowe is a public figure. I'll have to make amends somehow."

"*Uncle Tom's Cabin*!" Tennessee laughs. "We can call it *Uncle Tom's Crisis* now."

June 1868
The Manhattan Club
96 Fifth Avenue

As Reuben Buckman Claflin begins to nod off, he is overcome with a rush of joy known only to fathers. It is not through his own efforts, but rather those of his daughters that he is able to sit dozing amongst civilized men in a rarified corner. New York City is indeed a land of marvels.

Buck wakes with a start. Looking around, he recognizes an old acquaintance. Why, it's Jesse Grant! Father of the general everyone knows will soon become president. Jesse is with a younger man and greets Buck with much enthusiasm. They order some cognac and discuss the passage of time, and how extraordinary the years have proven to be.

"Tell me about those girls of yours," Jesse says, then chuckles reciting, "Three sisters fair, of worth and weight, a queen, a city and a state," a verse he'd made up years ago for Buck's three youngest children.

A treasured memory of a trick dances in Buck's mind. It always sent shivers of delight down his daughters' backs. "Give it here, give it here," he'd say, handing them a smooth golden-colored stone, no bigger than a penny. Buck would then open his mouth, and they'd place it on his tongue. Pretending to swallow it, he'd show he had nothing up his sleeves, nothing in his mouth, nothing in his hands. He'd tell the girls—Victoria, Utica, and Tennessee, the three from Jesse's verse—"Clap two times!" and Buck would gasp, pulling the stone from behind the ear of the girl sitting nearest him. It was marvelous. Every single time.

Buck smiles. He says nothing of the years since the War. No one wants to hear about failed marriages, intemperance, lies, or disappointment. The old men order more cognac.

Buck says, "Victoria has an uncanny gift. No rapping or tapping, like those Fox sisters. None of that. She just goes into a trance, and her insights are extraordinary. Our youngest, Tennessee, she performs a magnetic healing that awakens the youth and raises the vigor of a man, such as yourself, to one's, shall we say, former vitality."

"I daresay, one is never too young to awaken one's vigor," Jesse's companion observes. Buck raises his eyebrows, nodding in agreement.

"Claflin," Jesse Grant says, "this is my good friend, Luther Challis."

"Challis," Buck says, "what is it you do?"

"Stocks, mostly. I'm an investor." Challis smiles. His teeth are spread widely within his mouth, the space between them suggesting he's a few teeth short. But he is impeccably dressed. If Buck should lean forward, he'd see his own reflection in the shine of the younger man's boots.

"My youngest, Tennessee," Buck says. "She's most taken with learning investment."

"That's unusual," Challis says. He imagines someone restoring his vitality even as she studies the stock market, "for a woman."

Buck nods and agrees, "I think you'd find her very unusual, indeed."

From the *Lycoming Chronicle,* Williamsport, PA 1858

A CURIOUS FACT – We are informed that Miss T. Claflin is astonishing the citizens by her extraordinary clairvoyant powers. She is visited daily by many who are anxious to convince themselves of her apparent supernatural powers. She gives any information requested and answers all questions with singular accuracy.

To test her supernatural claim many have asked her the question, "how much money have I in my pocket," and received in all cases correct answers to the astonishment of all present. Gives the age of the questioner, or of his relations, with the number of brothers and sisters, with their residence, names, etc. Can tell the contents of pockets or carpet bags with astonishing accuracy.

July 1868
17 Great Jones Street

No one else is in the reception room. "Tennie! Was machst du da?" Her mother, Roxana, gasps and tries to grab the portfolio from Tennessee's arms. Inside it are clippings from before the War. In Ohio, then in Indiana, Pennsylvania, and Illinois, Roxana and Buck Claflin ran the show. Sometimes in a hotel, sometimes out of a tent. All their daughters performed, but Tennessee was their youngest child, and from the age of eight she was the main attraction.

Mother and daughter struggle by the stove, the top of which is open, waiting to receive more of the crumpled clippings.

"Stop it, stop it!" Roxana cries. "Why do you do this?"

"It's ancient history, Ma." Tennessee is trembling, the portfolio clutched against her chest. "Those days are over. Even Vicky says it's best forgotten. And, the Colonel—"

"The Colonel—" Roxana nearly spits at the mention of Victoria's husband, Colonel Blood.

"The Colonel says it's my chance to make a clean start of it."

"Why? Why should you do that?"

Tennessee cannot believe Roxana is so delusional as to ask such a thing. There can be no defense let alone explanation for what happened at the Fox River House.

"That woman had been dying from the cancer regardless of the ministrations you gave!" Buck had shouted at Tennessee. "How could we have known her family would lodge a complaint?"

Or that there'd be an arrest warrant for manslaughter? Manslaughter. The part of Tennessee's skin which has been threatening to flare, shoots fire down the inside of her arm. To answer will only summon the anguish from those years, those days. But this is not her mother's fault. Loving and resenting her together is too complicated.

"Vicky and Colonel Blood rescued me when they took me away from that kind of life." It is impossible for Tennessee to keep the sob from her voice, "They are the best friends I have ever had—"

To which Roxana wails, "Herr besuchte uns!" and runs upstairs, weeping.

In front of the house at Great Jones Street is a small patch of lawn surrounded by a wrought iron fence with a gate which prevents stray pigs wandering in off Lafayette Street from sullying the stoop. Everyone agrees, the arrangement is splendid. The house is large enough for the four sisters' parents, three husbands, and assorted children. The fifth sister, Meg, who is Roxana and Buck Claflin's eldest daughter, lives uptown with her own family.

That evening, Buck makes the introductions. "Mr. Challis has been a railroad man and now operates on Wall Street. Speculation in gold, isn't it?"

Tennessee thinks her father's friend bows too deeply to be anything other than mocking. As he straightens up, she recognizes the look he gives her. It doesn't take much to smell a rat. Tennessee crosses her arms, waiting.

Challis says, "Miss Claflin, do you find my bow impertinent?"

Colonel Blood has coached Tennessee on her use of English, so she's ready with the comeback, her smile demure. "Indeed, I find it nothing less than obsequious."

It surprises her when Luther Challis roars with laughter.

He becomes a frequent guest at Great Jones Street. Like Colonel Blood, he served under General Grant, and they exchange stories while Challis admires Tennessee, his eyes watchful, eager to assist in her mastery of finance.

Challis takes a pair of greenbacks from his billet-fold. "What do you see in my hand?"

"A pair of dollars, of course."

"But are they? They're just paper indicating that they're dollars." He takes out a coin. "If I hold up this, what do I have?"

"It's a silver dollar."

"So, which one is more valuable?"

She points to the coin. "This one, of course."

"Buy gold, Tennie. Buy as much as you can."

"But what about the greenbacks?"

"They're only paper. Lines of credit."

Challis treats Roxana with deference and insists on carrying the cake plates into the kitchen with Tennessee, leaning next to her when they put the dishes down. Challis stands waiting, as though he had asked if there were any more cake to be had.

"I shan't consider you romantically," Tennessee warns.

He smiles. "Is that because of your disposition, or is it something other?"

Three years before, there'd been a husband who held up his hands, covered with sores. "One night with Venus, a lifetime with mercury, is the saying, ain't it?" Since that day, she can only assume that what has plagued her is indeed the French disease. Scars of Venus, courtesy of a devil who gave her the scaling which crawls across her hips, down her inner thigh with an itch, something fierce. This evening finds Tennessee's legs and belly covered in her mother's lungwort liniment, then wrapped in muslin strips to mitigate her symptoms.

Tennessee answers, "Do you not have a wife in Kansas?"

Challis takes the last macaroon from the dessert dish. He throws it into the air, catching it with his mouth like a seal. He chews and swallows, then leans toward her, his face only inches from her own. "Miss Claflin, I fail to see the import of this question."

He places a mighty slap on her rump and leaves to join the others. She hears him say something which makes Roxana laugh. The hand on her person aside, Tennessee is forced to admit that Luther Challis is easy to be around.

Victoria's son, Byron, is almost thirteen, but he more closely resembles a boy half his age. "Come here, darling, give Mama a squeeze." When he puts his arms around her, there's the pang of never knowing. Was it from being dropped, or his father just a drunkard that destroyed this child's intellect?

She pulls away to study him and sweeps the hair from his eyes. "You're such a big boy, Byron. Go with Zula and the Colonel. Go on now."

Buck waits for his grandson to leave the room; he wants Victoria's full attention. But she is deep in thought, arranging herself on the divan.

"About the show," Buck says.

She isn't quite ready, vexed that she is still consumed with Zula and Byron's father. Oh, the countless sorrows from having lived with an addict. She gives herself a little shake. Why does her ancient heartache continue to plague her so? She and Buck need this moment alone.

This room they call the library is in the front of the house. She can look out the tall windows and watch her beloved new husband, Colonel Blood, take the children outside. The sky is somewhat overcast, but he'll bring them in if it begins to rain. Buck is speaking and Victoria's mind has wandered off.

Mistakes, errors. Dr. Canning Woodhull and what happened to dearest Byron. Victoria has always claimed her parents forced her into marriage, but even she admits that's just a ruse. She had been fourteen and burning with desire, anxious to lose her embarrassing crazy parents. To get away from her father and her Uncle Thankful and his family. At times there'd been as many as two dozen children under one roof. Besides, Canning was handsome and appeared to have resources. One of those missteps when one marries for love. She sighs and turns her attention back to her father.

"You know Tennie's war chest is considerable."

"Yes," she answers.

13

"My way of thinking is, if we continue with the healing and the clairvoyance, you'll earn enough that you and Blood can pay me back."

"Pay you back? But that money is Tennessee's."

"Oh, Vicky. It's Tennessee's in name only. Who do you think worked as her agent, and booked her the jobs? Who organized the provision for this family? Tennie may have the talent and she may have the gift, but it took her father's love and expertise to supervise this endeavor."

"How can you dare to claim such a thing, Pa?"

"It took every last ounce of my strength and my ingenuity as the Cancer King to ensure the 'The Magnificent Child' was successful."

"And the arrest warrant? How successful was that?"

"That's not fair. That woman would have died regardless of Tennie's ministrations. How was I to know they'd lodge a complaint?"

They are at an impasse. Victoria says, "Tennie is done with the show, Pa."

"Hmm."

They sit in silence.

"One good client," he says. "You only need one."

"Well, it isn't going to be Harriet Beecher Stowe."

"Ah well," he says. "She is only the most revered and well-loved woman in America!" and then laughs heartily. Eventually, shaking her head, Victoria laughs, too.

After a few moments, Buck says, "A man would probably be better. Then Tennie can put the full force of her gifts, as it were, to use. We just need one good client. When she's got him, you can take care of the rest."

"How would I do that?"

"With the spirits of course. Once a believer, always a believer."

Victoria leans back on the divan. Why not? Tennessee is twenty-four years old and knows her way around. She's been a married woman! One does what one must. Buck is right. With one good client, they won't need to do the show. They won't need to do it at all.

"**NOTE.**—All clairvoyants must use great caution in matters of sex. Abstinence is good, totally so, is better, for an error in that direction is fatal to clear vision, or its perpetuity when possessed."

-from *The Guide to Clairvoyance,*
by PB Randolph

MUTUAL AFFINITIES

"The mediums who practice this branch of the 'profession" are the lowest and vilest of all...I will here confine my remarks to the men who practice this business. The women 'healers' are not fit to be mentioned even in an *expose* of Spiritualism...He usually assumes the trance, and then commands his subject to undress entirely, as 'magnetism' will do no good unless he applies it to the naked body."

-from *Mediums Unmasked*
by Julia E. Garrett

October 1868
10 Washington Square

THE AFTERNOON IS unseasonably mild. Tennessee follows the Commodore's secretary up a flight of marble stairs into a room sparkling with sunlight. She is forced to squint and shades her eyes with her hand. The Commodore is sitting in a winged chair. He nods at his secretary, who withdraws, discreetly closing the doors. On the walls are countless depictions of ships, every shape and every size, paintings of horses, photographs of locomotive engines and portraits of children. The Commodore watches her take in the surroundings.

Her hat is tilted low on her forehead. Once her eyes have adjusted, she returns his gaze. "What ails you, sir?" Her voice is soft; she remains in the center of the room.

"This region, on my right side." He gestures, not moving from his seat.

"Please stand, Commodore, and I will attend to your pain." She walks toward him. "First, I must ask that you remove your jacket and your shirt, sir. Please allow me to help you."

Vanderbilt stands and towers over her. He removes his garments while she touches the impossible softness of his perfect frock coat and his impeccable white shirt. She chooses a small armless chair and gestures for him to sit down. She looks at the Commodore's hands resting on his knees. Grief and loneliness pour off him in waves.

"He is so very well connected," Victoria had insisted. "Why do you hesitate? With his money and influence, imagine what I might accomplish."

Tennessee did not answer, "You mean like in Cincinnati?" where they'd been run out of town, accused of the most outrageous behavior. Not that Tennessee wasn't guilty, but still...

Tennessee kneels in front of his chair. "Commodore. Watch my hand, sir." She moves her fingers, offering a benediction inches away from the old man's face, and he visibly relaxes.

The Commodore smells of tobacco and sandalwood and cloves. And something else she didn't anticipate. He smells of kindness. She gently waves at him. He is indeed, in a trance, a somewhat hypnotic state.

Silently, Tennessee removes her hat and jacket, inhaling the scent of him again. It's anybody's guess how long she has until she's covered in lesions or until she goes mad.

When she'd made enquiries, people were quick to say terrible things. That he'd placed his late wife in a lunatic asylum whenever she displeased him. That he had scorned his children and molested the servants.

She unbuttons her skirt then her petticoats. They collapse in a heap of taffeta and wool. She kicks them to the side and steps behind the motionless Commodore. To begin the healing gestures, Tennessee taps his back with her hands. She blows away his bad energy then places her hands on his forehead, gently pulling his head back onto her naked chest, her fingers stroking away tension on his shoulders and his neck. She knows he'll be kind.

Naked, save for her stockings and boots, she wanders to the other side of the room. She examines the paintings and photographs and studies a few of the statues purchased on the other side of the world. She removes the combs and snood from her hair, which falls to her waist, then returns to the Commodore, who remains profoundly still.

No one can argue there's any harm done in sharing a mutual affinity. Tennessee quickly counts to herself. It's been three years since a man has touched her in tenderness. It isn't as if she's compromising her virtue. With that charlatan Jack, there wasn't tenderness, either, only lust, on both their parts. She positions herself astride the Commodore. Her skin shows no sign of her illness. When he opens his eyes, he'll only see her body, alive and close enough to do anything, anything, that he chooses.

She whispers into his ear, "Commodore Vanderbilt, sir. When I tell you, please open your eyes, as slowly, sir, as you may. I am close to you and your discomfort has been removed. I come to you as a friend. When you look upon me, you may avail yourself of my person as you like." Tennessee moves closer to him than before, her hand on his shoulder. The wool of her stocking catches upon the fabric of his trousers.

"Commodore Vanderbilt. I am your friend." Her voice is soft. "I offer you everything I am, but you must tell no one what transpires in this room. Should you tell them, I will cease to perform your healing. Do you understand, sir?"

He mutters, "Yes, yes I do."

"Then please, as slowly as you may. Open your eyes, Commodore. The pain is gone. You may take what you will."

Cornelius Vanderbilt opens his eyes and is presented with her perfect fragrant bosom, her young body rocking astride his. His lips open, and she moves her hand from his shoulder toward his face. She gently enters him, sliding her thumb softly into his mouth. With her other hand, she touches herself until her back arches with desire. She reaches her hand inside his flies, checking for his response. When the Commodore shudders, life charges through his old veins and he roars as if a much younger man. He grabs her tiny waist, while she stays firm, and they move together. When she comes again, he knows he isn't dreaming, but that he is alive and that their coming together makes her so as well.

Everything is still, save for the clock in the corner of the room. Tennessee's blue eyes meet his, and he studies the strange girl, who only moments ago had stood before him with a promise to cure his pain.

She strokes his cheek with her graceful hand. "You must drink more water, Commodore, if you are to live as you should." Gently, she dismounts and begins to dress.

Vanderbilt seems profoundly overcome, at a loss for words. She twists her hair into its combs and snood. She puts on her hat and ties the ribbon.

"Do you feel better, sir? Was this helpful to you?" Tennessee tilts the hat forward and gives it a tug, so it rests at a rakish angle. "Would you like me to visit again?"

Tea and crumpets are on the table adjacent to the bed. Tennessee lies next to him, completely naked, her hair covering her to the small of her back. Vanderbilt is amazed. He is hard as a rock and they have yet to fuck.

"Commodore."

"Yes, my dear."

"I am going to heal you this afternoon, but alas, sir, I cannot put you in my mouth, nor sir, inside my body."

"What?"

"I am cursed, I am ashamed to say."

Everything alive and throbbing in Vanderbilt turns cold as before.

The truth is too cumbersome. "I was attacked. I may not take a lover sir, for fear of giving him my illness. I can still treat you, and you will be healed, Commodore. But I cannot put you inside me. I am so sorry and so ashamed." Once again, he is rendered speechless.

But then coming moments later, he wonders whether his soul had left his body and upon returning, brought the gift of joy back with it. He looks over at Tennessee, who meets his gaze with a blissful smile. She gives him a little squeeze and pats his leg as she climbs down from him, arranging her plump young self alongside his tired old frame to catch forty winks before she heads home.

———

From the journal of Tennie C. Claflin:

> *Every day, Cornelius and I share breakfast at his office. We read the papers together, discuss economics and affairs of state. I can't pretend I don't enjoy it. Usually by the time his business associates appear, we are so doubled up in laughter that they daren't know what to think! In the afternoons if the weather's fine, we go in the trap for an adventure. But yesterday was inclement, so we retired to Washington Square for healing and self-edification. I happened to sit down at his piano forte, and Cornelius asked me to play something. When I told him I had no learning in piano forte, he said, "Well, we must remedy that."*

———

Zula, who is eight years old, closes the curtains in the library.

"Do a good job. Make sure it's dark," Tennessee instructs her.

Curtains duly drawn, Zula sits at the round table and shivers with expectation. Utica, the sister closest in age to Tennessee, lights a candle and her singular beauty is illuminated by its glow. Tennessee hands Utica a white shawl. Utica drapes it over her head and shoulders then sits down at the table, a vague distant expression on her face, as if she were deep in thought.

"Have we started?" Zula asks Tennessee.

Looking at Utica, Tennessee says, "Yes I think so." She adds, "Utie will be the Marvelous Child and I will play the customer."

It seems only fair. Life for Utica hasn't turned out as they had all hoped.

"But you were the marvelous child!" Zula says.

Utica's second husband has been sent packing, and her acting career appears to be stalled. The list is endless.

"Do you want me to do it or not?" Utica asks them.

Tennessee puts another shawl over her own head. "It will be more fun if Utie does it. I haven't played it in years and Utie is an actress, after all." She sits down, in a bereft manner.

Utica lifts a hand. "Spirit!" she cries. "You are among friends. Beside us are my dead brothers and sisters—"

"Who died?" Zula whispered to Tennessee.

"Shh. I'll tell you later. It was long ago." Tennessee clears her throat and whispers to Utica, "Deliver my soul—"

"Oh, that's right. Deliver my soul, oh Lord, from lying lips and a deceitful tongue."

"Amen," Zula whispers.

Tennessee then says, "He wasn't but eighteen years old," and thumps under the table with her fist. Zula jumps in surprise at the thumping. A sudden banging on the door causes Tennessee and Utica to jump as well.

Their older sister, Polly looks in. "Tennie, there's a piano. It's compliments from Commodore Vanderbilt."

A pianoforte rests on the sidewalk. "Where do you want it?" asks the mover.

Later, two other men knock at the door. "I am a piano teacher," says one.

"I teach dancing," says the other. "Commodore Vanderbilt has ordered lessons for whomever in the household would seek instruction."

When her family gives her a look, Tennessee laughs. "Oh, the Commodore is most wonderous kind."

Brilliantly colored leaves float down to the pavement and the days are shorter with a chill in the air. Buck and Tennessee share a hansom cab. He muses how his once Marvelous Child now keeps her thoughts much to herself. He says, "Have you told the Commodore about Jack Barthels?"

"No, I'm not going to."

Buck folds his copy of *The Revolution*, which Victoria has shared with him. As a father of daughters, he finds it most edifying. "Heed Miss Anthony's words, Tennie."

"What are those?"

"She says, 'I do not consider divorce evil by any means. It is just as much a refuge for women married to brutal men as Canada was to the slaves of brutal masters.'"

The carriage stops. Tennessee watches pedestrians walk past them. She decides to remain silent.

———

Cornelius Vanderbilt collects her from Great Jones Street at dawn with his favorite trap for racing and his two fastest trotters. The morning sun peeps through Rose and crimson clouds as they arrive at a field in the upper-most part of Manhattan. The Commodore's valet and groom are waiting outside a solitary campaign tent on the edge of a bluff. Hot tea, sausages, and persimmon cakes are served, and the Commodore is brimming with excitement. "Stay inside, Sparrow. I will collect you when we are ready."

Tennessee obediently waits as instructed. Suddenly, she hears rumblings and shouting. It seems to go on endlessly until she can stand it no longer and steps outside.

A red balloon, as tall and as wide as the house at Great Jones Street, floats before her, its basket held down by three servants awaiting orders from a tall, ginger-haired man.

Cornelius calls out, "Ah, Tennie C., there you are. This is your surprise, my dear!" and he climbs into the basket, followed by the pilot.

The ginger haired-haired man bows. He looks to be the same age as Tennessee. "Mademoiselle?" He kneels on one knee, braces his gloved hands together, and lowers them for her to step on. She does so, and he hoists her up, murmuring, "Attention, et voila!" then smiles at her.

I know you, his smile says, which the spirit confirms is true.

She blushes and looks away.

Vanderbilt takes her by the waist and lowers her into the basket next to him. The ginger-haired man remains in the field, and whistles for the servants to release the ropes tethering the basket. He and Vanderbilt salute each other. The basket lurches, then begins its ascent.

Tennessee's heart is suddenly in her throat. She cries out in surprise, "Is this quite safe?"

Up and up again, as the Commodore shouts, "Not at all! Capital, capital!"

They catch the wind floating south over the Hudson River and across the cliffs of New Jersey. They pass over small villages and farmlands that sparkle with frost. Field hands wave, shouting at the balloon, and its passengers respond in kind.

Landing in Bayonne, the Commodore's sloop returns them across the water, and they sit on deck under fur blankets, marveling at possibilities for the future as the ship pulls alongside its slip in New York Harbor.

They go to the Commodore's offices. The building is empty, save for a night watchman. Hand in hand, they climb the stone stairs to Vanderbilt's suite. The sky outside is filled with color, much as it was earlier in the day.

Yet, the evening light creates shadows across the old man's face. "My eldest boy, Billy," the Commodore says. "I look forward to your meeting him. Then we shall all be a family. Billy will be like a brother to you, Sparrow." He takes her hand and kisses it. "But this mourning period for my late wife is such I fear it will be some time before we can venture out in company."

"Would you like to pray, Cornelius?"

They kneel, facing one another. "My darling girl." He takes her other hand and holds it to his cheek. "Ah, Tennie," he says. "I do love you. I truly do."

THE GRAND DOMESTIC REVOLUTION

November 1868

17 Great Jones Street

THE HANSOM CAB is Victoria's preferred form of transport. Inside, one is anonymous, at liberty to conduct business, the sound of the horses masking discussion from prying ears. Often, in the mornings, Blood hails a hansom cab and they squeeze inside, pulling dusty woolen blankets over their knees, which they press very close to one another, their gloved hands laced together, Victoria's head resting against the Colonel's shoulder.

Outside, the wet streets are mobbed with carriages and life. She peers out as they explore the city, from Union Square down Broadway to the harbor, over to Wall Street and the Stock Exchange while Blood waxes philosophical.

Sometimes Victoria asks him, "Why did you leave your perfectly decent life and marriage, Colonel?" She knows his answer but loves hearing it again.

"Because, my darling Vicky, upon meeting you I realized that to live with anything less than complete passion was to enslave myself to the hypocritical confines of the system."

"It is, isn't it?" she says tenderly.

"You know, I am convinced that since the War, everyone in the country also believes this, whether they realize so or no. It's simply a question of enlightening them."

At night, after the children have gone to bed, before the lamp is extinguished, they nestle in their embrace. "You are magical, Vicky," he says.

She is so happy and content with this man, it is all she can do to keep from purring. "When we met on that day in St. Louis—"

"You mean when you came for the session?"

"Yes."

"In those days, I thought love was over for me. But then, well, you know I was instantly overcome upon seeing you, Colonel."

"You said, 'Deliver my soul, O Lord, from lying lips and a deceitful tongue.' Do you remember?"

"Of course, I do." She moves closer to his warmth. "It's the prayer to keep a spiritualist pure of humbug." And as he kisses her on the neck, she is glad they have agreed upon what should happen next.

As if he has read her mind, Colonel Blood says, "You will enlighten the masses to emancipate themselves from the shackles of hypocrisy, my darling. That's what you will do. Here in New York, you shall take your place in history."

To Colonel Blood, Stephen Pearl Andrews is more than a genius. He is a visionary, with a singular, radical view. Andrews believes that women are men's equal in every respect.

At Great Jones Street one night, Blood says to Andrews, "There's something I'd like you to witness." Blood is eager to demonstrate that Victoria (she still calls herself Mrs. Woodhull) has a talent, a gift, really, which is very rare indeed.

He picks up a book, then changes his mind. "No, no. It would be better were you to select it."

Pearl Andrews (his friends call him Pearl) obliges and chooses a small volume. It is Emerson's *The Conduct of Life*. "This is a splendid tome. Did you enjoy it?"

Andrews begins to hand it to Colonel Blood, who shakes his head, insisting he continue to hold the book. "If you please, Pearl, choose any page that you will and show it to Mrs. Woodhull."

Andrews thumbs through the pages. Blood adds, "Choose something challenging. You do her a disservice should it be simple."

Andrews offers Victoria the book. "Here you are, my dear."

After a few moments, Victoria gives the book back to Pearl Andrews. She closes her eyes, then speaks in a clear fluid voice, as though every utterance is her own.

"We say love is blind, and the figure of Cupid is drawn with a bandage round his eyes. Blind: yes, because he does not see what he does not like; but the sharpest-sighted hunter in the universe is Love, for finding what he seeks, and only that; and the mythologists tell us that Vulcan was painted lame and Cupid blind, to call attention to the fact that one was all limbs, and the other all eyes. In the true mythology Love is an immortal child, and Beauty leads him as a guide: nor can we express a deeper sense than when we say…"

Victoria opens her eyes and smiles at Andrews. "Beauty is the pilot of the young soul."

The clock chimes the lateness of the hour. Andrews exchanges a look with his host. Through Mrs. Woodhull's flawless parroting, Colonel Blood has provided the vessel through which Stephen Pearl Andrews might share his philosophy. "Mrs. Woodhull," Andrews whispers. "How extraordinary! You are endowed with perfect recall."

The sergeant at the precinct looks up from his paperwork and studies Victoria, for just a moment. He says, "Your concern for your neighbor is commendable, Mrs. Woodhull. However—" He raises his hand before she can speak. "The lacerations Mrs. Lockner suffered are of no consequence. Mr. Lockner was inebriated and is therefore not responsible for the injury he caused his wife."

The sergeant waves her away with his hand. "There's nothing more to do at this time."

The position of the law is an outrage. She has to say something. Don't cry. Don't you dare let him see your tears, she scolds herself. Say something! "I take it then, Mr. Lockner must kill Mrs. Lockner, in sobriety no less, before you'll do anything about his abusing her?"

"Quite so. That is the law." The sergeant returns to his paperwork and does not look up. "Good day, Mrs. Woodhull."

They are expecting an early snow, and the pavements have been freshly salted. Around her, the merchants shutter their storefronts. Colonel Blood would never, never raise his hand against her, nor indeed any woman. When she'd been with Dr. Canning Woodhull, she either had to dodge his blows or scrape him off a doorstep. And every time, after sleeping it off, Dr. Woodhull swore he'd change.

For nearly a decade, she believed him because she loved him. Victoria blinks away the tears, grateful that the Colonel's superior being has healed her broken heart. With love such as his, everything is possible. But she does not understand why the Colonel has recently brought up the need for her blessing should he choose to bed another woman. Blood has assured her, it's a beautiful and natural extension of Free Love's philosophy, not a justification for promiscuity. When the desire makes itself known to them, as Blood says it inevitably will, they should express their love by blessing each other's union. Victoria's heart is pounding. Why has he even addressed this notion? There must be someone. She pushes the thought out of her mind.

In the garden behind 17 Great Jones Street, the children spin Byron around. He closes his eyes and pretends to count while the others run and scatter inside the house. When he opens his eyes, he makes his way toward the outhouse first, but there is a boot sticking out from behind the privy. Byron trots across the dormant vegetable bed and shakes the boot. It's attached to a foot and a leg, which then stretches, and out comes a filthy, sleepy man.

"Byron?"

Byron's eyes grow wide. How does this man know his name? Byron turns on his heel and runs up the stairs to his grandmother.

After a few moments, there is a soft knock on the kitchen door. Roxana asks, "Yes?"

"It's me. I have arrived from Missouri, Roxana. It's me. Canning Woodhull."

At dinner, Victoria will not be swayed. "He mayn't stay in this house with his intemperate degradation."

Blood looks over at her father, Buck, and Ben Sparr, the husband of Polly, one of Victoria's older sisters. Buck picks something out of his teeth and keeps his own council.

Finally, Blood says, "And to your children, Victoria?"

"What of them?"

"How will you say that their father was here, he came to you in rags, with nothing to eat and you sent him away? Is that what your Lord Jesus Christ and Heavenly Father would do?"

Victoria says, "I stopped believing in God some time ago."

Tennessee is grateful Roxana is in the kitchen and not present to hear this.

"Now, Vicky," Buck says softly.

Victoria announces to the table, "If there were a God, much of what happens would never come to pass. Look at Byron."

Buck says, "Come on, now, Vicky. You don't have to be so hard on people all the time."

Suddenly, the door flies open and Byron bursts into the room, a folded paper swan in the palm of his hand. "Mama, look." He holds up the origami, kisses the bird, and hands it to her.

It was in Cleveland, before the War. She had only met him one other time. *Dr. Claflin's Cancer Cure All* was prominently displayed on the side of Buck's wagon. He and Roxana had walked into town to sign a lease. Tennessee and Utica were tending to the laundry by the river. Being fourteen, Victoria had preferred to stay and guard the inventory while she read an old copy of *Uncle Tom's Cabin*. She was quite alone. It was summer, and his shadow cooled her from the hot afternoon's light.

"Well, Miss Victoria. We meet again." When she looked up, Canning crouched down to where she sat. The time before, when she'd first made Canning Woodhull's acquaintance, he'd rubbed her lips with fudge and kissed her on the mouth.

This time, outside the wagon, he reached into his pocket to offer her a little folded paper he held in the palm of his hand. "How do you find Cleveland?"

Victoria marveled at the offering. How beautiful. It was an elegant simple swan.

"I find it quite well, thank you. My parents are looking to settle here."

"And you? Would you like to settle here?" He offered her another one. It was a pretty paper flower.

She took the flower from his outstretched hand. She had never seen such tokens before. "That would depend."

"On what would it depend?"

"With whom I am settling."

"Ah. Well, a doctor needs a wife."

Then he had looked at her feet, which were shod in old, tattered shoes. "I should like to marry you, Victoria," he had said, and caressed her ankle. He put his hands on her knees and bowed his head on top of her legs, exhaling in such a way that she felt as though a sunbeam shone upon her. "Will you say yes?" he had asked.

When Tennessee and Utica returned from the river, Victoria stood next to Woodhull, ready to leave, her clothes rolled into a bundle by her side. "This is Dr. Canning Woodhull," she had said, and handed Tennessee the book by Mrs. Stowe.

Utica looked at them both rather doubtfully. "Where are you going?"

Canning had started to laugh. Each girl was lovelier than the next and here was he, choosing the ripest for the plucking.

He offered both girls their own paper flowers. "Well, we're going to get married of course."

Years later, Victoria still wonders whether she'd been trapped by enchantment.

———

Roxana gives Canning a thorough scouring then inspects him for lice. Morphine and alcohol have left few signs of the once handsome man, filled with ideas on magnetism and scientific innovation. Even after several weeks at Great Jones Street, he still seems woefully underfed. His hands tremble, spooning the broth-soaked bread into his toothless mouth.

Roxana leans toward him across the table, "But what is this Social Freedom Andrews is always harping on about?"

Canning swallows the last mouthful of broth. "Well, Mother," he answers, "Social Freedom rejects the State as it currently exists."

Upon entering the kitchen, Blood hears their voices. He stops short of the doorway, just out of sight. He didn't know that Canning called her Mother.

Canning delicately dabs at each corner of his lips and continues. "It also denies the legitimacy of the Church."

Roxana puts her hand on Canning's forearm. "Vicky said nothing of this to me."

"I can well imagine why. Those who practice Social Freedom, no doubt Colonel Blood and now Vicky, too, believe that marriage is a form of sexual slavery, endorsed by the Church."

"No!" Roxana is aghast.

Stifling a moan, Blood leans against the wall. He can almost hear Canning smile as he repays Blood's kindness with a little slander, just enough to make things difficult.

As the days pass, Blood can't bring himself to confront Canning. The man truly is an invalid. How will it look if Blood reveals that he's been eavesdropping?

"You gave them this Social Freedom idea. It's because of you," Roxana mutters, then scurries away, before Blood can protest that she is mistaken, that Victoria and Tennessee are capable of thinking for themselves.

It's because of the War, he wants to say, *of which he himself is a veteran*, that every thinking person is now concerned with individual liberty!

But no matter what efforts Blood makes to put things right, Roxana meets every one of his overtures with hostility.

Visiting with Pearl Andrews one evening after supper, Blood watches him admire Utica as she carries something through the room.

"Mrs. Woodhull's sisters are most unusually beautiful," Andrews observes.

"They are," Blood agrees.

"No doubt, you must take great pleasure in availing yourself of their amative attributes as well."

Blood thinks a moment before answering. "The Claflin sisters and I do not have that sort of arrangement." He refills Andrews's glass before pouring some more for himself.

"But, my dear fellow, you must take advantage of their feminine wiles. As sovereign of yourself you must exercise the freedom to move between willing and able partners. One might even say it's your obligation, as head of this household."

By which he means Utica, of course. Blood smiles and shakes his head. No harm is meant, and no offense taken.

PLACE THE SIN WHERE IT DESERVEDLY STANDS

"If the very fussy ladies of both sexes of the genus prude who have lately been hounding the unfortunates from public places of amusement - if these we say, wish to prove their sincerity in their work, let them practice prevention and avoid persecution. Let them cease harrying the immoral women who are irreclaimable, and whose vices are to a great degree the faults of society and of immoral men and let them strike at the root of our great social evil."

-from *Talks and Essays*,
by Tennessee Claflin Cook

December 1868
Greenwich Village

"I'M NOT WEARING the bonnet." Tennessee hands it back to Roxanna. "I can never see left or right." Being small, she prefers the top hat and wears it *à la française,* which lends her height. On the hat's rim she's woven flowers and a lavender-colored veil. "That bonnet makes me feel blinkered, like a horse."

"But the rain, Tennie," her mother frets.

Tennessee ventures forth with her mother's list. But Roxana was right. In the rain, the flowers wilt and the veil is a mess.

Tennessee emerges from the apothecary musing over her change and Roxana's list. Anemone seeds, cinnamon, mug wort, gladiolus pods, and donkey milk, which will be boiled together and blended into a creamy paste. Roxana insists this poultice, when rubbed across the chest, is an unparalleled preventative from any myriad of complaints.

The rain tapers off to a drizzle, and the streets are slick underfoot. Tennessee decides to count her change again. Standing at the curb, as she begins to look through her purchases, her hair falls loose. Struggling with her hair and the wet veil, she attempts to sweep its netting back but steps into a couple just behind her.

There is an awkward scuffle, and the lady cries out, "What is that?"

Tennessee spins around as the gentleman and lady recoil in distaste.

"What is that?" the lady says again. She looks Tennessee directly in the eye, then shrinks in disdain.

The man sizes up Tennessee. "One of Red-Light Lizzie's no doubt."

He has wide lambchop sideburns and his voice is distressingly familiar. Tennessee looks at him and wants to say something, but then she missteps and loses her balance, dropping her acquisitions and her fist full of coins.

She hears him say, "Home, Walter," and is aware of a footman opening a carriage door.

Struggling to get up off the pavement, she sees the gentleman follow the lady into the carriage.

"Yes, Mr. Vanderbilt," the footman says.

Roxana's precious ingredients have spilled open in a puddle. Worse still is the realization that the man was Billy, Cornelius's eldest son. Sighing, Tennessee picks up her coins. The street stinks of manure and urine.

From the journal of Tennie C. Claflin:

Cornelius is decided. He'll take me to John Aspinall Roosevelt's estate in the New Year. Mr. Roosevelt has challenged Cornelius to a race, between his ice yacht and Cornelius's private locomotive. He frets the odds are skewed, as Roosevelt's first mate set a record crossing the Atlantic a few years back, but I've assured him, the locomotive's technology will outpace any vessel, steered by mere human skill and wind. Cornelius liked that, I daresay. He is also decided that the Roosevelts' is the ideal place to become acquainted with his son, William, and William's wife, who've also been invited.

Cornelius said, "What could go wrong?"

What could go wrong, indeed.

January 1869
Hyde Park, New York

The Roosevelt sled meets them at the closest point of the tracks to the Rosedale estate. Hot bricks are placed at their feet, and they nestle under fur skins, arriving warm and pink at their destination.

Tennessee's modest room overlooks the river and her dressing room discreetly joins the Commodore's. After luncheon, the menfolk retire to the study and the ladies to the sunroom.

Mrs. Roosevelt plays Mother, pouring tea into delicate cups on saucers which her footman delivers to each guest while they buzz about the latest scandal at a neighboring estate.

"Of course, she blackmailed him. She may have been a servant, but she had his letters, dontchaknow…?"

Tennessee wonders if the phrase, 'dontchaknow' is the latest in society slang.

35

"When he attempted to eradicate the situation, the wretched girl died the next day—"

"Better that than the shame of yet another mewling bastard in the world!"

"My dear!"

"It's no mystery why she won't permit any Irish amongst the staff."

"And what about that gold-digging actress?"

"How grotesque, to have a child out of wedlock. The disgrace, it's perfectly mortifying. And so cruel for the young man's family."

"A word or letter shared by the wrong party and one's entire reputation destroyed."

"Slander, dontchaknow. That's all there is for it. He should sue that hussy for slander."

Mrs. Roosevelt nods sympathetically. "At least Mr. Howe is a most brilliant attorney." She pours another cup of tea and turns to Tennessee. "Tell me, Miss Claflin, what is your experience with the law?"

Everything stops. Does someone know about Ottawa? Or Chicago? The footman brings her cup and saucer.

Be calm, she warns herself. Make like it's a reading.

Tennessee smiles. "Indeed, I studied law at my father's knee as a child, his being a most respected attorney himself." She looks at each woman as though they are her closest friends. "In fact, prior to my arrival in New York, I spent the last six years thinking of little else." Which is true enough. She continues, "But any lady who commits herself to writing does so at enormous peril to her person, does she not? I believe that one is well advised to either say nothing or to burn the correspondence. Don't you agree?"

"Indeed, quite so," one of the women answers.

A footman whispers in Mrs. Roosevelt's ear. Tennessee wonders if the look her hostess gives her is out of curiosity or poorly concealed dislike. "Ladies," Mrs. Roosevelt says brightly. "Mr. and Mrs. William Vanderbilt are here."

Mrs. Vanderbilt does not convey a flicker of acknowledgment as she brushes past Tennessee to kiss the woman on her right. Admiring the way she cuts her father-in-law's consort, the other ladies follow suit. Within moments they, too snub Tennessee.

Following luncheon on the second day, she excuses herself and happily ventures outside instead.

Snow swirls and dances around her, everything shining in its white glow. Walking south, she comes upon a lonely orchard, the trees wrapped in burlap until the spring. A solitary figure moves slowly toward her, shouldering a backpack, his progress assisted by snowshoes. They are completely alone, so Tennessee meets him halfway.

He peers at her out from under his fur cap, his beard caked with snow. He shouts to be heard above the wind. "Hello! Aren't you lost?"

"No, are you?"

The man leans on his walking stick and catches his breath, realizing it's unnecessary to shout. "No, no. I'm here in a professional capacity."

"To race?"

"No, I'm here for the *Tribune*. To cover the race."

"You're a journalist."

"Yes. Are you?"

"No! I'm…I'm…" The Commodore would be livid were she indiscreet—what if Jack Barthels reads a report in the paper? She tells herself not to be ridiculous. Jack can barely read, and besides, he is God-only-knows-where anyway. They tromp back through the snow, retracing her footprints, the frozen river on their left.

"Are you a Roosevelt?" he asks. His eyes are very blue.

"No. Are you?"

"No." They continue a few more paces. "Who did you come with?"

Rather than answer, she smiles with her perfect dimple, achieving the desired effect.

"Are you here with the Commodore?"

Tennessee raises her eyebrows in response.

The man continues. "You're Mrs. Woodhull's sister, aren't you?"

"I am." Careful, she warns herself.

He nods and pauses for a moment. "Ladies treating you well?"

She looks at the smoke from the estate's chimneys floating toward the river. "The mendacity with which they discuss each other warrants ventilating, I daresay."

"So, you're a progressive?"

To which she nods, beaming at the thought of recounting this conversation to Victoria.

Floor to ceiling books run the length of the room and are accessible by means of a ladder. Two winged chairs face the fireplace, their backs to the rest of the library, in the center of which is a round table with a large bowl of oranges. Whistling under her breath, Tennessee begins to search the Roosevelt collection and climbs a few rungs up the ladder.

"Ah, Miss Claflin, fancy you're being a reader." He does have the same voice as the Commodore. She turns to face William Vanderbilt. If she descends the ladder, he will loom over and put her at a disadvantage.

She descends two rungs and puts herself at his eye level. "Yes, I always strive to learn things should the opportunity lend itself."

"Really, to what end, pray?"

"Well, if I learn enough, perhaps I might become a writer."

At this, he throws back his head and laughs. With some dismay, she observes it's very much like his father's laugh.

Wiping at his eyes and nose with his handkerchief, he answers. "Miss Claflin, are you familiar with psychology?"

"Please, enlighten me." Tennessee smiles, noting how Cornelius Vanderbilt's jaw is chiseled and strong, while his son William has lambchop sideburns to augment a weak chin.

"It's a science concerned with one's character. Once you've acquainted yourself with psychology, you'll discover that the nature of your association with my father indicates you have a licentious susceptibility. Whilst you may refrain from the expression thereof, it is nevertheless in your character and is immutable, making you forever enslaved thereof as well. A very unfortunate position from which a woman, such as yourself, might struggle to be a writer, Miss Claflin."

"I so wish you'd call me Tennie, as your father has insisted that I do call you Billy." His nonsense is impossible to follow, so she says again, "Billy."

Does he recognize her from the street outside the apothecary?

"Ah yes, Tennie." He clears his throat. "So, as to your becoming a writer and whether my father might support you in such endeavors, I have it on good authority, he doesn't give much thought to you doing anything other than seeing to his comfort. That's certainly the consensus of my sisters."

She waits for him to leave, but he makes no sign of moving, so she says, "I must continue in my search for a book. Heaven forbid someone mistake me for being an illiterate from Red Light Lizzie's." She catches the faint glimmer of recognition on William Vanderbilt's face. "Perhaps I'll read something to do with psychology. Billy."

Tennessee turns to face the bookcase and climbs a few rungs so her bustle will be at his eye level. She moves her backside just so, wiggling it for good measure. She looks over her shoulder at him. "Oh! Excuse me, I thought you were gone."

Having been caught in the act, the scarlet William Vanderbilt beats a hasty retreat.

"HA!" Another male voice laughs.

Oh, no, she realizes someone else had been in the room. Slowly, she turns around.

The ginger-haired man from the balloon stands up from the winged chair. "He is such a horse's ass!" he exclaims.

Unnerved, Tennessee wonders why her heart seems to be fluttering. The ginger haired man had not been present at lunch nor the previous day. He adds, "Well, I'll say this. There's nothing worse than the repressed lust of a God-fearing bully, what."

"That's quite true." Tennessee descends the ladder.

"You want to write?" He hands her a large magazine. "Give this a gander."

"I am afraid I do not know—"

"James Gordon Bennett." He bows.

Now her heart is hammering. She can sense that his is, too. She says nothing.

James Gordon Bennett straightens himself up and adds softly, "Junior." He helps himself to an orange, then bites into it through the skin. He says, "If you want to make someone like Billy Vanderbilt feel it in the balls, just write about him. That's how you get them."

At supper, Mrs. Roosevelt says, "Mr. Bennett brought us persimmons from his hothouse. Mr. Bennett, you are a perfect guest." Bennett raises his glass to his hostess then smiles at Tennessee, just as he had when he helped her into the balloon.

She looks away and attempts to listen to the very attractive E.C. Stedman who is sitting on her right. "All struggle is a class struggle, Miss Claflin." His breath warms the air as he speaks. "Wealth relies upon controlling those who toil for the benefit of the elite," Stedman whispers, softly, to her alone.

"Why, I think so too!" she whispers. "My brother-in-law has instructed me in these same ideas. That goods are fairly traded only when the price is the same as what it cost to manufacture them. Cost the limit of price, as it were."

The candlelight, the wine, enjoying the admiring looks from the other men at table, Tennessee winks at the Commodore, then holds his gaze, until it is he who blinks and looks away.

Later in bed, he wraps her long, braided hair across his throat. "To keep me warm, by God. Important to protect the larynx this time of year, isn't it?"

"That's what they say." Nestled in the crook of his arm, she is so warm and cared for that the unfortunate exchange with Billy dissolves to nearly nothing.

"I've been giving it some thought, Tennie."

She squeezes him in response.

He continues, "We need to contract our arrangement."

She begins to nod off, murmuring, "How do you mean?"

"I think we should be married."

Her heart lurches her wide awake. "Complications will ensue."

"And it shall be an adventure." He gently tugs on her braid. "You like that, no?"

"Oh, Goat. I beg you."

"Tennie C."

What reason can she give? That the authorities in Ottawa, or Jack Barthels, or any number of soldiers she touched, lied to, might seize an opportunity. Instead, she says, "Were we to marry, I would have nothing of my own with which to protect, my—"

"What, Tennie?"

"My own self-interest." Why can she not say "my individual sovereignty"? Instead she whispers, "I must master something."

"But you have many times over. As a medium…"

"I shan't do that again."

"Your healing."

"That too, I prefer to do only with you, Goat."

"I see. You need to protect your own self-interest."

"Yes, yes I do. I must practice my individual sovereignty. That I am my own person, mistress of myself, beholden to no one." There, she has said it.

"All right, Tennie C. Claflin. I love you." He holds her tightly to him and she nestles closer. "I love you for the very zeal," at this he chuckles, "with which you seek your individual sovereignty."

The next morning the sun dazzles through a pure cloudless sky. Like the Hudson River's surface, trees and stones, railings and footpaths are covered in a thick layer of ice. Roosevelt's ice yacht, the *Icicle*, is sixty-five feet long, sleek with massive sails and rudder, essentially the deck of a schooner on skates. Cornelius and Tennessee, Billy and his wife, and several other guests board the solitary, private car being pulled by the locomotive. A gunshot signals the start. The frozen river curves, and the train tracks run close to its edge. The locomotive takes a small lead. Tennessee and the Commodore observe the ice yacht from their perch by the window. He puts his arm around her waist, indifferent to the other guests.

She says to him, "Cornelius." Her voice is too soft to be heard by the others. "Should I accept, your brood will be in such a palaver that you'll be denied visits with the grandbabies and prevented from pursuing your life's work."

"My life's work. Tell me, Sparrow. Besides your individual sovereignty, what do you see as your life's work?"

The *Icicle* keeps pace with the train, its crew on deck facing down river. She watches James Gordon Bennett lean into the wind, his black scarf fluttering behind him, like a pirate. "Something like what the gents are doing, operating on the Exchange, writing a missive, perhaps."

"How much money do you have, Sparrow?"

"Of my own? In all, it's a good penny. I have nearly sixteen thousand."

"Let's invest ten of it. Give me that sum and we shall see what we can do for your self-interest. That should set you up. Then you can use it, toward your life's work." Vanderbilt beckons to the steward, "More coal."

Tennessee grasps his large hand so that it encircles her closer to him. "I'm not quite sure how I'll go about it. But the Exchange and writing, ventilating hypocrisies that are unfair. That shall become my life's work." She looks out the window. The ice yacht catches the wind and sails past the train.

PART TWO

WHAT IS SEDUCTION, WHAT IT IS NOT

"Do spirits exist? Is there anything apart from the solid, the tangible, the senses of man, the bulk of nature? Can intelligence exist without a body? Is the world of soul within the world of flesh, or is the world of flesh within the world of spirit? Which is the real thing, the material or the immaterial?... If we are, really, alone in the world; if nothing is believable—and therefore possible—but what is demonstrable; if human reason is everything, and common sense the true guide and the only guide; why, then... the sooner we close the account with this outside phantom-world the better! In this case AWAY WITH IT!"

-from *Seership! The Magnetic Mirror,*
by Paschal Beverly Randolph

THE UNVEILING

January 1869
27 Boylston Street, Boston

PASCHAL BEVERLY RANDOLPH pours one pint of madeira into his preferred pitcher, then carefully adds ten grains of iron phosphate to it, followed by two ounces of loaf sugar. Randolph leans back in his chair, thoughtfully stirring the mixture. After a few moments, he pours himself a hearty glassful and takes a sip. The proportions are perfect. He drains the glass and copies the formula into a small journal. He writes,

> two teaspoonfuls of this, taken night and morning, will cause Scrofula, Humors, and Diseases of the Liver, to fly like fog before the morning blast, AND UTTERLY ROUT ANY CANCEROUS TAINT, AND CURE THE WORST SYPHILIS, that ever poisoned human blood, or doomed innocent children to premature graves, under the mild names of 'Scrofula' and 'Salt Rheum.'"

Paschal pauses a moment and pours himself a second glass. He writes, "The name of this preparation is Humor Cordial."

He looks at the papers on the edge of his desk and fingers through one of his current projects. *The Guide to Clairvoyance and Clairvoyant's Guide, a Practical Manual for those who Aim at Perfect Clear Seeing and Psychometry.* Paschal decides to insert a chapter on hashish, of which he's taken perhaps a bit too much earlier this afternoon. Important to caution users against that tendency.

Surrounded by his bookplates, medicinals, and herbs, he is comfortable in his position as an eminent clairvoyant practitioner. That he considers himself and most of his colleagues to be frauds is simply an unhappy detail. One day he'll be called upon to address his chicanery, so he's writing a memoir, an account of spiritualism writ large with clairvoyance, in particular. He hears his landlady moving around downstairs. They've been together a little less than two years. He pours himself the last of the wine and studies one of his landlady's publicity notes. All in all, it's a been a good run, but he wonders how much longer they'll continue their deception in such epic proportion.

> Printed for People of Common Sense Only
>
> Everyone wants to consult the Future and know what awaits them in the coming days. Read on and find out how it can be done.
>
> On April 27th, 1867, an extraordinary occurrence, demonstrating an Ethereal Power took place in the ROSICRUCIAN ROOMS, 27 Boylston Street, BOSTON, MASS, an institution established by myself, and fitted up in a style of magnificence never before attempted for a like purpose, on this continent. The world-famous Clairvoyant, PB RANDOLPH who probably has no equal living to-day, in his specialty and he has been giving many curious proofs of his amazing power of developing clairvoyance by the "DISTANT WILL'"' — for he rendered a lady perfectly clairvoyant in eight minutes.
>
> At the Rooms, Clairvoyant Examinations are daily made, Circles for Development; Clairvoyance, Psychometry and Mediumship are held. Grand Levees, on Wednesday Evenings, for the cultured and refined only. Attendance by card.

From the unpublished memoir of Paschal Beverly Randolph:

By the end of the War, having lost everything several times over, I eagerly accepted Mrs. Crook's proposition. She had seen me perform in San Francisco, during the fifties, but I can't take credit for those readings. At the time, I had been graced with an assistant who had an extraordinary aptitude for all things spiritual. She was an actress and a tragic little thing, unhappily married and woefully homesick for her family. In the evenings, she brought her little boy with her. He was a simpleton, yet made no argument about curling up, going right to sleep as she began the show. But once the actress, her name was Victoria, returned East, my own misadventures and my wanderings began, ending only with the debacle in New Orleans.

Before his untimely death, Mr. Lincoln had suggested I go to New Orleans to assist in the creation of a school for Negroes. Fifteen months and one murdered president later, a delegation of 130 black citizens convened at Mechanics Hall. The object was to protest voting privileges being denied them. Consequently, New Orleans' mayor directed the police to subdue, beat, or kill any black men who resisted, surrendered, or fled the gathering. Those who resisted were beaten, those who surrendered were shot. Negroes were dragged off street cars, out of their homes, and slaughtered. More than 240 Negro citizens died.

After the Massacre in '66 (white folk call it the Riots), our persecution by those sworn to uphold the law became a matter of daily life. So, I left that place, where my body had been persecuted by bare-faced hatred, and came to Boston. In Boston, it is now my very soul that is persecuted by artfully concealed hypocrisy.

However, I have enjoyed the patronage of Mrs. Crook, at 27 Boylston Street, and established my Rosicrucian Rooms to practice the art of magnetic mirrors, soul blending with the dearly departed, and sex magic (Mrs. Crook's devotion to the last is for reasons I shall not discuss in these pages). At times, my business is most lucrative. But my seership and mysticism are often plagued by inconsistencies and ambivalence. As previously mentioned, most of us in the business are frauds. Yet, I wrote about my three specialties at length and the books have sold well. Recently, I have come to enjoy frequent trips to New York City, my native home, which provide a much-needed respite from Boston's stifling social pretensions. In New York, I have had the good fortune to rent lodging on the ground floor of a guest house presided over by Mrs.

Annie de Wood. The attractive Mrs. de Wood's write-up in the Gentleman's Guide *speaks for itself:*

> 105 West Twenty-Fifth Street is a 3-story brownstone house, furnished throughout with the most costly and newest improvements. Her gallery of oil paintings alone cost $10,000. Rosewood furniture, immense mirrors, Parisian figures, &c...Her house receives the patronage of distinguished gentlemen from foreign countries. This is the best house on Twenty-Fifth Street.

Both my landlady and the girls in her employ are enthusiastic consumers of all things spiritual, especially magnetic mirrors and soul blending. Happily, my business and that of Victoria and Tennessee now frequently overlap.

Randolph stops writing. Doctor-patient confidentiality prevents him from elaborating further.

Victoria had introduced them toward the end of the War. It was on the road. Randolph was on his way to New Orleans; the Claflins were headed to Cincinnati. Inclement weather had made travel most perilous and the tavern was filled to capacity.

"He brought it upon her, pity's the truth of it," Buck had said. "The poor child was married to a scoundrel." At the time, the old man's candor had Randolph at a loss for words. Buck continued, "From one medical man to another, I would appreciate you're making an examination. She is my youngest and I am loathe to see her so poorly."

Randolph had followed him up the stairs to her room. An oil lamp on the dresser revealed the ceiling's water stains and it was cold enough to see their breath. The patient's mother and Victoria stood watch over Miss Claflin. Thanks to a bedwarmer, she showed no sign of discomfort.

"Little sister," her father had said. "This man's a doctor. He's come to examine you. I said it's fine." Then he took the others with him and closed the door behind them.

Tennessee had looked at Randolph for a moment and asked, "Are you a darkie?"

To which he merely raised an eyebrow in response. Her voice was soft. "Were you a contraband, you know, fugitive, a runaway?"

"No. I was not." Randolph found her impudence not unattractive. He decided an absinthe tincture laced with laudanum was the proper approach and poured the medicinal into a cup. "Were you?" He offered it to her, and she drank it down. It took but seconds for the woodworm to do its magic.

She snuggled further under the blankets. "I wish that I were."

"Why do you say that?" And then he realized she was crying. He took her hand. "Sometimes it does a body good to share what gives us sorrow. Are you mourning the loss of your husband?"

"No."

"A soldier, perhaps?"

She nodded. "Yes. He was the one that I loved. But he's an angel now." And she wept tears of such pathos that they just sat quietly, until she said, "I'm a spiritualist, you know." As expected, the absinthe had begun to work, rendering her nonchalant.

"Indeed, I have met your sister, Victoria." Then he said, "Miss Claflin, should I have a look now?"

To which she waved her hand, "Please."

With her nightgown up around her waist, he began his examination and said, "I too, have worked in the spiritualism business."

"Is that so?" She perched up on her elbows. "Tell me your name again?"

"I am Dr. Paschal Beverly Randolph."

"Well! How do you do, Doctor."

Knowing those in the business to be the frauds that they were, he then asked, "Tell me, who have you bamboozled with your wares, Miss Claflin?"

"I don't bamboozle," she said. "My spirit guides come and do the work for me."

"Your spirit guides. Who are those?"

"Hester, Odessa, and Delia. My sisters who are in Heaven."

Was she bluffing? Perhaps it was just the medicinal. Or was that part of the act?

He held the lamp high. Her tender white skin, inflamed and scarlet through the fine hair, was angry in places with what appeared to be silver flaking scabs.

Oblivious to the exam, she said, "Much the same as that girl you like. What's her name, Cora Hatch? You like her, don't you?"

His patient winked at him. How did she know that?

"Ah, ah, ah! You'd like to be more than her friend, wouldn't you?" Tennessee wagged her finger. "I can see, it's written all over your face. But we need friends, don't we? My sister, Victoria, is my very best friend."

At that moment, Randolph had little doubt. Miss Claflin's malady was the Great Pretender. He knew of a specialist in Cincinnati reputed to cure those afflicted by means of a mercury vapor over which the patient perched as could be tolerated. A punishing treatment for an even worse disease. Despite his years of research, Randolph had never attended a college of medicine, so his expertise was limited and Miss Claflin deserved better than his humble treatment might provide. So, Randolph restored her nightdress and tucked her covers back around the bed.

"You aren't afraid?" she asked him.

He turned down the lamp and, in the dimness, she appeared little more than a child. He sat back down beside her and she took his hand.

"Well," Randolph answered, "all we can do is try."

She whispered, "Will you be my friend, Doctor?"

He answered, "Yes. I will be your friend." Then he whispered a prayer his mother had taught him and added, "I, too, have my spirit guides who look out for me."

She murmured, "Your two little ones?"

Yet again! How could she have known this? He had never told Victoria about them. How was it Tennessee's humbug and magic were rolled into one?

Afterward, he handed Buck a small box whose contents were an oriental hemp he called Dowam Meskh. "Have her smoke some of this tonight. She will sleep and not wake until midday. Here is a list of herbs you should acquire as soon as you're able, in addition to their preparation."

Everyone Randolph had met in this business, including himself, was a fraud. So how did Tennessee Claflin know about Cora Hatch and the grief for his two late children? "Your daughter is remarkable," Randolph added, and bowed to the old man. "Good night."

—⁓—

"I know that some people will blame me for thus alluding to the victims of folly, carelessness, ignorance, or ungodly debauchery, but all objections must stand aside before the potent fact these terrible ailments are as widespread as civilization. A remedy for the fearful thing is needed, ... I feel, not only that I am doing a good act, but also putting a stop to much of the imposition practiced on the suffering and unwary, by unprincipled dabblers of medicine."

-from *The Unveiling, or What I think of Spiritualism*, by Paschal Beverly Randolph

January 1869
Pfaff's Tavern, 647 Broadway

The Vault at Pfaff's has a reputation. Waiting outside, Tennessee suspects the same could be said of herself, but she'll have Pearl Andrews as chaperone. There will be nothing untoward. By five o'clock the city is submerged in darkness and she watches the lamplighter slowly shuffle past her as he brings the street out of the gloom. When she smiles at him, he mutters, "What I wouldn't give for a bit of that," and tips his hat with a laugh.

Finally, Andrews arrives, and they go downstairs, beneath the street level. There is a large fire in the fireplace and all of the tables are full.

Pearl Andrews crows, "As you see, my dear, the beer and conversation are flowing!"

The group of artists and writers who gather here call themselves Bohemians. She looks about. With a flash of pleasure, she sees EC Stedman. He waves them over as if their meeting were purely accidental. At his table are several women, whom Stedman introduces as actresses and a writer. The barkeep, Mr. Pfaff, comes over and Tennessee shows off her German.

Eventually, Andrews says, "Not only is Miss Claflin's sister, Mrs. Woodhull, a spiritualist, but Miss Claflin herself is clairvoyant and performs magnetic healing."

One of them exclaims "Is that so?" And they begin to ask if she can do a reading right now, this moment.

It irks her that Andrews would put her in this situation. These women are actresses and Tennessee hasn't rehearsed in months.

"Well," Tennessee demurs. She looks about the room. An old drunk is playing the piano. "The conditions, perhaps are not—"

"Oh, please." The women have come to life, imploring her with sounds and looks.

Tennessee's smile is tight. She pulls at a miniscule hole in the finger of her glove until she spies her friend in the back of the room. Dr. Randolph. He'll get her out of this.

Tennessee stands and says, "I would need assistance. From a neutral party, perhaps." She raises her voice to be heard across the room. "You, there, sir. Sprechen Sie English, bitte?"

Randolph looks up. He has already been there some time. It takes a moment for him to realize it is Tennessee who is calling out to him in German.

"Yes!" he says.

"I say, good sir. I seek assistance."

He wonders why she does not use his name. He takes in Tennessee's table. Perhaps it's a ruse. He runs his tongue along the roof of his mouth. He hopes he won't be expected to speak too much. He weaves his way across the room. Tennessee slips a tiny square of magic paper, which is flint, covered in gunpowder, into his hand.

The lights are lowered, and the table is cleared. Everyone in the tavern is hushed. She reaches in her pocket for her own tab of magic paper. Since the age of eight her mother has insisted, "You must always carry this, Tennie. You never know when you'll be called upon to use your powers."

It's ancient stagecraft that any carney knows how to use. Ah, but do they use it well? She asks Mr. Pfaff for a large empty bowl. One is brought and placed in the center of the table. She then asks Stedman to provide a sheet of paper, which he does, tearing some from a small tablet in his pocket.

"Please," Tennessee says, "tear off a piece and write a secret wish upon it. Then fold it and place it in the bowl."

Like obedient children, they pass the paper around, small pieces torn as several pencils are shared, and the participants scribble down their fondest wish.

She goes over to the pianist and whispers to him. He nods, then begins to play some Bach. *O Haupt voll Blut und Woden*, one of Roxana's favorites. Graceful and slow, everyone knows it. Tennessee smiles to herself and fingers the flint and second piece of flash paper in her pocket.

"I would ask that you place your hands upon the table. If you know this music, you may hum along." She wonders what humbug she can pull out of her hat. "First! I will begin with a poem, to absent friends."

Randolph is staring at her. She hopes to God he's got matches for that flash paper she just passed him. He must have some. She gestures with her empty hand toward the rest of the room and says, "It's called, *The Drunkard's Wife*."

> A step! Hark! It is he: I was not dreaming!
> I know too well that heavy, trembling tread—
> He comes! his eye with wine-cup frenzy gleaming;
> I am a drunkard's wife —would I were dead!

> He knows me not: he looks on me with scowling;
> He sings foul curses in my trembling ear—
> My heart! the tempest that without is howling,
> Is not so fearful as the storm that's here!

Everyone is caught up in the poetry, and Tennessee uses that second to jet the flint and paper into the bowl. There is a tiny crackle, and a flash of color. Everyone jumps with a collective gasp as their wishes ignite and go up in flames.

Tennessee closes her eyes, "Albert!" she cries and begins to sway.

One of the men says, "Yes."

Thank God, Tennessee thinks. Thank God. The spirit is present.

"Albert Richardson, you shall marry your lady love, and…and," the residual smell from the tiny explosive fills her nostrils. She is at New York Harbor. It is summer, and she is running. Tennessee opens her eyes. Randolph watches her. In her mind, he moves his lips, but she cannot hear what he is saying. There is a buzzing in her head.

She turns to one of the women, "Ada Clare!"

"Yes!" the woman cries.

"You shall tour to great success!" The buzzing grows louder. Tennessee does not say, but your writing shall fail. You will be bitten by a rabid dog and then die. Nor does she say that Albert will be killed by his lover's ex-husband.

She doesn't say these things because she stills sees Randolph moving his lips but she is unable to hear him. All eyes are on her, but she is looking at the bowl. There is enormous pain and she glances at Randolph, please, please, she tries to communicate. Just then, he nods and, unobserved, throws his flash paper into the bowl.

This second spark sends a thrill through the participants. The room is strangely silent. Her head pounding, Tennessee resumes her recitation and the hackneyed poem takes on a sorrowful truth.

> My husband! how in other days I loved thee!
>   Thou brought'st me here, a trusting happy child,
> Our home was heaven, e'en like the heaven above me;
>   Now—'tis the home of dread and terror wild.
>
> Yet I would love thee still. Why wilt thou wander
>   From me, to linger with the demon, wine?
> Are they who lure thee there truer and fonder
>   Than I? Their tones more dear to thee than mine?
>
> He heeds not. Ah, Death, take us o'er the river—
>   My babe and me—to yon fair, blissful shore!
> There my rent heart-strings never more shall quiver—
>   There I shall be—a drunkard's wife no more!

Tennessee sits, her hands folded on her lap. Everyone at the table now wants to confide in her and share their deepest secrets. She speaks to some part of them, in a way they can't quite understand.

Albert Richardson is watching her, and they meet one another's gaze.

He smiles and says, "Bravo, Miss Claflin!" He claps heartily. "Very stirring recitation!"

She looks at him. The buzzing inside her head only quiets when she hides away the knowledge that he'll be dead within the year.

"Indeed!" the others echo and join in the applause.

Mr. Richardson lifts his glass. "As Miss Claflin so eloquently said, 'To absent friends.'"

WHILE MAN IS A COWARDLY LIAR, WOMAN IS EVEN MORE DANGEROUS

February 1869
17 Great Jones Street

MR. STEDMAN OR Mr. Bennett. She knows Cornelius proposed only when he saw their admiration for her person. Tennessee pushes her writing tablet aside. Mr. Bennett or Mr. Stedman. Besides, what if that scoundrel, her ex-husband Jack, were to surface? Then what? No one knows about the marriage. Better that everyone should assume there has never even been one.

Since the session at Pfaff's Tavern, attempts at writing have been for naught. Both Stedman and Bennett waltz back into her mind. If she were to get married and take a lover, how might she confess that she has been cursed with her affliction? What would that say about Cornelius?

"Oh, stop!" she says to the empty room.

She picks up the magazine James Gordon Bennett gave her. She looks at Mrs. Stowe's editorial for what must be the umpteenth time.

Alas, if only she could avail herself of Mrs. Stowe's wisdom. She reads the piece again.

How may I know that I may make a Writer?

It is not enough to have a general desire to write; the author must have a very particular and definite conception of something she wants to say. We would say to such a person, "Is there any subject on which you feel so deeply and vividly, that it seems to you that you have something to say on that subject?" If it be so, then try to put that something into the very clearest, plainest, and simplest way that you can. The best directions for writing, whether in prose or poetry, that we have ever heard were given by a shrewd clergyman to a young poet: "FIRST THINK WHAT YOU WANT TO SAY AND THEN SAY IT."

There is a knock on the door. Tennessee looks up, annoyed. "Come!"

It is Zula. A man is standing in the shadows behind her. "You have a visitor," she says, then skips away.

"Mr. Stedman," Tennessee is still for a moment. "To what do I owe your visit?" There is a heavy snowfall outside. She decides only a fool would not know to what she owes his visit.

"I felt I owed you the courtesy." He removes a sheet of paper from inside his chest pocket. "This is my report of the race. I want to assure you, there is no mention of anything we discussed, nor the visit at Pfaff's Tavern." He hands it to her. "At all."

"Thank you," she murmurs, aware that she is becoming strangely warm. "Why don't I find us some refreshment?"

She retreats to the kitchen and scurries about, rattling cups and saucers. Why does she sounds so breathless, and, even worse, why is she so pleased with herself that he should be there at all?

If an intimacy with Stedman goes nowhere, then any disclosure of her affliction will be for naught. Mr. Stedman or Mr. Bennett. The thought of it makes her hands shake. There could only be the shame of having compromised herself by sharing her most painful secret. Tennessee purses her lips and struggles not to spill the water from the kettle.

Out of the corner of her eye, she sees Utica and Canning Woodhull in a passionate embrace by the pantry.

"For mercy's sake!" Tennessee slams a tray onto the table. Utica looks over and smiles at her like a cat.

Tennessee brings the tray, shaking in her hands, to the library. When she places it on the table beside the settee, she is struck by her guest's handsome profile. She stops trembling and sits next to him on the settee.

In his hands are two slim volumes. "These are for you." His hands are soft and cared for. "The first is a collection of my poems. From when I still believed in goodness and had faith in mankind."

"You no longer do so?" Not only is Stedman a journalist, he's also a poet, and part-time financier, too. Accomplished, as well as good-looking.

"Miss Claflin, with the exception of your graceful company, the War has proven that anyone's faith in mankind is woefully misplaced." She gazes at his beautifully carved lips and straight white teeth. "This second book is a manifesto as it were, of progressive ideas expressed in German and then translated into English by a Mr. Morton who like you, is female."

Flattered by the gifts, Tennessee looks at the title. *The Communist Manifesto*, by Karl Marx and Friedrich Engels, as translated by Howard Morton.

She realizes she'd better say something. "May I offer you some tea?"

His face is inches from hers. "You know I came here for more than tea."

Is he there because he imagines she'll have little pretension when it comes to the bedroom, or is it because of her proximity to a great man? She stands up and so does he. Her heart is pounding. She decides it doesn't make any difference one way or the other.

Stedman presses himself against her and she does not resist. When he begins to raise her skirts, she longs to kiss him but remembers her arms and belly are wrapped in muslin. She pulls out of his embrace instead.

"Mr. Stedman." She takes a deep breath and is trembling again. "I regret we may not be as familiar as you would have me give over to you, sir." She doesn't want to explain why. She grabs the doorknob behind her, should she need to make a hasty retreat. She whispers, "My only, nay, my greatest desire, is that we may in friendship further acquaint ourselves."

Flushed and embarrassed, she gives him a moment to salvage his dignity. Stedman reaches for the cup and quickly drinks his tea. "Thank you for the refreshment." He looks out the window. "The weather seems to be letting up. Thankfully, my skis should have me home in little more than an hour."

She barely has the strength to speak. "Where is your home?"

"Just north of Kip's Bay."

Silently, she leads him to the foyer.

He clicks his heels. "I shall see myself out."

The snow has been reduced to flurries. She watches as Stedman, bundled up in his furs, fastens on his skis. He stands, framed by the pristine white stillness, and salutes her, then pushes off with his poles, skiing into the night.

Tennessee returns to the library. Her tea is now cold. She paces the room and places her icy cold hands on either side of her face. Her cheeks are burning. She sits at the piano.

The Commodore enjoys Schumann, and Tennessee has learnt *Album for the Young* as a surprise. It soothes her, lifting the cover off the keys and turning up the lamp to read the music. She begins the first part, *Melody*. Moving her hands, seeing the notes, hearing the music within, she begins to calm herself. What a gift Cornelius has turned out to be. Every moment with him is filled with mutual discovery, not to mention the physical pleasure it pleases them both to provide each other. He never asks about the muslin bandages nor does she explain what they are there for. It's enough to be together.

She moves on to *Soldiers' March*, and then plays the *Humming Tune*.

Recently, Cornelius had so well advised her on an Erie trade that she and Victoria walked away with more money than either of them had ever dreamed of possessing in their lives.

Thanks to Cornelius, one might even argue that the Claflins are now rich. Rich! But to what end? Some of their neighbors are considered wealthy, such as the Lockners down the street. But it makes little difference for Mrs. Lockner. Sometimes, if one stands in the back garden, one hears her cry out as dreadful Mr. Lockner crashes the furniture in their house. Once, Mrs. Lockner fled her home, her face covered in blood. And even though Mrs. Blake took her in, she thought it not her place to report Mr. Lockner to the police. But Victoria did so, within a moment's notice. However, as far as the police were concerned, Mr. Lockner wasn't to blame. He had been drunk and what could be expected? Wives are the property of husbands and that is that. The whole thing was nothing less than a scandal.

Tennessee turns the page in front of her. She plays *The Poor Orphan Child*. Buck, despite everything, would never expect any of his daughters to stay with husbands who no longer pleased them. Never. Thank God for small favors. Cornelius. If she marries him, she will once again be someone's property. But perhaps she loves Cornelius after all. She decides she will tell him so. The thought of him listening to her play, of his foot tapping to the music and his off-key humming along makes her smile.

She will tell him tomorrow. Goat will be so happy. She will tell him that she loves him.

Night gives way to morning. Snow drifts cover the street-level windows, and the city's livestock, if they're they fortunate enough to have shelter, wait for their masters to dig them out. Beasts without shelter have either frozen or suffocated during the blizzard. Their corpses are sent to the slaughterhouse once the roads are clear.

No amount of poultice seems to work. Roxana puts her hand on Tennessee's brow then makes a clucking sound as she crosses the room to pull the drapes back.

"Don't! Don't open them."

"Shh. Tennie. Just a little bit."

"No!" Tennessee pulls a pillow over her face.

"What is vexing you so?" Roxana snatches the pillow away then tries not to gasp. The lesions are inflamed and raw, covered with blisters, as are Tennessee's hands and feet.

Tennessee starts to weep. "I saw a woman on the street. Her face had been…" It is impossible to say and too terrible to describe. "I am so afraid one day, one day my nose will fall off." The sobs turn into a wail. "I am a leper."

"No, Tennessee. Sht." Her mother sits on the bed. "You are not a leper."

"It could happen. It happens to old whores! I have seen them."

"No, no. Shh. You are not a whore. We put on the compress and find Dr. Randolph. Just stay in the bed. Maybe we should be leeching you."

Roxana brings her a glass filled with amber liquid. Tennessee drinks it, her insides roaring as if they are on fire and she begins shaking. "No leeches. No, thank you." She wags her finger at Roxana. "And no enemas either, Ma. I know you." Her bones seem to snap apart as she attempts to lie back down. Suddenly drowsy, Tennessee sighs. "The last thing I need is mustard up my ass."

"We get you the syringe I think and use Doc's stash."

Tennessee starts humming fragments of Bach from the old days in Ohio. "No, Ma. No thank you. Do you remember singing? Just to get the music out?"

"You have fever, Tennie," Roxana says. "You are not in your right mind."

———≈———

As soon as his sled can get through, the Commodore summons Mrs. Woodhull. "I will send my physician to you."

"Oh, that is very kind. But, Tennie is—she will see no other medic than the one that has treated her these last few years."

He answers, "You insult me, Mrs. Woodhull. Tennessee apprised me of her condition. I can assure you I understand her concerns most intimately."

Victoria stands up. "Commodore, she has my solemn vow that I will discuss her condition with no one. I regret to say, not even with you."

———

It is night when Tennessee opens her eyes and the windows are open. She adjusts the stocking cap that had been placed over her head and feels the hot brick under the covers. It is still warm. She sees Paschal Randolph watching her from the corner of the room.

"You aren't cold?" she asks.

"Well, it is brisk."

Her lips are chapped, and he hands her a glass of water, which she gulps down.

Finally, she says, "So! Dr. Randolph. What brings you to Great Jones Street?"

"I thought I had a standing invitation," he says, turning up the lamp. A lesion, grey and seeping pus where it isn't red and chafed, is situated just above her dimple. No doubt it is impetigo rather than a secondary development of the French disease.

During his examination she says, "I believe this is the first time I've worn this chapeau in your company."

"Indeed, if you borrowed your father's eye patch, I would mistake you for a pirate." Which makes her chuckle and he joins in until they are both laughing.

But she can see the concern under his mirth and she begins sobbing, "My life is over! My nose will fall off and then I will die."

"No, No. Your nose will not fall off. All will be well."

She swallows and whispers, "Oh, God. It will. I saw that woman."

———

"You must receive them." The Commodore's eldest daughter is adamant. "They are family and she is newly single, Father. It's the Christian thing to do."

Rather than cross his daughter, Cornelius Vanderbilt welcomes his cousins, Mrs. Crawford and her daughter, Frances, whose nickname is Frank. When Frank leans forward and softly kisses the Commodore's cheek, there is no mistaking. Frank is thirty years old, slim, elegant, and a member of the family. Moreover, Frank is available unlike Tennessee Claflin who is twenty-four, voluptuous, ambitious, a possible interloper, and otherwise indisposed.

May 1869
10 Washington Square

"Happy Birthday to you, Cornelius!" Tennessee says. "I have brought you a gift."

The butler directs the enormous package to be placed against a bookshelf, then closes the doors behind them. Finally, they are alone.

"Where did you receive the funds to purchase such a gift?"

"From the proceeds of my seed money, Goat. That you so kindly invested for me."

"Ah yes, the seed money."

There is a moment's heavy silence. If she asks about cousin Frank's now frequent visits, he will only lie. It is better to negotiate an unspoken agreement and ignore Frank's increasingly prominent role in his life.

She asks, "Are you going to open it?"

"Remove your clothing." He has never spoken to her thus.

"Cornelius."

"I want to see you. Take them off." She complies, watching him look for signs of her infection. To the naked eye, there are none.

"Will you see the painting now?" Tennessee tears away the brown paper, revealing the canvas. *Aurora* is a life-sized allegorical Tennessee as naked on the canvas as she is standing before him.

He holds out his hand to her. "Are you sure you are quite well?"

She nods, and he crushes her to him, crying as though he were a child.

REFORMATION OR REVOLUTION, WHICH?

"The right of citizens of the United States to vote shall not be denied or abridged by the United States or by any state on account of race, color, or previous condition of servitude."

-XV Amendment to the U.S. Constitution

May 1869
Steinway Hall

SITTING AMONGST THE sea of women, the one who comes to mind that day is Randolph's mother. She had been born into slavery but died free in New York City a few days shy of his eighth birthday. He'd been told the yarn that his father was a Randolph of Virginia and a known kinsman to Thomas Jefferson. But that made little difference when he was orphaned, a child amongst the thieves and gangs in Five Points. Now, decades later, he feels his mother smile at him, even as she was fading from the world. "Paschal," she whispered, "you must try, sweet child, try as much as you can."

He had wanted to sob and hide himself within her love. Instead, he struggled to appear brave, so she would be proud and believe that he was strong. Then she closed her eyes and said, "We must try if we are to be happy yet in this world."

The ladies on either side of Randolph smile prettily, and he nods, as a well-to-do, "representative" American Negro man, perfectly at ease in his skin. How ironic, then, that what one appears to be and what one truly is are so often at odds with each other. He often jokes with his friend Frederick Douglass about appearances and perception. Whereas Fred's looks do not morph into transformations at will, Randolph can shift and change, depending on his mood or the political temperature in which he finds himself. When Fred asks why Randolph does this, Randolph cannot say whether it is due to a Dionysian urge or simply self-loathing.

And the Fifteenth Amendment to the Constitution? Well, that is for him. So, at this moment, on this day in Steinway Hall, Dr. Paschal Beverly Randolph is a man of color. The next day, he'll decide whether or not to be a swarthy Spaniard.

Mrs. Cady Stanton's fury that the cherished word "sex" has been excluded from the Amendment is indisputable. But as she drones on and on, venting her spleen, Randolph begins to realize that she is denying his rights as a human being.

Irritation morphs into resentment, which begins to grow and harden in the pit of his stomach. Frederick Douglass walks across the stage and Randolph marvels at his equanimity. It is a quality, Randolph must admit, which is sorely lacking in himself.

> There is no name greater than that of Elizabeth Cady Stanton in the matter of woman's rights and equal rights, but…I must say that I do not see how anyone can pretend that there is the same urgency in giving the ballot to women as to the negro. With us, the matter is a question of life and death…at least in fifteen states of the Union. When women, because they are women, are hunted down through the cities of New York and New Orleans; when they are dragged from their houses and hung upon lamp-posts; when their children are torn from their arms, and their brains

dashed out upon the pavement; when they are objects of insult and outrage at every turn; when they are in danger of having their homes burnt down over their heads; when their children are not allowed to enter schools; then they will have an urgency to obtain the ballot equal to our own.

There is a hush in the crowd. Fred has drawn a line in the sand. Randolph doesn't realize he is beaming from ear to ear until he notices that the women who had smiled so prettily before have now turned away, stone-faced. Randolph gets up and leaves the building. Fred has spoken the truth! Those silly white women and their mewling, beating their chests as though they're the ones who had spent centuries in chains.

Randolph has been wrestling with sobriety, but the speeches give him a throbbing headache. He needs fortification, without delay. Something transformative, perhaps Irish lightening, to block the hollowness that overwhelms him, because he knows. He knows that despite the speeches, despite the War, nothing will change. Not in his lifetime.

June 1869
118 East 23rd Street

Tennessee and Victoria have squeezed in at the back of the room which is so crammed with bodies, there is barely space to breathe. A young woman addresses her comments to the group:

> It is an insult to the entire mass of women in the United States if Negroes, Chinese, and every description of ignorant and brute male foreigners are granted suffrage while women remain excluded from that right. I trust the Fifteenth Amendment will not receive support in as much as it asserts itself in spirit, that every man, no matter how degraded, is the superior of every woman!

The audience boo and hiss, vigorously fanning themselves. The windows have been painted shut and the air is stifling. The organizers are concerned someone might faint.

> In regards the voting of Negro men, not only are white women more fit to vote than they, but so are Negro women, as well.

To which there is hearty applause. The speaker sits down as Miss Anthony makes her way to the front of the room.

She looks up from her notes. She seems cool and elegant, indifferent to the sweltering temperature. Her clothes are understated, cut from the finest cloth. "Many of you have expressed reservations about attendance at our gatherings, either in part because of your religious faith or whether your husband approved your attendance. But it matters not whether you are married or what may be your religious creed. We must meet to ensure the passage of female suffrage, and I have received letters from Memphis, Tennessee, and from Louisiana, Texas, and Mississippi requesting that we establish chapters of the National Women's Suffrage Association in those places. To do so will necessitate additional contributions. To that end, we will meet tomorrow evening at 23 Avenue D in the Seventh Congressional District. We shall also choose delegates for the Saratoga Convention, which will be the thirteenth and fourteenth of July."

Afterward, Victoria approaches the women who are the organizers. "My name is Victoria Woodhull."

"How do you do, Miss—?"

"Mrs."

"How do you do, Mrs. Woodhull?"

"I should like to offer my services as delegate for the Saratoga Convention."

But the tight smiles with which Victoria's offer is met informs her immediately that with this group, a lady does not announce herself. She must be presented properly, with letters of introduction, antecedents, or contacts.

One of them says, "Mrs. Woodhull. Delegates are only nominated once they've made substantial contributions to the cause."

The other adds, "Contributions are made following receipt of one's references."

"Of course," Victoria answers. "Forgive my presumption. You're not about to nominate a delegate off the street. For all you know, I could be a rabble rouser, or even worse—" At this, she smiles widely, "one of those advocates of Free Love."

THE GRAND ORDER OF
RECREATION

June 1869
New Dorp, Staten Island

IT IS BARELY summer, but the streets shimmer with the heat, sum-moning pesky reminders of sanitation challenges and cholera outbreaks from years gone by. Anyone with the means flees the city in pursuit of clean air.

Commodore Cornelius Vanderbilt finds it the perfect opportunity to take to the waters and to show Tennessee his favorite cove on Staten Island. His cat boat speeds them across the Upper Bay as Vanderbilt chats with its pilot and Tennessee faces the open water. Removing her straw hat, her hair blows loose, and she shields her eyes from the bright sun. Seagulls and salt and bright clean light shine around her. She feels reckless and daring and salutes the sailors on neighboring vessels, "Ahoy, maties!"

To which they wave and respond, "Ahoy!"

A horse and trap are kept for the Commodore at his dock. As they ride over to the farm, Tennessee decides she will not go with Victoria to the suffragist convention in Saratoga. Cornelius spends his summer in Saratoga. It would be awkward were he to learn Tennessee prefers to rally round women's rights rather than be at his side. Particularly were she to see him with his cousin Frank. She pushes the thought of cousin Frank out her mind.

They dine on fried fish, cucumbers soaked in vinegar, and chilled white wine, then walk to a secluded cove. The sand is hot underfoot, and there is only nature and ocean and sky.

Cornelius throws his hat down and undresses.

"It will be cold," he says, "but most invigorating." He stands before her, colossal and strong. Uncharacteristically, Tennessee feels strangely shy.

He kneels down. "May I assist you, Sparrow?"

She nods, and he undresses her, placing her garments next to his in the sand.

The freezing water brings every nerve to life. The Commodore whoops and dives under the small waves and grabs Tennessee's ankle. She squeals, and he reemerges, shouting and splashing like a young boy. She lets him think she cannot swim, and he holds her as she kicks in the water. Afterward, they lay on the warm sand lulled by the cove's peacefulness. The city's chaos seems far away.

"Cornelius."

"Yes, my dear."

"Have you ever wanted to be an acrobat?"

"An acrobat? Zounds, I've never given it any thought. Why d' you ask? Do you have a penchant for tumblers?"

She chuckles and says, "Well, since we were on the balloon, I've often wondered if your legs are strong enough."

"For you, Tennie, my legs will always be strong enough." Lying on his back, he bends his knees with his feet in the air and she clambers on top, resting her shins on the soles of his feet, balancing one another by holding each other's hands, concentrating as hard as they might.

"Can you manage?" he says.

She answers, "Yes I think so."

"Are you ready, Little Sparrow?"

"Yes, Goat. I am ready."

Carefully, he releases her hands, and her arms extend as he straightens his legs. Propelling her higher into the air, she looks out over the ocean, like a conquering goddess on the masthead of one of his ships.

"Capital!" Tennessee bellows.

"Here! Here! Capital!" He shouts in response.

"Capital!" they roar together. "Capital!"

Sailing back to Manhattan, they snack on lobsters and corn.

The Commodore gestures at her, "Miss Claflin, the sun has turned you nearly as pink as the shell of our dinner."

"Alas, I may be found unfashionable," she replies between mouthfuls. "What say you to an unfashionable friend?"

"I have no interest in the fashions of the demimonde, little Sparrow."

"Are you so indifferent? Are you just an old Goat, who can come and go as you please?"

"I am, I'm not ashamed to say."

The sun has left stripes where his eyes crinkle from smiling. She reaches up to touch them, and he grabs her hand and holds it to his lips. A seagull hovers on the rail, watching the mismatched lovers embrace, then turns and flies away.

———

The heat continues unabated. Victoria's son, Byron, has given up bathing. His long, matted hair smells most unnatural, but Victoria cannot bring herself to cut it. From the parlor, Tennessee watches Roxana hold the scissors and approach Byron in the hallway. Polly and Victoria sit in their undergarments, fanning themselves. Byron's bloodcurdling screams force them to cover their ears.

Polly says, "If it were me, I'd tether him to cut it. Really, Vicky." To which Victoria closes her eyes, pretending she doesn't hear. Polly was the third child born to Buck and Roxana and is cut from a very different cloth than Victoria or Tennessee. She has had five children, two husbands, and a past everyone knows is best forgotten.

There is a shriek as Roxana struggles to chase Byron up the stairs.

Ignoring Polly, Victoria says, "Were you to formalize your arrangement with the Commodore, Tennie, you know you would never want for anything."

This time it is Tennessee who closes her eyes to pretend Victoria hasn't spoken. Blackmail, bigamy, general hangers-on. Visions of Jack selling their story to the papers. What kind of sovereignty would she enjoy then?

As if on cue, Polly asks, "Does he know about Jack?"

Tennessee wonders whether that isn't a thinly veiled threat. When she doesn't answer, Polly raises her eyebrows. "You would hate for him to learn about that, I daresay. Imagine the cost to the Commodore's good name. My goodness."

Byron bursts into the room like a smelly cloud. He stands behind his mother, panting, followed by the defeated Roxana who collapses next to Tennessee. Tennessee stands and takes the scissors from her mother.

"Byron, look at me."

He whimpers from his corner.

"No, don't be afraid," she says. "Watch." With two snips, she cuts off her hair, just above the nape of her neck.

The others gasp and Tennessee collects her hair off the floor. "Look! It's so cool. It feels wonderful."

She turns to Victoria, "Vicky, blow on my neck."

"What?"

"Blow on my neck." Tennessee stands next to her, then sighs and smiles broadly. "It feels so cool!"

Byron walks over to his mother that she might blow on his neck, too.

Tennessee shakes her head. "It won't work, Byron. You need short hair for it to work."

"Tennie's right, Byron. You need short hair. And then it will feel so cool."

He stands still. While Tennessee cuts the offending locks she says, "The Commodore needn't fear for his good name, Polly. I shan't be marrying him anytime soon. No need to fear blackmailers just yet."

Byron stands in front of his mother, and Victoria softly blows on his neck. He sighs and gives her a big smile.

———

"Where is your hair?" The sky is an ominous grey, and the swimming lesson is suddenly less appealing.

She turns so the Commodore might admire her profile. "Do you like it?"

"You look like a boy."

"I cut it, so Byron would do the same."

"Your hair was your crowning glory, Tennessee."

"Indeed, Cornelius. That's why I brought you this." She slides a box across the table. Inside, wrapped in tissue paper, her hair has been woven into an elegant series of knots entwined with lilac-colored velvet and cords of silk. "This should keep you warm, lest you find your throat chilly of an evening."

She watches him push the box and its contents away. They both prefer to say nothing rather than goodbye.

The carriage waits in the driveway. Tennessee climbs in and with her mind watches Cornelius summon his cousin Frank and Frank's mother, Mrs. Crawford, to Saratoga. There has been no discussion, but Tennessee knows what will come next.

"At last I find you, Miss Claflin." That unmistakable voice wakes her from her daydream. William Vanderbilt opens the door and sits beside her. The driver cracks the whip, and the horses pick up speed, headed toward the dock.

"I had mistaken you for a boy. Dressed like that, it's little wonder the Commodore banished you today."

Tennessee does not to respond to this, because her mariner's shirt, trousers, and cap are very comfortable. She is indifferent to humidity, which cannot be said of William Vanderbilt. He removes his hat and fans himself with it. "How fortuitous! Pater's interest may have waned, but, despite your outlandish getup, I, too, need magnetic healing." He gives her a hard look. "It is your expertise, is it not?"

"Billy, I no longer practice. Your father was my only remaining client."

"Indeed, why should you continue to service others when his is a mighty revenue stream unto itself?"

"Actually, Cornelius is managing my nest egg whilst I strive to become adept at my new profession. As we discussed at the Roosevelts'."

William Vanderbilt raises an eyebrow. She can see he's quite forgotten the substance of their conversation.

"I might be a journalist and ventilate truths for readers who have no idea of the corruption and hypocrisy in which pillars of society, gentlemen such as yourself, surround us."

When he doesn't answer she says, "Why don't I refer you to a colleague?"

"Oh, Miss Tennie C., this chestnut does not fall far from the tree. It is your healing exclusively I seek." Which prompts an awkward scuffle wherein the hunted eludes the hunter, until he forces himself upon her with a kiss. His eyes are closed, but hers are open. She lowers her teeth on to his lip until he recoils, "Ow, you bitch!"

Trembling, Tennessee grabs her cap then hands William his hat, which has fallen to the floor. He wipes his mouth and his brow with his handkerchief, smearing the blood from her bite across his forehead. "Miss Tennie C Claflin, one can't help but enquire, are you even literate?"

She imagines him explaining his blood-streaked face to his wife and father. "Why don't you wait to see what I publish and find out?"

William Henry Vanderbilt is in his fiftieth year. He understands more than most that what we perceive to be one kind of thing often turns out to be another. He knows she won't say anything, and neither will he. He has met Tennessee now on several occasions. He still finds her an incorrigible, slutty little gold-digger. If she is not undressed with her legs open at their next meeting, then he dearly hopes that this encounter will be their last.

They arrive at the marina. "Good day, Billy. Be kind to your father. He loves you very much." She slips from the carriage, and quickly climbs aboard the catboat. The skipper eases the vessel into the open water. Tennessee turns to face William. She reminds herself she does not give a toss that Cornelius's children prefer Frank Crawford. Besides, the attempted assault is yet another reason not to be a Vanderbilt. Bully for the Vanderbilts. Bully for them!

"Well, Tennessee," she says to herself. "Well done."

"You hussy," William Vanderbilt whispers. She gives him a friendly salute and turns to face Manhattan. Only then does she begin to sob, grateful the wind is too loud for the skipper to hear her cry.

WHAT IS WOMAN?

August 1869
Long Branch, New Jersey

THEY ARE AT the grandest house on the beach. Earlier, there was a storm, but the clear night sky is awash with starlight, reflected on the ocean. The tall French doors are open, and guests lounge on the terrace, chatting and laughing as couples dance across the parlor floor.

The day before, while still in the city, Victoria had said, "An invitation from Mr. Luther Challis comes with every possibility. You must go. Challis is very well connected."

To which Tennessee remained silent. Victoria continued, "I thought you liked him. And besides, it's not as though you're a blushing virgin."

Luther Challis crosses the terrace and hands Tennessee a glass of summer punch. "Tell me your picks this week, Tennessee."

"Well, I've been studying the balance sheets as you recommended, and…"

"And?"

"Jay Cooke's backing the cables that supply Morse. Coal has been edging up as of late."

"Anything we have a chance of shorting to hedge our bets? We know your sister enjoys a rather unusual insight into these matters."

"It's not unusual at all."

"And the word on gold?"

"Mr. Drew's already drained the Erie of its holdings in gold, Challis. Everybody knows that."

Was that Stedman at the other end of the porch? She turns away to look at the surf, lest Challis notice her cheeks are burning. Tennessee takes a deep breath of night air then turns back to him, "I believe Colonel Jim Fisk, Mr. Corbin, and Mr. Gould are the authorities in that department."

Challis says, "Is it true, as rumor has it, that you're now free of all encumbrances?"

Tennessee raises an eyebrow and curtseys. "I have always been, and shall always remain, free of all encumbrances, Mr. Challis."

"Now, that's a pity!"

"But I still require the services of a dancing partner." She gives him her best dimpled smile.

"Well, then, drink up! Let's see if we can't wreak some havoc in this sleepy coastal town."

The party is in full swing. Through the French doors she sees James Gordon Bennett arrive with a famous actress.

A heated argument begins at the far end of the terrace. Looking over, she sees E.C. Stedman appeal to someone's better nature. Calm down, she tells herself.

Next to Stedman is an attractive, heavily pregnant woman.

"Who is that?" Tennessee asks.

"Mrs. Stedman, of course," Challis says.

"Oh, of course."

"She's taking her accouchement here. Far more comfortable than in town this time of year."

Downing the rest of her drink, Tennessee holds up her glass to Challis. "Let's have another and then dance till they throw us out."

Roxana is awake when Tennessee creeps into the room they're sharing with the children. Tennessee slips her nightgown over her head and leans down to kiss her.

Roxana grabs Tennessee's hand. "Tennie, 'as the serpent beguiled Eve through his subtlety, so your mind shall be corrupted from the simplicity that is in Christ.'"

"Good night, Ma." Tennessee lies down as her mother sits up.

Roxana says, "Mrs. Julia Grant's party for the tent meeting, Tennie."

"Hmm?"

"You must come with. We must pray together for Utie and poor Byron if for no one else."

"But we can pray here."

"No, no, we must be in Nature. In the tent. The Reverend Osborn and Mr. Stokes will lead the group. Come, Tennessee. We must pray together. For Utie and for Byron."

From her spot in the ocean, just beyond the waves, Tennessee observes James Gordon Bennett and his man drag a dinghy onto the shore. She lets the tide carry her a short distance further down the beach. Thoughts of Cornelius, when they splashed together, shouting "Capital! Capital!" make her heart ache.

Her tears mix with the seawater. "Pull yourself together," she mutters, watching the bathers on the beach. Soft white sand and blue, blue sea. The undertow is terrific, and waves crash over her. She realizes the tide is too strong to swim up current, past where Bennett has set up his boat.

When she walks by him to return to the house, he bows and says, "Miss Claflin, I presume?"

Tennessee nods. "Indeed. Mr. Bennett."

"You are a jaunty and veritable mermaid in your swimming trunks, I daresay."

She chuckles at this, even though she prefers not to answer.

"May I accompany you?"

"Mr. Bennett, did I not see you with Miss Markham?"

"Ah, I returned her to New York. She suffers from seasickness, and this time of year is overwhelmingly nautical. Besides, I wonder…"

His voice trails off and he shrugs, walking with great long strides toward the houses. Tennessee must take two steps for every one of his. She glances up at him. His handsome face is bronzed, his eyebrows and moustache bleached blond from the sun. His enormous hands are freckled, and his legs and feet are pale. She realizes she is smiling at the white legs transporting this great lumbering man beside her.

"What do you wonder, Mr. Bennett?" she asks.

He stops walking and points at an elegant yacht moored in the ocean. "That's my boat, the *Henrietta*."

"Who is Henrietta?"

"My mother." He suddenly smiles. "Would you like to go on deck?"

"Now?"

"Why not?" He appears no more imposing than a freckle-faced farm boy.

Tennessee laughs and says, "Yes, I would."

Abruptly they change course and return to the dinghy. Bennett and his man push the boat into the water and row past the waves. Aboard the *Henrietta*, Bennett gives her a sweater to wear over her damp suit and shows her every detail of the yacht. Afterward, they sit on deck and feast on grilled halibut, corn on the cob, peaches, and champagne.

"I wonder if you're not somewhat like me, Miss Claflin."

"Like you?"

"You're a lone wolf. You'd rather go it alone than play along with everyone's hypocrisy. Because at least at this juncture, I'd say it's little more than that."

"Hypocrisy. Hmm." She thinks about the ladies at the Roosevelt house. "When we met, Mr. Bennett, each one of those so-called virtuous women made a great show of pretending she wasn't available to the highest bidder. I did find it most hypocritical."

"Should I appear with a companion who is not in society, but whose company I enjoy, Miss Markham, for instance," he says, "society is then closed to me, if its daughters cannot vie, as it were, for the contents of my wallet."

The sun is low in the sky. The yacht gently rocks in the water and they watch the houses darken in shadow. Bennett looks at her and she senses his heart beating.

Finally, he says, "It's time to conquer some uncharted waters, or at least get to Newport. Would you like to come along?"

It occurs to her that he knows about Cornelius, too. She realizes Bennett is still speaking. "Perhaps you would need to fit me in though, between…" Has all this just been a ploy?

A moment ago, if he had kissed her, she would have gladly reciprocated. Now, it seems, a slap might be more in order. Instead, she says, "I don't know what you take me for, Mr. Bennett, but I am here in the company of my mother and family."

Embarrassed, he stands, offering her his hand. "One of the crew will row you back."

She can still feel his heartbeat, but his offer has spoiled the afternoon. She pulls off the sweater and hands it back to him. "Thank you for the loan of your sweater. Good night."

Three wagons bring supplies for the two dozen families. While the men pitch tents and debate where to hold the revival meeting, Tennessee dons her swimming costume. She does feel jaunty and mermaid-like at the same time. The weather is sublime, and she digs for clams with Zula and Byron. Afterwards, they lie down on the water's edge, reading the clouds in the sky. In the evening, the families gather around the campfire to sing hymns, and Tennessee sees Stedman, across the flames, next to his wife and three young sons.

He sings loudly, his face ruddy from the sun and now the campfire. Does he see her as well? She feels a strange lightness looking at Stedman's boys, holding hands, their arms crossed right over left. The verses are sung in rounds. The air is sweet and sparks from the fire jump into the night sky.

The next morning is spent in prayer as the sun rises over the ocean, followed by an abundant feast and more religious service.

Tennessee wonders whether Bennett was right. She does feel like a lone wolf, and it fills her chest with sorrow. She sneaks away and walks south in her straw hat and sailor suit. Away from the encampment, past lonely fishermen's shacks and the occasional jetty, the sorrow turns to grief. She goes as far as the sandy beach will take her. When she looks back at the white peaks of the camp, their resemblance to the tents from the War sear her with the injustice of it all. Performing her sessions, conducting readings. There had been hundreds, perhaps thousands. Everyone knew those boys would die, and they knew it, too. Still, they'd each pay her to read their palms and not say what she saw.

What a disaster those years had been! If she wasn't taking their money, she was cheating them at cards, with that charlatan, that Jack, the contaminating bastard.

Why did her parents condemn her to such a life of humbug? After the woman in Ottawa died, how could Buck still put her to work and continue selling the elixir? How can she possibly pray to, let alone love, the Lord who let such things come to pass? God doesn't love her. He certainly didn't love those million souls He'd kept in bondage, nor those boys He killed in the War. With a sob, she thinks about the dead woman in Ottawa. Why is it that God loves Buck and Cornelius, and men in power who take and steal and humbug to further their own ends? Tennessee begins to weep, because it seems to her, that is who God truly loves.

Desperate to be done with it, she rips off her clothes, yelling into the surf. "I do not love you, LORD! I do not!"

The surf roars in response and Tennessee shakes her fists at the ocean. "I do not love you! I am free to do whatever I choose!" She tears into the water yelling and beating at her chest, "I am the Sovereign Of Myself!"

She plunges into the waves, is knocked over and swallows a mouthful of water. Still, she swims toward the horizon.

"WAIT."

A giant wave rises above her. She holds her nose and ducks to let it rush over her head. She reemerges.

"WAIT!" a lone figure calls from the shore.

Tennessee rolls onto her back. She sees a pair of seals watching her, curious for what will happen next.

"My God!" she yells and shakes her fist at the sky. "Have I got to live this life always? Can I not even take my life in PEACE, Lord?!"

The male voice swims closer. "Are you injured?"

A wave rolls her closer to him.

It is Stedman. He is not much of a swimmer. "Swim back! Please." He appears to struggle in the water, turning his back to the surf. "Miss Claflin!"

A massive wave crests, rushing toward shore. She rides it to push him out of harm's way. "Get behind me, Stedman!"

"WHAT?"

The ocean heaves its force on the pair, spinning water and sand. When she is upright and breathing, she sees he is the same. They drag themselves to the water's edge. He does not react to her nakedness.

He wipes his brow and beard. "Why did you say, 'Get behind me Satan'?"

"I said, 'Get behind me, Stedman.'"

"Oh."

She turns her head away lest he see her disappointment at having been rescued thus.

"Miss Claflin." He gently touches her shoulder. It is simply too much. She brushes his hand away. This beautiful man with his pregnant wife and three young boys, traipsing behind her or whatever he's been doing and robbing her of her moment to—

Tennessee whirls around and strikes him as hard as she can. "How dare you! How dare you take it upon yourself?"

"What would you have me do?" He raises his arm in front of his face and grabs her other arm. "Leave you to drown and say what?"

"God damn you!"

"I saw her drowning, but she didn't want to be disturbed."

"Get away, get away!" she yells, and flings sand into his face. She runs to her clothes, throws them on and continues running until she reaches the camp.

Later, at the hymn sing, Roxana collapses in a swoon. Naturally, Stedman is one of the men who assists her back to their tent. Roxana is put to bed, and Tennessee walks him outside. The night sky is brilliant with stars. She says, "We must return to Long Branch. This religious diet is too rich for us, I'm afraid."

Stedman sees the shadows in her gaze and nods. "Get behind me, Satan." He shakes his head. "That's what I thought you said."

Even in her wretchedness, she can't help but smile. "Good night, Ned. Thank you—for bringing my mother back. Thank you."

From the journal of Tennie C. Claflin:

17 Great Jones Street is being painted, so all of us in town are staying with Meg on 26th Street. New York in August is deliciously quiet. I have begun to write my essay, "What Is Virtue, What It Is Not." However, EC Stedman remains shamefully more on my mind than the Commodore has ever been. And what about that rake, James Gordon Bennett? What he said about hypocrisy feels quite true, and much to my regret, I wanted to kiss him as well. And that invitation to Newport? Out of the question. As for Stedman, he is very bold, but would he ever want me on his arm? Of course not. That is his wife's privilege.

Downstairs there's laughter and a hullabaloo. Meg calls, "Tennie, you have company!" Has Stedman come back?

She races downstairs and finds Luther Challis. "Hello. What brings you here?"

"Dealings with Colonel Fisk and Mr. Gould." Luther's eyes sparkle. She brings him into the parlor. He is holding a rucksack. "Heed what I tell you about gold, my girl. Look!" He sits down and takes out several pints of champagne.

"How kind. Thank you, Luther."

"I know it's your favorite. Tennie, Tennie C…You'd do wise to advise your patron as much."

"My patron? As much about what?"

"Gold, gold! Listen." Luther has difficulty speaking. "Your arrangement with the Commodore's been discussed at some length. We all know why you were with him. And it was commendable! You're helping your sister's cause, what." He is quite drunk and leans toward her. "Now, he's through with you, so listen, listen. Listen, to me, my girl."

"Sit down, Luther." Obediently, he does so, and she sits next to him. He says, "Why wait? Now the Commodore's wrapped things up, forego it all. Just come to Luther."

"Luther…I will never have—"

"I brought you this, dear." He takes a package wrapped in lavender tissue from his rucksack. "Listen to me, Tennessee."

She begins to speak, but he puts his thick finger over her lips. "Listen. About the gold. I daren't speak about it with Vanderbilt, or anyone. Save for you, so listen. It's going to rise at the end of September. Buy as much as you can in the next weeks. Tell your ex-lover, Old Father Time, to do the same. If it's too awkward, have your sister do it. In a trance, what—"

Challis taps his chest with his fist. "Champagne gives a man gas!" He lets forth a rumbling belch. "Ah, Tennie, you're something. You're something naughty, aren't you?" He goes to kiss her, his mouth open and his tongue protruding.

"You should go home, Luther, you're drunk."

"But I got this for you." The lavender package falls off his lap. "Gold, Tennie. Buy as much as you can, before it's 130." He leans back, closes his eyes, and passes out cold. She unwraps the package. It's a pretty camisole.

In the morning, Meg is fit to be tied when she finds Challis has been sick beside the divan. "What an appalling example for the children. Really, Tennie!"

"I didn't know! I'd already gone to bed!" Tennessee protests.

"Really, Tennie," Polly chimes in. "You're such a whore. You parade about with your illicit nonsense for the children to see, and Ben struggling to find work. When I think, how we could just go like this," Polly snaps her fingers, "and tell those Vanderbilts a thing or two about where you've been and what you've got."

Polly plunges a soiled rag in the bucket of soapy water. She straightens up. "But that's what you get, living with little more than a whore."

Utica adds, "Challis comes here so Tennie will service him. Why pay at Hotel de Wood when he can come here, and she does it as a favor?"

"Do you speak of yourself, Utica?" Tennessee asks.

"I've seen you! I've seen you and your different men. Not only Challis. What about that poet?" Utica smiles at her discomfort. "And Dr. Randolph, with his magic mirror?" Utica says, an inch from Tennessee's face.

"That is false."

"I hear you running baths, rubbing yourself with Ma's revolting liniment. How else are we going to pay our bills? Buck's fees at the club are fierce, Tennie. I've heard him say so."

The clack from Tennessee's hand on to Utica's cheek makes everyone freeze.

"You bitch!" Utica screams. "Whore!"

In a flash, they are kicking, pinching, tearing at each other's clothes and hair. Polly runs to get her husband. A small table falls over. A china shepherdess crashes into a million pieces. Ben grabs Polly's bucket. He pours it over them. The putrid water calms things down.

"Have some brandy, Utica," Ben says.

"You're less nasty when you're drunk," Tennessee mutters. She looks at her writing tablet. It's dripping wet and the ink has run off the page.

COST THE LIMIT OF PRICE

September 1869
37 West Twenty-Seventh Street

WHEN MRS. VIRGINIA Grant Corbin learns of the Commodore's nuptials, she promptly arranges a luncheon. Old Jesse Grant, who is the father of Ulysses and Mrs. Corbin, is emphatic that "his people" should be received. Upon their arrival at the Corbin house, Buck, Victoria, Colonel Blood, and Tennessee are met with great enthusiasm. Roxana is otherwise indisposed but sends her kindest regards. In attendance is also Mrs. Corbin's sister-in-law, the First Lady, Mrs. Julia Grant. The President, Ulysses Grant is unable to attend, but sends one hundred lobsters, which are steamed, peeled, and served in molded salads on beds of sliced alligator pear.

Best wishes for the future and a sparkling Riesling are in abundance.

Before the ladies retire and the gentlemen go for their cigars, Victoria murmurs to Cornelius, "The spirits advised, it's imperative to buy gold before it's 130, Commodore, then sell it at 150, sir. Commodore," she puts her hand on his arm, "it will be that high very soon."

"We must consult before the end of the week, Mrs. Woodhull."

"Yes, we must. Indeed."

He watches Tennessee leave the dining room. "Additionally, I'm sure there is some way we can front you a sum, so that you, too, might profit from the gift of the spirits. You and your sister have been," he pauses for a moment, "most accommodating."

Later that night, before going to bed, the Commodore stands in his dressing room, and holds the length of Tennessee's hair, tied with velvet ribbon. His wife calls him from their bedroom. He studies the braid a moment longer and then carefully wraps it in its tissue paper. He moves it to the very back of his glove drawer where it will be found after his death, mused over and thrown away as only so much rubbish.

———

"Well?" Polly and Ben Sparr are alone in the kitchen. Ben begins writing another letter and does not answer. Despite his beautiful penmanship, he's left an inkblot on the paper.

How frustrating! Polly wipes away an exasperated tear. It's as though she weren't the one, all those years ago, whom Buck had offered up to those inclined, and she had willingly cooperated, for the good of the family! Victoria and Tennessee make no such sacrifice, yet they have coin in abundance. All Polly has is her brood and a dreamer for a husband.

She looks through Tennessee's journal. There is Commodore Vanderbilt, of course, that smarmy Stedman the poet, Challis is also a must, and why not that odd-looking senator who came for dinner?

She tries again with her husband. "Ben, tell me what you penned in your letter."

Ben Sparr clears his throat. "Dear Sir: Your intimacy with Tennie C. Claflin and Mrs. Woodhull is known…I know also that you have a wife and family. Now I am down on my luck, and I want three hundred dollars out of you. You may call this blackmailing. But I have you right."

"That's pretty good." Polly smiles. "I should ask Ma to dress as a poor woman and drop these off. She'll do it, she likes a little play-acting. Besides, she owes me a favor."

———

James Gordon Bennett studies the note and then writes to Tennessee.

My dear Miss Claflin:

An old woman claiming to be your mother left this letter with me. She said that she had been told to get $300 out of me for it, but as she couldn't read, I believed that she did not know what she had been put up to. I told her it was no use. That my intimacy with you was honest, square, and pure. I gave her three dollars because she said she hadn't a cent. I asked her why she didn't go to you. She said Sparr told her that if she did, you would send her to the island. I write this to put you on your guard…the parties behind your mother mean to do you harm.

September 24, 1869
Wall Street

Many years later, the day will be known as Black Friday. On this day, the last Friday in September, as prearranged, the price of gold continues to climb.

Outside the exchange, errand boys run back and forth, relaying messages of how much to buy, when to hold, when to sell. Men leave their offices, crowding the pavement. Soon, they struggle to navigate between one building and another. No one knows when, or even if, the price of gold will plummet to its original value. All one can do is speculate.

A boy knocks on the door of the carriage Victoria has hired for the day. She peers out and he hands her a note. She gives him a penny then sends him on his way. Glancing at the message, she turns to Colonel Blood and whispers, "We need to sell, all of it. Right away."

Wordlessly, he leaves the carriage. Minutes pass. Outside, the horses shift, tensing as the uncertainty around them gives way to a tide of mounting chaos. But, it occurs to Victoria that she is happy, as happy as she had been when Colonel Blood took her away from St. Louis. Eventually, the carriage door opens, and the Colonel is sitting beside her. She can see from his smile that he has been successful. "Oh, Colonel," she murmurs. They kiss tenderly. Then she says, "I shall walk home, I think," and slips out of the brougham before he can protest.

The National Guard arrives to quell any rioting. Soldiers jog heavily past her, their bayonets pointed upright. But as sometimes happens in a city like New York, just a few blocks around the corner, everything is peaceful. Indeed, it all seems a world away.

———

Despite running with a different crowd, James Gordon Bennett likes Colonel Jim Fisk. He admires the fact that Fisk is self-made and so matter-of-fact about it, too.

As friends, Bennett and Fisk share enormous appetites, but they are also a study in contrasts. Fisk enjoys audacity in financial ventures, whereas Bennett is considerably more cautious. For Bennett, chicanery on Wall Street is not as compelling as racing on land or sea. But whenever he invites Fisk to join him, Fisk always begs off, stating that he is partial to the act of remaining alive instead.

The walls at Colonel Jim Fisk's apartments are papered with red velvet damask. No expense has been spared and the sitting room is furnished with gold leaf tables, marble columns, massive palms, cheetah skins, and tiger skins scattered on silk Persian carpets.

Bennett watches as a little boy wearing a turban, a small child really, expertly pours green liquid into a chilled crystal goblet. The boy then places a sugar lump onto a slotted spoon and slides the spoon across the top of the glass. Water is then drizzled over it, melting the sugar, diluting the absinthe. He carries the drink over to Bennett. Fisk is already on his second absinthe, and waves the boy away, saying, "That business with the gold on Friday, I had nothing to do with the sell-off, you know. Gould was unloading his hoard while I was still driving up the price! It was nothing less than nefarious."

"Your own partner undermined the strategy you concocted together?" Bennett lights a cigarette.

"Indeed! He sent the boys out to sell, whilst my lot was still buying it up!"

"Was Butterfield in on it, too?"

"Well, he is at the Treasury. We got him through President Grant's brother-in-law, Corbin."

"I see."

"I know a good many were wiped out, but the inner circle did well enough."

"The inner circle? Who was that?"

"Unhappily for them, not the Corbins! But Vanderbilt yielded quite a few million. I heard Tennie's sister, Mrs. Woodhull, she did very well. Someone said three quarters of a million or thereabouts."

Bennett allows the boy to refill his glass. Fisk gestures to his own and continues. "Of course, everyone Gould was buttering up, they made money. His dance card will certainly remain full."

Bennett puts his cigarette out. He thinks the absinthe packs a wallop.

Fisk says, "But here's the thing, Jimmy. I am utterly peeved with Gould. He netted a good seven million at least, if not more, and I'd be exaggerating if I claimed to have done better than two or three. I think it warrants ventilating."

"Really?"

"You should expose the whole lot of 'em in your paper."

"That would be the president's sister and brother-in-law?"

"The Corbins, yes that's right, and of course, his wife, Julia."

"Mrs. Julia Grant?"

"Yes, and Butterfield, Assistant Secretary of the U.S. Treasury. Then Jay Gould, of course. Who am I forgetting?" The men drink in silence until Fisk adds, "I'll send you the list."

Suddenly, Bennett feels very tired. The president's sister, as well as the first lady. Thank God he is headed to Paris in the morning.

Fisk is still talking. "Perhaps you'd do me the favor to keep me out of it. But what I'll give you is enough to take them down. The entire Grant administration. The whole lot of 'em. Those scoundrels."

December 1869
425 Fifth Avenue

The sleeping form next to James Gordon Bennett Jr. brushes the strands of hair away from her mouth and yawns before she scratches her nose.

Bennett checks her evening slipper on the bedside table. There is still some champagne in it. It's warm and a little flat. She is likable enough, though, this one. Nice singing voice, still starring in that absurd musical, *The Black Crook*. But they enjoy the same things. A bit of carousing and evenings concluded with sex. It works out not too badly, really. She opens her eyes and turns over to face him. "Well?"

"Yes."

"I wouldn't say no to a bauble or a token, Mr. Bennett."

"No, I don't imagine you would."

"Colonel Fisk has advised me to accept nothing less than that which is worth my weight in gold."

"Did he now? I am surprised that you'd divulge our arrangement to Colonel Fisk."

"Well, he advises me. On all matters. Romantic and financial."

"Ah." James Gordon Bennett watches Miss Markham find her stockings. She slowly puts them on. She steps into her petticoats and then her skirt.

"Hand me that, would you?" She points to the shoe on the table.

Bennett obligingly wipes out the last drops of champagne with a corner of the bed linen.

He hands her the shoe. "And how did you make out during Colonel Fisk's last foray into the gold market?"

Pauline Markham chuckles as she arranges her ample bosom and her corset. "Very well indeed, thank you. Colonel Fisk invested everything I had. He sold after the gold began its descent, alas, but I can't complain. How about you?"

"I missed that caper altogether."

"Well, you're rich enough already, Mr. Bennett. Now how's about my trinket?"

Bennett gives her a brief glance and strolls over to his dresser. The top drawer is lined in velvet. Various pocket watches, gold chains with which to secure them, lorgnettes, cuff links, tie pins, shirt studs, and the like are carelessly scattered within.

"Miss Markham, perhaps I can interest you in this." It is a small gold brooch of the *Henrietta*.

Pauline Markham wags her finger gently at him. She has but little interest in any aspect of a piece other than its worth. "Thank you, no. I really hate boats. These cuff links are nice, though." A pair of square-cut emeralds that match her catlike eyes.

"Consider them yours," he says. "Will I see you at the French Ball tomorrow?"

"Not I!" She says and turns toward the mirror. "I have a reputation to protect."

He bends over the speaking tube in the wall, which transports his voice down to the servants' quarters. Watching her primp in front of the mirror, he says into the tube, "Have Dixon see Miss Markham home, would you?"

A disembodied voice responds. "Yes, Mr. Bennett. Right away, sir."

From the journal of Tennie C. Claflin:

I like to play cards. I do. If I had won my hand, it would've been ten dollars in my pocket. But I did not win. Rather, it was Luther Challis who won the other night. He suggested rather than paying him ten dollars, that I agree to meet him at this year's Masked Ball. I invited Victoria and Utica to come along for the adventure, and Paschal Randolph will act as chaperone. I told everyone at home we were going to a recital. I know deception is naughty, but it's so easily contrived when well planned! I spent a tidy sum on the costumes, too. Victoria and I are dressing as shepherdesses, Utica will be a shepherd, and Pascale, of course, will play the wolf. Our frocks are sumptuous. Lace cascading from open sleeves and enormous straw hats perched on specially designed hairpieces lend us ten inches' advantage in height. Of course, bodices are worn very tight in such a getup. I daresay, it makes it difficult to breathe.

Victoria adjusts her cleavage in the mirror. "Miss Anthony will be obliged to acknowledge my seriousness when I make a donation and move to the front of her suffragist queue now, won't she?"

Tennessee raises an eyebrow, "Particularly if you go dressed as you are."

Victoria chuckles. "The Colonel would be scandalized, too, should he recognize me thus!"

They venture forth, filled with the thrilling, dangerous element of being amongst the revelers, everyone masked, undercover, out in public.

Victoria's brooding persists. "Even were I to pave the streets with gold, some of the suffragists will still find me unsuitable."

Paschal Randolph answers, "Your unflinching candor when it comes to independence and relations between the sexes is heightened by your singular beauty. It makes for a potent brew."

They cross Fourteenth Street and he adds, "That you are not only a revolutionary in theory but also a woman of action sets you apart." They approach the Academy of Music. Formally dressed men descend from their carriages while a sea of color and feathers swarm the entrances.

"Please continue!" she cries. "It does my heart good to receive such encouragement."

Randolph says, "It will be your cross to bear, as long as you are fighting for the cause of women."

Spectators crowd the pavement and policemen clear a path. Utica takes a nip from a small flask and passes it to Randolph. She holds her fingers to her lips to keep the flask their secret. Randolph has a swig, and gasps. Irish lightening, a type that has long been banned, its strength known to be sometimes lethal.

Utica laughs, declaring, "What mischief awaits us tonight!"

From the unpublished memoirs of P.B. Randolph:

Revelers overwhelmed every inch of the space. I pushed back my mask (a wolf's head, no less), in an effort not to fall over myself. Thankfully, Tennessee had purchased a box on the orchestra level, furnished with a settee, table and chairs, a cold banquet, and an abundance of champagne on ice.

I finished the flask and basked in the pleasure of being with friends for whom I've been my best self. Alas, at times, they are the same people with whom I've been at my worst. With Tennessee and Victoria, we discussed clairvoyance and individual freedom. With Utica, I rarely remembered what, if anything, we ever discussed at all. But Utica had such charm and beauty that if we both made it home, then it hardly seemed to matter.

My next memory of the ball was literally from under a table. Everything was silent. I climbed out. The hall was empty, and the street doors were open. It was daylight.

From the journal of Tennie C. Claflin:

We all had a great deal to drink, but that does not excuse my failure to prevent what happened from taking place. Luther Challis found our box and climbed in over the side.

"Which one of you is which?" he asked, although he knew very well. Then he placed his hand round my waist. "Come with me, Shepherdess. Let's trip the lights fantastic."

The orchestra was playing my very favorite song from The Black Crook. *It is a polka and impossible to resist.*

When you want a kiss or favor,
you're on your best behavior,
you naughty, naughty men.
You may talk of love and sighing,
say for us you're nearly dying,
All the while you know you're trying to deceive,
you wicked, wicked men!

Challis is not a bad dancer. We whirled round the floor, spinning, laughing, and stopped only for champagne, the evening a rush of pleasant chaos, until the scream and then a crash.

Everyone froze for a moment. It was silent. A woman had fallen over one of the balconies. Not two seconds later, the orchestra resumed playing, louder, faster. All became topsy-turvy. It was difficult to stand. I had to sit down.

Across the floor, shoulders above everyone else, was James Gordon Bennett Jr. waving his arms like a madman. He seemed so foolish, I resumed laughing and staggered back to the box. Then someone tweaked my bottom. It was Challis.

He said, "You may be a shepherdess, but I know you are a wolf in lamb's clothing, too." He goosed me again and went to open his flies.

"Luther, desist!" I pushed him away. No harm was meant, and none taken. It was then we saw the little shepherdess wandering through the dancers.

Luther Challis shouts. "Over here! We've food and drink!"

"Hello!" she answers, her crook weaving back and forth.

"What is your name?" Victoria calls out to the girl who scoots up over the railing.

"I am Bo-Peep, of course." She lifts her mask. It is doubtful she is more than thirteen years old. Bo-Peep makes a boozy wink at Tennessee. She then sits on the settee and within moments is passed out.

"Well, I'll go find Utica, shall I?" Victoria says.

Tennessee attempts to stand, but the room still spins. No sooner has Victoria gone then Bo-Peep comes to. She is up halfway, leaning on her elbows. Luther sits next to her and says, "Here Bo, try a little bubbly."

He props her up, so she leans against him. "That's a good girl." He puts the bottle to Bo-Peep's lips and her head lolls back.

"Luther. Leave Bo-Peep alone!" Tennessee stands and needs the chair for support.

"Tennie, mind your business." He smiles and strokes the girl's tiny flat chest. "Bo is happy here. Aren't you, my dear?"

"What?" Bo's head nods back, and she is out again.

"Challis, you rogue!" Another man in a mask and Harlequin's cap straddles the railing and climbs into the box. "My goodness, but there are two of them."

"Yes, but that one's no fun," Luther says, pointing at Tennessee. "However, our Sleeping Beauty is quite defenseless."

At which point Challis stands, undoes his flies again, but this time he pulls the helpless Bo toward him, hoisting up her petticoats. "Hold that one, will you?" he says to the Harlequin.

"Luther, stop it!" Tennessee cries out. Challis's friend grabs and holds her tight.

You take us from our mothers,
Our sisters and our brothers,
When you get us, flirt with others
Oh, you cruel and wicked men.

No one comes to their aid when Tennessee screams, begging them to stop. The party remains in full swing. The Harlequin's lips brush against her ear, "What did you expect? It's what you're here for, isn't it? It's comme il faut, bitch."

Which makes her realize that anyone asked is of the same opinion. All women at the Ball have agreed to be taken, simply by showing up.

Luther Challis lets the girl fall back on to the settee and buttons up his flies. He thrusts his hand under her skirt, then holds up a bloody finger and wags it triumphantly. "You see? You see! I win the prize. I found my cherry first! You owe me fifty dollars."

The Harlequin releases Tennessee and she crumples onto the floor.

Challis says, "Here's an idea. Let's take her to Mrs. de Ford. We'll have turns at her over the weekend. You don't have any plans, do you?"

"I do now! I'm spending the weekend at Mrs. de Ford's." They laugh and slap each other on the back, leaving with Bo-Peep hoisted over Challis's shoulder.

Victoria returns to the box alone. "Utica's been arrested."

"Why?" Tennessee wipes her eyes. "Where is Paschal?"

"I don't know."

Tennessee's finery is in ruin, and the make-up runs down her face. "Vicky, I saw them—that poor girl." Suddenly she is sobbing. "I did nothing to stop them!"

"Shh," Victoria says, "Let's go home."

Outside, the night is bitter, and the streets are deserted. Tennessee wonders if they should go to Mrs. de Ford's. She thinks about what James Gordon Bennett had said. "You want to get to someone like that in the balls? Ventilate it. Get them in the press."

PART THREE

FAME

"When a dog bites a man, that is not news. But if a man bites a dog, that is news."

-Charles Dana,
proprietor of the *New York Sun*

WHEN A MAN BITES A DOG

January 1870
Madison Square Park

THE WINTER SKY turns a magical pink and snow flurries are whirling in such a way that they dance, floating up rather than down. Tennessee emerges from the Hoffman House Hotel. She pauses on the curb, about to cross the street, when she hears a whistle and a cry, "Hey, Babs! Hey, Toot! Mommy, Poppy!" Whereupon a four-legged flash of fur speeds out of Madison Square Park. On Tennessee's left, a pair of sleds are racing down Broadway.

The spaniel stops, stock still in the middle of the street.

"Get out of the way, out of the way!" the drivers shout, whips waving in the air, the horses foaming and snorting, but the dog is confused, still in the middle of the street.

Tennessee dashes forward. She grabs the dog, tumbling onto the opposite curb, missing the sleds by moments.

Her heart is pounding and the blood roars in her ears, the spaniel trembling in her arms. It takes a moment to catch her breath. Furious, she carries the dog toward a lone figure surrounded by a pack of small dogs.

"Oy!" she shouts. "Did you see what just happened? Did you?" It is James Gordon Bennett. "Mr. Bennett!" Her heart is still racing. "We might have died."

"Hells bells! From the look of it, you very nearly did, Miss Claflin."

She is surprised he recognizes her under the scarves and hat.

"That was very brave. Thank you." He takes the spaniel in his arms.

"Hmm." Tennessee turns away and marches toward Twenty-Third Street, vaguely puzzled that she is smiling.

"Mommy!" She hears him scold the spaniel. "What have you got? Drop it. Drop it!" Within an instant, he is walking alongside her, the dogs at his feet. "What are you doing out in this weather?"

She struggles to frown, but the dogs are so playful, it is impossible. "We're setting up shop across the street."

He gives her a strange look. "At the Hoffman House?"

"We're going to be brokers. My sister and I." The dogs joyfully cavort around them. She says, "If you really love them, you'd keep a better eye on them."

"You're quite right. I apologize. To you and to Mommy." Then he holds out a small, white ball of fluff in his enormous gloved hand. "So, what should we do about this? It was Mommy's prisoner."

The tiny white barn owl in the cup of his hand struggles to right itself. "Oh—oh." He says, removing the glove on his other hand with his teeth to create a shelter for the owl. The enormous eyes in its flat round face look up at Tennessee.

"Don't look at me," she says to the owl.

"Let's just take it to the house. Then we can—where is it you live?"

"Great Jones Street."

"I'm on 38th. We shan't be a tick." They approach a gleaming black sled. The dogs and Tennessee climb in and Bennett jumps in beside them. "Home, Dixon," he says to the coachman.

425 Fifth Avenue is on the east side of the block, its entrance on Thirty-Eighth Street, with a circular driveway behind a tall, ivy-covered fence.

"Let's go in, let's go in," Bennett says.

Polished wood and burnished gilt frames glow in the soft light. Tennessee's feet sink into an exquisite carpet underfoot and the room's elegance exudes every comfort.

Bennett speaks to the footman, who bows and quickly fetches a small box. "Ask Mrs. Mack for some socks and my grey muffler, perhaps."

He stands on the hearth, gently stroking the bird. "Chirp, chirp," he whispers to it, then puts it into the box, tucking his socks and scarf around it. He says to Tennessee, "You know, the owl is my spiritual guide."

"Really?"

"Being clairvoyant, I would think you'd know that."

To which she raises her eyebrows and remains silent. After relinquishing the bird's care to the footman, Bennett says, "Should I take you home, or will you stay for refreshment?"

Tennessee realizes she has yet to cease smiling and is suddenly reluctant to leave.

"I think we'd be wise to have soup and some libation before venturing out," he says.

"And we must consider what to feed your bird," she replies.

"That's right!"

A small table is set up by the fire and they dine on consommé and Cornish game hens.

Bennett looks up from his meal. "Is this in very poor taste, considering our guest?" he asks, at which point she begins to laugh and so does he.

Afterward, he drives her back in a different sled, a sporty cutter, designed for two. Bennett stands and cracks the whip. The horse leaps forward and the cutter almost flies past the other sleds on the street. Bennett whoops, leaning into the snowy wind, just as he had on the *Icicle*. The freezing temperature nips at their skin. It is exhilarating. Tennessee laughs and joins him, shouting and whooping, too.

They arrive at Great Jones Street, and he gives her a considered look. Finally, he says, "Miss Claflin, this stock brokerage venture—you're going to want a lot of press."

"Yes, yes, we will."

"The *Herald* is at your service then. The rest will follow suit. Within hours, I might add."

For a moment, they are both silent. Finally, Bennett says, "I am sure I don't need to caution you."

"Against what?"

"The press. Things will get out of hand. They invariably do." He helps her out of the sled. "But you'll cross that bridge when you get to it."

He stands very close to her. Tennessee says, "What do you think of ladies working on Wall Street, Mr. Bennett?"

When he doesn't answer, she asks, "And of women's suffrage in general?"

He holds up his hands. "Miss Claflin, I am apolitical. The *Herald's* function is to be purely independent in support of the facts. Nothing else." He bows, then climbs back in the sled. "Oh, by the way..."

"Yes?"

"I've decided to name the bird after you." He cracks the whip. "Miss Tennessee!"

NEW YORK HERALD

January 22, 1870. THE QUEENS OF FINANCE. A New Phase of the Woman's Rights Question. The Lady Stock Operators of Wall Street—The Firm of Woodhull, Claflin & Co.—Vanderbilt Proteges—Interview of a *Herald* Reporter with the Future Princesses of Erie."

Reporters attending their first day in business are many. Tennessee spins in the Colonel's chair and says, "Why don't we invite that yummy Whitelaw Reid of the *Tribune* to dinner? He might follow the excellent example set by the *Herald.*"

She pretends to study a balance sheet as yet another reporter waits for her to look up. She whistles an owl's "who, who," then laughs, "We do not want flattery. We ask to be taken for exactly what we are good for, as men are."

But everyone knows that will never happen. Women must be one classifiable commodity or another. She wonders why people will not admit that females are still traded as if they were so much chattel. Society ladies merely hawk their wares for a higher sum than those who barter and are paid for by the hour.

⁓

A copy boy leads Tennessee across the lobby of the *New York Herald*, and she spies her reflection in the polished stone columns. Everything is pristine, of the latest technology and innovation. Powered by two steam engines, at a rate of thirty-five horsepower each, massive printing presses are visible through a row of windows along the inner wall, operating almost ceaselessly, turning out the next issue.

The copy boy steps aside. He speaks, then listens through the brass end of a speaking tube. "Yes, sir. I'll bring her right away, sir."

They step into a lift, which begins its ascent. On each floor she sees journalists at desks, arguing at large tables. Proofreaders examine copy. Typesetters pour over proofs at tall walnut desks, while clerks conduct business with the public.

Tennessee asks the operator, "How many people work at the *Herald*?"

"Oh, a good five hundred, Miss. We're by far the most widely read paper in the country."

On the fifth floor, the caged doors open. Light pours in circular windows which grace every wall. James Gordon Bennett gives her a deep bow. The entire floor is his office. He leads her to a leather chair across from his massive desk.

"Thank you for the kind notices, Mr. Bennett."

"Miss Claflin, the *Herald* celebrates those who not only *are* the news, but those who make it as well. You and your sister do both."

"I should like to entice the *Tribune* to follow suit."

He frowns and sits behind the desk. He leans back and puts his feet up. "Well, Whitelaw Reid at the *Tribune* is quite the enthusiast when it comes to great thinkers among the fairer sex."

"You don't find it remiss my courting the opposition, do you?"

"On the contrary!" Bennett swings his feet down and leans forward. His eyes sparkle and he smiles. "You need the press, Miss Claflin. As much press as you can handle."

───⁓───

That night, James Gordon Bennett Sr. and Jr. dine at their home on the corner of Thirty-Eighth Street. The younger man pushes his plate away and lights a cigarette.

His father says, "Jimmy, you might as well out with it. What is vexing you so, lad?"

"Fisk wants the *Herald* to expose the Black Friday cabal. He's still miffed that Gould got out quicker than he did."

"And will you run the story?"

"Pater. The president's sister- and brother-in-law are in as deep as Butterfield and Gould."

Bennett Sr. knows his son lacks the nerve to expose the administration. So, he asks, "What else have you got? What news of the pixie Tennie C. Claflin?"

"She wants to win over the *Tribune.*"

"Ha! It will never happen. Horace Greeley is too curmudgeonly to grasp the gossamer of her fairy dust." The old man studies his son. "Jimmy, you look as smitten as your crony Van der Bilt. She won't win over the *Tribune.* It would be like raising the dead."

James Gordon Bennett Jr. shrugs and struggles not to smile. "Pater. Rumor has it she does that, too."

From the journal of Tennie C. Claflin:

We have moved house. Standing on the roof at 15 East 38th Street, I can see as far as the Battery where the East River meets the Hudson and still admire the stars of a clear evening. The house is palatial, and the bedrooms are many. Besides Ben and Polly Sparr's brood, the two maids, and Canning

109

Woodhull (whose room is behind the larder), there is even accommodation for gnarly Pearl Andrews as well. Coincidentally, the James Gordon Bennetts, father and son, reside, dare I say, only fifty paces from our door.

Indeed, our fortune has been so extraordinary that I made it my business to present Ma with something I've long admired in Mr. Tiffany's window. She was in the kitchen when I found her, supervising the maid's tussle with a fish.

"Mater!" I said and showed her the Macassar wood box. I opened it to reveal its silver serving spoons and forks, in addition to the service for twelve.

She closed the box and said, "Take it back." Seeing my dismay, she added, "Your one sister lies with he who degraded your other sister and this sister thinks nothing to have that Blood here in my house."

"Ma!" I explained, "Victoria speaks for us. For all of us. She is going to be Presidentess of these United States, Ma."

To which my mother quoted scripture, "As silver is melted in the furnace, so you will be melted in the midst of it: and you will know that I, the LORD, have poured out My wrath on you."

Hard-boiled quail eggs and sherry are served to stimulate the appetite. Mr. Charles Dana of the *New York Sun* explains, "Mrs. Woodhull, you must employ something other than charm to advance your agenda."

Whitelaw Reid of the *New York Tribune* adds, "This city has no shortage of accomplished women writers. What sets you apart must be something altogether different."

Bennett says, "The challenge will be your credibility."

"Why, because we are women?" Victoria asks.

"No, because you are without pedigree," Dana answers. "Without the endorsement of the suffragists, the Stantons and Anthonys, you are considered sensations who only take attention away from them."

"But what if the very sensation of us worked to drive the sales of a paper as well as discussion of the cause?" Tennessee asks. "We might be considered sensational enough to put the cause on everyone's lips, do you not think?"

Bennett laughs, "She has a point there. Well played."

The loveliness of the Claflin sisters and abundance of wine quickly dispel any awkwardness the journalists might have, particularly as raw oysters on the half shell make their way round the table.

Victoria asks Mr. Dana, "How can I make my feelings, indeed the convictions of my very soul, known to the public; should I not have a platform nor an invitation from which to speak?"

"Mrs. Woodhull, your husband will concur, what you must do is write." Mr. Dana swallows the liquid of the creature sliding down his throat. "My compliments. These are delicious."

"Commodore Vanderbilt sent them over this morning." Victoria smiles at Tennessee.

"Should one fear that being prominently featured in the press would provoke those who might do a person harm?" Tennessee asks.

Bennett says, "In what sense, Miss Claflin?"

"Well, blackmail, or skeletons in the closet, or those who want to embarrass one." Tennessee turns to Mr. Reid. "After all, the power is with the press, isn't it?"

There is a brief silence. She continues, "Look at the murder of Albert Richardson. It matters not that he was murdered in cold blood, in a public place, in front of a witness. Mr. Dana's newspaper has turned his killer's obvious guilt into a justification for those opposed to women's freedom. Hasn't it?"

Someone clears his throat, but no one cares to answer.

Tennessee says, "The *New York Sun* will win Daniel McFarland, who is a murderer, the acquittal."

"No, no." There is a general negating sound from the newspapermen. "That shan't happen," Dana says.

Utica speaks for the first time that evening. "Oh, I believe it will. The public, if not the jury, has been manipulated to believe that McFarland is the injured party. Men hold their wives to be property forever, don't they? Whether they be divorced or no."

Tennessee turns to Bennett. "Isn't that so, Mr. Bennett?"

Bennett says, "Being unmarried I don't quite see it from that angle. But, if you have the affection of the press, anything is possible."

Victoria says, "Then it's a sign. We will produce our own press. Then we can discuss our agenda and what we think is important."

"Great journalism rests on the ability to report a story regardless of what your personal politics might be," Mr. Dana says.

Victoria smiles. "There is much said about what Mr. Greeley's personal politics at the *Tribune* might be."

"Mr. Greeley's commitment to the Fifteenth Amendment is much to his credit," Whitelaw Reid replies.

"Ah, but when will the Fifteenth Amendment include women, too?" Victoria asks.

"You have us there, Mrs. Woodhull. When indeed?" Whitelaw Reid turns to the others. "May I raise a glass to our kind hostess and her exceptional hospitality?" Mr. Reid stands up and says, "To Mrs. Woodhull."

The others join in. "To Mrs. Woodhull!"

PROGRESS! FREE THOUGHT! UNTRAMMELED LIVES!

"Many a good story has been ruined by over verification."

-James Gordon Bennett Sr.

April 1870
44 Broad Street

"While others of my sex devoted themselves to a crusade against the laws that shackle the women of the country, I asserted my individual independence; while others prayed for the good time coming, I worked for it...I have deliberately of my own accord, placed myself before the people as a candidate for the Presidency of the United States."

-Victoria C. Woodhull, *New York Herald*, April 2, 1870

From the journal of Tennie C. Claflin:

When I handed Victoria's editorial to James Gordon Bennett, he wrote across the top, '1ˢᵗ Pronunciamento' in blue pencil as if it were the most natural thing in the world. Then he picked up one of his dogs, I believe it was Mommy, and perched her on his shoulder.

"I like you, Miss Claflin," he said. "You're beautiful and audacious. You and the Woodhull will swash buckle your way to the Capital on the coat-tails of Anthony and Stanton, reinterpret the Constitution and have Mrs. Woodhull run for President! It's great copy."

What is it about this man, with his foolish smile and adoring spaniel?

He continued, "You know, if one were to make the most of recent events, any politician running for president could do worse than to have Fred Douglass at his side. Or her side." Still smiling, he added, "And about your dinner engagement. I expect a full report. From one paper proprietor to another."

It is odd. Every time I see Bennett, there is nary a trace of the notorious roué whom polite society gossips about. Stranger still is that his enthusiasm and support for Woodhull & Claflin's Weekly only serves to increase his esteem in my eyes. It is most unsettling.

———

Whitelaw Reid takes her to Delmonico's. Within moments, the waiter brings over a bottle of champagne, sent compliments of Mr. Bennett, who is dining across the room with Miss Pauline Markham.

When Bennett and Markham leave the restaurant, they pass their table. Reid stands up and he and Bennett whisper something in one another's ear as they shake hands.

"To the protectors of the Free Press!" Reid says.

"Dear fellow, there's no such thing!" Bennett replies, and they both roar with laughter.

The following afternoon, Tennessee sits opposite Bennett at his desk. He asks, "So? Do you like him?"

"I like Reid fine. Don't you?"

"What I'm trying to ascertain is whether it would be fruitful for your business to have a closer association with him."

"My brokerage business or my newspaper business?"

"I don't believe Reid dabbles in the market. It would have to be the newspaper, I suppose."

"Enlighten me with your thinking, Mr. Bennett, if you would be so kind."

"Well, you might pen a letter to Reid, enquiring as to what his designs on you deign to be!"

"And what should I say?" She blushes but refuses to look away—after all, he is complicit in this foolishness, isn't he?

"Well, something light. What time did you get home?"

"Oh, it was toward one, I think."

Bennett raises an eyebrow.

"Does that offend you in some way?"

He clears his throat and begins to scribble. "I trust you rested well last night and that you find yourself refreshed therefrom. For myself..."

"Is that what you write your friends after an evening's entertainment?"

"Say, how about something from a song perhaps? Something from *The Black Crook*."

"That's my favorite show. 'I'm lonely today,'" Tennessee begins to sing. Bennett laughs and joins in the next line.

She smiles at him. "You're not much of a singer, are you, Mr. Bennett?"

The stock market is more volatile than anticipated. Before, they had played gold on the margin, but the results are no longer lucrative. In an effort to economize, they've moved their offices to 44 Broad Street where one isn't subject to the leering eyes of all and sundry. Moreover, Broad Street is only a few minutes stroll from the *Herald* offices at Broadway and Ann. Tennessee lights her pipe and imagines her next visit with Mr. Bennett.

Outside, someone rings the bell, which is followed by a sharp knocking on the door. The office boys have gone for the day. Blood and Victoria are out interviewing printers for the paper.

Tennessee puts away her hash medicinal and opens the door a few inches. "May I help you?"

The man says, "Miss Tennessee Celeste Claflin, this is a summons for an unpaid debt."

Chicago. Bennett did warn her. The coverage in the papers would bring out those from the past, those with an axe to grind. He did say it might get out of hand.

Where there has been a hollowness, the stuff in her heart comes crashing through, flooding the back of her mind and her eyes. She must not cry nor dare say a word.

The man says, "You are to appear in Essex Market Court. You have been served."

<center>~~~</center>

She says nothing to Victoria, nor indeed to anyone. But somehow, it's in the papers.

"Despite every good thing I have done for you, you leave some scandalous business in your wake!" Victoria is livid. "This will damage the respectability which I am striving to exude." She grabs the white pipe out of Tennessee's hand. "And stop smoking! It blurs your capacity for excellence."

Tennessee tries to object, but Victoria cuts her off. "Don't argue. You know I speak the truth. Just stop it." She wags her finger in Tennessee's face. "When Miss Anthony comes to do the profile, there must be no, not even a whisper of, impropriety. Do you understand?"

From the journal of Tennie C. Claflin:

Miss Anthony is said to favor simplicity, so we wore our navy silk jackets and skirts. Despite Vicky's admonishments, I did sneak a hearty dose of hashish medicinal, and the anxiety of recent events melted away, so we made a most relaxed, smiling impression upon our guest. We sat at the burled wood table (yet another gift from Cornelius) and I served tea while Vicky described our history to the readers of The Revolution.

Miss Anthony said, "The challenge looms before us, with the vote beyond our grasp."

"Well, if it is our right, and the law cannot be denied that it is so, then it is up to us to exercise it," Victoria declared. "I promise you, Miss Anthony, with the next election cycle, I for one shall exercise my right and vote. Whether I am permitted to or not."

"Yes!" Miss Anthony agreed. She then added, "Quite so."

Afterward, Miss Anthony said, "Mrs. Woodhull, our readers and sisters in the struggle will find your venture most uplifting." She then turned to me and added, "Likewise, Jenny, that you follow in your sister's footsteps is an inspiration to us all. Mrs. Woodhull, Jenny."

Honestly. Did she really forget my name?

"Miss Claflin, please take the witness stand."

She walks to the box, allowing her skirt to sway, pretending she is neither angry nor embarrassed. She lifts the veil of her hat, ignoring emotions her past mistakes threaten to unleash. She calmly exchanges glances with the plaintiff's attorney and gives the judge her most beguiling smile.

The judge says, "Miss Claflin, it is the Court's understanding you left Mr. James Blake an unpaid balance for the following items." He reads from a list: "Bloodroot, one box of ley, one syringe, an ointment prescription, one quart of alcohol, one bottle of sherry, court plaster, morphine, bay rum, one ley cup, and various other sundries too numerous to mention. The arrears come to a total of $125.70."

Tennessee doesn't notice the reporter from the *Herald* who is sitting in the back of the room, frantically writing. They are all on strict instructions from the boss. Wherever she turns up, Miss Claflin is to have complete coverage.

Miss Tennie C appeared in Court attended by her partner, Mrs. Woodhull, in all her charms of manner and of dress. Her dress was of black silk velvet. She had a fashionable chignon, surmounted by a hat, bonnet, or whatnot, of the latest Paris style.

"Do you recall said purchases?"

"Honestly your Honor, I do not." Make it seem like nothing, she commands herself. "You see, there's another woman who lived in Chicago the same years that I did. We were often mistaken for one another. I am sure he reads a description of that person."

The judge is not unkind. "That may be the case, but it is indeed your personage that stands before this court. Therefore, I find you liable for these arrears and order you to pay said debt without delay. This court is adjourned."

"Onward and Upward! Victoria C. Woodhull, future Presidentess!" is written across the front page of *Woodhull & Claflin's Weekly* premier issue. They are indeed making a splash. Notices are complimentary. Tennessee stands on a chair and holds up the paper. Everyone cheers and Colonel Blood kisses his beautiful wife full on the mouth.

Tennessee crows, "*Woodhull & Claflin's Weekly* is the only paper in the world conducted absolutely upon the principles of a Free Press!"

"That's sweet, Tennie," Blood laughs, "but there's no such thing."

YOUR NAMESAKE REQUESTS YOUR COMPANY
AT HER SEND OFF NAME THE DATE BENNETT

Bennett smiles when she emerges in her breeches and jacket. Silently, she climbs into the trap beside him. They race up Fifth Avenue, past the Croton Reservoir, past the unfinished cathedral, past the construction site of William Vanderbilt's monument to himself. They turn left at the Central Park and fly past every other horse and carriage. Tennessee feels the warmth of his leg next to hers. She wonders if sitting next to him might be the most comfortable place to be in the world.

At Fort Washington, they walk directly to the river's edge, to a dock on the other side of the railroad tracks she'd ridden with Cornelius. Bennett helps Tennessee down to a dingy and rows her over to a magnificent schooner in the middle of the river. "This is *Dauntless*," he says. "I'm going to put her through her paces at the end of this month."

"Here in New York?"

"No, no. From Ireland to Sandy Hook lighthouse. Against the *Cambria*." They stroll the length of the deck.

"How long will you be gone?"

"Difficult to say, really. We allow thirty days there, thirty in London and Paris, visit the mother and sister. Then, God willing, not much more than a fortnight to race. In all, ten weeks."

"Why do you do it, Bennett?"

"Why do I race?" He looks down for a moment. "Because, Miss Claflin, I am addicted to the idea of finding men as foolish as myself who will work together, in a vast ocean on one tiny vessel, simply to go faster than the others, by catching the wind and setting one's rudder so, in the face of every danger." He steals a glance at her. "It's both a weakness and a flaw."

The air is perfect. They stand wonderfully close to one another. The river flowing around the yacht causes their hips to sway. "Do you waltz, Miss Claflin?" he asks.

"I enjoy waltzing very much."

"Me too!" he says, and sweeps her into his arms, humming *The Blue Danube*, which she knows, too. Both humming louder than the other, they dance on the deck, up and down and up again, the one hundred and twenty feet of the schooner's length.

Afterward, her host rows them back to the dock. She draws her knees up to her chest and wraps her arms around them. "Thank you, Bennett."

He raises an oar in response and whistles *The Blue Danube*.

"Really," she says when they head back to the house. "That was the most edifying afternoon I've had in some time." Bennett takes her by the hand and leads her over to a shady spot near the porch. He puts his fingers to his lips and then points toward the tree.

"Shh," he whispers. "Look." Tennessee does and sees nothing. Bennett stands with his hands on her shoulders, and softly calls, "Who! Who! Miss Tennessee, who!"

She thinks, what a pity this handsome fellow will turn out to be crazy. Suddenly, there is a whooshing sound, and the owl, much grown, alights onto the bottom branch.

"What do you think?" he whispers into Tennessee's ear.

She looks up at him and he smiles down at her.

She whispers back, "I think it's grand."

———

"Well of course, Mr. Gerber, most of our readership is women. If they know of your excellent service, then naturally it follows they will purchase your insurance against the untimely demise of their husbands. How does the Declaration of Independence put it? It's self-evident."

The man's gaze is fixed, just below Tennessee's left shoulder.

"So, would an eighth of a page for the next ten weeks suit? Or would you prefer a quarter page with a small illustration?" She pulls the paperwork from the valise and stretches slightly, arching her back as she takes the lid off the pen and hands it to him. "Sign here, Mr. Gerber, and you'll see your business increase ten-fold within no time at all."

She leans over the desk as he signs, her breast not a millimeter above his hand. "Let's do the quarter page then." The button of her jacket brushes against his wrist. She quickly draws in her breath and sighs, smiling at him, her eyebrows raised. "Thank you! Thank you, so much, Mr. Gerber."

———

Tennessee says, "But selling an advertisement, nothing changes for it. They buy it when I sell it. We are only richer for cash and ad space."

"But that's the critical component, Tennie," Blood responds, "for the success of the paper."

"I would much prefer to try my hand at writing. Vicky?"

The future Presidentess does not answer.

Tennessee tries again with her brother-in-law. "Colonel. Couldn't I write something?"

"Such as what?"

"Something. Say, the life of the working woman at large. Or what it is like to be a woman and *not* running for president. I could write something on those Communards in the Social Party or, what is it, the National Labor Union."

"I think she should run," Victoria says.

No one responds to this. Victoria continues, "Why shouldn't she? Tennie can run for Congress. She's at least as capable as I am." Victoria adds, "Then it will be a family affair, won't it, Tennie?"

To which Tennessee starts laughing, "Oh, it would!"

Victoria joins in. "Tennie for Congress! I think you should do it."

Tennessee says, "I'll write something about our constitutional rights. Pearl, you'll clean up my grammar, won't you? And Colonel, you could work on my prose." Tennessee can't stop smiling. "And I'll just sign my name to it." She looks at Buck and asks, "Where's the harm in that?"

July 1870
The Central Park

Tennessee wears her preferred linen trousers and jacket when E.C. Stedman comes to Thirty-Eighth Street. He says that his wife and children are in New Jersey. They walk up Fifth Avenue, and the streets are all but deserted. Standing beside Stedman, Tennessee imagines she cuts a jaunty figure in her linen suit and boater. They enter the Central Park and walk to the boathouse.

"My platform will be predicated on the rights of individual sovereignty," Tennessee explains.

"Which is what, exactly?" Stedman asks her.

"Well, that one is free to choose to do as one will. Regardless of one's sex. That and the right to do as one will one day a week."

"Tennie," Stedman asks, "if you could do anything you want, anything at all, what should it be?"

"Well, apart from running for Congress, I would, well, I should write."

They rent a rowboat and Tennessee climbs in. Thoughts of Bennett and dancing on his schooner creep into her mind. In the center of the lake, Stedman leans back, and they float, silent in their own thoughts.

Eventually, he says, "I think, Tennie, should you decide to write, you might elevate the conversation and discuss those aspects of a woman's life which function to suppress her natural attributes or inclinations, such as your own."

"I don't even know what that means," she replies. Humming *The Blue Danube*, dancing on deck, flashes before her eyes. She moves to the other side of the boat and it tips dangerously. Stedman barely seems to notice. She sits next to him and gives him a close look. "Ned, what is it that vexes you so?"

He struggles to suppress a scowl. "How do you know I am vexed?"

"I'm clairvoyant." She splashes water at him.

"You wanted to come to the park. We came, as you wanted."

"But we're not sharing a great many laughs, are we?"

"How should we share many laughs?"

"We are to make one another laugh! Like this." Tennessee stands in the boat again, rocking it. "Perhaps I should take my leave." She makes as if she'll jump in the water.

"No, please. Please stay." She sits down again.

"You have a very long life ahead, Edmund Clarence Stedman."

He doesn't answer. She tries again. "All will laud you for your place in poetry."

"I am hardly writing now." A tear begins its descent down his face.

"Ned!"

"I have lost everything."

"Oh, Ned."

"Ten thousand dollars in the market." He looks away. "It isn't really mine."

So, that is what he wants. The air is soft and she watches the other boaters. Stedman is not a bad person and he did save her life. Quietly, she says, "Ned. I can make you a loan. I have that kind of money." If Victoria knew she were doing this, she'd be furious. "But you mustn't tell anyone. It has to be our little secret." As they return the boat, it occurs to Tennessee that Blood might find out, though.

They walk south along Fifth Avenue, the streets empty save for a coach and four. It slowly passes them and then stops at the corner. Tennessee whistles to the driver, who raises his whip to acknowledge.

They make their farewells, and she climbs into the cab. Stedman waves and turns east, walking away from the park. The coachman climbs down from the box and looks into the cab.

It is James Gordon Bennett. "Miss Claflin, I presume? Just the person I'm looking for." He doesn't wait for her reply but climbs back up to his seat. The horses begin to trot.

Tennessee sticks her head out of the window. "Hey!" She has to shout to be heard. "Are you following me?"

He answers over his shoulder. "What are you doing uptown?"

Happiness sears through her. "Following a person is really rather rude, you know."

"But your namesake has been asking for you."

"Who?"

"That's what she said. Exactly that."

Tennessee knocks on the ceiling. "I'm coming up."

Bennett pulls the horses to a stop. She climbs up and sits next to him. "Mr. Bennett, you'd best not be following me."

"I had no idea you'd be here. But you're the only girl I know who wears trousers in this neighborhood, and when I saw that curvy shape in the jacket, I had to stop."

She smiles and says, "I don't believe you."

They ride a few blocks until she says, "I'm sorry about the race. Two hours—that must have been infuriating."

His playfulness vanishes. "It's nothing when I consider the crewmen we lost."

"What?"

"Two of them, overboard." He clears his throat.

"Bennett, I had no idea."

"I owe their families some assurance or...It's unspeakable, really."

They ride in silence, the afternoon now shaded by Stedman's near ruin and the death of two innocent men. How precarious it all is.

Abruptly, Bennett returns to his former self. "How's your summer?"

"Not without its challenges, I daresay. Friends who only visit if their wives are out of town, other friends who pose as wandering coachmen, and then there's the volatility of the market."

"And *Woodhull & Claflin's Weekly*?"

"My efforts have been confined to advertising. Everyone seems to think selling is my forte."

"I'm sure they're right."

"Ha! Don't look at me like that. Keep your eyes on the road."

"At your service." He taps his finger against the brim of his absurdly tall coachman's hat. At Sixty-Third Street, he comes upon a post, jumps down, and ties the horses. They make their way to the menagerie the authorities have declared is a zoo. A lion yawns from behind his cage. They stop to consider him.

Tennessee glances up at Bennett then over to the indifferent cat. "He looks not unlike you," she says.

"Do you think so? I wondered if we mightn't be somehow related."

They stroll along until they come upon a caged bear. The bear attempts to make the most out of not much more than a puddle from the previous night's rainfall.

"If I were him, I should break out of this place," Tennessee says. "Consider it. All these beasts people assume have no feeling. Imagine, one night, when the public least expects it, there is a mighty roar!"

She throws back her head and roars. The bear looks at the small crazy woman, her hands clawing. "Then, the creatures break free, tearing their captors to pieces, and stampede down the Mall, over to the Avenue, brutally destroying everyone and everything that impedes their progress, as they make their way back to the jungle and to freedom! ROAR!" She removes her lilac gloves from her pocket. Sighing, she sits on a bench. "Have you ever thought about that?"

When he doesn't answer, she carefully puts the gloves on. "Well, I have, I can tell you, Bennett. I have thought of it often."

ONWARD, CHRISTIAN SOLDIERS

January 1871
Washington, D.C.

IN WASHINGTON, THE puddles are veritable lakes, drenching skirts and cloaks alike. But, upon arrival at the Willard Hotel, a short wooden ramp is slid under the doors of one's carriage, mitigating the slushy wet underfoot.

A footman grips the impeccable lady's hand as she descends. "There we are, Miss Anthony," he murmurs.

Following Miss Anthony is her friend and fellow crusader. "Madam," the footman says. He bends his knees to support the lady's considerable weight.

Mrs. Stanton is as stout as Miss Anthony is slim. They are always among the first to arrive at the National Women's Suffrage Association convention. Later, they will be joined by Mrs. Hooker and Mrs. Mott. Mrs. Davis and Miss Stone are not expected until early the next day. The convention will take place at Lincoln Hall and at the last moment, the organizers have invited Mrs. Woodhull to join them. Her memorial at Congress has created such a stir that everyone agrees. Mrs. Woodhull is a sensation.

Upstairs, in the suite he rents when Congress is in session, Senator Benjamin Butler studies Victoria Woodhull. The desire in his gaze is betrayed by the failure of his eyes to focus on her face. But the senator is too powerful for Victoria to care about eyes that do not align, or a stature which more closely resembles an egg rather than a warrior. She takes his hands in hers. He is quite alone, the poor man, as his wife is in Germany to seek medical treatment.

"Regardless of the reception yesterday," the senator says, "eventually, Congress must concede. As an American, Mrs. Woodhull, you are a citizen. As a citizen, you have the right to vote."

<hr>

Lincoln Hall. Backstage, every trial, every heartache is spun together into a chorus which whispers to Victoria, this is your destiny. She has never felt so well, yet she has never in her thirty-two years been quite so afraid, either. Black dress, white rose at her throat. The sounds of the audience pouring into the auditorium and even the traffic beyond are drowned out by the booming of her heart hammering inside her body. Quiet, quiet, she thinks. She takes a deep breath through her nostrils, her lungs expanding inside her ribs. Breathe.

"Mrs. Woodhull?" It is Mrs. Isabella Beecher Hooker. Mrs. Hooker's eyes are clear, and she resembles her older sister, Mrs. Harriet Beecher Stowe. But Mrs. Hooker's smile is kind.

Victoria clasps her hands in front of her waist as they walk to the stage, squeezing her palms to still their trembling. Stepping forward, she feels herself waver.

Mrs. Hooker puts a firm hand on the small of Victoria's back and whispers, "We have all waited so long for this moment."

Victoria glances at her. Mrs. Hooker gives her a gentle pat, the way one does a child needing a Dutchman's courage.

Victoria looks out at the audience. She finds the lights.

> "It was an honest zeal which first influenced me to appear before the public as a champion of a cause, which receives alike the jeers of the common multitude and the raillery of the select few."

Be stronger, Vicky! she warns herself. Be strong.

> "It is an honest zeal in the same that inspires me with confidence to continue before it as its advocate, when but too conscious that I am of that portion of the people who are denied the privileges of freedom;"

Say it again. Say it louder.

> "who are not permitted the rights of citizens; and who are without voice, in the pursuit of justice, as one of that sovereignty to whom this Government owes its existence, and to whom it will be held accountable, as it holds all accountable who set themselves against Human Rights."

Breathe. Look at them. Breathe again.

> "I come before you to declare that my sex is entitled to the inalienable right to life, liberty, and the pursuit of happiness. The first two I cannot be deprived of, except for cause, and by due process of law…I ask the right to pursue happiness by having a voice in that Government to which I am accountable. I have not forfeited that right, still I am denied."

We are equal. Women are equal to men. There is nothing to stop us from saying our piece.

While Victoria continues to speak, it begins to occur to members of the audience that with Mrs. Woodhull, it just might happen. Even in the largest hall of the nation's capital. Women nod at one another. For every time they've had something to say, they've been relegated to silence, because they have no "voice." But Mrs. Woodhull proves that they do have a voice.

It is time to be heard.

In the box closest to the stage, Tennessee's eyes are damp with pride. She reaches in her pocket and touches her talisman, a piece of mirrored shard Victoria gave her in Ohio, on the slope behind the mill. Tennessee was seven years old.

Victoria had shown her the two small shards of a mirror. "Look, Tennie. Watch this." Victoria turned the mirror back and forth. It was just after dusk. A star was caught in its reflection and cast a light into the darkening sky.

Tennessee gasped with pleasure. "How do you do that?"

Victoria laughed, "'Tis a mystery."

"Do you have one for Utie?"

"No," Victoria had said. "It's just for you."

For Tennessee, it was the most entrancing thing imaginable. "What makes that happen, Vicky?"

"It's the angel spirits talking to us. When I leave here, and I will, I'll hold my piece this way. If you do the same, we will always be in touch."

Victoria is still speaking.

Tennessee considers, that if legislators agree that the colored man should have the vote, then what about their wives and mothers and their sisters and daughters and their aunts? If we have our freedom, then we must have the right, too.

"I have the right; it is my right," Tennessee whispers, "I have the inalienable right."

Yet, the spirit is clear. Men in power, despite their encouragement, aren't about to share anything. Anything at all.

The room breaks into thunderous applause. Tennessee holds up the shard. It catches the light in its reflection. Victoria sees the reflection and smiles. She is radiant.

There is a reception afterward. Before joining the others, Tennessee sends a telegram to everyone at home.

STUPENDOUS STOP NOTHING SHORT OF GLORIOUS ALL HAIL OUR FUTURE PRESIDENTESS

To James Gordon Bennett, she writes, "WHAT A NIGHT."

Tennessee hears two women chatting behind her. "My dear! Did you know that Dr. Taylor hosted a séance where the Woodhull was medium?"

"Doesn't Mrs. Harriet Beecher Stowe take the cure at Dr. Taylor's?"

"Indeed, Mrs. Stowe was there with several other eminent citizens, besides."

A servant offers Tennessee a small sandwich and glass of champagne. Holding the sandwich and sipping her champagne, she continues to listen.

"What are they?" a woman asks the servant.

"Birds' tongue in olive and anchovy paste, madam," he answers.

Tennessee steps behind a potted palm that she might have a better view of those in conversation.

"Afterward," the woman confides, "Mrs. Taylor said that not only did Mrs. Woodhull have the audacity to offend Mrs. Stowe—"

"My dear, what did Mrs. Woodhull say?"

Suddenly a crush of people reaches for new trays of food and drink. The potted palm shifts slightly, and Tennessee is pressed against a bald man who eats his sandwich then runs his fingers through his moustache before wiping them on his waistcoat.

Snippets of other conversations float toward them.

"I understand Horace Greeley was very taken with that kind of thinking in his youth."

"Charles Dana, too. After all, they're newspapermen."

Tennessee discards her sandwich in an umbrella stand. The bald man watches her do so. Embarrassed, she meets his gaze and smiles, her dimple showing. Another group of women move past them. One says, "I might as well tell you. It will come out eventually. Mrs. Woodhull is divorced."

"What!" The group stops.

"That won't do, will it?"

A waiter refills Tennessee's glass. Still looking at the bald man, she drains her glass and then licks her lips. The waiter offers her more, and she shakes her head.

She hears someone say, "My dear, you know what they practice in Oneida, New York." At which point, Tennessee turns and sees a woman raise her eyebrows and say nothing.

"Communal marriage" was the answer. "Yes, that."

The other lady guffaws, "My goodness! The mind reels."

Tennessee makes her way to Victoria and Senator Butler. As she moves past another couple, the woman says to the man, "I am amazed Isabella Beecher Hooker would be on stage with a woman whom her sister believes to be a strumpet."

The man answers, "Oh, the Beechers are hardly in a position to comment. Henry Ward Beecher preaches to at least twenty of his mistresses in church every Sunday."

Elizabeth Cady Stanton and Susan B. Anthony watch the crowd. Mrs. Stanton observes, "It appears Mrs. Woodhull has inspired more enthusiasm in the last thirty days than we may have done in the last thirty years."

"I imagine it's the newness of her." There is something about the Woodhull that does not sit right with Miss Anthony.

"Susan, she has beauty, she has brains, and evidently, very deep pockets."

"Courtesy of Commodore Vanderbilt?" Miss Anthony asks.

"I don't believe that matters anymore."

The man who had licked his fingers and ran them through his moustache bends over Victoria's hand. "Your style has some swagger, Mrs. Woodhull, but you could stand to emulate, or at the very least, steal the techniques of a few of our greats."

Tennessee admires her sister's aplomb, ignoring and dazzling the man at the same time. Tennessee asks, "Who, pray tell, are a few of our greats?"

The man says, "You're the sister, aren't you?"

"I am."

"Quite the dynamo—You give good copy, Miss Claflin."

"So, who are a few of our greats?"

"Well, there's Mr. Twain of course, oh and Miss Dickenson is spectacular, and Mr. George Train, he's very colorful. And then there's Reverend Beecher. Watch how he delivers a sermon. Riveting. No doubt about it. Once one has mastered what promises to be a singular style, then, we'll be able to book you."

Tennessee whispers into Victoria's ear, turning her away, "You won't need the likes of him to address people, Vicky. He's just a humbugging carny. I can spot them from a mile away."

The man taps on Tennessee's shoulder. "Like it or not, your sister's views and now your experience with the press and with the government make you, but more particularly her, a commodity. And as such, she owes it to herself to get on the road and to speak out."

"And what do you make off her back, simply for sending the telegrams and booking the room?"

"I make twenty percent of course."

"Gross or net?"

He smiles. "Net." It is no secret Anna Dickenson has made him a fortune. "So, what would suit you, Miss Claflin? Taking the road on your own and working one circuit as Mrs. Woodhull does the other?"

"Oh no. That wouldn't suit. The show is hers. I am here for reinforcement."

He smiles broadly, "I'll say."

"Do you subscribe to our point of view? Where do you stand on the issue of suffrage?"

"Does it matter?"

"I should think so."

"Miss Claflin, may I ask where you stand on the universal rights of man?"

Tennessee answers without blinking. She reads everything assigned to her without exception. "I stand in appreciation of Mr. Thomas Paine's sentiment, 'Whatever is my right as a man is also the right of another; and it becomes my duty to guarantee as well as to possess.' Which is to say, women must share the same rights as men."

The man opens his mouth to speak, but Tennessee continues, "And, of course then, if one were to examine the economic implication of that sentiment, the troubling aspect is if the proletariat organizes to overthrow the bourgeoisie, the proletariat then becomes bourgeois by default and therefore loses its integrity as the proletariat in the first place. The way I see it is a question of property—ownership is not without its challenges. Much akin to the divorce debate."

"That's very true."

"It's quite a pickle. But, apart from that, I most certainly identify with the worker."

"Somehow, despite your resplendent finery, that doesn't surprise me."

He smiles even as he thinks, I will never book you. You're obviously overeducated whores with an axe to grind and you'd be the death of any standard. No, I won't book you. Not in a million years.

At the house on Thirty-Eighth Street, Colonel Blood rereads Tennessee's telegram. It's late and everyone has retired for the evening. Blood takes his glass back to the kitchen and sees her, lit by the glowing embers. Utica appears so vulnerable, as if she were translucent.

Blood kneels beside her chair and Utica looks at him. She is forbidden to drink. Her only comfort lies in morphine from Doc Woodhull's needle that everyone pretends isn't tucked away in his room. She points at the telegram in his hand. "Another triumph, Colonel?"

"What's that, Utica?"

"For you and the Woodhull." Utica turns back to the fire. "Oh yes, and plucky Tennie C."

"What vexes you, Utica?"

"Why do they get to have something to fight for or believe in? They have money, they have friends! They make fortunes, and everyone lauds them." She is only inches from Blood's face. "I, too, have studied these questions. I, too, have views worth discussing! I know that marriage," here she mimics Victoria, "'binds a woman, both soul and body and delivers her over to tyranny and lust.' I know that."

Utica smells of roses, and is it bourbon? "Have you been drinking, Utica?"

Her pupils dilate a fraction, inviting him to move closer. "Just a little." Her lips part, and he admires the beautiful teeth all the sisters have in common.

"Utica."

"Shh." She lifts his hand and puts it to her breast. He can feel there is nothing between her skin and the soft wool. "I am so lonely, Colonel."

He can barely hear her whisper. His heart begins pounding in his groin. The amative impulse makes his trousers impossibly tight.

Roxana silently pads into the room. She sees his hand on Utica's breast. "I knew it!"

Blood stands, hoping the darkness conceals his erection.

"You are a snake." Roxana grabs the broom leaning in the corner, "and you prey upon the innocent! Herr beschütze uns!" she shrieks, striking at Blood, flailing at him as if he were an unwelcome rodent. He dodges her blows.

"Quit!" he roars. "Quit I say, old woman!" He grabs the broomstick in one hand and catches himself before his other hand strikes her cheek. It is the first time Blood has risen his hand in anger toward her. But, God knows, she's given him every reason to do so.

He glances at Utica. "Say something."

Utica ignores them, humming as she rocks the chair.

Roxana grabs the broomstick free. She strikes Blood as hard as she can. "You prey on us! You take our money, and have Vicky spend it with no regard, no regard for our…"—Roxana's eyes narrow until they are slits, sparkling in contempt—"privacy!" she hisses just as Polly Sparr enters the kitchen.

"Shut up, old woman!" Blood leans toward Roxana and shakes his fist at her. He doesn't bother to dodge her blows nor explain himself to Mrs. Sparr. "Just shut your venerable mouth or I will put you over my knee and strike you senseless." With that, he leaves the room and brushes past Polly who is rooted to the spot.

Roxana's mouth drops open, but nothing comes out. She straightens her back and looks at Utica who is now twirling a lock of her hair.

Roxana mutters. "Herr beschütze uns, Herr beschütze uns."

It is impossible to sleep. When the door of his bedroom opens, Blood isn't surprised. She is holding her cat, which springs from her arms and stretches beside him, purring and kneading the blanket as Utica slips under the covers.

Before he can protest, she places her finger on his lips. "Shhh."

Blood doesn't know how he'll tell Victoria. Any discussion with Roxana is impossible. And everything was witnessed by Polly. Polly will tell her husband, Ben, who will use it to further his own ends. Wearily, Colonel Blood mounts the stairs. He looks at the door of the bedroom he shares with his wife. She will be away for at least another day. He pauses for only a second, then enters Utica's room, takes off his boots, and collapses on the bed.

When Victoria returns from Washington, she is bursting to share every aspect of the trip. Upstairs, in their room, still in her traveling garments, she is filled with the joy of seeing him. She removes her gloves and asks, "How are things at the *Weekly*, Colonel? Did you keep all the imps and urchins in order?"

He looks at her gentle, elegant face. "Your mother and sisters were not without their usual challenges." How to tell her? "And Ben Sparr seems to think I have a position for him when I do not."

"Is there nothing you can do for him, Colonel?"

Blood rubs his face with his hands. He will have to come out with it. It was simply physical weakness. In fact, it reassures him that of all the women in the world, his wife is the most—

"Colonel?" She looks at him oddly and removes her bonnet.

"Victoria." How to tell her? "Darling, Vicky. Utica. Utica and I…"

There it is. Free Love, right in front of her own foolish face. Victoria whispers, "I see."

"And your mother." He is too lame. Blood thinks, how could he do this to her? She is blameless. "Then Polly walked in…"

"Please don't say anymore. I am very tired from the journey." She stumbles toward the dressing room. Blood tries to follow her, but she waves him off. "No, please, Colonel. It's all right. I just need a moment." She turns to face him. "It's all right." Softly, she latches the door from within.

Why? Her heart wails. Why is it that on the heels of every triumph there has to be some crashing defeat which undoes everything that came before it? She leans her head against the door as Blood stands on its other side, doing much the same thing. She wipes the tears from her face and forces herself to smile. "Did I tell you, Jim?"

He winces. She never calls him Jim.

"I've now been invited to speak to the American Women's Suffrage Association. You know, the opposing suffragists, in Boston."

February 1871
New York

"My dear, when Victoria Woodhull, that free loving hussy, lay her eyes on his, he abandoned his wife and child, and now they are here in Boston, destitute, I tell you—it will not stand. She must not be permitted to speak here. The

good people of New England should not subject themselves
to such salacious scandal. One can only imagine what will
come out of her torrid mouth next. "

-Harriet Beecher Stowe to Fannie Fern

It is with some relief that Colonel Blood watches Victoria leave the office
for her ride with Miss Catharine Beecher. Relations have been unusually
strained, despite Victoria's claim she supports the tenets of an open marriage. Blood notices a mousy young woman standing in the threshold of
the office.

Blood approaches her. "May I help you, Miss…?"

"Swindell," she says. "The name is Annie Swindell. I opened an
account here last year with all my savings. It was five hundred dollars. I
just received my statement." He can see Miss Swindell's hand is shaking.
"It says there's only eighteen dollars left in the account!"

Blood recognizes his own handwriting on the piece of paper. "Please,
do come in."

"Miss Beecher. It is such an honor." Victoria climbs into the hansom cab,
still wincing when she considers that unfortunate séance at Dr. Taylor's.
If only she had confided in Mrs. Stowe instead of insulting her. She could
have told her how she and Tennessee know *Uncle Tom's Cabin* forward
and backward, almost better than their Bible. If only things had gone
differently.

The carriage moves forward. Miss Beecher speaks first. "Mrs.
Woodhull, I shan't waste our time by pretending it wasn't dear Belle who
interceded on your behalf."

Victoria says, "I had mistakenly believed it was your reverend
brother."

"Certainly not. Henry believes…." At this Miss Beecher trails off.

"Indeed, what does he believe?" Glancing at the older woman, Victoria reminds herself, win her over, win her over, so she takes a deep breath and recites,

> Awake, from the dream of thoughtless pleasure!
> Awake from the reveries of selfish care, and save your-
> selves and your country, ere it be forever too late!

Catharine Beecher's mouth falls open with pleasure. "How come you to know my words?"

"*The Duty of American Women to her Country* was one of two books to which I dedicated all my energy during my time in California. Indeed, some fifteen years ago."

Catharine Beecher chuckles. "I hope your other book was the Bible."

"No, Miss Beecher." Win her over, Victoria warns herself. You must win her over if you are ever to make peace with Mrs. Stowe. "It was but another one of yours. *Physiology and Calisthenics.* Having been an ardent enthusiast of Mrs. Stowe's I then devoted my energies to your work. I tell you most unequivocally I followed the regimen prescribed in *Calisthenics.*"

"Did you really? How edifying."

Victoria feels herself beginning to blush. It always happens when she speaks from the heart. "I mistakenly believed the exercises you prescribed would cure my beloved son, who alas, has a deformity of his mind."

The women ride together in silence, and Victoria prays for the presence of mind to stop speaking. Alas, it is not to be. "Miss Beecher, may I enquire as to whether you still believe women should forego their citizens' rights, even as they are compelled to pay taxes and yield their bodies at the whim of their husband, whether he be fit or no in his capacity as her spouse?"

"Mrs. Woodhull."

"As for *Physiology and Calisthenics,*" Victoria says, "I must say, you are a quack."

Catharine Beecher's face freezes in horror.

"You did little more than humbug your devoted readership into believing that by following the prescribed regimen all would be well. I can assure you that whilst in California, we were not well. Not at all."

It is impossible to stop now. "The word in Washington is your reverend brother believes all women should be free to yield their bodies to whomever they so desire, whether it be conjugal or outside of the marriage bed altogether."

"Mrs. Woodhull! How dare you? Reverend Beecher is a true and faithful husband."

"Oh. So, there's no veracity to the legend he is most unhappily married?"

"Well, Mrs. Beecher is not…." Once more, at a loss, Miss Beecher's voice trails off.

"She is not?"

"I will no longer speak of this, Mrs. Woodhull. This is the most salacious and contemptible discourse I've been affronted to. Driver, stop! Stop this instant." The older woman prepares to descend the carriage, but Victoria lightly jumps out in her stead.

Catharine Beecher shakes her gloved fist at the younger woman. "Mrs. Woodhull. Victoria Woodhull, I shall strike you dead."

Victoria laughs, "Well, strike as much and as hard as you please. Only do not do it in the dark so that I cannot know who is my enemy! Good day." With that, Victoria walks, her heart still hammering, sedately away from the carriage, grateful for the unusually fine weather.

Afterward, when Isabella Beecher Hooker enquires of Victoria as to how the visit with her eldest sister went, Victoria tells her she thought the carriage ride went very well. When Harriet Beecher Stowe asks Catharine Beecher the same question, Catharine informs Harriet that she believes Victoria Woodhull is insane.

April 1871
Brooklyn

Reverend Henry Ward Beecher turns the pages of *Woodhull & Claflin's Weekly* and admires its banner. PROGRESS, FREE THOUGHT, UNTRAMMELED LIVES!

"They are the sort of people whom debt collectors seek out and prosecute across state lines." Observes his sister Harriet as she pours him a cup of tea. "I have no doubt you came across the report on Miss Claflin's dalliance with the law."

The Reverend makes a noncommittal clucking of the tongue and helps himself to a powdered fig.

"Did you see that woman's printing of the George Sand story?" Harriet asks him.

"Sister, I am surprised you deigned to even read *Woodhull & Claflin's Weekly.*" He brushes the sugar from his fingertips.

Ignoring him, she continues, "You know, Henry, George Sand actually lived outside of marriage with that poet de Musset, and afterward she published *every aspect* of her adultery with him and his grossness to her." It pains Harriet to even describe this to Henry, but still, she soldiers on: "Under the title *Elle et Lui*, a novel which I have read…And then de Musset's brother published his side of it, under the title *Lui et Elle*, which I have also read." Henry raises his eyebrows, so she says, "Between the two, it is about as vile a slough as I ever saw. That woman, Sand, in spite of her exquisite French, is the animalism and atheism of this century impersonated."

Henry thinks he could stand to do with some animalism.

"Henry." She refills his teacup.

"Hmm?"

"Should American women go down this path, this insane, Free-Love-depravity path, they will do it out of ignorance and fear, because the men will be free to choose and to choose and to choose again. Watch." Harriet pours a spoon of sugar into her tea, points the spoon at her brother, then returns it to her cup, stirring furiously.

The reverend runs a hand through his leonine hair and stretches on the divan, to imagine such a world. "Well, it is all highfalutin ideas and castles built on clouds at this juncture, Harriet." Pity though, he thinks. He resolves to make a point of reading Madame Sand.

The suffragists prepare for the New York convention, gathering at homes in and around the city. Soon, their tongues begin to wag as their brows become furrowed.

"My dear, the views expressed in that paper!"

"One has heard the most extraordinary reports of Mrs. Woodhull's comportment, from speaking without cessation to random men in the carriage of a train, to blackmail, should one publicly denounce her views."

"Her lack of antecedents would not concern me, were she not so…," the speaker's voice drops sotto voce, "so boldly ambitious."

Letters are exchanged quickly, without delay. A woman around whom there are hints of shady dealings, divorce, and worse cannot be in a position to lead the National Women's Suffrage Association. Yet, in addition to Mrs. Hooker and Mrs. Stanton, both Mrs. Mott and Mrs. Davis are also much taken with Mrs. Woodhull. Mrs. Stanton decides to set everyone else straight.

> In regards to all the gossip about Mrs. W. I have one reply to make to my gentlemen friends…If all 'they say' is true, Mrs. Woodhull is better than nine tenths of the Fathers, Husbands and sons…

Bennett is in his office at the *Herald* pouring over several maps, a small dog draped across his shoulder. Tennessee strides over to him and raises her fist but spins away as quickly as she had approached him.

"Ah!" she shouts.

SWINDELL SWINDLED!

The headline of Bennett's other paper, the *Evening Telegram* is nothing less than dreadful. "Did you not like the headline?" He says, "You know, my intent was to be somewhat lowbrow. 'Swindell Swindled!' It has a snappy sort of appeal."

"Bennett."

"I warned you. I did."

"Yes, you did."

"And the *Herald* gives you the very best press whenever it can, doesn't it?"

Tennessee nods. He returns to his maps. "You look ravishing in that getup." He adds, "Mommy thinks so, too. Don't you, Mommy?" The spaniel wags her tail as Bennett rubs her back, "So. How'd things go with Miss Swindell?"

"The charges were dropped, thank God. The Colonel has offered her a position, to compensate for her losses."

"How is the venerable Colonel?"

"He's fine, Bennett. Thank you."

"Delmonico's tonight? I'm feeling rather peckish." They walk to the elevator. He grabs his hat from the hat stand.

She says, "Perhaps home would be best."

"Of course, we don't want to blow our cover, do we?" Standing on her left, he taps her shoulder from behind her right.

"Bennett!"

"Tennie C.," he murmurs just under his breath, "brutally destroying everyone and everything that impedes her progress, as she makes her way back to the jungle and to freedom!"

The elevator doors open. They step in, the dog following close behind.

May 1871
15 East 38th Street

Trembling, Victoria tears the letter open. A kind word from Mrs. Hooker is all she needs. Mrs. Hooker asks after her health, the details about the pending Apollo Hall speech, and then, there it is. Rather than reassurance, is the criticism.

> *I want you to use nice paper hereafter, plain envelopes. You are no longer a banker nor businesswoman, but a prospective queen—a lady in every sense of the word. Those envelopes have been a dreadful eyesore to me for a long time… and so mannish…If you are to be our accepted standard bearer, be perfect, be exquisite in neatness, elegance, and decorum. You have the means, and the furnishings in your house show that you know how to use them.*

Victoria folds the letter back up. Her old sadness shifts to make room for the feeling of inadequacy.

———

"Right, so if you travel by Kingsbridge Road and cut over at 120th to Eighth Avenue, it should take you forty-seven minutes to the tip of the Central Park. That's halfway back to our street. You have two horsepower in the trap with Daisy and Maisie here. That's fair, isn't it?"

"How well they run the course will determine whether it's fair or not."

The horses pull at the reins, Tennessee sensing them itch to leap forward.

Bennett finishes checking his horse. He climbs into a shiny new brougham. "Bruno here is going to take the Public Road along the river. Then we have to make that left and go another mile, so it seems to me it's quite fair."

"Well, then, I'll see you anon!"

The reins in her hands and the beautiful horses' smooth gait, racing down the avenue, is heaven. She arrives at the northernmost end of the Central Park in no time at all. The trees are white with blossoms and the previous evening's rain has made everything fresh and clean. They are coming up on their fiftieth issue of *WCW*, and one can say, without equivocation, the paper looks good. Tennessee's prowess selling ads seems boundless and the circulation numbers are healthy.

There is no sign of James Gordon Bennett. Tennessee climbs off the trap and gives the horses a carrot. She sits on a group of rocks, then leans back and closes her eyes. The last two Sundays she and Victoria have taken the ferry to Brooklyn and attended Plymouth Church. As Mr. Redpath predicted, Victoria is much taken with Reverend Beecher's charisma.

"He radiates such compassion and tenderness for his flock," Victoria said. "It's God's mercy for all people, whether you agree with the substance of his message or no, whether you find him a sympathetic character or not. He is perhaps the greatest pastor our society has seen— or will see for any time." Victoria resolved, "I must meet him. Face to face."

Tennessee turns over and drifts off to sleep.

"Your money or your life!" Something is stuck into her lower back. She tries to turn but the voice growls, "Don't move, wench."

There is no one in sight. She has the shard in the pocket of her skirt. The whip is on the trap.

"HA!" she shouts, spinning around, throwing herself at the knees of her assailant. Completely off guard, Bennett topples over her, laughing. "I'm winded, Tennie. How did you learn to do that?"

"You rogue! We might have been hurt." She hands him a carrot. He eats it in silence. She says, "What happened to you? I thought you'd been spirited away."

"The harness was rubbing on Bruno here. It seemed kinder to let him walk."

"You're full of surprises, aren't you, Bennett?"

"Not so full of surprises that I won't race you the last seventy blocks to the house."

"But what about your horse?" He helps her to her feet.

"I gave him a lambskin. He's right as rain now." Bennett helps her get back on the trap. In a flash, he is on the brougham. "Last one there must do something very illicit to the other. Adios!" With a crack of the whip, the brougham leaps forward.

"Hey!" She watches them grow smaller in the distance. Tennessee stands and cracks her whip overhead, shouting, "Yah! Yah! Come on, girls!" as she races to close the distance between them.

WHAT IS VIRTUE, WHAT IT IS NOT

June 1871
44 Broad Street

WRITE EVERY DAY. Tennessee sits at her desk scribbling what amounts to not much more than lists. The Victoria League, the People's Party, The Equal Rights Party, the Cosmopoliticals, the Suffragists, the Spiritualists, the Pantarchists. Momentum, she thinks to herself. They need to keep up the momentum. It is imperative they generate as many interested parties as possible. Elizabeth Cady Stanton, who leads the NWSA, has been most sympathetic despite the bad publicity, but Miss Stone and Mrs. Livermore particularly, from AWSA, seem to relish it. They've been quoted saying hurtful things about licentiousness and other indecencies with nary a provocation.

Blood says to Victoria in the far corner of the office. "One might argue that the Victoria League, such as it is, is easily misunderstood to indicate the Queen of England." He takes Victoria's hands. "But the Equal Rights Party or the People's Party speaks precisely to your platform. Doesn't it?"

Tennessee weighs in, "But what about the Communists and their International?"

She doesn't add that the correspondence with Mr. Marx has been— it's difficult to say, really. Pearl Andrews introduced them to Herr Sorge and Victoria invited them to meet at the *Weekly*, but there is something Tennessee can't quite put her finger on.

Instinct warns her to refrain from speaking too much German with those men. They are happy to be accommodated by the sisters but are pointedly disinterested in Victoria's political agenda. Why do they not think women's rights are citizens' rights? But if Tennessee were to say anything, it will make for ill will, which isn't the purpose of this alliance. It isn't the purpose of the alliance at all.

———

Reverend Henry Ward Beecher's coachman discreetly places *Woodhull & Claflin's Weekly* with other less reputable material inside the *New-York Tribune*. Once Mrs. Beecher retires upstairs to prepare for her day's obligations, the Reverend opens the newspaper, takes a piece of toast, and lathers on the marmalade from Harriet's citrus farm. Delicious. He sees the editorial from Miss Tennie C. Claflin. She's bold. Very bold.

> I will tell you confidentially, that since Mr. Andrews is chief of the Pantarchy and Victoria is chief of the Cosmo-political Party, I have taken it into my head to be chief of something, so I shall take it on my hands to carry out this special enterprise. I may perhaps want the help of my friend the Commodore, Rothschild, or whoever else has a few hundred thousand to spare, but I can't consent to touch a dollar on any terms that would trammel me in the least in my operations.

———

Miss Susan B. Anthony begins to read.

> I just want the privilege of showing what my own genius can design and realize.

This phrase alone compels her to put the paper down. This is sensationalism only! Her heart starts pounding. Why does Miss Claflin sabotage herself with her own ostentation?

How frivolous, Miss Anthony thinks and puts the paper by the grate to be burned.

At his home in Pleasantville, Horace Greeley finishes the last of his morning's gruel, sips his dandelion tea, and turns to the second paragraph of Miss Claflin's editorial. The audacity, he snorts to himself.

> I will have a grand city home, such as the world has not seen, where men and women of letters and genius, great artists and the like, and especially the great leaders of reform of all sorts, shall be as much at home as myself and shall form the nucleus of a social circle which shall be filled in from every rank in life, according to merit.

Mrs. Woodhull and her sister are self-serving opportunists, pushing the female suffrage debate only as a means of notoriety. They are obviously prostitutes, and little else.

It has been weeks since Stedman has seen Tennessee. He has fallen behind on the loan installments, but she hasn't reproached him nor sought to embarrass him in any way. He leans back and reads her editorial.

> What I contemplate is to obtain the lease of one of the large hotels and make it the headquarters of the new "Republican court," the focus and center of the intellect, science, taste, religion, fashion, and representative excellence, in all spheres, of this country and to some extent of the world, as the nucleus of the higher and better style of the society of the future.

Stedman knows he owes her an enormous debt of gratitude. He decides he'll repay the rest of the loan before the summer's end.

Tennessee watches Paschal Randolph finish the last sentence under his breath. He puts down the paper and has a sip of tea.

"So?" she asks. "What do you think?"

"I would attend your Republican Court and avail myself of its every aspect with relish!"

Colonel Blood says, "Vicky, if I might have a word."

Victoria follows him into the back office. A moment later, they reemerge, and he leaves in his jacket and tall hat. Victoria sits at her desk, deep in thought. Knowing when to keep her own council, Tennessee bends over her work until a marshal is shown to her desk and presents her with his credentials.

"Where might I find Colonel James Harvey Blood?"

"And your business is, sir?" Tennessee asks.

"I have a warrant for his arrest."

A few doors down from the Essex Market Police Court is Ludlow Street Jail. When they descend their hansom cab, the sisters see a pair of black-guards enter the building in shackles. One of the prisoners receives a smart blow from his captor.

Tennessee pats her sister's arm. "Well, at least they haven't thrown the Colonel in the clink."

Victoria whispers. "I should die were I so confined."

In the courtroom, the judge says, "Well, Colonel. It appears you're not guilty of anything apart from living with your wife and not agreeing with your mother-in-law. The complaint is dismissed unless you insist on a trial."

Blood answers without hesitation. "I do. I do insist." Looking at Victoria, he says, "To clear my good name."

That afternoon, across New York Bay, a Mr. Bowen arranges to meet Reverend Henry Ward Beecher and the Reverend's former best friend Mr. Theodore Tilton at a neutral party's home for lunch. Reverend

Beecher is America's preeminent clergyman and is compensated as such, earning $100,000 a year as pastor of Brooklyn's Plymouth Church. It is Mr. Bowen who hired him to serve in that capacity twenty years earlier.

The reason for the lunch is the upset, left in the wake of the Reverend's several friendships with his female congregants, most recently with that of Mrs. Tilton. The irony is not lost on Mr. Bowen. Bowen's own wife, while on her deathbed, several years before, confessed to having an affair with Reverend Beecher as well. What is the saying, something about Job—and bad things happening to good people? Bowen can't remember. The important thing is to contain the scandal. Protect the reputation of the church and simply contain the scandal.

―――

The luncheon party's host shows the esteemed guests into the library. He slides the tall pocket doors shut and goes to the sideboard to decanter some Madeira wine. Each man takes the offered glass. The four of them chat and gossip as if the reason for the luncheon had never occurred.

"Mrs. Woodhull enjoys the patronage of the troll," Reverend Beecher says.

"Which one?" Bowen asks.

"Senator Butler—the senator is quite alone," Tilton says.

The pastor looks up. "Well, not as alone as he was before Woodhull's arrival in the capital." Which makes them all laugh.

"Do you think she'll achieve it?" asks the host.

"Does it matter?" Bowen answers. "It gives them something to latch their talons on— moving from one grievance to the next, as the fairer sex is so fond of doing."

"So, do be a good fellow." Beecher nods toward Tilton.

Tilton shakes his head. "I have no desire to engage with Mrs. Woodhull."

"I've heard she's very charming," Bowen offers.

"You would be doing everyone a service by distracting La Woodhull," Beecher adds.

"And you? Were you doing me a service when you distracted my wife?" Tilton says.

Reverend Beecher's eyes mist over. They had once been the very best of friends. That it all came undone by Tilton's neglect, yes, Tilton's neglect of his bride, is not so surprising, really.

"Alas, I have prayed about and mourned the loss of your good opinion since time immemorial," the Reverend says, and helps himself to a mincemeat tart. "But I can't take on La Woodhull just now, we have a huge class of first-year communicants, and what with the Passion Plays…" He consumes the pie in one mouthful, then gives a beseeching look to his former protégé. "Be a good fellow. I will consider myself in your debt."

———

"All rise. The court is in session."

Colonel Blood sits next to his attorney. Victoria and Tennessee are behind him in the first row. At the plaintiff's table, Roxana is with her attorney, flanked by Polly and Ben Sparr.

Roxana is called to the witness box and cries out, "Judge! My daughters were good daughters and affectionate children!" She stands, trembling, and points at the Colonel. "Till they got in with this man, Blood. He has threatened my life several times."

Colonel Blood turns scarlet with indignation. Victoria looks at her hands and Tennessee feels the room become unnaturally quiet.

Roxana continues, her voice trembling. "I'll tell you what that man Blood is. He is one of those who have no bottom in their pocket; you can keep stuffing in all the money in New York, it never gets full up. S'help me God, Judge, I say here, and I call heaven to witness that there was the worst gang of Free Lovers in that house in Thirty-Eighth Street that ever lived—Stephen Pearl Andrews and Dr. Woodhull and lots more of such trash!" Roxana is distraught. She puts her handkerchief to her mouth, sobbing. Her lawyer leads her away, back to her table.

Then Colonel Blood testifies. Tennessee turns and looks around the nearly empty courtroom. There is no one there from the *Herald*. Thank God.

Alas, she is mistaken. The next morning, it is clear, a reporter from the *Herald* was there after all. After she reads the paper, Victoria locks herself in her room and Blood escapes to the office.

———

There is no embellishment. It is simply the testimony, reported, verbatim. That Dr. Woodhull lives in the same house as Colonel Blood and Victoria. Roxana's attorney then asked whether Dr. Woodhull stays in the same room, or indeed, shares the same bed with them? Which so infuriated Colonel Blood, that he refused to answer.

———

"Bennett! This is dreadful! How could you? Vicky is beside herself."

It is raining. From his office window, James Gordon Bennett watches the mayhem below, while he is cool and dry, surrounded by his dogs, his maps, and now graced by his favorite newsmaker.

Tennessee says, "I thought you were my friend." She doesn't know whether to scream or to sob. Instead she takes his offered glass of elderberry wine.

"Tennessee, I am your friend. You know if it weren't the *Herald*, it would simply be every other paper. I can't excuse myself, just because we're friends. Can I?"

"No."

"Your mother's comments were very moving, I daresay." He looks at the paper then smiles sweetly at Tennessee. She scowls back at him.

"If I had known that all this was going on but a few doors from my own home," he says, "I would have invited myself over every single night."

The next morning is brilliantly sunny. Gentle breezes roll nefarious city smells away and thanks to the *New York Herald*, the courtroom is packed.

The previous day, her attorney had cautioned Tennessee, "It is imperative the judge believe you are answering in all seriousness." When directed, she sits in the witness box.

"Give it a moment's thought before you speak, Miss Claflin," he advises.

The damage is already done. She looks at her attorney's kind face. Why not tell the truth? She waits for what seems an eternity. Finally, she says, "I never knew the Colonel to use any violence toward mother. He only treated her too kind. In fact, I don't see how he stood all her abuse." Tennessee opens her purse and holds up a handful of the correspondence she's intercepted. "I have some letters here, supposed to be written by my mother for the purpose of blackmailing different eminent persons in this city."

There is a rustle in the courtroom. "But Miss Claflin," the attorney attempts to get her back on point. "What was the reason your mother quarreled with Colonel Blood?"

She looks over at Roxana, sitting sadly between Ben and Polly Sparr. They're the ones who should be under scrutiny. Not Colonel Blood. Tennessee points at her brother-in-law. "The letters were written by this man, Ben Sparr."

There is a gasp among the spectators.

Tennessee continues, "My mother can't read or write. She is insane on spiritualism. But she is my mother and I love her. She has not slept away from me five minutes until lately."

"You and your mother have been on most intimate terms?"

"Yes, I used to tell fortunes with her. She wants me to go back into that business. But Vicky and Colonel Blood got me away from that life. They are the best friends I ever had. Since I was fourteen years old, I have had to keep thirty or thirty-five deadheads—"

"Deadheads, Miss Claflin?"

"Hangers on. You know, freeloaders. I am clairvoyant. I'm a spiritualist. I have power and I know my power. Many of the best men in Wall Street know my power. Commodore Vanderbilt knows my power." One can almost hear the pencils scratching on the notepads, scribbling down every word.

Tennessee glances at Victoria. The courtroom is very still. She turns back to the lawyer.

"I have humbugged people, I know; but if I did it was to make money to keep those deadheads."

⁓

Bennett puts down the paper. The *Female Financier Feud* is flying off the presses. It has sold even more copies than Stanley's search for Dr. Livingstone in Africa.

"Tennessee! Tennessee," he says. "Mrs. Stanton and Miss Anthony won't think much of your hullabaloo with the thieving sisters and hangers on."

"What do you mean?"

"To discuss humbugging whilst practicing clairvoyance?" Bennett raises his eyebrows, "And still sleeping with your mother? Yet I persist in asking you to sleep with me."

"Stop it, Bennett. You have Miss Markham and the entire chorus of *The Black Crook* lining up to sleep with you. I am not blind."

He looks back at his paper and reads: "I've kept thirty-five deadheads and had to humbug to keep them." At this he starts laughing.

"Stop it! It's not intended to be funny."

"Oh, you naughty, naughty Ten," he laughs.

The Commodore stands, facing the window. She can see the *New York Herald* on his desk. "COMMODORE VANDERBILT KNOWS MY POWER" screams across the headline.

He continues to look out the window, "You told the press you practice humbug."

"Oh, for mercy's sake, Goat." She throws up her arms. "A lot of it is, and you know it. How could it not be?"

He spins around and roars, "I don't waste money on humbug!" He is trembling. "I'll not be made a fool and you make a mockery of us."

"I have not made a mockery of—"

"You connive to swindle money from unsuspecting folk. It makes you a charlatan, Miss Claflin."

"And you cornered the Erie stock to destroy the value of those honest investors' shares, Cornelius." Tennessee is astonished that tears have begun running down her cheeks. "Who's the charlatan now?"

"You are to be held to a higher standard, Miss. That is business."

"I have never humbugged you, Cornelius."

He studies her for a moment and says, "I thought you were a woman of virtue, Tennessee."

She answers, "I thought you were my friend."

"I am not your friend. I do not know you. I am not your friend, after all." He rings a small bell on his desk. A footman enters. "Tell Sims to draw up a cheque for Miss Claflin. I believe the number is ten thousand."

Tennessee cries, "How dare you? I don't want the damn money!" She brushes past the servant and lets herself out of the house.

Ten minutes into her walk, it occurs to her that may have been a stupid thing to say. She had given him half her entire nest egg. "Damnit, all to hell!" It's the same amount of money she'd lent Stedman. Ten thousand dollars. She'll have to take care of it later.

Why is it that hypocrisy is not only prevalent in society, but in language as well? The words flow from Tennessee's mind onto the page. She will say her piece.

VIRTUE, WHAT IT IS AND WHAT IT IS NOT.

...A free man is a noble being; a free woman is a contemptible being. Freedom for a man is emancipation from degrading conditions which prevent the expansion of his soul into godlike grandeur and nobility, which it is assumed is his natural tendency in freedom.

Freedom for a woman is, on the contrary, escape from those necessary restraining conditions which prevent the sinking of her soul into degradation and vice, which is, all unconsciously, assumed to be her natural tendency.

"Whatever possessed you to think that I would tolerate this?" Tennessee is finished with these people. "Ben does nothing but hooey and peddling shoe polish as cough remedy."

Polly puts her hands on her hips, "I don't know what you're talking about." Everyone in the kitchen grows quiet.

Tennessee holds up the letter intended for Bennett and looks at the others. "Let's ventilate it all, Polly. Your encouraging Ma to bring this suit has ruined Vicky's chances of going to the head of the platform for the NWSA, let alone the AWSA. Let's just get everything out in the open!" She turns to Ben Sparr. "Ben, why don't you tell Polly how I've had to kick you out of my bed and why I sleep with our mother?"

There is a collective gasp in the kitchen.

She adds, "It's to protect me from the likes of you."

Polly whispers, "Ben, is that true?"

Utica says, "I don't mind sleeping with Ben. He's a bit rough, but all in all..."

Tennessee says, "Shut up, Utica."

Polly's face crumples into tears. "You're lying. You're lying! Ben, how could you?"

"Why should you have any problem with what I do?" Ben says, "I make sure we're safe in your mother's house."

Victoria says, "You mean your sister's house."

He continues, "And besides, you're through the Change now and Utica's willing."

Tennessee watches Victoria blanch. Colonel Blood's face is scarlet, and he looks at the floor.

Tennessee waves the letter under Polly's nose. "Own up to it! This is the kind of person that you are and have always been. Like a parasite, sucking my lifeblood, and never satisfied, always wanting more."

"It's hardly sucking your lifeblood when I was the one passed back and forth to keep the landlord from kicking us out of house and home!"

Which is the truth. It was during the fifties. Roxana had condoned it, too.

Utica says, "No, I don't mind at all."

Suddenly, Roxana wails and strikes at Ben Sparr. "You're wicked, wicked! A son of the devil with your Free Love, shaming one daughter with the other! Oh, heavenly Father." She is trembling but appears to be calm. "Get out, Benjamin Sparr, get out, Colonel Blood. Heraus!"

"I will not get out," Blood answers. "This is my house."

Victoria says, "You mean your wife's house."

Polly weeps in the corner and Roxana throws her preferred kitchen utensils into a bag. "Oh, the shame of it," she cries.

"I can't take another moment. I must leave," Tennessee mutters, and slams the front door behind her.

Utica yawns and walks down the passage behind the kitchen. She knocks on Canning Woodhull's door.

"Come in," Canning is lying on his bed, reading a small book.

"What's that?" Utica points at the book.

"This?" He smiles at her. "It's to do with the Faraday Effect and its role in diametric magnetism."

"Oh." Having little interest in diametric magnetism, Utica lies down next to him. "Do you have anything for sharing?"

"I might. What's going on out there?"

"Polly's just realized she married a villain. It's the usual thing."

———

From the journal of Tennie C. Claflin:

Yesterday, Ben Sparr was found dead in Jersey City. Polly accused Vicky of poisoning him, but the coroner insists that Ben somehow bumped his head. The coroner does not go so far as to add during a drunken stupor, but he doesn't need to. It's implied. Alas, the unspeakable mess of it all!

———

It exasperates Reverend Beecher that the agape he has with his female parishioners is so often misconstrued by their husbands. He wants to shout that if Tilton had not been dipping his pen in several other inkwells, the exquisite Elizabeth would not have been left alone, nor would she have responded to the Reverend's amativeness with such profound depth!

Kneeling before his former protégé, the Reverend shifts his weight from one knee to another. At fifty-two years of age, kneeling is not as easy as it used to be. He imagines the younger man's wife. Life can be cruel. It is most unfortunate. The Reverend grabs the fauteuil for support as he stands up.

"I held you in the highest regard." Theodore Tilton says, unable stop his voice from trembling. He pinches the bridge of his nose.

"I know." Beecher looks at the ground.

"And that you should touch my property with your person, leaving her with child!" Tilton's tears begin flowing and there is only rage, white and searing. It dazzles everything with light. Tilton finds it difficult to breathe and stumbles from the room. He fears he might have a stroke.

IT MAY BE THAT SHE IS A FANATIC, IT MAY BE THAT I AM A FOOL

July 1871
44 Broad Street

"IS THE RUMOR founded on fact?" Victoria waits for Tilton to account for himself. Her skin glows in such a way that Tilton finds he has to restrain himself from reaching out to touch her. She is not tall, but despite the difference in their height, he sees her at eye level, rather than looking down. It is most unnerving.

Tilton doesn't realize that Victoria uses an apple crate's advantage when working at her husband's standing desk. She steps down and crosses to the sitting area. "Tell me, do you really believe marriage without love is a sin against God?"

He tries to speak but nothing comes out.

"Don't look so amazed, Mr. Tilton. I am a voracious reader, and always catch the latest issue of the *Independent*. Your editorials were most stimulating. When did you write that? I understand you are between engagements now." She rings a bell on the table beside her. "Will you have tea?"

Blushing, he sits down where she indicates. When the office boy brings a silver tea service to the table, it appears, like Mrs. Woodhull, to glow from within. Of the items on the tray, she says, "A gift from Mr. Tiffany; he's a faithful advertiser for *WCW*. Have you read my paper, Mr. Tilton?"

———

Back in Brooklyn, Reverend Beecher asks, "And your reception was…?"

"She could not have been more accommodating. Mrs. Woodhull is, in fact…" Tilton takes moment to search for the word. "The lady is transcendent. That's all there is to it."

"You should win her over," Henry Bowen says. "Offer to do her bidding,"

"Write something for her. Whatever she needs," Reverend Beecher chimes in. "You were a confidante of President Lincoln! Men in power have flocked to you."

Tilton looks at the man who has made him a cuckold. "You needn't attempt to persuade me, Reverend. Mrs. Woodhull's company is most singular. In fact, I am sure you would find her very much the same as I do."

"Really?"

"Without a doubt."

———

"Mrs. Woodhull."

"Please, call me Victoria."

Everyone at *Woodhull & Claflin's Weekly* waits for Tilton's response, so he says, "Victoria, I will write a biographical portrait of you, to attract and galvanize a large number of readers." It would be dreadful should they suspect him of having been put up to it by Bowen and Beecher. Just do it, he thinks. Take the plunge. "I will compel them by the pathos of your struggles during those early days and contrast them with the lofty heights of your more recent triumphs."

Victoria remains utterly still. The chance to wipe away the scandal of Roxy and Blood's tawdry havoc in court hangs like a golden ring. If this works, she'll salvage her dignity. She'll convince the public she is respectable after all.

Blood prompts, "Such as the brokerage, your newspaper, the memorial to Congress."

Victoria asks, "You don't think a straight narrative of my upbringing would yield the same fascination?"

"In my editorial opinion?" Her eyes are so beautiful, Tilton thinks, like the color of twilight. He replies, "No. I do not."

"The greater the pathos, the keener the sympathy," Pearl Andrews says. "One's readers prefer drama and conflict, Victoria."

"As demonstrated by the attention we received from the trial," Blood adds, turning away from the group. He mutters to no one in particular, "It pains me to say."

Tennessee watches Victoria study their father. Theodore Tilton cannot know about the girls being told what sacrifices had to be made or what it was to do the show and humbug the innocent. Tennessee is quite sure. Tilton has no idea.

Victoria murmurs, "Yes, I suppose that's true."

Tilton crouches beside Victoria's chair and whispers so only she can hear. "Then perhaps we might consider those moments when all seemed to be lost and, uh…" Looking at Victoria, he realizes he might be falling in love with her. "Embellish them, as it were."

Victoria glances at Buck, then smiles weakly and says, "Well, I'll let you decide that."

———

Bennett rows Tennessee out to the yacht. They enjoy an elaborate picnic on deck and watch the sun go down. She's taken to playing the concertina, and figures out the notes for a shanty, singing so softly Bennett can barely make out the words.

While money lasts, I spend it fast
get drunk as drunk could be
And when me money is all gone

On liquors and the whores,
I make up me mind that I am inclined
To go to sea no more

"Tennie. You should take the summer off. Even suffragists need a respite from time to time."

"But I'm already booked. We're meeting with the 12th International to discuss labor conditions."

Bennett groans.

"Do you not think we should demand an eight-hour workday? Or that women should earn as much as their male colleagues in laundries and at work?"

"Tennie."

"Mr. Tilton supports this notion. So does Miss Anthony. How much do you pay your typesetters, Mr. Bennett?"

He takes out his toothpick and says nothing.

"And how much do you pay women who work in the same function? Oh wait!

Let me tell you how much Mr. Jones at the *Times* pays them."

"I can only thank God and the Heavens you do not work for me, Miss Claflin."

"The *Times* pays the men fifty-five cents per thousand ems set, and the women barely forty cents for each thousand ems they set. Does that seem fair to you?"

"Beware the incongruity that you side with workers yet reap the rewards of their oppressors."

"Would you prefer we sing, Bennett?"

He nods, and she leans against him. She plays the opening bars on her concertina. The boat sways very gently in the water and the sky is dark.

"Du bist die Ruhe," Bennett sings. His German is flawless, but like Cornelius, he sings off-key.

"Oh Bennett." Tennessee looks tenderly up at him.

"Yes, Tennie?"

"You really are a terrible singer, aren't you?"

So much life! Being with this woman brings him so much life. Bennett's heart is pounding, and the air is bracingly clear. After they say their farewells, his driver takes him to the Union Club. His mates are there, plotting the Newport season.

By one in the morning, after they've finished off the '52 whiskey, someone cries, "Fire!"

All hell breaks loose and smoke billows out of the kitchens as firemen lean their ladders on the outside of the building.

"I've got it, I've got it!" Bennett yells, attempting to climb the first ladder.

"No sir!" The fireman shoves him out of the way.

"What? You scoundrel!" Bennett takes a swing at the fireman who deftly steps aside.

"Hose him down, Jerry!" shouts the lieutenant. The fireman turns the water on Bennett full blast. "You need to get out of the way, sir!"

The next afternoon at the club, Bennett asks, "What happened last night?"

Someone shrugs. "You made a complete fool of yourself, as usual."

Bennett says, "I must send the fellows in that brigade new slickers. I've never been so wet in my life."

The cross breeze makes the roof at 15 East Thirty-Eighth Street a perfect place to sit in the evening. Victoria spreads a large blanket and scatters several pillows. Theodore Tilton watches the soft wind blow her unruly hair irresistibly across her face.

"It is most painful to be cuckolded," he says, "particularly when the offending party is someone you've held in the highest esteem."

"I know what it is to be betrayed. By my own sister no less."

"Tennie C.?"

"No, no. Utica. She, she is often intemperate. It is how I came to understand that while marriage has outlived its usefulness in society, we should still find a solution with the greatest compassion for everyone, shouldn't we?"

Tilton says, "Victoria, read this and tell me what you think."

She looks down at the paper as Tilton leans back on one of the pillows. She begins to read aloud:

"A Legend of Good Women" by Theodore Tilton

"If the woman's movement has a Joan of Arc, it is this gentle but fiery genius. She is one of the most remarkable women of her time. Little understood by the public, she is denounced in the most outrageous manner by people who do not appreciate her moral worth. But her sincerity, her truthfulness, her uprightness, her true nobility of character, are well known to those who know her well."

She stops reading and looks at him. "Oh Theo, you are indeed my very best friend, aren't you?"

Theodore Tilton whispers, "Yes, Victoria. I will be your very best friend."

From the journal of Tennie C. Claflin:

Since our disaster in court, there've been few invitations to leave town, which matters little, because the Colonel is all consumed with the Weekly, and Victoria is all consumed by Mr. Tilton. I should lie were I to pretend I don't miss the incorrigible Mr. Bennett, but such is my cross to bear. Before his departure for Newport, he sent me the most marvelous gift. Mr. Edison's Universal Stock Printer for Gold and Stock. Now I can sit all day at 44 Broad Street, watching ribbons of white paper indicate the ups and downs of the market's value. Much like my emotions, I suppose.

In fact, everyone is on edge. Last week, mobs of Irishmen took to the streets because City Hall would not let the Protestants (much to the relief of the Catholics) mark their Orange Parade. The governor even sent out the National Guard. But someone in Tammany relented, so the parade took place yesterday afternoon at 2 o'clock. By 4 o'clock, 60 marchers were dead, not to mention 100 other casualties, in addition to 22 police and two guardsmen. Yet another summer's day in New York City.

The missives are scattered around the house.

> *My dear Victoria, put this under your pillow, dream of the writer, gather the spirits about you, and so, good night.*

—Theodore Tilton

Tennessee finds another on the hall table.

> *My dearest Victoria, I made haste, while yet able to sit up, for I am giddy with xxxxxx this morning.*

—Theodore

Victoria hums as she sits at her secretary, skimming through the evening paper.

"Perhaps you neglected to put these away?" Tennessee places the notes on the desk.

Victoria feigns surprise. "Oh, did you find those?" When Tennessee doesn't answer, Victoria smiles and says, "Ah, then Colonel Blood will have noticed them," and returns to her reading.

Tennessee shrugs and goes upstairs to her room. On the console in the center of the landing is yet another.

> *The Reverend will meet you, Victoria, after his business.*
> *I imagine near ten. And you shall have as long as you both need together.*

—TT

It is Sunday, July 30. A visit to Staten Island is the perfect escape from the city. Tennessee walks through the harbor, past the day's catch, mountains of fish waste, netting, and dank coiled ropes along the pier. To the tattooed seamen and various naval officers, she more closely resembles a boy than she does a woman, with her short hair, dressed in her sailor's garb. At the battery, the crowd impatiently waits on the dock while passengers are loaded onto the *Westfield* ferry.

She sees Randolph near the kiosk. He seems preoccupied and she wonders if he's been drinking. "Doctor! Have you forgotten your swimming trunks?"

"Alas, I shan't go in today," he says. He is swaying just enough to give her concern.

"I thought you would come in the ocean with me." Her pout lasts only a second, fading as the mutual affection flows between them. The sun has showered her with freckles and her smile opens wide.

He says, "You know, you are my very favorite—"

"Favorite what, Dr. Randolph? Radical? Cosmo-political? Communard, nay Reformer!"

"Indeed, of all—" But his words vanish in a flash of darkness.

The explosion's boom shakes the ground. Tennessee's spirit slips away from her body and she watches herself reaching for Randolph. They float through the air. Litter and burning chards of wood dance in slow motion around them, then crash into each other's arms in a heap on the corner of the green.

Everything is silent. Stunned, Tennessee blinks. The sky is a dazzling blue and she struggles to focus. "Pascal?" Her vision clears as the scene from the séance at Pfaff's replays itself, silently.

He moves his lips, but she can hear nothing. She is afraid to move. The smell of oil and fuel makes it impossible to breathe. Suddenly, the sounds roar around her. There is screaming and the sobs of tens of hundreds and a bell clanging. She struggles to get up.

Confusion and mayhem are everywhere. Randolph helps her to her feet, and she collapses in his powerful embrace, "You're all right?"

She nods.

"Stay here," he says, and heads toward the crowd.

There are anguished screams from the water, hot oil scalding the water's surface. Flames engulf the ferry. Men throw burning wood shards off the boat into the water, unwittingly injuring those struggling not to drown. Women and children are sobbing everywhere. Limp bodies are placed on the street as men attempt to halt the traffic.

A horse rears up in panic and tramples a boy who runs underfoot.

"Tennessee! Miss Claflin." William Vanderbilt's coachman gestures at her. William is inside the carriage, beckoning. "Come with me, come away from this—come with me now."

She approaches. "Was this your ship?"

"My cousin's. Come."

"No! I am needed here. No, no."

"Are you quite mad?"

"No! Billy. You must stay. You must stay and help."

"I'll send reinforcements." But she has already returned to the crowd. She finds Randolph lifting the mortally wounded onto a wagon. He looks up for a moment and when he sees her, gestures to where she can offer her assistance.

———

At last, the good Reverend Beecher. Victoria is taken to a room filled with as many books as can be fit into every possible space. The maid leaves, closing the door behind her, and Reverend Beecher says, "These volumes are my weakness."

She smiles and faces a bookshelf as if to study the titles so that he doesn't see her take a deep breath. Just get to the point, she thinks, and get the job done.

Watching her admire his collection, the Reverend considers his conversation with Theodore Tilton and can't help but wonder where this visit will go.

Victoria turns to look at him. "For one who has the power to put those that pursue me at bay, you certainly have been elusive, Reverend."

"Oh Mrs. Woodhull, I am your humble servant. Albeit one with many masters."

There will be no pretense, no hullabaloo. She says, "Would those masters include your congregants amongst whom your amative prowess has been so much discussed?"

Touché. For a woman who is reputedly illiterate, she is really very good. He realizes she is still speaking.

"You would do me a great service, Reverend, indeed, all of my sex a great service, were you to call off the wrath of both Mrs. Stowe and Miss Catharine Beecher. I should find myself completely in your debt and very much obliged."

"My dear Mrs. Woodhull, my sisters are free thinking women. Far be it from me to induce them in any way. Besides, is there not some foundation in their antipathy toward your enthusiasms?"

He picks up a tray of his preferred sweets, those being dried fruits sprinkled with powdered sugar and offers her one—"Fig?" —which she accepts and puts on a small plate he gives her with the other hand.

She places the plate beside her lace gloves and says, "My goodness, it is becoming so much hotter this evening than I'd anticipated." Victoria raises her chin and delicately fans herself with her hand.

Watching her move the air near her throat sends a brief thrill down the Reverend's back. She moves closer to him and he feels himself blushing with pleasure. "Indeed," she says, "I can only surmise your reputation's veracity—"

Before he knows what is happening, her graceful hand has firmly coaxed his amative nature to its fullest extent. "Unless I experience it myself." Her gaze does not waver from his. "You understand, don't you?"

When she kneels down he grabs the edge of his desk, compelled, as the moth to a flame, and surrenders to the flash of oblivion.

She stands back up and his shoulders are limp. His mouth is numb with sin and desire. Victoria removes her hat. "Undo me," she says.

Obediently, the Reverend unfastens the hooks within which she is confined. She leans forward and kisses him in such a way he fears he may have died and gone to heaven.

Slowly leading him away from the front of his great desk, she gently pushes him to his knees, and raises her foot onto a chair. From her pocket, she hands him a silk oblong bag, concealing a carved phallus the length of his hand. Never has a woman presented him with this! He has only read and dreamt of such things undercover in the dead of night.

"You know what to do, Reverend."

Trembling, he reaches out to touch her. Her skin is exquisite. She says, "First me and then you."

The *Westfield* ferry disaster results in nearly a hundred dead. Countless more are injured. It is after two in the morning when Tennessee opens the door at Thirty-Eighth Street. She enters the house, beyond numb from the shock of the day's events.

Tennessee is mounting the stairs as Utica emerges from Victoria's room. Utica puts a finger in front of her lips. "Shhh." But then she sees Tennessee's face in the moonlight. "What happened to you?"

"What are you doing, Utica?" Tennessee whispers.

Utica shrugs. "I just want to experience his technique."

Victoria returns before dawn. Quietly, she opens the door and passes the front sitting room. Canning and Byron are asleep, curled up on the sofa. She thinks to kiss them goodnight but changes her mind and goes upstairs. Inside her bedroom, she walks past Colonel Blood's sleeping form and retires to her dressing room to catch a few hours' rest.

The dates have already been set. It is impossible to back out now. When Tennessee announced her campaign, Victoria donated one thousand copies of Mr. Marx's *The Civil War in France* as a gift to the Internationals. Not wanting to owe Victoria anything, Herr Sorge, the head Marxist, then endorsed Tennessee's candidacy to represent the German-speaking community.

The cable comes the day before her scheduled appearance at Irving Hall. It is from Bennett who is still in Newport. "BIST DU BEREIT," it reads. Yes, Tennessee whispers to herself. I am ready.

At the hall, she declares, "Solange ich Sie im Kongress vertreten werde - wenn durch Ihre Stimmen Sie mir dorthin senden sollen - werde ich darauf bestehen, dass die persönliche Freiheit jeder Person unberührt bleiben soll!"

The man from the *Herald* approaches her when she descends the platform. "Miss Claflin, would you be so kind as to translate for our readers?"

She realizes she has not stopped trembling since the explosion. "I said, if elected I shall insist on individual freedoms for everyone, mandating an eight-hour workday, particularly for children, and a day of recreation wherein one might drink beer, so long as it does not disrupt the peace."

The president of the German American Citizens Club presents her with a large bouquet and pledges his support for their nominee for Congress, Miss Tennessee Claflin.

Buck is not in attendance, but Roxana is bursting with pride.

Afterward, a brass band plays outside on Thirty-Eighth Street. Before Tennessee steps on to the balcony, Victoria says, "I thought you were going to talk about the *Westfield*."

"I couldn't," Tennessee's trembling has only become worse. "How can I say that capitalist greed, in overloading a boat that isn't seaworthy, far outweighs the safety of working families and children?" The absurdity of her campaign strikes her like a slap. "No one wants to hear that! Please. It won't change anything."

She wonders if she is coming down with a fever. "It's meaningless. Everyone knows it's just for show."

"Tennie—"

"No, don't Vicky. Tomorrow, let's put an end to it."

Victoria stands in the shadows as Tennessee waves at the crowd. Canning and Utica are in the back garden. Blood and Andrews are at the office. Tilton is still working on her biography for *The Golden Age*.

As for Henry Ward Beecher, what is there to say? The Reverend and Victoria understand one another. Perhaps they are even cut from the same cloth. She folds the eviction notice the landlord just delivered back into her skirt pocket. Blood will deal with it. He'll figure out a way to buy them a few more months at Thirty-Eighth Street. In the meantime, she'll have to think up something new with which to fascinate the Reverend. Henry Ward Beecher has warned Victoria, he doesn't like to be bored.

September 1871
The Herald Building
Broadway and Ann Street

Bennett hands Tennessee a cup of tea. "I'm very much looking forward to it. Buffalo Bill Cody and Wild Bill Hickok as well as a few of the lads. It will be the perfect diversion."

They study the countless maps spread out upon his desk. He stands behind her and enjoys the scent of her hair. "Do you think I'll bring home a squaw for wife?"

"She'd be a refreshing change from some of the other females you cavort with."

"Miss Claflin! Do I detect a note of jealousy?"

"Mr. Bennett, I'd be on a fool's mission were I to presume any rights to you. How many are on your trip?"

"We are ten in Cody's party. The entire corps is made up of three hundred, I believe. Twenty or so wagons, several for the porcelain and wine, then of course there's accompanying staff."

"That will be two buffalo per man, then."

"What's that?"

She squints then closes her eyes. "The total number you'll kill in the herd." She opens them to see him watching her just a few inches from her face. "Enjoy your hunt, Mr. Bennett. Those buffalo will be near vanished before long. Ah, well!" She pats his cheek and then finishes her tea in a gulp. "For myself, Vicky's got the Spiritualists and whatnot next week. I do envy this epic freedom you so enjoy."

"Come with me."

"I'll go with you as far as Thirty-Eighth Street. And then my other duties must prevail."

There is a rap at the entrance to his office and a copy boy hands him a telegram.

Bennett reads the cable and smiles, announcing, "Well, bully for that! Stanley has found Livingstone. My God. I suppose I should pay his expenses after all."

"What did he say?"

"I'm sure it was the usual thing. 'Dr. Livingstone, I presume?' He'd better not sell his story to the *Times*."

They make their way to the elevator. "Buck thinks the *Times* is the only real paper."

Bennett slaps her rear end. "The *Times* is the real paper?" Not too hard, just with his hat.

"Hey!"

"Two buffalo per man, that's not so bad."

"Get back to me in twenty years. We can discuss it then."

———

Two private Pullman cars from New York to Chicago convey Bennett's entourage through Illinois into Missouri, across the Mississippi, heading south until they arrive in Topeka, and rendezvous with their guides, Buffalo Bill Cody and Wild Bill Hickok.

In addition to Bennett, and his close friends, the Jerome brothers, their company also comprises several generals, and a few New York businessmen, one of whom is Luther Challis, his having profited mightily from the railroad's expansion across Kansas.

There are twenty-five wagons in all. In addition to the dry goods, Persian carpets, linens, crystal, and china, there are three traveling ice houses to chill the game, the produce, and the wine. As Buffalo Bill leads them further into the heart of the Great Plains, its original occupants observe this masculine spectacle, bemused by the wagons' nightly square formation spreading across several acres, inside of which sleep some of the nation's wealthiest and most decorated gentlemen.

In the evenings, Leonard Jerome plays a small guitar and sings while the others sit around the campfire, nursing their brandy snifters, enjoying their fine cigars. They recall their time in the War, consider their fortunes, and silently reflect on their loved ones back home.

Challis is surprised. "You aren't familiar with the Rosicrucians and Paschal Beverly Randolph?"

"Should I be?" Bennett gives a mighty stretch and blows smoke rings as he leans back in his chair.

Someone says, "Randolph wrote *The Master Passion*, didn't he? Describes how partnering with a woman might open the gates to all that would be possible."

"I don't know how I missed that." It is then that Bennett sees the owl, quietly perched on one of the wagons. He stands up to take a better look. The bird's white face is inscrutable and watches him, unblinking.

The man continues, "One's diet is critical. No potted meats or stimulants and the like. And you need to practice some air bathing, too."

"She can't be a virgin," Challis adds, "or another man's wife."

"Prostitutes are also out," the man continues. "And she must reciprocate. That much is paramount. She also has to be of exceptional intelligence, or else there's little point in the exercise."

Bennett sees the owl is now in shadow. He studies the stars behind its silhouette. He only knows one woman who fits that bill.

"So," Bennett says, "imagine one finds such a person, one practices a diet free from potted meats, and that person is willing and able to reciprocate. Then what?"

"One must abstain from intercourse for forty-nine days. Then love becomes the conduit that leads to magic and all that one's heart desires."

"Really?"

"Sex power is God power, according to Randolph. Jay Gould swears by it."

"That scoundrel. Of course, he does. And I'm sure Mrs. Gould is happy to oblige!" They all roar with laughter. Bennett watches the bird fly away and listens to the guitar, filled with his own thoughts.

Catharine Beecher looks up from her needlepoint at her brother, Reverend Beecher. "Henry! Mrs. Woodhull must not dare to present herself in Connecticut."

He coughs, then takes a sip of his tea.

Harriet Beecher Stowe adds, "This is all Belle's doing, shaming us, shaming the family by consorting with those Free Lovers."

Reverend Beecher lowers his chin so that it touches his foulard. Harriet is his respected and beloved sister and he does not wish to offend.

But it is time to clear the air. "If memory serves me correctly, Harriet, I have published as many as six of the articles you have written against Mrs. Woodhull in the *Christian Union*, haven't I?"

"You have."

"Would I be correct in assuming that if we move forward with the rather flamboyant Audacia Dangereyes whom you created in *My Wife and I*, you would no longer need to vent your spleen against this lady?"

"Brother," Harriet says, "it is not my intention to draw that individual, but rather to draw attention to that sort of class." She thinks for a moment, then adds, "Of person."

"I am reassured then that your fifty thousand readers don't doubt that for a moment."

To which Catharine Beecher exclaims, "Henry, are you not in the least bit concerned that Belle has been seduced by a woman whose heart is little better than that of Lucifer?"

Harriet nods in agreement. "Belle's attachment to that woman is most unnatural. Do you not think so, Henry?"

Reverend Beecher, for his part, thinks it best to remain silent.

As a diversion, for their last evening in camp Buffalo Bill hires a few braves to stage a gag raid of sorts. Catching wind of the scheme, Leonard Jerome joins the native company in the proceedings, whooping loudly, wearing only a loin cloth and war paint, which adds to the hysteria when the raid takes place. Their efforts pay off, and no one is hurt, much to the amusement and delight of the company. And Tennessee's count was correct. They slaughter more than six hundred buffalo, two hundred elk, and smaller game besides. All in all, it is most entertaining.

Tennessee chuckles and reads aloud to Victoria and Blood.

"Dacia was in high spirits, jaunty as ever…'f I see a man that pleases me,' said she, 'I shall not ask Priest or Levite for leave to have him.' This was declared with so martial an air that I shrank a little, but she relieved me by saying, "You needn't be frightened. I don't want *you*. You wouldn't suit me. All I want of you is your money.""

"Mrs. Stowe has a forked tongue," Victoria says, thinking how dare Reverend Beecher publish this in his paper? Did those nights with him mean nothing? She wants to scream.

"Oh, Vic, honestly, Audacia Dangereyes resembles yours truly more than she does you." Tennessee continues to read the paper.

"That's not the point." Victoria sits down and buries her face in her hands.

Blood strokes the back of her head and she looks up at him, remembering the moment that they met. *Deliver my soul, O Lord, from lying lips and from a deceitful tongue. Amen.*

He hasn't lied. He has been honest, and it devastates her. Blood does not ask, and she refuses to volunteer. The truth is, Tilton's amative nature has possibly saved her sanity. As for Reverend Beecher, do they have an understanding? Well, as Buck used to say, one must make sacrifices.

The Colonel says gently, "Just attempt to forget it."

She snatches her hand from his. How could she forget it?

"Vic." Tennessee does not look up from her paper. "He means Audacia Dangereyes."

If Tennessee finds no fault with Mrs. Stowe's serial, then, Victoria decides, she should be the one to read Mr. Tilton's profile to the family. She summons them into the parlor and says, "Tennie's reading this aloud for everyone's benefit. It will be published in the next day or so, and you should be prepared."

Tennessee turns up the lamp. "It begins with a quote from Scripture, Ma."

"Oh, that's good," Roxana says, "to start with scripture."

Tennessee reads, "He that uttereth a slander is a fool."

Roxana smiles, "Klar, Proverbs, ten eighteen. Very nice. I like that young Tilton, don't you, Buck?"

"Shh," Buck murmurs, and watches Victoria sit down next to Zula. "Read, Tennie," he says.

In Homer, Ohio, in a small cottage, white-painted and high-peaked, with a porch running 'round it and a flower garden in front, this daughter, the seventh of ten children of Roxana and Buckman Claflin, was born September 23rd, 1838.

Tennessee scans through and says, "Something, something about being named for the Queen, and one day seeing the Queen and Windsor Castle, my goodness." She stops and clears her throat. Frowning slightly, she says, "Here we go."

It is pitiful to be a child without a childhood. Such was she...She was worked like a slave—whipped like a convict. Her father was impartial in his cruelty to all his children...In a barrel of rainwater he kept a number of braided green withes made of willow or walnut twigs, and with these stinging weapons, never with an ordinary whip, he would cut the quivery flesh of the children till their tears and blood melted him into mercy. Sometimes he took a handsaw or a stick of firewood as the instrument of his savagery.

Buck says, "Now, Vicky. I was stern, but you can't say you were denied affection."

Victoria smiles and says, "Tennie, go on."

The mother, who has never in her life learned to read, was during her maidenhood the petted heiress of one of the richest German families of Pennsylvania, and was brought up not to serve but to be served...The father, partly bred to the law and partly to real-estate speculations, early in life acquired affluence, but during Victoria's third year suddenly lost all that he had gained and sat down like a beggar in the dust of despair.

Her mother has on occasions tormented and harried her children until they would be thrown into spasms, whereat she would hysterically laugh, clap her hands, and look as fiercely delighted as a cat in playing with a mouse...This eccentric old lady, compounded in equal parts of heaven and hell, will pray till her eyes are full of tears, and in the same hour curse till her lips are white with foam. The father exhibits a more tranquil bitterness, with fewer spasms. These parental peculiarities were lately made witnesses against their possessors in a court of justice...At times, they are full of craftiness, low cunning, and malevolence; at other times, they beam with sunshine, sweetness, and sincerity. I have seen many strange people, but the strangest of all are the two parents whose commingled essence constitutes the spiritual principle of the heroine of this tale.

Roxana stands up. "I wish you to stop now."

Buck says, "Mother, let her finish."

Roxana shakes her head. "Reuben Buckman Claflin, you know I was never an heiress in Pennsylvania."

"They said it for circulation, Ma," Tennessee says. "To sell the paper. You don't mind, do you?"

"Yes, I mind! I mind very much." Roxana stands to take her leave. At the door she says, "And it is a sin against God to describe your mother as having white foam on the mouth. As if I am a rabid dog! Es ist ein jammer schade, Vicky."

Utica starts to laugh. She wipes her eyes and says, "Well, I love it. I think it's perfect."

PART FOUR

INFAMY

"Do you believe I could have taken her to my heart as I have done, if I did not believe her true and pure?"

-Isabella Beecher Hooker to
Harriet Beecher Stowe

WHO IS THY NEIGHBOR?

November 1871
Brooklyn Heights

REVEREND HENRY WARD Beecher traditionally spends All Saints' Day in seclusion. It is the one day of the year he permits his wife to mourn their family angels with him. Of their eleven children, four are buried out west and three are buried in Brooklyn. Over the years, Mrs. Beecher has, without comment, learnt to accept her husband's position. It cannot be said, Mrs. Beecher is nothing if not stoic.

No sooner is their sad visit concluded and his wife retired to her room than the maid informs the Reverend that Mrs. Woodhull is in the parlor.

Mrs. Woodhull. So lovely if not the tiniest bit of a menace. Reverend Beecher requests they be brought a pot of tea and goes to the parlor to receive the good lady.

"Reverend!" Victoria stands by the window, where the afternoon light graces her to striking effect.

"Mrs. Woodhull." He watches her untie her bonnet and loosen her curls. God, she is beautiful, he thinks. Their visits over the summer had been most edifying. Such a pity they could not continue as they had. But only a fool would ignore that she is a loose cannon, liable to fire if not treated with care.

She hands him a portfolio which he had failed to notice when greeting her. "This is the speech I will make at Steinway Hall. Whatever suggestions you might have would be so appreciated."

Beecher opens the folder and skims the text.

He reads aloud, "'1. Every living person has certain rights.' Very good, yes. 'Order and harmony can alone be secured etc.' etc. But Mrs. Woodhull. This is very good. You shall acquit yourself well in the presentation of these ideas."

"Thank you. The other purpose of my visit is to seek your assistance, which can hardly surprise you, in silencing those who would remove me from the public arena."

"And how might I do that?"

She gestures at the portfolio in his hands. "By endorsing these same truths which I've put forward. Suffrage and constitutional equality for women, Free Love or the abolition of marriage as we know it."

"Alas, Mrs. Woodhull, you come on a day which has me woefully unprepared to discuss these…"

"Those evenings last summer, Reverend, could not have happened had you not shared my sentiments in these matters."

"Indeed, but should I do so, I would be abandoning my flock. The very tenet of marriage bonds them to their belief in God the Father."

"You will not stand next to me?"

"Mrs. Woodhull." Reverend Beecher puts down the portfolio. "Today I stand next to no one, other than my dead children, whose passing I mark and observe on this day only. The housekeeper will see you out."

At 425 Fifth Avenue, they both know they should be content, as they normally are, to be together, but the thought of voting at the polling station has Tennessee on edge.

"Tennie," Bennett repeats for the twentieth time. "For one to make profits, those who actually do the work must earn *less*."

"I am not suggesting you should cease to be wealthy." Don't get angry, she warns herself. "I am suggesting you should care more about the common man."

For some reason Bennett finds that funny. "And what, Miss Clairvoyant-Claflin, Former-Consort-to-Commodore-Vanderbilt himself, do you understand about the common man?"

She wonders if he still has no idea.

"My father came to this country with nothing. Nothing." Bennett continues, "And he built the *Herald* up, without assistance from those whose wealth you are so eager to disperse as you see fit. He did it on his own, Tennie. That's how it works here. You have to do it on your own."

"Have you done it on your own, Jimmy?" She never calls him that.

"Of course, not. The sailing, well, I don't know." He does not want to argue. "Tomorrow you'll get enormous coverage, and you will look as beautiful as you always do," which is meant as a peace offering. Too late to stop himself, he says, "So don't confuse your rights with overthrowing those in power you mistakenly imagine to be evil oppressors."

To which she remains silent.

Her hair is too short to pin up. If he pulls it gently away, he might reach over and kiss the space between her collar and her neck. He clears his throat, "Tennie, when you move from one platform to the next, you invariably upset the apple cart and-"

"Is that why you didn't expose Black Friday in '69?" She disappoints herself by wanting to strike back.

"How do you know about that?"

"Fisk told me he ventilated everything, but you refused to print the story."

"Don't run with the International. You'll make trouble for yourself you just don't need."

"It's my duty to state my objection to the French government's execution of those boys!" She wishes she hadn't started yelling again. "Don't tell me you approved of their deaths."

"Whether I think it was just or not has nothing to do with your naïve enthusiasm for blasted communards!" He wishes he could just stop yelling.

"The march isn't for another six weeks."

"The police are going to ban the demonstration. I've received a letter to run in the paper."

To which she is silent again. Bennett curses himself even as he says, "Don't do it, or -"

She cries out, "Or what, Bennett? Are you forbidding me?"

He knows better than to answer.

"Perhaps you've forgotten," she says softly, "I am a free woman and conduct my affairs as such. Please, don't get up. I'll see myself home. As you so often remind me, it's just a few paces."

From the journal of Tennie C. Claflin:

We were several carriages in all. Mrs. Daniels from Boston and Mrs. Cuppy Smith rode directly behind us. Dear Judge Reymert was our escort. He is nearly as tall as the Commodore and in his stove pipe hat is even taller. When we arrived, not one of the men outside the polling station commented on our presence. Indeed, they invited us to move to the head of the queue.

We entered the polling booth and Victoria whispered, "If your name was on the ballot, I would have voted for you."

"I would vote for you too, Vic," I answered.

She said, "Next time, perhaps you shall."

From **The World**, November 8, 1871

"I can't take it," said the inspector.

"You refuse to take my vote?" rejoined Mrs. Woodhull.

"We can't receive it," was the reply.

"By what right," continued Mrs. Woodhull, "do you refuse to accept the vote of a citizen of the United States?"

"By this," said the man, producing a copy of the first constitution of the State of New York, which reads "all males," etc.

"But refer to the second article," replied Judge Reymert. "You will there find that all citizens are entitled to vote."

"We haven't a copy of the second constitution here," said the inspector, "and even if we had, I could not take the vote."

"Why?" asked the judge.

"Because we were told to refuse."

"I challenge you," continued the judge. "Will you swear?"

"No."

"Then I will send for a copy of the second constitution, which completely kills the first, and then see upon what authority you refuse to take the lady's vote," threatened the judge.

A messenger was thereupon dispatched to fetch the required book. Meanwhile, Mrs. Woodhull crossed to the side, and the balloting went on briskly. When the constitution arrived, Judge Reymert found the place and, approaching the inspectors accompanied by Mrs. Woodhull, requested the officer to read the article which specified that no citizen shall be deprived of his privileges or immunities, etc.

"I can't look at it," replied the man.

"Can you give me a reason? asked the judge.

"I can give you no further information on the subject" was the response.

"Are you aware that you are liable to pay a penalty of $500?" queried a bystander.

"I know nothing about it," responded the officer.

Mrs. V.C. Woodhull then withdrew. Miss Tennie C. Claflin then tendered her vote but the same answer was vouchsafed as in Mrs. Woodhull's case. The party then retired. Mrs. Woodhull's indignation was scarcely controllable.

James Gordon Bennett remembers Mrs. Woodhull's words from her column in the *Herald*:

What may appear absurd today may assume a serious aspect to-morrow, and the party espousing this woman question will be the dominant one in the hereafter.

Using his blue pencil, he scrawls it in the margin and sends it to the copy editor.

To Tilton, Bowen and Beecher's host, the thing about Reverend Beecher's affair with Theodore Tilton's wife is that everyone knows. How the Beecher sisters can pretend *not* to know is unfathomable. That Mrs. Woodhull should be relied upon to say nothing about it while Beecher's sisters abuse her in the press is also, to their host, inconceivable.

Tilton is the first to speak. "Reverend, Victoria is going to ask you to preside when she speaks at Steinway Hall."

Beecher murmurs, "I cannot think what I might say should she do so."

Bowen says, "What is the name of her talk to be?"

Tilton answers, "Principles of Social Freedom."

At this, Mr. Bowen warns the clergyman, "If you sully the name of Plymouth Church in any way, Reverend, I will see you ruined as long as you are living on this Earth."

———

No one else is at home. Reverend Beecher is accomplished at compelling others to fulfill his needs and Mrs. Woodhull presents herself at just the moment to do so. He takes in her vaguely distracted air. "Please," he murmurs.

"Reverend Beecher." Victoria realizes her voice is trembling. "Without your endorsement, I am but a chattering bird, without the benefit of your edifice upon which I might rest."

Exquisite Mrs. Woodhull. He thinks how easily he might have fallen in love with her and whispers in her ear, "May I offer you release?"

That all her efforts are reduced to this leaves her nothing to do but whisper, "Yes."

He locks the door of the library and pulls her skirts above her waist. Watching for her reaction, he spits in his hand and places it between her legs.

The Reverend mutters, "Give over. Give over to me, Mrs. Woodhull."

Beads of sweat form on the Reverend's cheeks, his blue eyes are unblinking.

Victoria closes her eyes, her self-respect crumbling in despair.

"Show me that you like it. Show me you do, Mrs. Woodhull." Finally, he gasps and shudders.

Victoria slides onto the floor and leans against the arm of the sofa. He pours them both a glass of brandy. She drinks it back at once. He sits on the sofa, his knee alongside her shoulder.

"I believe your indiscretions with Mrs. Tilton, and indeed, the rest of your female congregants, will only be forgiven in this world and the next were you to come clean, Reverend," Victoria says. "Please, I beg of you."

He kneels beside her and his gaze droops into a sorrowful arc. Tears begin to stream down his cheeks. "My dear Victoria." He takes her face in his hands. "It is I who must beg you. You've got to let me off. I should die in shame if my flock felt I had betrayed them."

Too late, she realizes her grievous error in believing that they had an understanding. She doesn't know who she despises more, Reverend Beecher or herself.

———

"It's just too long. I should want my supper and a glass of beer before the speech is at an end," Tennessee says when the Colonel hands Victoria a newer version of the speech.

Victoria looks at the pages. "What is this?"

"We have misgivings about Pearl Andrews's text. It's too dry. You might lose them."

Victoria throws the pages on the ground. "How dare you? It's too late for that now! Besides, Pearl is the only one who hasn't strayed from the path. The only one."

Victoria runs upstairs and flings herself on the bed. Blood follows and sits down next to her. He puts his hand on her back.

She turns over, shouting, "Don't! It's too late," then bursts into tears.

"Oh, my darling, Vicky."

"Tilton has usurped your place in my affections, Colonel." She has to pull herself together.

"Vicky."

"I will present Pearl's earlier text." She walks over to the small sink and turns on the faucet. Nothing comes out. Like my life, she thinks, pouring what is left from a pitcher into the basin. She splashes the cold water on her face.

⌁

Theodore Tilton finds Victoria at Steinway Hall, alone in her dressing room, sobbing. She dares not share her distress from the visit with Reverend Beecher, nor his claim were he to be exposed he'd be left with no other option but to take his own life. She had wanted to scream, *then take it!* But she did not say that. Instead, she continues weeping until Tilton soothes her nerves, which he does with little fuss. When it is time, he smiles at Victoria from the podium until she smiles back. He winks at her then looks out into the packed house.

> Ladies and Gentlemen. Happening to have an unoccupied night, which is an unusual thing for me in the lecture season, I came to this meeting actuated by curiosity to know what my friend would have to say in regard to the great question which has occupied so many years of her life…

Victoria steps forward. The applause is deafening. With a deep breath, she plunges right in:

> It has been said by a very wise person that there is a trinity in all things. Religious freedom, political freedom, and social freedom, while Religion, Politics, and Socialism are the Tri-unity of Humanity. There is also the beginning, the end, and the intermediate space, time, and motion, to all experiences of space, time, and motion, and the diameter, circumference, and area, or length, breadth, and depth to all form.

Whitelaw Reid from the *Tribune* says to one of his reporters, "Here we go. Pearl Andrews's Surd, Absurd, and Abso-surdism?"

"Is that Uno-duo, trifecta-mundo, what is it?" The men stifle a guffaw and struggle to pay attention.

Victoria continues, reciting the speech as written. Her mind wanders over to her husband. She misses their former closeness. She can see him in the wings, watching her.

> Now, let me ask, would it not rather be the Christian way, in such cases, to say to the disaffected party: "Since you no longer love me, go your way and be happy, and make those to whom you go happy also."

Oh Jim, she thinks. I do love you so. She chides herself, Breathe. Speak loudly. Think of the cause which is greater than oneself.

> "Thou shalt not covet thy neighbor's wife." And Jesus, in the beautiful parable of the Samaritan who fell among thieves, asks: "Who is thy neighbor?"...In the same spirit I ask now, who is a wife? And I answer, not the woman who, ignorant of her own feelings, or with lying lips, has promised, in hollow ceremonial, and before the law, to love, but she who really loves most, and most truly, the man who commands her affections, and who in turn loves her, with or without the ceremony of marriage; and the man who holds it can now be asked: What is the legitimate sequence of Social Freedom? To which I unhesitatingly reply: Free Love, or freedom of the affections. "And are you a Free Lover?" is the almost incredulous query. I repeat: I am; and I can honestly say, in the fullness of my soul-

Suddenly, from the audience, there is a shriek. It is Utica. "How'd you like to come into this world not knowing who your father was?" She springs up from her seat. There is dead silence. Roxana gasps and pulls on the edge of Utica's cloak. Utica slaps her mother's hand away.

Someone shouts at Utica, "Ya, ya, we've had enough of the likes of you!"

The blood rushes into Victoria's cheeks. She thinks, You harlot, Utica. I'll get you, you whore.

Utica is forcefully led from the hall, squirming as she is escorted out, yelling, "This is my sister! This is what I have to live with!"

Victoria watches, waiting for silence. She says,

> And to those who denounce me for this I reply: Yes, I am a Free Lover. I have an inalienable, constitutional, *and natural right to love whom I may, to love as long or as short a period as I can; to change that love every day if I please, and*

with that right neither you nor any law you can frame have any right to inter-
fere. And I have the further right to demand a free and unrestricted exercise
of that right, and it is your duty not only to accord it, but, as a community, to
see that I am protected in it.

The audience begins to clap and whistle. Emboldened, she cries,

I tell you, my friends and my foes, that you have taken hold of the wrong end
of this business. You are shouldering upon Free Love the results that flow from
precisely its antithesis, which is the spirit, if not the letter, of your marriage
theory, which is slavery, and not freedom!

The cheers are deafening, and Victoria knows, this is the one. This is
the speech for which she'll be remembered.

Buck and Roxana sit opposite Tennessee and Victoria in the carriage
taking them home. Buck wipes his glasses with his handkerchief. "Very
brilliant, Victoria," he says. "Very well argued. Tennie, mind you, watch
over Vicky. You're not as high strung as she and your medicinal talents
will be of some service, I wager."

"Yes, Pa," Tennessee answers. She squeezes Victoria's hand and
Victoria holds on.

Buck puts his glasses back on. "But how you're to sell this whole
free-love arkymalarky humbug rigamarole to God-fearing Christians is
anybody's guess."

"It isn't for sale," Victoria sighs. "There is nothing about love that is
for sale. It is meant to be offered at will, in a state of grace, for free."

"Herr besuchte uns," Roxana mutters.

Leonard Jerome joins Bennett at the Union Club, and they share a '57 claret.
"It surprises me you weren't out with your brothers of the press tonight."

"Oh, I attended." Bennett lights a cigarette. "For an audience of three
thousand people to applaud or even listen to the sentiments expressed
there is a deplorable state of affairs."

Jerome says, "I've always found her fascinating."

"It was the most astonishing doctrine ever listened to by an audience of Americans." Bennett finishes the claret. "And the *Herald* will say as much, I can assure you."

———

From the unpublished memoir of P.B. Randolph:

Over the years, some of my books have been widely sold. Magia Sexualis *has never gone out of print, and* Seership! The Magnetic Mirror *has also been a favorite. But the reader should not confuse my frank discussion of soul blending or sex magic as an endorsement of Free Love. On the contrary, this practice often results in the most egregious corruptions. However, as a friend to Mrs. Woodhull, as well as a tenant of the attractive Mrs. de Wood, I knew it politic to keep my views on these matters to myself. At least for the time being.*

Besides, affairs in Boston had not gone well for me. The authorities shuttered my Rosicrucian rooms. Then I was burgled, and my bookplates were stolen. Frantic, I made an unwise decision to entrust my copyrights with someone who proved to be a charlatan. Catastrophe and misfortune became my constant companions.

Tennessee called upon me at Mrs. de Wood's with a solution. "Jim Fisk is your man," she said. "I'm sure of it." Filled with a new sense of hope, I offered to walk her home. She stood on the pavement as I locked the wrought iron gate to the terrace. She continued, "Jim Fisk is a believer, Paschal. He has spoken very highly of your work. He'll be a most suitable patron."

Arm in arm, we moved onto the sidewalk. She added, "If you were to perform a reading, Fisk would be more than happy to…"

Two men ran down the front stairs, narrowly missing us. To avoid a collision, the taller one shoved me, shouting, "Watch it!"

It was James Gordon Bennett. He stopped, stared at me and then at my companion. She stood as if frozen.

I said, "Excuse me!"

James Gordon Bennett said nothing. He simply stared at her and she stared at him. Next to Bennett, I recognized the other man, Luther Challis. Tennessee did not acknowledge Challis. We knew why they were there. With a most spectacular rudeness, the two men crossed the street and walked in the opposite direction.

I said, "You're strangely silent, Miss Claflin."

She said, "I'm just thinking of the paper's next issue."

———

Tennessee bends over her writing tablet and whispers, "Want someone like that to feel it in the balls? Write about them."

Woodhull & Claflin's Weekly, December 16, 1871

"I have conceived an intense indignation, amounting almost to hatred...for men, especially in their mean and hateful treatment of women of our class — intimate with and caressing us in private and coolly passing us by without recognition before the world...If you, as a social reformer, have any need to see more behind the scenes and to understand the real state of New York society better, I will give you access to my two big books...You will find in them the names of all classes — from doctors of divinity, to counter jumpers and runners for mercantile houses. Make what use of them you please.

With love and admiration, Mary Bowles."

Mary Bowles is an old name she uses to go incognito. Goddamn James Gordon bloody Bennett Jr. Ha, bloody, ha, Tennessee thinks. Let him put that in his pipe and smoke it.

———

Tennessee stomps her feet and blows on her hands. The protesters congregate outside Cooper Institute and some rabble-rousers perch in the trees, shouting, "Oy, I'm a Free Lover. I'll have at you, Tennie!"

Ignoring them, she pulls her red gloves higher up on her wrists and pushes her peaked cap forward in the way that she likes. Victoria steps closer to her and Colonel Blood places the harness around Tennessee's waist to support the banner's weight. It reads, "Complete Political and Social Equality between the Sexes."

The drumbeats begin. The crowd has grown in number and force. Everyone falls in line. There are thousands more marching than expected. They begin to move forward. Drummers flank the procession. Black-plumed horses pull the symbolic funeral wagon honoring the martyrs of the French commune. Slowly, slowly, over to Broadway, west on Fourteenth Street. Up Fifth Avenue. The procession slows. When they stop outside the Union Club, Tennessee looks up. She sees him, watching from a second-floor window.

Her banner is the largest. She shifts its weight from one hip to the other, then balances it with her left hand and flamboyantly extends her right hand and salutes him.

Inside the Union Club, standing next to Bennett is his guest, the Czarevitch Grand Duke Alexi, from Moscow. "In Russia we do not tolerate such flagrant display." Alexei says, "The authorities always control such disturbance."

"Indeed?" Bennett responds. "Do they do it like the French?"

"Ha! Yeah, just so. But sometimes we do not round them up. We just shoot 'em in the street. Oh, oh." The Grand Duke points to some thugs who push to get through the crowd. Bennett's throat is dry.

Suddenly, the thugs break through, kicking and punching the demonstrators. Several fight back, One of them comes dangerously close to Tennessee. Bennett sees Blood and another man—it's Theodore Tilton—help Victoria into a carriage. Tennessee stands fast, but a ruffian shoves against her, causing her to lose her grip on the banner. She staggers to keep hold of it. Another man (it looks like that Negro he'd seen her with at Annie de Wood's) blocks the ruffian and Tennessee leans against the Negro. Bennett's heart is beating very loudly. He takes out his handkerchief to seem as though he needs to wipe his nose.

After a moment, Bennett turns to his guest. "Just shoot them, really?"

"Yes, that's right." Alexi nods. "That's how we make it in Russia."

———

Tennessee scours the *Herald* for a write-up. There is nothing. Furious, she writes back to Mrs. Bowles.

Woodhull & Claflin's Weekly, December 23ʳᵈ, 1871

I shall be happy to receive you at my home at any time...In respect to the books you speak of, I do not know what use can be made of them, for my sister and myself have scrupulously adopted the policy of avoiding personalities when possible. But the time may come when that policy will have to be abandoned, for our enemies do not scruple to resort to them in the most scandalous manner...

———

The maid informs Tennessee that Mr. Bennett's driver is at the front door. Tennessee comes down, and he gives her a deep bow. "Mr. Bennett has asked that I deliver this to you, with his compliments for a very Merry Christmas, Miss Claflin!"

It is a large square box. "Dixon, how thoughtful. And would you please be so kind as to deliver a token in return?" Tennessee hands him a small box.

Later, only a solitary lamp shines from a window at Bennett's house. She opens the box. Inside are two large black books. They are blank ledger pages. On the inside of one he's written,

When you keep tally, I should like to be at the top of your list.

-Your humble obedient servant,

JGB

On Christmas Eve, Bennett opens her gift. It is a rosette of the Bennett Clan tartan. The blue on the tartan reminds him of the color of her eyes.

THE IMPENDING REVOLUTION

January 1872

15 East Thirty Eighth Street

SOMETHING CATCHES IN Theodore Tilton's throat and he can't quite clear it. Swallowing, he holds Victoria's hand. Finally, he says, "Horace Greeley has decided to run for president."

"Good!" Victoria smiles, "He will be a most worthy opponent."

"He has asked me to run his campaign."

"Why wouldn't he? You're brilliant. You had the ear of the late Mr. Lincoln. Too bad for Horace Greeley that you'll be at my side."

St first, Tilton does not answer. Finally, he says, "The thing is, Victoria, I've decided to accept Horace's offer. Your profile, what I wrote, it's still..." He cannot begin to describe what it feels like to be a source of such unbridled ridicule, all because of that absurd article. It takes a moment for her to grasp his meaning. When she snatches her hand away, he murmurs, "This is the moment for me."

"The moment for you?" Victoria stands up. She wants to cry out, "No wonder your wife loved Beecher!" Instead, she says, "You will never find as loving a friend as you had in me. Never. This time next year, Horace Greeley's presidential aspirations will be but a memory." Victoria storms from the room.

Across the foyer, through a pair of French doors, Tilton sees Tennessee at the dining table, her back to him, newspapers and reams of manuscript in front of her. He decides not to say goodbye. As soon as he retrieves his things, Tilton goes through the front door, down the steps, and makes a right turn. He never crosses Victoria's threshold again.

Tennessee looks up. The papers are filled with the murder of Colonel Jim Fisk. Fisk's spirit seems very close. How many times had he been a guest in their home? A dozen at the least. And at least that many times when they lived at Great Jones Street, too. He could be dishonest, but Fisk had always been generous. He had lent his support to all soldiers who fought in the War. Tennessee decides she should do the same. She will volunteer her services to Fisk's regiment immediately.

The door behind her opens. Wordlessly, Utica stumbles in and collapses upon a fainting sofa in the room's bay window. The cat who had been asleep on Tennessee's lap hops down and crosses over to Utica, jumping upon the sofa to perch beside her. Utica ignores the cat and simply stares straight ahead.

"Where do you go?" Tennessee asks her.

"Hmm?"

"Where is it that you go when you've taken your syrup?"

"Oh, that place," Utica answers softly.

"What place?"

"The one where it doesn't matter." Utica's eyelids flutter and she barely manages a smile. "The place where it just doesn't matter."

Tickets to the lecture are oversold and the hall filled beyond capacity. Blood says, "Just get on with it. Then they'll open the doors, so everyone can leave."

"Wait one second," Tennessee protests. "Everyone has worked very hard on this speech, and Vic will say it properly, so it is understood."

Victoria whispers into Tennessee's ear, "This isn't the time."

Tennessee pulls back, "Then when, Vicky? When is the time?"
Victoria does not bother to answer but crosses the stage. The crowd
roars its approval. Eyes blazing, she cries out, "Does the impending revolution imply a peaceful change or a bloody struggle?" To which they clap,
cheer, and whistle. Victoria nods at them.

Oh, the stupid blindness of this people! Swindled every day before their very
eyes, and yet they don't seem to know that there is anything wrong, simply
because no law has been violated!"

Gradually, the audience quiets down. She continues.

A Vanderbilt may sit in his office and manipulate stocks, or make dividends, by
which, in a few years, he amasses fifty million dollars from the industries of the
country, and he is one of the remarkable men of the age. But if a poor, half-
starved child were to take a loaf of bread from his cupboard, to prevent star-
vation, she would be sent first to the Tombs, and thence to Blackwell's Island.

But it is asked, how is this to be remedied? I answer, very easily! Since who
possesses the accumulated wealth of the country have filched it by legal
means from those to whom it justly belongs—the people—it must be returned
to them, by legal means if possible, but it must be returned to them in any
event. When a person, worth millions dies, instead of leaving it to his children,
who have no more title to it than anybody else's children have, it must revert
to the people, who really produced it.

These privileged classes of people have an enduring hatred for me, and I am
glad they have. I am the friend not only of freedom in all things, and in every
form, but also for equality and justice as well. These cannot be inaugurated
except through revolution.

Jim Fisk's regiment finds Tennessee's offer to be of service laughable, as
does, once the word is out, most of the press. However, some friends of
Paschal Randolph don't find her offer funny at all. The 85th Regiment
Veteran Guards who are colored soldiers and known as the Spencer
Greys, ask if she will stand in as their colonel. Tennessee answers that she
would be honored.

March 1872
15 East Thirty Eighth Street

Byron lies down next to his father, his hand over the dead man's eyes.

"Papa is in heaven now." Victoria says to him, "We must leave Papa with the angels, darling. Come with Mama, come along."

When Utica sees a reporter hanging around outside, she tells him Doc Woodhull was poisoned, but everyone knows he died from excess with the bottle and needle. Utica is distraught, but then astonishes everyone when she volunteers to dry out.

"I think something's wrong with my kidneys, Ma," she says.

"Soon, you will be well, Utie," Roxana answers, having long been concerned with Utica's color and the contents of her chamber pot. Treatment is a chance for recovery. Enquiries are made and everyone is guardedly optimistic.

Paschal Randolph accompanies Buck and Utica on the ferry to the Asylum for the Inebriate. For five dollars a week, Utica will enjoy much privacy and some comfort. She walks toward the building ahead of them, as if lost in a dream.

"You seem to be our friend indeed when it comes to tending my family, Doctor," Buck says, grateful for Randolph's company, unaware of the younger man's shame for the many times he's been happily plastered with her.

"Life gives but few opportunities to demonstrate true friendship, sir," Randolph replies.

Later, Buck says, "You'll do just fine here, Utie," He hopes she does not notice his eyes are full of tears.

Randolph tells her, "When we see you again, you will be restored to health."

"Visit me," Utica whispers.

Her father embraces her, then blows his nose as he and Paschal retrace their steps to the ferry.

Because of Victoria's very public views, the other parents at the lycée have requested that Zula not return after Easter recess. Zula is a loyal daughter, but to be turned away from school because of her mother— it is the first time Zula has ever associated shame with being Victoria's daughter. And now, they are losing the house. The servants are let go, and Buck sells every stick of furniture that does not belong to the landlord. All of which makes for a trying day.

Victoria and Tennessee are the last ones to leave the office. An early supper for just the two of them, somewhere quiet, is very much in order. Delmonico's is on the way home. Tennessee sees the table by the window is free. The sisters sit down.

"Ah, Mrs. Woodhull, Miss Claflin." The waiter approaches them. "Ladies, you are how many this evening?"

Victoria answers, "It's just us two."

He bows deeply and makes a hasty retreat.

In the far corner at the rear of the room, James Gordon Bennett has been dining with railroad men and financiers. As usual, he sits with his back to the wall. While the conversation around him progresses, he watches the drama unfold at the table by the window.

Signore Lorenzo Delmonico, followed by the waiter, approaches the sisters and bows, as did the waiter, who bows again.

"Ladies," he leans over and whispers, "it pains me to say it, mi molto dispiace, you are our great customers. I much regret, but we cannot have unaccompanied women at Delmonico's."

He rearranges the salt and pepper shakers, then slightly moves the forks, as if describing the specials on the menu. Victoria's cheeks flush a brilliant pink.

Tennessee stands up. "Excuse me a moment." Lorenzo Delmonico moves her chair out of her way. As she leaves the dining room, she sees the shock of ginger hair in the far corner. She nods at Bennett, as he does to her.

Outside, a hansom driver is feeding his horse. "You there," Tennessee calls to him, "I'll need a ride in a few minutes. Are you hungry?"

He nods, "I'll be ready for my soup tonight, yes, miss."

"Before we go, follow me inside, please." She strides back into the restaurant, followed by the driver.

Signore Lorenzo continues to rearrange the forks and knives, whispering rapidly, "I am delighted, no, it would be my great privilege to say you ladies came to make use of our facilities. But you must understand, my customers."

Tennessee gestures at the chair next to hers. "Have a seat." The driver doesn't understand. "Please, sit down." He removes his top hat and sits down.

Tennessee smiles at Signore Lorenzo. "We'll have soup for three."

As Bennett's carriage turns on Thirty Eighth Street, he signals to his driver fifty paces shy of his driveway. The carriage stops and he watches a large wagon being loaded outside number 15. Lest there be any press around, Bennett stays put and sends Dixon to find Tennessee.

She emerges from the house, wearing trousers and a shawl over her head. When she climbs in beside him, Bennett is suddenly overcome and doesn't trust himself to speak.

She smiles, "Mr. Bennett, I presume."

He answers, "I came to lure you over for a nightcap."

"Well, I'm rather ensconced in this business of moving in the night."

"Oh no. Not back to Ohio?"

Tennessee thinks his question strangely out of character. "No, to my sister Meg's .It will be crowded, I grant you, but we have little choice, I'm afraid."

He realizes their knees are touching. "How was the soup?"

"Absolutely delicious."

He touches the edge of her shawl, brushing a strand of hair away from her face. Tennessee slides out of the carriage. "It's good to see you, Bennett. Thank you for coming by."

In the morning, she receives the telegram.

RESERVATIONS MADE IN YOUR NAME AT GILSEY
HOUSE, BWAY & TWENTY NINTH STREET
SUITES 30-34 WITH OUR COMPLIMENTS JGB

Victoria raises her eyebrows and Tennessee shrugs, saying, "No doubt, it's out of neighborly concern."

May 1872
Washington Heights

COME TO DINNER WILL MAKE AMENDS FOR WOEFUL
ABSENCE OF COVERAGE JGB

At Fort Washington, the dogs clamor over themselves, circling Tennessee in the courtyard. Bennett Sr. is in the foyer. She embraces him, and they make their way to the library. The doors to the porch are open and the early evening light on the Hudson bathes everything in color.

"Miss Claflin, I presume?" Bennett Jr. hands her a glass of champagne, as his father shoos yet another dog out of an armchair. Bennett gives his father a glass and stands beside Tennessee without touching her, then changes his mind and has her sit next to him on the bench by the fireplace.

"Vesuvius," he says, "is the next expedition. We will photograph it from a balloon."

"Imagine," Tennessee says, "the thought of you in a balloon above an erupting volcano."

NAKED TRUTH

"Would you like to join me?"

Bennett Sr. weighs in. "Tell us news of the winsome Mrs. Woodhull, Miss Claflin. Are her political aspirations moving apace?"

"I do believe the future looks bright for her campaign, Mr. Bennett."

"And will you be her running mate?" the old man enquires.

"Mr. Bennett, is this off the record?"

"My journalistic career is long behind me now."

"Ah! Well, I see my service playing out from behind the scenes, I think."

"Then who the devil is going to run with her?" Bennett Jr. asks, "I dread to think it might be that windbag Andrews." To which Tennessee laughs but says nothing.

After dinner, Mr. Bennett Sr. recalls the old days, being poor in Boston, scratching out a living in Charleston.

Suddenly Bennett Jr. turns to her. "Tennessee, how much school do you have?"

"Less than three years in all."

"I have none."

"Really! Mr. Bennett Senior, I am surprised you did not send your son to school."

"It was enough he should learn to fend for himself. Everything else he picked up from tutors in France. Tomorrow marks the lad's thirty-first birthday. From all reports, I'd say he's suffice."

When Bennett walks her to her room, he holds her hands to his chest and whispers, "May I kiss you, Tennessee?"

Surprised, she shakes her head and murmurs, "I would loathe for you to catch what I've got," which he takes to mean a myriad of things. He kisses each of her palms instead, and bids her good night.

Afterward Bennett sits on the lawn and drinks the bottle of brandy his father saved from the day of his birth. A dog howling at the moon wakes him after midnight and he staggers back to the house.

———

After a medicinal of six raw eggs, Worcester sauce, and horseradish, James Gordon Bennett Jr. cleans his teeth and calls her room from the speaking tube in the kitchen. "Oh Miss Claflin! Miss Tennie C. Claflin!"

When he enters and places the breakfast tray on the table by her bed, she pulls up the blankets. "Will you come to the convention tomorrow?" she asks.

"If anyone observed me, the perception would be misconstrued— either coming or going."

Tennessee leans over him to pour the tea. "Wear your coachman's getup." She offers him the cup. He shakes his head. She has a generous gulp then slathers honey on the fresh warm bread and takes a hearty bite. "Delicious," she says, chewing.

"I do so long to kiss you."

Smiling still more, she offers Bennett the bread instead, to which he roars, grabbing it with his mouth out of her hand. He gobbles it down in one bite and collapses on her as she squeals with laughter and the dogs begin to bark.

He groans, "I certainly gave myself a humdinger last night," then rolls over and plumps the pillow under his head. He considers his paper and the woman beside him. The *Herald's* belligerence toward the Woodhull and People's Party has been the right move for sales. No one suspects, not for a moment, that he is deeply and irrevocably in love. The reporter he'll send to the convention will be undercover. As he closes his eyes and nods off, Bennett decides he'll send a woman.

———

To Susan Anthony, it is very clear. Mr. Steinway has generously lent her the venue with the understanding they are to discuss *no issue other than suffrage*. But Elizabeth Cady Stanton has now added her name to Mrs. Woodhull's list of supporters. Once again, everything could be thrown asunder, particularly if they stray from their purpose just to flatter Mrs. Woodhull. It is unfair. Moreover, it is unjust. It is also, quite frankly, unworthy of Mrs. Stanton.

Miss Anthony weighs her words. "Lizzie, we have crossed this nation over countless miles for more than a generation. This convention cannot and will not play second fiddle to Mrs. Woodhull's presidential campaign."

"Susan, open your mind."

Miss Anthony hears this as though a hammer were struck between her eyes. Mrs. Stanton continues to speak. It is almost unbearable to Miss Anthony, particularly when Mrs. Stanton says, "Mrs. Woodhull brings more to bear than any of our efforts thus far!"

In her mind, Miss Anthony sees the years, the unrelenting sacrifices, the trains, the carriages, and the *closed minds* which she herself worked so hard to open.

Finally, she says, "Lizzie. Mrs. Woodhull cannot take the platform at Steinway Hall."

"Oh, now, surely you don't mean that!"

"The Hall has been donated in my name and I expressly forbid it." For the first time in their very long friendship, there is nothing left to say.

Mrs. Stanton gathers her things. "If that be the case, then, it pains me to say this." Mrs. Stanton counts to three before speaking, "After the convention tomorrow, I will resign from my position as President of the National Women's Suffrage Association."

They have stood side by side, for more than twenty years. That Victoria Woodhull is the person who comes between them breaks Susan Anthony's heart. Both women keenly feel this.

"That's all," Mrs. Stanton says, and softly closes the door behind her.

The next day Susan Anthony keeps the proceedings centered around suffrage only and stands behind the lectern, a delicate gavel in her right hand.

"Resolved," she says, "that since the right to vote is a right of every citizen of the United States, it is the duty of all patriotic women to exercise this right in the coming presidential election, and the duty of all patriotic men to remove the obstructions now blocking their way." She looks up briefly and then continues, "Resolved, that as Cincinnati has refused—"

"Let's discuss the rights of Labor!" a man calls out.

Miss Anthony frowns, then continues, "Whereas Horace Greeley as editor-in-chief of the *New York Tribune* has for the past four years lost no opportunity to ridicule and falsify the spirit and purpose of the suffrage movement of this country…"

Victoria's supporters ignore Miss Anthony, chatting amongst themselves.

Miss Anthony strikes the lectern with the gavel. "Out of order!" she shouts. "And what about the illegal taxation of my estates?" a man shouts back.

"This is for woman and woman alone!" Miss Anthony cries. "There will be no side issues."

Victoria realizes the day must not end without acknowledgment of her purpose. But Miss Anthony intends to do just that. Victoria strides over to the doorway on the left of the proscenium, goes through it, and walks onto the stage.

The crowd roars its approval.

She stands not five feet from Miss Anthony. With both hands extended toward the audience, Victoria cries out, "My friends! All of you, each and every one of you, deserve to be heard!"

"VICKY! Vicky!" The energy in the audience rises up. Claps and whistles and cheers drown out anything resembling decorum.

Miss Anthony slams the gavel down with greater force. "Out of order!" she cries.

"VICKY! VICKY!"

"OUT OF ORDER!" The cheers drown out Miss Anthony's voice and gavel.

Victoria says, "I invite you all to join with me tomorrow morning at Apollo Hall, where we will raise up our arms and create a new party!"

The cheering becomes a frenzied pitch. Victoria quiets them down again. "Tomorrow, at the Apollo Hall, the People's Party shall be renamed. We shall call ourselves The Equal Rights Party!" This is met with wild cheering and applause.

"Out of order!" If Miss Anthony weren't so livid, she'd burst into tears. Backstage, she finds a stagehand. He is cheering, too. Upon seeing her, he stops.

He puts his cap discreetly in his pocket. "Yes, Miss Anthony."

"Turn out the lights."

"Miss Anthony?"

"I don't care how you do it! But you must do it now. TURN OUT THE LIGHTS."

The stagehand shuffles over to the gas. He closes the footlights. Victoria looks up and then out past the cheering crowd toward the back of the hall. She sees Colonel Blood and Tennessee. The stagehand turns off the dimmers and the floods on the stage. The house lights go dark. Everyone is silent. Colonel Blood opens the door to the street and the sunlight pours in.

——◊——

Victoria Woodhull for president. Frederick Douglass as her running mate. The celebratory ruckus continues late into the evening. But Tennessee can't stop wanting to steal away and ring the door at 425 Fifth Avenue, to go inside and to never leave.

——◊——

"We must invest the funds from the campaign contributions with symbolic significance," Victoria declares. No one speaks, so she continues,

"Such as the diamond mines Senator Butler has been asked to vouch for. They've hired a surveyor. If all reports bear out, the returns could be astonishing. Diamonds and precious stones. Not negotiable, but ethereal and dazzling."

"I did not see these stones." Blood is dubious.

"Oh, Colonel. They were magnificent. Mr. Tiffany examined them himself. Not three doors down from sister Meg."

"Vicky, the mines depend on too many variables," he says.

"Then we will insure them! Surely the cost of such a thing offsets the risk. Colonel, I spoke with Ben Butler and General McClellan. There is going to be a major expansion at that mine. How wonderful to be a part of such a project and enjoy stupendous returns not more than a dozen weeks from now."

"That the returns should be so generous, Vicky, in and of itself indicates dreadful risk."

She sighs, "So, what are you proposing?"

"That we buy Western Union bonds and place the balance with Jay Cooke. We must be conservative, my darling. Everything else we do is not."

New York Times, June 2, 1872
Obituary of James Gordon Bennett Sr

It is with deep regret that we announce the death of Mr. James Gordon Bennett, the founder and proprietor of the New York Herald, in the seventy-seventh year of his age. Mr. Bennett died at his residence in this city at 5:25 o'clock yesterday afternoon, after a lingering illness. The career of Mr. Bennett may be not inaptly likened to one of those Spring days whose morning is dark with overhanging clouds, and inclement with tempestuous winds and storms, while the remainder is warm and bright with all the splendor of sunshine. There have been few men so absolutely self-made as...

The diamond investment is a disaster. Blood was right to put the rest of their money with Jay Cooke, who is nothing if not conservative. To keep

Victoria's campaign afloat, they will have to put the paper on hiatus. No sooner is publication suspended then the rent at 44 Broad Street is raised by a thousand dollars a year, payable in advance.

"You understand," the landlord says, "one must pay New York prices."

From the journal of Tennie C. Claflin:

425 Fifth Avenue has been draped in black. He saw me amongst the mourners, but made no sign to indicate our friendship, either to his mother or to his sister, and my heart tumbled down against my side. Greeley and Reid from the Tribune, Mr. Dana from the Sun, Mr. Samuel Clemens, and Mr. Barnum were all there. Everyone listened to the dogs, confined to the carriage house, yelping for their freedom.

Afterwards, we passed number 15, and I wondered if any of this would have occurred had we not been living but a few paces away.

Colonel Blood finds a new office, four doors down and several hundred dollars a year cheaper. There is a knock on the door, which is now kept locked.

Victoria cries out, "If you are the bearer of bad news, please desist!"

The voice in the hallway says, "Telegram!" She opens the door. It is for Tennessee.

DINNER TOMORROW JGB

During the ride to Fort Washington, heat from the silver scales threatens to erupt over her entire body. The temperature is stifling, and everything is at sixes and sevens. When she arrives at the house, Bennett is standing in the courtyard. No sooner does she descend the carriage than she bursts into tears. Bennett says, "Tennie, whatever is the matter?"

To which she cannot speak, but merely sobs all the harder.

"Is it the paper?"

"Yes. No! Yes."

"You'll have the resources again, you will."

To which she mumbles something nonsensical and retreats to clean her face and hands. Thankfully, there is no sign of the rash, although her face is red and mottled from crying.

"Pull yourself together," she warns the mirror.

Their meal is served on the porch. Bennett prefers to not speak during dinner, and she can't stop yearning for the comfort of his embrace. But it is as if they have never been together, which drives her mad. How can she be the sovereign of herself if she feels as she does?

From where they sit, the light overlooking the river shimmers in the heat. It is still oppressively warm. Thankfully, there is a bowl of ice on the table. She hopes he does not notice when she wraps some in her napkin and then hold it to the base of her throat. But he does notice, and takes another piece, wrapping it in his own napkin to place on the back of her neck.

"Does that feel better?" he asks.

She nods, silently grateful to feel his hand, if only through the wet napkin. Bennett gestures to where the water has stained her neckline and says, "You will do it."

She realizes she must tell him. She must be transparent and fearless.

"Bennett," she says. "Jimmy. I've come to understand you may be the love of my life and I fear I mean almost nothing to you."

"Oh, now." He pushes his chair away from the table. He lights a cigarette and says, "I think that's a gross overstatement."

"Don't you see? This is little more than a diversion for you, and for me this is the business of my life!" She bursts into terrible sobs again. How can she have been so stupid? It is impossible to stop crying.

The wretchedness of losing the paper, losing their house, their office, the death of Bennett Sr. and the likely absence of Bennett Jr.'s love crashes through her as he brings his chair next to hers and she weeps into his shoulder.

"I'm ruining your shirt," she sobs, through her snot and tears.

"Oh, I have another one, very much like this," he says, which makes her sob all the harder. "Tennie." He says, "its demise is of little consequence."

Gradually, only the hiccups and embarrassment from caring too much remain. She straightens up, and he gently rubs her back, as though she were a small child wrestling with the first of many disappointments. "Come, I'll take you home."

Wordlessly they get into the carriage, but before Dixon pulls out of the driveway, Bennett says, "Will you look at something with me first?"

She nods, too exhausted to speak. They head north along the Hudson and arrive at a field, where a dozen hot-air balloons wait for the call to inflate. First one, then the other. Silently, majestically, all of them rise. The pilots in their baskets signal and the ropes are released. The sky turns pink and the evening sun begins its descent as the balloons move through the sky across the river.

"Where are they going?"

"Only to Weehawken." Bennett chuckles and kisses her hand. "Do you like that?"

"Yes." She thinks of the day she first saw him. "I love you."

He keeps her hand in his and they return to the carriage, silent until they arrive at the Gilsey House.

"Don't fret," he whispers. "You'll find a way to resume the paper." He traces the outline of her face with his, their lips barely brushing. "I'll see you after summer."

WOULDST THOU HAVE A
SERPENT STING THEE TWICE?

Summer 1872
48 Broad Street

P. B. RANDOLPH finds Tennessee curled up in the back of the office, gazing out the window, the complete works of Shakespeare on her lap. The pathos on her face is so tragic that Randolph begins to laugh and after a few moments, in spite of herself, she does, too.

"You are a natural talent," he says. "You need something to occupy your energies." Randolph points at the open page of her book. "You should consider a theatrical venture!"

Tennessee looks across the room at Buck, snoozing in an upright chair with a copy of the *Times* folded across his stomach. Zula sits in a corner, working very hard to concentrate on her own reading. "Well, let's include Zula," Tennessee says. "She's a natural talent, too. Zula, if I were to play Portia, would you be Jessica?"

"Who is Jessica?" Zula asks.

"She is Shylock's daughter. We'll have Buck play him."

"What do I get to do?"

"Oh, you get to elope! But Randolph, who will play Antonio and Bassanio?"

"A couple of your Spencer Greys have been actors, I believe."

Victoria crumples up the letter she was writing and starts over.

"That would be capital," Tennessee says. "A good deal more entertaining than matters of the military, I daresay."

Victoria shushes them and bends over her letter.

> *My Dear Mr. Beecher,*
> *It is with some trepidation I write to you, recalling with much fondness our very pleasant visits during what is nearly a year ago today. As I am sure, no doubt, you are aware, the fight against me...*

She frowns and begins again.

The following evening, Paschal Randolph and two of the Spencer Greys he'd recruited for *The Merchant of Venice* wait for Tennessee in the lobby of the Gilsey House. The night clerk clears his throat as she passes the front desk.

"Miss Claflin," he says, drawing himself up to his fullest height, flaring his nostrils. "Miss Claflin, should you gallivant with people of this order—"

"Do you mean veterans who served the Union during the War?"

"I mean Miss Claflin, should you choose to associate with random soldiers who are not of our class—"

"By which you mean who are not white."

"It will necessitate my evicting you to guarantee the wellbeing of our other guests."

"Don't be absurd. You are not their mother." Tennessee prepares to leave with the lieutenants and Paschal in tow. Remembering something, she comes back, "You might want to watch yourself, lest good Dr. Randolph here conjure up some of his voodoo who-do charms against you. Good night!"

But when Tennessee returns from rehearsal, her clothes are in a pile on the pavement outside the hotel, on top of which sits an envelope. *"Sister, we are at the office. Thanks to your spirited brashness, we have been kicked out, and told to find lodging elsewhere."*

A stray pig sniffs around a pair of her shoes. Tennessee shoos at him. "Get, get!" she shouts. Thankfully a hansom cab pulls over. Without wasting a moment, she flings her belongings and then herself into the carriage.

———

Reverend Henry Ward Beecher sighs when he reads Victoria's letter.

His wife asks, "What is it, dear?"

The Reverend shrugs, "Just another congregant asking for the moon and sixpence, of course. Alas, I cannot help her. The Lord only helps those who help themselves."

November 1872
48 Broad Street

Bennett was right. They have found the resources to get the *Weekly* back into print.

"Do you think I'm a blackmailer?" Victoria asks Tennessee.

Tennessee glances at her own article, "The Philosophy of Modern Hypocrisy, Mr. LC Challis the Illustration," and says, "You are very persuasive. But you fight for those who can't fight for themselves. I don't see anything wrong with that."

**THE BEECHER-TILTON SCANDAL CASE.
THE DETAILED STATEMENT OF THE WHOLE
MATTER BY MRS. WOODHULL.**

Reporter—Do you not fear that by taking the responsibility of this exposé you may involve yourself in trouble? Even if all you relate should be true, may not those involved deny it in *toto*, even the fact of their having made the statements?

Mrs. Woodhull—I do not fear anything of the sort. I know this thing must come out…

———

With the paper's rebirth comes a glamorous energy. Pearl Andrews hums under his breath. He will be the Duke and Buck will play Shylock. Paschal Randolph is Bassanio, Tennessee is Portia, and Zula is Shylock's runaway daughter, Jessica. Annie Swindell agrees to play Nerissa and Stedman is Antonio. The two lieutenants who are actors are the Princes of Morocco and Spain and double as the clowns. Several friends send over fruit baskets and cake and everyone is in costume.

Andrews in his doge's hat steps forward with a portentous rumbling. "What, is Antonio here?"

"He'll be here later," Tennessee answers. "Zula, what's Antonio's line?"

Zula calls out, "Ready, so please your grace."

Andrews says, "'I am sorry for thee; thou art come to answer?' Is that right, Zula?"

Zula nods. He continues, "A stony adversary, an inhuman wretch/ incapable of pity, void and empty/ from any dram of mercy."

Victoria and Blood sit in the corner reviewing orders for the paper. George Blood, the Colonel's brother, checks the ledgers and Victoria glances at the article for the millionth time. It is quite perfect. A reporter had interviewed her, and she simply recounted everything she knew. It will rock those Beechers to their core.

<hr />

Formidable in his black Shylock robe, Buck extends an arm, reciting with gusto,

> So, can I give no reason, nor I will not,
> More than a lodged hate and a certain
> loathing I bear Antonio,
> that I follow thus a losing suit against him.
> Are you answer'd?

Paschal as Bassanio, responds,

> This is no answer, thou unfeeling man,
> To excuse the current of thy cruelty.

Buck declares,
I am not bound to please thee with my answers.

Paschal asks,
Do all men kill the things they do not love?

Buck replies,
Hates any man the thing he would not kill?

Paschal says
Every offence is not a hate at first.

And Buck answers,
What, wouldst thou have a serpent sting thee twice?

Zula says, "That was really good! It was perfect."

An office boy whispers into Tennessee's ear. She brings a copy of the paper outside and Dixon holds open the carriage door. She climbs in and her knees touch Bennett's when she sits down beside him.

Noticing the mortarboard cap and lawyer's gown he asks, "What are you wearing?"

Tennessee beams. "How do you like it? It's for the courtroom scene. I am playing Portia. We were going to do it at the Academy, but they just canceled our booking."

"So where will you go?"

"The Liberal Club I imagine."

"I'm sorry I'll miss it." For some reason Bennett can't stop smiling and his heart is bursting. They sit back, and she rests her hand on his arm as he flicks through the paper. "Oh, here's your mentor, Mr. Karl Marx."

"Bennett."

"And Luther, Luther Challis, finally facing the music, eh. I saw you that night in '69, didn't I?"

"You were dancing like a mad man."

"Probably from the thrill of seeing you." Bennett puts down the paper. "Do you know who Henry Bowen is?"

"Yes, of course."

"Tennie, Henry Bowen is the power and money behind Reverend Beecher. You and your sister are stirring it up, aren't you?"

"Yes, we are."

"Listen to me, William Howe is your man," Bennett says. "He worked for Pater, takes care of me. With this Beecher-Tilton thing, all hell will break loose, Tennie."

Tennessee smiles. "Somebody told me, it isn't enough to be the news, sometimes you have to make the news as well."

"As for Howe, you know I can't foot the bill. If I do, it will come out."

"We will be all right."

Bennett chuckles, "The Beecher-Tilton Scandal, who, who!" To which she laughs and lets herself out of the carriage. He says, "Tennie, I…"

But she has already gone back inside.

…I believe it is my duty and my mission to carry the torch to light up and destroy the heap of rottenness, which, in the name of religion, marital sanctity, and social purity, now passes as the social system.

Reporter.—You speak like some weird prophetess, madam.

Mrs. Woodhull.—I am a prophetess—I am an evangel—I am a Savior, if you would but see it; but I too come not to bring peace, but a sword.

The preorder sales for the November 2nd issue surpass anything they'd dared hope for. The *Weekly* is hot. They are back in the game.

Henry Bowen folds his copy of *Woodhull & Claflin's Weekly* before throwing it in the fire. It matters not that the claims in Mrs. Woodhull's paper are true. That she has ventilated them leaves him no choice but to punish her and those responsible for the paper's publication, immediately. He tells his servant, "Send for the District Attorney and send for Anthony Comstock. That will be all."

—•—

> Mrs. Woodhull.—Mr. Beecher told me that marriage is the grave of love, and that he never married a couple that he did not feel condemned.
> Reporter.—Was Mr. Beecher aware that you knew of his relations to Mrs. Tilton?
> Mrs. Woodhull.—Of course he was. It was because I knew of them that he first consented to meet me. He could never receive me until he knew that I was aware of the real character he wore under the mask of his reputation.
> Reporter.—Do you still regard Mr. Beecher as a moral coward?
> Mrs. Woodhull.—A few days before the lecture, I sent a note to Mr. Beecher asking him to preside for me…He said he agreed perfectly with what I was to say, but that he could not stand on the platform of Steinway Hall and introduce me. He said, "I should sink through the floor. I am a moral coward on this subject, and I know it, and I am not fit to stand by you, who go there to speak what you know to be the truth; I should stand there a living lie." He got upon the sofa on his knees beside me, and taking my face between his hands, while the tears streamed down his cheeks, begged me to let him off.

"Ha, ha!" Tennessee crows when she and Victoria leave Broad Street for the Jersey City ferry with three thousand copies. But then they are stopped at the corner by a deputy sheriff. He politely informs them that they are being charged with sending pornography through the mail. Blushing, he adds that the charge is also for publishing obscenity. Then he arrests them.

The Merchant of Venice is canceled.

There are half a dozen reporters waiting at Essex Market Court.

"How did you know to expect us?" Tennessee asks. One of them tips his hat and enquires what she's heard from Luther Challis.

"I've not heard a thing. And in fact, we've yet to be notified what exactly is obscene in this paper."

"It's the phrase 'token virginity,'" the reporter says. "That's pretty strong stuff, Miss Claflin; ladies using such language."

Mr. Howe informs them, "The bail is going to be set at $16,000."

Tennessee cries, "What?"

Victoria says, "I don't understand."

"I have been advised that Mr. Luther Challis is filing a libel suit in the Jefferson Market Court. Please understand—this obscenity charge is in federal court where you can avail ourselves of the government's accommodations here at Ludlow Street. But as for the libel, ladies, if you post bail on Monday, Mr. Challis's charge will see you incarcerated within the day at the Tombs. It would be most unpleasant."

Harriet Beecher Stowe has no doubt that Mrs. Woodhull's persecution of her brother Henry is satanic. Even if she must do it herself, Mrs. Harriet Beecher Stowe vows the forces of Darkness must be destroyed.

Rochester, November 5th, 1872

Dear Mrs. Stanton,

Well I have been and gone and done it!! Positively voted the Republican ticket—straight—this A.M. at 7 o'clock—and swore my vote in, at that—was registered on Friday at 7. Fifteen other women followed suit in this ward—then in sundry some twenty or thirty other women tried to register, but all save two were refused...So we are in for a fine agitation in Rochester on the question.

Affectionately,
Susan B Anthony

The warden's wife gives them a drape so they might enjoy a modicum of privacy. Tennessee stands, stretching her arms out. "Take a deep breath, Zula. Your mommy persuaded them not to smoke while we're here. Isn't that good?"

"Guck mal, Zula! Mommy's place is not so bad, hunh?" Roxana's voice trembles as she peers behind the screen concealing the slop bucket. "Yeah, this is all right."

"When are you coming home?" Zula sits next to Victoria on the bed.

"In a few days. Be a good girl with Auntie Meg and help her look after Byron."

Zula's lower lip starts to tremble, and her eyes fill with tears.

Roxana gasps, "If she cries, I cry too."

"Please don't," Victoria says. "Draw the curtain, Tennie. We'll become copy if we begin to cry."

Tennessee does so, whereupon they huddle together, and silently weep.

President Ulysses S. Grant is reelected by a landslide. President Grant's opponent, Horace Greeley, the founder of the *New York Tribune*, returns home to mourn the loss of his wife, who has died only days before the election. He is prostrate with grief. Whitelaw Reid takes control of the *Tribune* and has Greeley committed to an asylum. One week passes and then another.

Ludlow Street Jail, November 16, 1872

To the Editors of the *Herald*:

What I desire to accomplish, and at which the public howls, is this: I desire that woman shall be emancipated from the sexual slavery maintained over her by man...They may succeed in crushing me out, even to the loss of my life, but let me warn them and you that from the ashes of my body a thousand Victorias will spring to avenge my death by seizing the work laid down by me and carrying it forward to victory.

Bennett lights a cigarette and looks down the long table at his dozen editors. He leans forward and says, "This is what we're going to do. Run the Tilton-Beecher scandal and the Challis rape. Run these pieces exactly as they were in *Woodhull & Claflin's Weekly*. Let's see if the authorities come after me. Let them come after the *New York Herald*."

<div style="text-align:center">~~~</div>

> *"I think the silence of the Beechers is a hundredfold more of an obscene publication than that of the Woodhulls, and the said silence is a thousandfold more potent in convincing people of the truth of that scandal than the evidence of fifty Woodhulls could be."*

-Samuel L. Clemens to
Olivia Lewis Langdon, Hartford
3 Dec 1872

TRIED AS BY FIRE

1873
Twenty Sixth Street

To Susan B. Anthony,

January 2nd, 1873

There is no time to indulge in personal enmity. I have none toward anybody, and I ask everybody to put aside whatever there may be against me and permit as great a unity as possible…I fear (the administration) intend to crush out, in your person, the constitutional question of women's right to suffrage…For myself I have a pretty large fight of my own on hand, but I can find time to do my share to assist you…Hoping to hear from you by return mail, permit me to subscribe myself,

your friend for the cause, Victoria Woodhull.

MISS ANTHONY DOES not answer her letter, nor does Miss Anthony speak to Victoria Woodhull ever again.

———

"To the editors of Woodhull & Claflin's Weekly —Please send forthwith a dozen issues of your November 2nd issue to the following address: James Beardsley, POST OFFICE Box 22, Greenwich, Connecticut. Enclosed is 12 dollars to cover post and parcel."

Signing with a flourish, Comstock chuckles.

Harriet Beecher Stowe beams at this. "Beardsley. That's a good name."
She appreciates how much Mr. Comstock's efforts further her own.

"It is, isn't it?" Comstock agrees. "And we'll do something for Jesus,
every day, every day."

———

At Broad Street, Colonel Blood thinks about those who've gone before
him. Communard men and women who dared to speak out. He wonders where they are now. He watches his brother George tirelessly sort
through the business at hand for the next issue.

Miss Swindell tactfully clears her throat. She stands next to his desk,
waiting.

"Yes?" he says.

She hands them the note from a Mr. Beardsley. "It's a request,
Colonel," she says, "for a dozen copies of the November 2nd issue."

George Blood looks up from his desk and says, "We shouldn't do it.
Consider the date."

"Well, we can't afford to turn away any business, however modest.
Besides the other papers have reprinted it. We can't be held culpable now,
can we?"

But as soon as Anthony Comstock receives the copies of the paper,
both Colonel Blood and his wife are arrested again.

———

There are now twelve people staying at Meg Miles's on 26th Street.
Roxana sorts the unmentionables too fine to go to the laundry in rows
along the long pine table in the kitchen. In the corner is a copper tub,
three-quarters filled with steaming hot water and eucalyptus. Covered in
liniment, Tennessee climbs in and takes a large swig of Fowler's solution.
The sores always come back in winter and soaking in a steaming bath
with the ointment spread from head to toe cures the aches and pains.

There is a loud banging at the door. "What can they want now?" Meg mutters and goes down the hall to answer it.

Tennessee hears men's voices, then Meg raises hers in alarm. "She isn't here! This is a place of quiet. No! I will not let you in."

There is a crash and what sounds like a scuffle. Tennessee sits up.

There are footsteps toward the other end of the corridor away from the kitchen. Roxana begins to flutter around the kitchen. "Kommst du herein. Herr besucht!"

Roxana sees Tennessee's clothes on a chair. "Oh Jesus Christ, you must dress!"

Tennessee springs out of the tub and Roxana thrusts her clothes at her. "Not here, not here. Hide behind the cupboard!" she whispers.

Tennessee takes a deep breath and struggles to slide behind the massive pie safe. She doesn't fit. The voices and footsteps are headed toward them.

"Oh, you're wet, you're wet." Roxana grabs a towel. "Schnell, schnell!" She thrusts it at Tennessee and begins wiping the floor with one of the petticoats.

Tennessee shoves her clothes into the pie safe. "Ma, let's move the table."

"What?"

"Move the table, move the table." Each takes an end, dragging it over to the tub. Stockings and bloomers tumble to the floor. Tennessee climbs back into the water and holds her breath. She sinks under as her mother slides the table over her. The door flies open.

Roxana sees Tennessee's shoes. She begins to sing *Von Himmel Hoch* as loudly as she dares, picking up the ladies' unmentionables strewn across the floor. She nudges the shoes out of the way. The only person there is the crazy old woman knee deep in laundry.

Meg stands with her hands on her hips. "Who do you hope to find exactly? If I tell you they've gone, then they have! No one is here but my mother. Now leave us to our folding for mercy's sake."

"Yes, Herr besuchte uns!" Roxana shakes out a pair of bloomers.

Seeing no one else in the room, the men take their leave. Meg quickly drags the table away from the tub and Tennessee sits up, sputtering.

Mr. Howe protests. "Judge, you have just rearrested Mrs. Woodhull for the original charge. She has already posted more than thirty thousand dollars' bond for her previous incarceration and a charge indeed for which she has yet to stand trial."

"I must insist upon another ten for her husband and herself," the judge says. "In addition to another five for Miss Tennessee Claflin. Once we find her. Flight risk, I'm afraid."

"Here's the pickle." Tennessee perches in a chair by the fire, the snow blustering around outside. One of the dogs is curled up on her lap and Bennett wraps an old lilac-colored stole belonging to his mother over her shoulders. "We cannot both post our bail and pay our lawyers' fees. I'm afraid we're not that rich."

He kneeled at Tennessee's feet and gently rubs them. "And your communard chums in the 12th International?"

"Don't be unkind, Bennett." Tennessee sneezes and blows her nose. She has certainly caught a chill.

He goes to his liquor cabinet and fetches a bottle and two glasses. "You could probably use some of this."

"What is it?"

"Slivovitz. Tastes of plum. It will do you a world of good. Now, tell me. Will you stay one more night, or am I taking you to join your sister in jail?"

Tennessee retires for the evening. Bennett pours himself more Slivovitz and wonders if anyone knows how deeply he is involved. If they did, it

CARRIE HAYES

would undermine what little credibility he barely has in the first place. The members of the press would have a field day if they found out. Christ! Why are things so difficult? He stands up and blurrily focuses on the two fireplaces. He sways and considers which one is real. He waves his hand in front of him. He finds the mantel and hangs onto it. Reaching down, Bennett undoes his flies and puts the fire out with a spray to rival any racehorse.

"My, my," he says to himself. "That Tennessee Claflin."

His valet checks on him and seeing Bennett extinguish the flames, shakes his head. It always makes such work for the char the next day.

In the morning, Bennett brings Tennessee a tray covered in delicious concoctions. Like every time before, he places it beside her and shoos the dogs from the bed. He lies down and groans about his headache.

She pours them a cup of tea. "You really shouldn't drink so much, you know."

"You're preaching to the choir, Miss Claflin."

"One of these days, it will get you into trouble."

"Which, I daresay, is something you know a great deal about. And you don't even drink that much, do you?"

"I'll miss you from prison, Bennett."

"I'm sure you will."

Within the hour of turning herself in, the fifteen thousand dollars they need for bail has been posted.

Everyone is silent in the carriage back to Meg's.

After dinner, Blood goes to check on the office. He turns up the lamps and sinks to his knees. The place has been ransacked. "WHORE" is written on the wall. Across the room is the drawing of an obscenity. Tennessee's stock ticker is smashed into pieces. The lithograph and duplicating press are in a heap on the floor. Filing cabinets and credenzas have been turned over, their contents torn in half, scattered through the rooms.

Blood covers his face with his hands and sobs as though his heart will break.

———

"Allow me to introduce myself," the man says. "Anthony Comstock, Bureau for the Suppression of Vice. At your service."

Luther Challis studies the card. Since the publication of that piece, Tennessee's article, every aspect of Challis's life has soured. Not that there aren't a few fellows who have patted him on the back and said nice work, well done. But even more of his circle now avoid him, particularly in the company of women.

Woodhull and Claflin, my eye, Challis thinks. It matters not that they were jailed with the obscenity charge. He wants those bitches to rot in hell for libeling him. He will ruin them, then he'll get the hell out of this godforsaken town and return to Kansas.

Luther takes a drag from his cigar. "Mr. Comstock, I will pay $100,000 if I must to see those harlots serve time for their offense."

———

The editorial staff of *Woodhull & Claflin's Weekly* are reduced in number. There are just enough funds to eke out an issue every Saturday. Contributing articles are always welcome and sales on the street remain brisk. Yet Tennessee is strangely preoccupied, unable to focus on work, the issue of suffrage, or indeed, much of anything at all.

———

New York Herald, April 1st 1873

It becomes our painful duty to announce the death of Mrs. James Gordon Bennett Sr. which took place yesterday morning at Konigstein, Saxony, after a brief illness. The office of the *Herald* will be closed today until 6PM.

May 1873
Washington Heights

To sit on the porch at Fort Washington in the enormous wicker sofa with a pair of dogs next to Bennett, who has another one on his lap, is heaven.

"Tennessee."

"Yes, Bennett."

"It turns out Mater had been ill for some time. For whatever reason, I can't say really, she preferred me not to know." He puts out his cigarette and looks at his schooner, anchored in the Hudson. "I suppose I wasn't much of a dutiful son, if she didn't see fit to tell me, was I?"

"Don't think like that."

"In fact, the physician sent for us against her wishes. Jeanette was in Paris and arrived a day late. Poor Mater. Poor Jeanette. The girl's pretty broken up about it." He looks at Tennessee. "We pass this way only briefly, don't we?"

"Yes, it's very brief. Bennett, I am so sorry." After a moment, Tennessee asks, "Why did your mother live abroad?"

"There was an incident when I was little. She insisted that we leave. My father, for his part, would not. Perhaps he could not."

"I don't understand."

"I had a younger brother, Cosmo, who died when I was eight years old. At the time, Pater would not endorse a certain New York politician. He went on about it at great length in the paper." Bennett was silent for a moment, then continued. "My parents were still in mourning and we were with my mother, walking home one evening, not long after she had given birth to a baby girl, and this politician's cronies set upon Pater with a horsewhip. It was quite savage."

"Did anyone intervene?"

"Actually, the police laughed and kept me off the assailants while my mother was forced to watch." Bennett drains his glass. "As you saw for yourself, Pater survived the thrashing, but my mother attributed the distress she experienced as resulting in my sister Clementine's demise.

"The poor thing wasn't three months old. The physician claimed it was failure to thrive. And of course, my mother blamed herself. So, she said, 'Jamie! Jimmy and I are leaving. You are welcome to join us.'

"But he preferred to stay and work on the *Herald*. I joined him here in the summers. He showed up in France often enough to have a hand in Jeanette's conception three years later. And there you have it. One happy family."

He clears his throat. "I'm going to put *Dauntless* through her paces in a few weeks. We'll do a slalom around a quartet of glaciers."

"In the spring?"

"It's up north. Bay of Exploits. In Newfoundland."

"Don't go."

Bennett shrugs "It's a dare, Tennie. It was made before Mater's—I can't very well decline the challenge. Besides, it's just the diversion I need at this point."

"The dogs will miss you a great deal."

"That's the wonderful thing about the little scamps." He picks up the spaniel on his lap and looks deep into its eyes. "This fellow only lives for now. Not for later, not for before, but just for now." He smiles at Tennessee. "Just like us, Tennie. It's for now. Just for now."

Colonel Blood struggles over how to proceed. It has taken weeks to put things right. How long it will take to recoup the funds lost from the vandalism at the office is impossible to say.

Everyone on the paper puts their best foot forward. Particularly Dr. Treat, a naturalist whose ideas are radical and whose contributions to the paper pour forth, regardless of the chaos in which they find themselves. Blood marvels at the good fortune of having such a prolific employee, as

Dr. Treat produces page after page, writing about corruption and conspiracy at Brooklyn's Plymouth Church. There seems to be no end to it. Remarkable, Blood thinks to himself. Just remarkable.

⁓

Tennessee notices Dr. Treat watching Victoria in a strange way. She goes to where he stands and asks, "What is it you see, Treat?"

"Her convictions, her humility, her determination. She is like a queen. Your sister reigns over everything that is noble and true."

"Ha! I wish you'd tell that to the authorities. But you know, you're not the first to say this. And you won't be the last." It is only then Tennessee notices Treat's persistent tick over his right eyebrow.

He gives her a strange smile and murmurs, "Miss Claflin, if I may be so bold, I might recommend some alternative medicinal for your..."

"My what?"

"Perhaps another time." He returns to his work. Tennessee wonders to what Treat is referring. No one discusses her health. It has to be something else.

Later, Tennessee and Victoria review the small ads in a quiet corner.

Tennessee says, "It appears Dr. Treat is under your spell."

"Really?"

"I wonder where the Colonel digs up these fellows."

"Treat lived in Vineland, but he's from Berlin Heights."

Tennessee shrugs.

"In Ohio, it's like Oneida."

Tennie raises her eyebrows. "Really?"

"Except I believe the arrangement is the opposite. I don't recall. And honestly, Treat eats too much garlic for me to pursue much of a conversation with him."

"Maybe he looks thus from that? In addition to a lack of male continence?"

"Tennie!" They both start to laugh. It seems like forever since they've shared a joke. They don't notice the policemen standing with Miss Swindell.

Victoria wipes her eyes. "May I help you?"

"Mrs. Woodhull," one of them says, "We have a warrant for your arrest, ma'am. For you and the rest of the staff of *Woodhull & Claflin's Weekly*."

No one speaks.

The policeman adds, "It's for libel, Mrs. Woodhull."

* * *

As Mr. Howe had predicted, they are taken to Jefferson Market Court. Its adjoining prison is called the Tombs. Howe takes Tennessee and Victoria aside. "While we were able to post bail for Colonel Blood's brother, Miss Swindell, and Dr. Treat, the funds at your disposal are not enough to cover bail for yourselves or Colonel Blood."

Being Friday afternoon, the bondsman who provides additional monies needed for bail is away for the weekend. As is the prosecuting attorney, the bailiff, and a judge.

Colonel Blood is taken in one direction and the sisters are led away in the other. A guard steers them through a series of doors. The air is foul, and it becomes very cold. Down an interminable passageway, lit only by a torch, their cell is little more than a cage butting into the corner of the building. It reeks of sewage.

"In here," the guard says. "Name's Sam. Only use it under pain of death."

It is three feet wide by eight feet long. There is a single cot and a slop bucket. The walls are dank with mold.

Sam's lantern is the only light. "You've got a window." He smiles, showing his rotten teeth. "It'll be daylight before you know it."

Tennessee sees an opening where the wall meets the ceiling. Several stars twinkle in the night sky.

By morning, word is out that the sisters are in. The press clamors at the gates for an interview but are turned away. The warden, like everyone else, has left for the weekend.

Bail is posted on Tuesday.

⌇

Silently, they repair to a large, comfortable apartment provided by a sympathizer. Buck has purchased all the papers during their absence and Tennessee brings them into the dining room. She looks at the piece from the *Herald* and then the one from the *Sun*. The *Herald* isn't very sympathetic. In fact, its coverage is appalling. She looks at the report in the *Sun*, which is all right. She takes the *Herald* and throws it into the grate.

Just for now, my eye, she thinks. To hell with his just for now.

⌇

Roxana tells the journalist that while Victoria is unavailable, Tennie C. is at home.

He says, "Miss Claflin, my name is John Green. I write for the *New York Sun*. It's no secret you've been unfairly persecuted. The *Sun* would like to do a piece about what I believe is the monstrous harassment you've endured since publishing the November 2nd issue of the *Weekly*."

John Green is tall, nearly the same height as Bennett. His skin is dark. His gaze is kind and steady.

"Mr. Green," she says, "won't you sit down?"

June 1873
East Thirty Fourth Street

From the journal of Tennie C. Claflin:

Since our interview, John Green has come calling on several occasions. We take long walks through the city and exchange ideas. I like John Green. Yesterday, he said that the world is not ready for Vicky. That she is too honest and too passionate. He then went on to say he believed men with power and money have little interest in fairness to the common man.

I asked, "What about fairness to women?"

To which he laughed and said, "Men aren't about to give it over."

We then stopped to rest in Madison Square Park, and he asked me how my clairvoyance manifests itself.

I did not tell him about my true moments, when I go to the place where I am my most private self. That when I am in the true place, there are no questions, nor are there any answers. There is only a vision which I accept because the spirit sees into my heart and it touches me.

Instead, I said to Mr. Green, "I daresay, it's a blessing and a curse. For us, without it, certainly in New York, there would have been no calling cards nor letters of introduction. Most certainly where Vanderbilt was concerned."

I could see him wondering what it was I actually did with Cornelius, so, I gave him my best smile and confided, "I'll tell you this, Mr. Green. I rarely conjured spirits."

———

Mr. Howe says, "The key, Miss Claflin, is to delay."

Tennessee relays this to Buck, and he agrees. "He's the best money can buy. I would heed his council."

Their old friend Judge Reymert concurs. "Howe is a master strategist. Your father's assessment is correct. The key to winning this thing is to delay."

"Utica! Why is your skin so white?" Roxana peers at Utica's makeup over her glasses. Triumphant in sobriety with a part in the chorus of *The Black Crook*'s traveling company, Utica's tour has concluded. She is home, in the bosom of her family.

"It's a lead paste, Ma. Don't you like it? It hides the tiredness."

"Why are you tired?"

Utica throws up her hands in exasperation. "Why wouldn't I be tired? I have crossed this country back and forth on the train, singing and dancing, never a moment to myself. I'm exhausted."

Utica takes a large dose of the Vin Mariani before dinner. With Vin Mariani, she doesn't crave liquor, nor does she need the needle. She enjoys the warmth sliding down her throat and smooths the white pancake around her chin to blend better with her neck. A little pinch to the cheeks and bite to her lips. Perfect!

Meg and her son, Duke, have joined them for dinner. Then Dr. Treat calls on them as well and sits on Utica's right. Everyone eats in silence. Victoria manages a few sips of soup then pushes the bowl away. Meg watches Utica closely, there is something about her which Meg cannot quite put her finger on.

"Don't you, sister?" Utica looks at Meg.

"Don't I what, Utica?"

"Don't you believe that Vicky and Tennie smothered poor Doc Woodhull?"

There is a collective gasp around the table.

"Oh Utica. That's a terrible thing to say."

"But it's true!"

Colonel Blood stands up. "No, I can assure you, it is positively not true."

Victoria unsteadily pushes herself away from the table and murmurs, "I am feeling unwell."

"He came to me." Utica turns back to Dr. Treat, who is so enthralled by Utica's loveliness, he cannot look away, even as he turns crimson with embarrassment. Utica puts down her fork and grabs his thigh. "He said they wanted to take the medicine. It was all he had, all he had in the world."

"Utica, you haven't gone back on it, have you?" Tennessee asks.

Meg says, "You're looking something odd, dear."

"Odd? Is that what you say to me? When every man in the company of *The Black Crook* is just waiting for five minutes with me! You have a gall, you know, Margaret. You're too old and too ugly for anyone to want you. I'm surprised Dr. Treat here doesn't have to fight you off!"

"Enough!" Blood roars. He quickly leaves the room. Victoria follows. Suddenly, there is a terrible crash. Tennessee runs out.

Meg says, "How dare you speak to me like this."

"How dare I?" Utica stands up and squints at Meg. She picks up her dining chair. "Watch this! And watch how I dare do this!"

Meg freezes, then ducks just in time as the chair is hurled across the table, smashing dishes and glasses in its way.

"I hate you. I HATE YOU!" Utica trembles, her eyes bright.

Meg grabs Duke. "Our Uti is out of her head. Please get the constable to assist us. Mercy! She may get ahold of the knives."

Tennessee begins screaming, "MA! Mama! Get a doctor, please!"

The Sun, June 7th, Mrs. V.C. Woodhull Dying

Pronounced dead by her two attending physicians. Subsequently showing signs of life, but still lying unconscious. Little if any hope of recovery. The breaking of a hard-working woman's heart.

"Mrs. Woodhull," the doctor whispers into Victoria's ear. "Lie still. No, no, don't move. There must be no fuss. Your very life depends upon it."

He beckons to Tennessee and Blood. "She's ruptured a blood vessel, possibly in her lung. It is critical she is not disturbed. If she does not rest, she will forfeit her life."

It is just before sunrise. Tennessee knows Colonel Blood loves her sister as much as it is possible to love another person. "Colonel. Jim," she whispers. "Vicky will live, Jim. She will live longer than either you or I will."

A telegram is on the hall table. Tennessee opens it with trembling hands

PERFIDY DISMAY SCOOPED BY THE SUN JOHN GREEN
THE SUN THE SUN JOHN GREEN COLOSSAL PERFIDY
JGB

The next week, they reported to Federal Court to face the original obscenity charge.

ACQUITTAL. The Sun, June 30th, 1873. New York City.

The prosecution opens; it proceeds; it closes—then what? Why, then, the learned judge of the United States District Court, who presides at the trial, informs the accused that there is no occasion for them to introduce any evidence in their defense; that no case has been proved against them...For the wrong which has been done to these women they have no redress. The injury is irremediable.

When Tilton and Henry Bowen arrive at their host's house, they find Reverend Beecher already stretched out upon the sofa. The Reverend says, "I care not for any documentation or letters Mrs. Woodhull might make available to you. I have little to hide."

Bowen can barely contain himself. "On the contrary, Reverend. It would seem you have everything to hide. Your pitiful efforts at dissemblance are a discredit to the good faith placed upon you by the five thousand souls who worship at Plymouth Church."

The Reverend looks around the room. Most of the furniture is covered in white sheets for the summer. The normally abundant liquor tray stands empty. Beecher sits up and turns to his host. "Might we open a window? It seems strangely close in here this afternoon."

PART FIVE

THE QUALITY OF MERCY

"Of course, in a novel, people's hearts break, and they die, and that is the end of it; and in a story, this is very convenient. But in real life we do not die when all that makes life bright dies to us."

- From *Uncle Tom's Cabin*, by Harriet Beecher Stowe

THE HUMAN BODY,
THE TEMPLE OF GOD

July 1873
Twenty Sixth Street

UTICA MOVES TO Meg's, where the infatuated Dr. Treat calls upon her every day. She pours out to him the heartbreak she suffers at the hands of her sisters. Dr. Treat listens but inches from Utica's exquisite face, and she allows him to inject her with enough sedative to render her oblivious as his sweating body stretches next to hers, his amative impulses staining his faded linen suit.

Meg puts her ear against the door of Utica's room and hears them snoring. She can't bring herself to tell her family that when Treat isn't sidling up to crazy Utie, he is exchanging confidences with Polly Sparr. Still, rumors of pandemonium and brawling begin to surface. Ten days later, Utica dies in her sleep. Meg tells Dr. Treat to please leave, which he does, shamefaced at having lost the special friend he considered a patient under his care.

The morning of the funeral, Roxana gingerly removes a pair of pearl earrings from a silk pouch and places the posts into Utica's ears. Then Tennessee slides Utica's wrap under her shoulders as the undertaker holds her body aloft. After the autopsy, unkind jokes purported syphilis as being the cause of death, but the doctor states it was Bright's disease. Utica's lifelong entanglement with the bottle caused her kidneys to just give out. She was thirty-one years of age, younger than Roxana was when she gave birth to her.

Roxana is past tears, past sorrow. There is only a pain which can never heal. She still thinks of Utica as a small child. How beautifully she sang! "She looks like my mama. I never mentioned that, did I?" Roxana strokes her dead daughter's face.

Tennessee shakes her head.

"I pray God, Tennie, poor Uti is the last of my children I shall see buried," Roxana whispers. "I cannot abide another loss. How I wish it were me in this coffin and not little Utica."

"Oh no, Ma." Tennessee's tears begin to fall. "Please don't say that."

Meg comes in and takes her mother's hand. "The hearse is here. They are ready."

Roxana says, "Bring your father and sisters in before we go. Not the little ones."

"Yes, Ma."

"And the priest."

"Yes, Ma."

Silently, she watches her youngest child, Tennessee, sing the note which helps the others find theirs. When they were younger, and Roxana sang with her girls, it was then she felt closest to the Holy Spirit. She knows that God forgives her. Over the years, in the back of the wagon, in the different places they rented, when Tennessee and occasionally Victoria would do that show. God forgives Roxana for those years, because He gave His only son.

Out on the street, the driver of the hearse removes his stovepipe hat to wipe his brow. The clouds in the sky are low and thick. Clearing his throat, he replaces the hat on his head, and patiently waits for the family to come outside. From the window upstairs, he can hear what sounds like keening. But then it transforms itself into women singing, one voice so tightly aligned with another he wonders if they are angels.

It is agreed, Treat must go. Blood insists that they take care of it before leaving for Chicago and calls him into the back office. Blood speaks first. "Your contribution has been inestimable, but we have to cut back."

Victoria says, "We simply cannot afford to keep you on."

Treat's facial tic begins twitching. "I see." He crosses and uncrosses his legs, straightens his back, and pulls at his fraying cuffs. He says, "It's a good thing I've prepared my pamphlet then, isn't it?"

"Your pamphlet?" Colonel Blood asks.

"Yes, on Tennessee's career as a whore."

A crash roars between Tennessee's ears, pounding just behind her forehead. "What?"

"Polly Sparr worked on it with me. We have accounts of the nights you spent with different men and the conversation Polly overheard about whoring with Commodore Vanderbilt."

This cannot be happening, Tennessee thinks.

"And of course," Treat says, "your late sister Utica's testimony."

Polly will deny it. Then again, perhaps they are in it together. Do not scream, she warns herself. Remain calm. Tennessee glances at Victoria who seems on the verge of swooning.

Colonel Blood stands up. Somehow, the ladies follow suit. "Dr. Treat," he says, "be advised, should you move forward with any pamphlet of any nature, we will sue you in a court of law."

Once inside the carriage, Blood tries to reassure them. "He's bluffing. Don't give it a thought." Victoria looks at Tennessee and says nothing.

It is a rare moment on the *Dauntless* that James Gordon Bennett prefers to sit in the cabin rather than on deck. But the weather is lousy. Another summer has passed without Tennessee coming to Newport. Now it is too late to ask her. But it would have been catastrophic had she been with him when Utica died. And why did Tennessee give that clown Green who works at the *Sun* the story about Victoria? It is beyond the pale. And why does he have to learn from his own man that Utica is dead? Why?

By the time he is back in New York, Tennessee, Victoria, and Colonel Blood are long gone. Again, he reads about it in the *Sun*.

⌇⌇

Tennessee sees Treat in Chicago, on the corner outside the auditorium. He seems to be laughing. The other spiritualists, as if embarrassed to be seen purchasing the pamphlets, are turned with their backs from where she stands. Mortified, Tennessee is rooted to the spot.

"Go inside, go inside." Blood ushers the sisters backstage. Victoria is the principal speaker after lunch. She must make her appearance. Her speech goes smoothly enough, until a man in the third row stands up. It is Mr. Cotton from the Chicago delegation.

"Well?" Cotton shouts up at her. He points to Treat's pamphlet. "Are these allegations true?"

Victoria narrows her eyes. She takes a step toward him. "If this convention wants to know anything special about my sexual organs let us have it understood."

Cotton persists. "But is it true?" Tennessee stands in the wings, her heart hammering. She wants to collapse.

Victoria pauses, then says, "Suppose he did tell the truth. Has Mr. Cotton ever had sexual relations with Mrs. Woodhull?" She waits. One can hear a pin drop.

"No," says Cotton.

"Do you know any man that has?"

"No."

"Then what in the name of heaven can you prove? Have you in your eagerness to do something for the public weal, which I suppose you consider in danger, come before this convention to arraign me for hypocrisy?"

The auditorium is completely still. Victoria draws herself up. "I hurl the intention back in your face, sir, and stand boldly before you and this convention and declare that I have never had sexual relations with any man of whom I am ashamed to stand side by side before the world with the act. I am not ashamed of any act of my life! At the time, it was the best I knew. Nor am I ashamed of any desire that has been gratified or of any passion alluded to. Every one of them are a part of my own soul's life, for which thank God, I am not accountable to you."

From the journal of Tennie C. Claflin:

We waited long after the auditorium had emptied but Treat was still there, selling his pamphlet. The man is demonic, for it must have been a devil that tapped him on the shoulder. He whirled around and saw me, crowing, "And she's a whore! At the New York Herald everyone's declared she's a whore!" It is beyond slander. That insane man shouted to someone who stood near him, "You've been hoodwinked. Ha ha! You go with the whore at the Herald!" It was then I realized the man standing near Treat was John Green, and that John was holding a pamphlet.

Sitting in the tearoom at the hotel, Tennessee studies her hands. There is no sign of an outbreak. She straightens the lace cuffs covering her knuckles and waits for Green to show up. She is on her second cup of tea when he walks in.

"I can only stay a tick." He looks around the room before sitting down.

She is resolved to stay calm and pushes the teapot in his direction. "I won't try and sway you either way, but it is lapsang souchong."

Suddenly Green scowls and says, "How do you think it's going to look should my colleagues learn I run with the whore at the *Herald*?"

"Gosh, John." The insult is so hurtful, it feels like hours before she can answer. "How do you think it's going to look should your colleagues actually believe I am the whore at the *Herald*? It's a conundrum, I daresay."

"I have enjoyed your friendship very much."

"But not enough to offset the pestilence Dr. Treat hurled about this afternoon."

"It's one of the trials of being in the public eye." He looks at her. "I should imagine."

"Compared to incarceration, it is but a hiccup."

"Tennessee."

"Please. I don't want you to plead or weep. That would be awkward, wouldn't it?" He doesn't answer, so she adds, "What Treat said is not true."

Green shakes his head and looks away. When he glances back at her, he sees she is gathering her things and has paid the bill. He says, "Take care of yourself, Tennessee."

"You can be sure I will, Johnny Green." She smiles brightly at him, blinking back the tears in her eyes. "Adios, Johnny. Au revoir."

———

That evening they board the train back to New York. What little remains from the diamond investment is kept with Jay Cooke whose firm is the most conservative of banks.

The New York Times,
September 20, 1873

THE SCENE IN WALL STREET – LIST OF SUSPENSIONS - THE GOVERNMENT TO BUY $10,000,000 OF BONDS TODAY - The excitement in Wall Street yesterday beggars all description. The trouble of Thursday was bad enough, but it was entirely eclipsed by that of yesterday. It is a singular coincidence that the gold corner of September 1869, when so many persons were ruined, and the culmination of the panic of 1873, when the finances of the entire country have been placed in the most dangerous condition, happened upon the same day of the week and in the same month.

No less than eighteen major banking houses collapse. While Tennessee, Victoria, and Blood journey home, the firm of Jay Cooke becomes bankrupt and its cash reserves are wiped out. By the time they arrive in New York, they are penniless.

———

James Gordon Bennett leaves the *Herald* on the corner of Ann and Broadway at noon. He pretends not to notice the men in search of work. Those who have juggled credit and debt from one day to the next are suddenly destitute, with wives at home and children to feed. Silent, the men stand, three or four wide in serpentine lines winding around one building and then another. Their umbrellas are open to protect them from the rain, dressed in their finest clothes, ready to work at a moment's notice. Bennett recognizes more than a few. He enters Delmonico's and takes a table where one might watch the goings-on outside yet remain obscured from the street.

He beckons the waiter. "Send for Signore Lorenzo."

When the proprietor appears, Bennett says, "I've taken a lease on 110 Centre Street."

Lorenzo nods, "Si, Signore."

"As much soup and as many sandwiches for these fellows as you can muster should do it. See they have enough to put in their pockets, too."

"Yes, Mr. Bennett. For when would you like to provide their meal?"

"This afternoon. Then every day. Until they're back on their feet. Just send over the bill."

"Yes, Mr. Bennett."

"They can't find work on empty stomachs, can they?"

"No, Mr. Bennett."

"Let's keep this between ourselves," Bennett says. "It might cause some hard feelings or be misconstrued, if my involvement gets out."

He spends that night at the *Herald* and reads the September 27 issue of *WCW* when he can't sleep. "Scarecrows of Sexual Slavery"—that looks promising. But when he sees *"THE AMERICAN COMMUNISM,"* he sighs and tosses the paper on the floor.

AFFIRM STATUS UPON ARRIVAL JGB

They move back in with Meg, who hands Tennessee the telegram. Her mind will not be still. Treat claims she was known as the whore at the *Herald*. Jack Bartels used to call her a whore. When the sisters fought, they always called each other so. Then Bennett saw her outside Annie de Wood's. But she saw him, too. So, what does that make him?

All those soldiers. There had been thousands, and everyone knew most of them would die. Yet she was paid to say nothing. I'll touch you. Give Buck the money. It was supposed to be different in New York. But it wasn't. I'll touch you. Give Vic the money.

Blood sees her huddled on the stairs. He crouches down next to her. "Treat used Utica's death, Tennie. To make you doubt. Everything."

"REFORMATION OR REVOLUTION, Which?" Both Victoria and Tennessee are on the program. Tickets are sold out within hours and there is a torrential downpour, steam rising off everyone's sodden garments. The audience whistles and cheers, stomping their feet, "VICKY! VICKY!"

They wait in the wings. Victoria seems reluctant to move. Tennessee watches Colonel Blood take Victoria's hands in his. Bowing their heads, their foreheads touch as he whispers to his wife. Tennessee watches Victoria's face slowly fill with color and come to life. Individual sovereignty and enduring love are not mutually exclusive. Not at all. Straightening her back, Victoria winks at Tennessee, then strides onto the stage. The crowd goes wild. Minutes pass. Finally, it is quiet.

> It may appear presumptuous, perhaps ridiculous, for a woman to talk to an audience composed largely of men, about politics and government. Men have had the management of these questions so long, it ought at least to be presumed that what they do not know is not worth talking about.

There is friendly laughter and some applause. Victoria's voice grows stronger.

> There are times in the affairs of nations when revolutions are not only necessary, but obligatory upon a people, and it is an open question if such a time is not now impending over this country. One of two things will surely be: There must be reformation behind the political scenes, or there will be revolution outside of them.

The audience roars its approval. Tennessee takes deep breaths. At last! It is her turn to follow. She will say her piece. Her heart pounding, she moves toward the stage.

Victoria shakes her head and reaches for Tennessee's hand. The crowd cheers, stomping their feet.

Tennessee shouts over the crowd, "I am going to speak."

"No, not tonight."

Is Treat in the venue?

Victoria won't let go of her hand. "They won't hear you. They're too riled up. We don't want a riot."

"But…"

"Come with me."

They step outside and are immediately drenched. Across the street, the black carriage is waiting. Dixon scrambles down, opens an umbrella, and runs to assist her. Tennessee turns to protest, but Victoria has vanished.

Bennett is inside the carriage. "Miss Claflin, I presume?"

They speed to Fort Washington in silence. He hands her cloak to the footman and they go upstairs to his quarters. She has never seen Bennett's rooms. Her small overnight bag has somehow been placed on his bed.

She says, "I am not your whore."

Bennett does not answer but steps into what she imagines is the bath-room; then she hears all kinds of water begin running behind the door.

He reemerges and says, "You need to warm up." Only then does she realize her teeth are chattering. She is shaking like a leaf.

Without further comment, he undresses then puts on an enormous dressing gown.

"I am not your whore," she repeats.

Very softly, he says, "Sit down, Tennessee."

She sits on the edge of his bed; her feet dangle above the floor. He kneels in front of her and gently removes her boots and then her stock-ings. He stands her up and carefully takes off her jacket and then removes her skirt and petticoat. Finally, he removes her camisole. He sees the lesion across her back and down the inside of her arm.

Our friendship is over now, she thinks, I am sure of it.

Bennett carefully touches the lesion. "Who did this to you, Tennessee?"

Tears of shame prevent her from answering. She does not bawl nor howl; the tears just come of their own accord.

"Tennie, do you take something for this?" he whispers.

She nods and says in a small voice, "I cannot wash without it." Not looking at him, she opens the bag and takes out a jar of Roxana's liniment and the box of muslin rags.

Bennett says, "I'll do it. It's all right. Shh." With tender hands, he covers every angry sore and abscess with liniment, then leads her by the hand inside the bathroom. Everything is marble and steam is everywhere.

It is impossible to see him. She takes an instinctive step back when she sees the floor to ceiling tower shooting jets of water beneath what seems to be a fountain cascading water into a drain on the floor.

"Hello! Tennessee!" Bennett calls as if he were far, far away around the corner of a mountain, barely visible in the clouds of steam. Perhaps I'm going mad, she thinks, and begins to chuckle at the absurdity of it all.

"Come with me!" he calls, still in his faraway voice. "It's not too hot!"

Then the water meets her body and she is laughing and crying at the same time while he gently bathes her. Careful not to disturb the liniment, he sings sailing shanty songs, unable to carry a tune, kneeling as he takes first her left foot and then her right, heeding that she feels safe within his care and love.

Afterwards, he wraps the muslin rags over her lesions and places the lilac-colored stole around her shoulders.

———

The sky is clear in the morning and the ground has hardened with frost. They take the balloon across the Hudson River as far west as they dare and pitch a small tent. They retire inside when the campfire no longer keeps them as warm as they are in each other's arms. The next morning, he struggles to inflate the balloon, laughing even as he curses, while she entertains him with impersonations of the season's personalities.

When they finally are aloft, Bennett says, "Tennessee. I think we need to get away from here."

"I thought we just did."

"No, no, I mean truly away, on another continent where we—oh, I don't know."

"I can't leave Victoria to face the trial alone, Jimmy."

Quite suddenly, he moves across the basket to embrace her, and it loses its equilibrium, causing the balloon to tilt and sway.

"Woah!" They hold onto each other in the basket's center. "No, you couldn't do that, could you?" he says sadly.

Afterward, Bennett returns to the *Herald* and Tennessee to the *Weekly*. They agree not to communicate unless events warrant it. After a fortnight, they agree again, but it is no good. In a ferocious embrace, hidden from view in the grand upstairs rooms at 425 Fifth Avenue, he persuades her that it will be all right, he will take the risk. There is nothing to fear. He has cleared it with a French physician and will use every precaution.

From the journal of Tennie C. Claflin:

It is no small shock that his tenderness yields such immeasurable joy. There are few words, only a great deal of laughter every time Bennett demonstrates his prodigious clumsiness with prophylactic engineering. Our days are now spent at work, reading, writing, and then meeting in the dead of night, when his carriage collects me, and I arrive, hoping he won't be too drunk to get it right.

So, why is it when we are happy, we presume its surfeit will spread itself to others? Yesterday, when PB Randolph lamented his chronic lack of funds, and the demise of the Rosicrucian rooms, I exclaimed, "But friend! It is you who said to me that we must try if we are to be happy in the world. Let me introduce you to Bennett. He is a believer. I am sure you will win him over and he'll champion your books."

Honestly, how can Bennett resist?

They stay up until midnight, when the carriage comes to collect her.

"It's quite all right, Dixon," Tennessee says, "this gentleman is a friend. He is here to meet Mr. Bennett."

The dogs yap, greeting Tennessee with enthusiasm and Randolph with suspicion.

Bennett's eyes sparkle when he sees the black man. "You're the fellow from the march."

"The march?" Tennessee says.

"In December, Tennie. When I was entertaining the Russian Duke." He nods toward Randolph. You're a communard, aren't you?"

"Mr. Bennett, I am apolitical." Paschal Randolph shakes his head. "I believe in harmony and the cultivation of a greater purpose between man and woman."

"Not with this woman, you don't."

Randolph's eyes widen, and Tennessee flushes in embarrassment. Randolph says, "Tennie C. is free to cavort with whichever man is lucky enough to win her heart."

"Bennett." Tennessee smiles brightly. "I've brought Paschal to do a reading for you. He's a true clairvoyant. Much better than I am. He's also written the most marvelous book."

"Hmmm. Well, let's have something to drink and hear what he has to say."

They sit at the small table near the fireplace. She pours them each a glass of brandy. Thoughts of Bennett holding the baby owl make Tennessee smile.

"Miss Tennessee asks after you all the time," Bennett says.

Randolph asks, "Who?"

"Exactly. That's what she says exactly." Bennett lights a cigarette, and Tennessee places a small candle in the center of the table. She knows he's quite drunk.

She raises her hands and flutters her eyes, gazing toward heaven. "Deliver my soul, O Lord, from lying lips and from a deceitful tongue. Amen." She holds each man's hand in hers. Bennett strokes her palm with his middle finger, and she raises an eyebrow causing him to smile. With his free hand, Randolph drains his glass. He refills it and drinks it down, then closes his eyes. They sit in silence. Tennessee senses the magic, and the room becomes palpably cooler.

"What is the date of my death?" Bennett asks.

"It will be close to the day you were born," Randolph answers.

"Don't worry," Tennessee says. "You have a great many years left."

"How do you know that?"

"Bennett," she whispers, "we're clairvoyant." She squeezes his hand, "You will be at least your dear father's age."

Randolph sways in his chair, humming to himself. "And because of you and your vanity"—he refills his glass and drains it again—"they will starve to death. Twenty souls."

"What?" The magic vanishes. Bennett leans forward. "I would never let a living creature go hungry." His cigarette ash falls across the table. He thrusts his pointed finger toward Tennessee. "Tell him."

"Your heart is like ice isn't it?" Randolph responds. He takes the last of the Slivovitz and knocks it back. She realizes he is as drunk as Bennett.

Bennett stares at his guests with contempt. "Get out," he whispers.

"The only place fit for you is the Arctic." Randolph begins laughing. "Isn't that right, Tennie? This rich fool's heart is made of ice!"

"Get out of here. Both of you. I'm not some gypsy mark you can humbug for your nefarious ends."

"There will be a magnificent journey to find the Northern Passage because you are jealous. You are jealous, aren't you? And your proud heart is like ice. So, you send them to the Arctic."

"Get out!"

Standing on the corner of Fifth Avenue and Thirty-Eighth Street, Randolph slips and falls.

"Paschal!" Tennessee helps him up, and he cries out in pain.

Randolph moans. "I have broken my arm."

"What?"

"I have, I have. It's the humerus. God, I did it as a boy."

"Can you walk? I don't think Mr. Bennett will provide us with a lift home."

———— ··· ————

In her will, Bennett's mother left him an early token she'd received from his father. It is an opal and diamond ring. The next evening, Bennett follows Tennessee into the sitting room and touches his waistcoat, feeling for the ring. He watches her stand beside the fire. Bennett decides he'll ask on bended knee and imagines slipping the ring on her finger. But somehow, the conversation turns, and he realizes Tennessee is still speaking.

"Randolph is a very accomplished wizard, even lauded by Napoléon III. He started a most important group, Bennett. I am amazed you've never heard of him."

Bennett shrugs and says nothing.

"The Rosicrucians. *The Master Passion*? Oh, for heaven's sake." Tennessee stands up. "Why were you so hateful to him? It's because he's Negro, isn't it?"

"I don't give a rat's ass about that." He looks at the fire and will not meet her gaze.

She must find a way for them to get along. "Then why?" There is no point in yelling.

Finally, he answers, "Because of you."

"What?" Bennett and Randolph must be friends.

"Because of how he looks at you. He loves you." He sits down and struggles to gather his thoughts. The moment is slipping away.

"Don't be silly." If she weren't so sad, she would find it funny.

"He loves you. Don't see him anymore." Bennett looks at her. "I don't want you to see him again."

"I will do whatever I choose with whomever I choose to do it." She is surprised that she is trembling.

"Not with me you won't." Bennett returns his gaze to the fire. So. That is that.

"No, perhaps I won't," Tennessee says. "You have never respected my individual sovereignty, have you? Don't get up. I'll see myself out."

From the unpublished memoir of P.B. Randolph:

To read between the lines, one could see that my friend was desperate for refuge. Somewhere she might wait out a few months to discern the right choice for herself, and any issue that was, to put it delicately, imminent. Since my own reconciliation with the lovely Katy Carsoun, it was all I could do not to wax rhapsodic about every aspect of our new baby boy. Life in Toledo is very good. The new subscriptions to the Brotherhood of Eulis will prove most lucrative. Soon, I will have put my financial troubles behind me.

From the journal of Tennie C. Claflin:

It is Christmas and the nausea has largely subsided. Bennett continues to make overtures with his telegrams, but it requires little effort to throw them into the fire unopened. When the box arrived on Christmas Eve, I placed it in a corner of the room where it has sat underneath Vicky's publicity materials.

The first stop will be Missouri, followed by Kansas, then Nebraska, Iowa, Michigan, and then back to Iowa, finally winding down in Illinois. As advance agent, I am to arrive ahead of the others ensuring everything is suitable for both our success and comfort. The Colonel will stay behind and tend the paper. Thankfully, there's been no further sign of Joseph Treat's pamphlet. In fact, there have been no signs of Treat whatsoever, which is a relief, because I should want to kill him were I to see him. In the mayhem that was my departure, I did not think twice when asked if I wanted Bennett's box included with my luggage, and said that yes of course, I did. Perhaps it is something to keep warm.

James Gordon Bennett has reached just about the limit in relations with the fairer sex. It is bad enough Pauline Markham hung around as long as she did. And now this business of being at odds with Tennessee Claflin has driven him to distraction.

At the end of January, there is an invitation to join the Brotherhood of Eulis. Several of his friends are in orders such as these. He recalls the cracks made about Jay and Mrs. Gould practicing sex magic. It certainly hasn't done that couple any harm.

Bennett will go to this retreat, in Tennessee, no less. Then make his way back east, take *Dauntless* out of dry dock, and chart a leisurely course back to Europe. He'll enter a regatta in the south of France, of which he is particularly fond. Then it will be time for Jennie Jerome's nuptials in Paris during the second week of April—that should be a great party.

Besides, the Challis libel trial is bound to be wrapped up in more controversy than Bennett has the stomach for. He picks up the Joseph Treat pamphlet. The damnable thing is that these missives often have an element of truth about them. He throws the pamphlet into the fire. It is best that he be far, far away; otherwise, the nearness of her will undo him. It will simply undo him.

The porter places the unopened box onto the freshly made couchette. Tennessee tips him, then curls up and closes the curtain. She has a swig of Fowler's Solution and takes a piece of licorice root to suck on for her stomach. Slowly, she opens the box. Inside is an exquisite lady's guitar, with a delicate pearl and rosewood inlay around the front of the instrument. The card reads,

> *This belonged to my mother. I know in your care, in your hands, it will become, as does everything you touch, music to my ears.*

For James Gordon Bennett, Tennessee Claflin is beautiful, kind, brilliant, and inappropriate in every way. His world revolves around the very rich, some of whom had dealt his late father a sneer of such contempt that it is impossible to see them and not be reminded of this. And Tennessee is like his father. She has little regard for convention and were she to be on his arm, he fears she would most likely not be received in polite society.

Is the fact that he cares an aspect of himself he finds disappointing? It chagrins Bennett very much to acknowledge that, yes, it does indeed matter to him. And while he has no reason for concern, he cannot help but fret that something may have transferred from that dear lady to himself. It is best that he be examined once and for all. The French are, thank God, much advanced in diagnosing and treating scars of Venus.

———

Few people notice whether anything is changed, as the gentleman's overcoat Tennessee wears conceals most of what is changing. When Roxana tells her that her color is full of life, Tennessee waves her hand, saying, "You know, I think I have a fever," to which her mother squints, shaking her head.

Tennessee is surprised that she is no longer comfortable listening to diatribes against marriage but prefers discussing the future of children and their rights instead. She often thinks of that girl at the Masked Ball and she wishes the *Weekly* went further in exposing those charlatans who consider themselves to be above reproach.

Once the trial is over, she'll go to Toledo and stay with Randolph and his wife. He has written Tennessee of his delight at being the proud father of a baby boy.

Tennessee imagines, her hand at her stomach, a baby boy. Wouldn't that be something? She knows she must make a decision. She is at least five months along. She plucks a few strings on her guitar. She will decide once the trial is over. Once and for all.

———

After the opening arguments, the judge tells the attorneys to approach the bench. "In light of the depravity and heinousness with which Mr. Challis was libeled, I will insist the defendants remain in custody for the duration of this trial." There is a hush in the courtroom. Zula's lower lip begins trembling. She looks up at Victoria who stares straight ahead.

Their new attorney, Mr. Brook, says, "Your honor, I must object."

"Overruled," the judge answers. "It will be unnecessary to set bail, as their daily business will be taken up by the proceedings of this court. Bailiff, conduct Mrs. Woodhull, Colonel Blood, and Miss Claflin to the Tombs." The judge bangs his gavel. "Court is adjourned until tomorrow morning."

Tennessee is sure she has misheard him. The bailiff leads the three of them to the holding cell. Victoria dabs at her eyes with Blood's handkerchief. He whispers something to her, and Tennessee turns away to give them a hair's breadth of privacy. She puts her hand on her stomach and feels the distinct nudge. Spreading her hand wide, she taps where the nudge had been. The nudge taps back.

The air is rancid. As many men are inside their cells as are hanging about the corridor, trading sundries and gossip. An old fellow is selling bread and another flasks of water. One of the residents calls out, "Well, hello, ladies!" as the sisters follow the guard to their cell.

Its door is open. It is completely empty. Several leaks in the ceiling provide an inch of standing water on the floor.

The guard wags his finger. "Now don't turn your nose up. This ain't a hotel."

Tennessee leans against the wall. All the cell doors are still open. It will be another hour before they are locked within. Victoria struggles to control her coughing and holds her hand over her right breast, gasping for shallow sips of air. She says, "Tennie, I can't breathe."

Tennessee pushes herself upright and makes her way out of the cell. "We just need something to sit on. I'll get you something, Vic. Don't fret."

Furnishings will have to be procured, which means money and they have none. The other prisoners direct Tennessee to a cell which appears to double as a supplies closet. Inside is the guard she recognizes from her previous stay. "Sam, Sam. What do you have for us to sleep on?"

"I'm sure we can find you something." He looks at her. "For a price."

"I can't pay you tonight," Tennessee says.

"So, you've shown up here, and you got no money?"

Tennessee swallows. The spirit has not said what will come next.

"Look, look at these lovely cots." Two rusted cots are leaning on a wall beside Sam's desk. "Perfect, wouldn't you say?"

She nods.

Sam smiles wide, revealing the rotten black holes where his teeth used to be. He calls out, "Hey, Bruno, you there! Get these cots in Miss Claflin and Woodhull's cell. *Macht schnell*, imbecile." Sam steps up to Tennessee. He grabs her breast. He closes his fingers around it and squeezes, twisting it very hard. "I am going to need payment, Miss Tennie C.," he whispers, licking his lips, "and if I can't get my dick wet, I'll think of something else."

You ogre from Hell, she thinks. "I know you will."

Tennessee watches as Victoria lies down, her breath labored.

There are groans from another cell somewhere inside. How is it possible that one could see New York City from the sky only to be reduced to this cell, with its chains dangling from the wall, and her beloved sister, now struggling just to breathe?

Tennessee's guts churn. There is just enough space for their cots and a few square feet for a chamber pot, but there isn't one. The doors of the cells are being locked for the night.

When the guard approaches, she summons her strength. "We need a bucket," she says.

The guard says, "I got strict instructions, nothing more for you girls till you've paid your debt to Sam."

The room is spinning. "Well! Then by all means, take me to him and I'll make the arrangements. Let's get that bucket."

The guard takes her back to Sam's office.

"Miss Tennie C!" Sam crows. "Ready to get your kit off?"

"Look, Sam. My sister's very ill. We'll need some Fowler's Solution first. And Sam, for mercy's sake. We need a slop bucket."

"Hmmm. Take this to the Lady President." He hands the guard a bucket. "And you. Let's see those tits."

"Fowler's."

"You're in no position to negotiate, bitch."

Must she beg or does she demand? Her heart is beating so, she can't tell the difference. Everything is spinning, like Chicago was before Blood had rescued her. Tennessee feels herself fainting, when the room is suddenly infused with color. Her spirit begins to leave her body and she says, "Come on, Sam, I'll let you do more than see them."

Sam narrows his eyes and waits.

She opens her coat. "Fowler's Solution, please." She undoes the hooks of her blouse. "A whole bottle, Sam." One breast is revealed, pink and white with no sign of the lesions which drive her mad to the point of tears, nor the nights she spends wrapped in her mother's smelly liniment and muslin. He hands Tennessee the bottle. It is full. She drinks from it. Her throat catches on fire and her stomach turns inside out. She puts the bottle in her coat pocket.

"Get out the other one," Sam says gruffly. "Come on, you cunt."

The damp of the prison has opened the cracks in her hands and fingers but as she faces him, her breasts pulled forward with her arms at her sides, she closes her eyes and sees Utica's spirit. She is humming Bach and the air smells of late autumn. Utica begins singing, and suddenly they are in a field filled with sunshine.

Overcome by the softness under his touch, something like shame washes over Sam. He chokes on a sob then withdraws, pulling her blouse back around her. He rehooks the fastenings himself. His hands are trembling and his trousers damp. He has been reminded of another time, so long ago, it is difficult to recall whether it was real or no more than a dream.

———

Bennett hires a private railcar as far as Chattanooga, then takes a stage-coach the rest of the journey. Fluids, his father used to laugh. Bodily fluids and the four humors. He had often warned Bennett, Jimmy, beware your fluids don't interfere with your humors! Well, he has allowed too many fluids with all and sundry. And yet, Tennessee never attempted to take anything from him ever. She had simply become closer.

The stagecoach pulls up to a battle-scarred mansion at the end of a long driveway. The furnishings are spartan. Bennett studies the aged landlord and his wife, who serve the evening meal. He has brought several cases of exceptional claret with him and is pleased to offer them to the couple.

Dinner is a pork stew followed by peach compote, which makes perfect sense, given that the host and his wife are both toothless. He wishes he had brought some of that excellent bread served on the train as well. Bennett says nothing to the other five men at the table. Food, wine, speed, sex.

In his room is a monk's robe he's been instructed to wear for the evening's commencement. Bennett checks his timepiece. He goes upstairs, puts on the robe, and leans back on the bed for a moment's rest.

In his dream, a magician places three cups upside down upon the table in front of him. Then, he takes a stone, no larger than a penny, golden colored and smooth, and places it in his mouth. Bennett is very young, just a small boy. Is it him or is it his brother, Cosmo? That's who it is. It's Cosmo. The magician smiles and opens his mouth. There is nothing inside, nothing up his sleeves. Bennett realizes Cosmo is sitting on his lap. The magician waves his hands, and presto! He is Tennessee Claflin's elderly father, and she is sitting beside them, laughing and clapping in pleasure. She whispers to Cosmo, "Clap two times," which the little boy does, and the old man reaches up and pulls the stone from Cosmo's ear. Cosmo cheers, then leans over to whisper something to Bennett.

The knock on the door is insistent. "Mr. Bennett! They cannot start without you."

———

"You were once great friends with Mr. Challis, were you not, Miss Claflin?"

"Indeed, I was."

"You were certainly great enough friends that you would feel comfortable asking him for two hundred dollars, would you not?"

"If you're referring to a solicitation letter, those were sent to any number of wealthy persons with whom we associated. We were raising money to pay for a speaking venue, which as you know, can be very expensive."

"You were not blackmailing him then?"

"With that letter? No. We were no longer friends, but far be it from me to blush when asking for donations from anyone."

"Thank you, Miss Claflin." Her attorney bows to the opposition's table. "Your witness."

Challis's attorney approaches her. "Hell hath no fury like a woman scorned. Is that what happened to you, Miss Claflin? Did Mr. Challis scorn you? Rebuff you in some way so that you saw fit to smear his name and destroy his reputation?"

"The events reported in my article actually occurred. They were true in fact and fair in comment. Nothing false or embellished in any way."

"Objection!"

"Overruled."

———

There are only six participants at the Brotherhood of Eulis convocation. Himself, Billy Vanderbilt's son Cornelius III, Thomas Carnegie, and a couple of other fellows Bennett doesn't know from Adam. Then there is the black man. Bennett knows he looks familiar but is distressed when he cannot place him. Randolph, Randolph. It is three quarters into the first night that he realizes it is Dr. Paschal Beverly Randolph, whom Tennessee had been so eager for him to entertain that night last autumn. Oh God, he thinks. He wonders if it was Randolph who had given her the pox. The Treat pamphlet making the rounds certainly implied— he does not allow himself to complete the thought.

Randolph, the wizard, gazes at Bennett with contempt. Suddenly it is impossible to hear the words being said and Bennett has no doubt. The blood begins roaring between his ears. That swine fucked his girl, ruining her health and her reputation. Bennett is decided. He'll challenge Randolph to a duel and then he's going to kill him.

———

From the unpublished memoir of P.B. Randolph:

The others returned to the house. I spoke first. "I have never known Tennessee Claflin in that way." The redheaded fool just stood there, so I added, "But I very much wonder what good turn you did her by bedding her yourself?"

Having spent a lifetime at the mercy of such rich, shallow bigots for no reason other than their moneyed whiteness, suddenly overcame me. It was time for retribution. "So now she must contend with not only the Challis prosecution but is in turn libeled herself. Did you, Mr. Bennett, call her your whore?"

"God damn you, you son of a bitch!" Bennett went to thrust his hands around my throat. "Don't utter her name in my presence."

Eluding his reach, I extended my arm. Hot energy sparked around us.

"Tennessee Claflin!" My voice rang out. "In the name of Tennessee Claflin, I curse you to a life of loneliness wherein you will lose the only love worthy of the name! I curse you."

———

The court breaks for lunch. In the holding room, their attorney says, "Well, I can't get you out."

No one else speaks. Colonel Blood eats his meal with intense concentration. Victoria pushes her plate in his direction, which he accepts. Tennessee leans back and closes her eyes. The flutters have stopped. There is only stillness.

Victoria meets the gaze of Challis's attorney from the witness stand. He says, "In your opinion, Mrs. Woodhull, should a woman desert her husband and live with another man, if prompted by such a desire?"

"If her will takes her away from a man, she surely ought to go," is her response. "I hold that any man or woman, whether married or unmarried, who consorts for anything but love, is a prostitute."

It is their third night. The cell is so cold, one can see one's breath. Tennessee gives Victoria the last of the Fowler's, then removes her coat to examine a new lesion. Watching her do this, Victoria asks, "When were you going to tell me?"

Tennessee puts her coat back on. "I had thought I would be in Toledo and it wouldn't matter one way or the other."

Victoria shakes her head. "How could you do this? Has it not occurred to you what would happen to a child you gave birth to?"

"What?" She is suddenly disgusted by Victoria's righteousness, so justified in everything she says. After what feels like an eternity, she answers, "It just happened, Vicky. There was some discussion about love, if I recall. Sometimes things just happen."

Victoria cries out, "But how could you be so selfish? With your disease you've condemned this child to a life of suffering, or disfigurement, or like Byron, unable to care for himself."

"Stop it!" Tennessee sits on the cot and pulls her knees up to her chest. "Stop it. O my God. Just stop." She rocks back and forth. Please, she thinks, let the baby be all right. Please. There is a roar, then a pounding, and her legs are covered in water. Moaning, she goes on all fours. "Vicky. Please. It's too soon, it's too soon."

Victoria puts a hand on her back. Its warmth calms Tennessee for a moment.

Victoria says, "Deep breaths. Stay like this. I will get help."

"Yes," she gasps. Another contraction pulls as if to rip her in half.

"Help! Help!" Victoria shouts. Cat whistles and shouting break out along the corridor.

"Quiet!"

"Help. Oh my God, please help us," Tennessee groans.

A lantern makes its way down the corridor. Sam shouts. "Enough of this claptrap!"

"Please, we need help."

He raises his lamp and looks in the cell, then turns on his heel and leaves.

"Please! Come back." Victoria takes off her coat. Minutes pass. She has Tennessee lie on her back. She puts the coat under her to use as a pillow, then places Tennessee's coat over her like a blanket. A contraction tears through Tennessee stronger than the first one.

An hour passes. Something seems very wrong. "Oh no, oh no." She grabs Victoria's wrist. "I was in love with him. Now we don't speak."

She is caught in another contraction when Sam reappears. He lets himself into the cell with two buckets, one filled with water, the other with rags. He kneels at the foot of the bed. Seeing the buckets, Tennessee recoils and cries out, "Oh no."

"It's for the best," Victoria whispers. "On your feet. You have to stand, dearest."

"No. No. Please, Vicky." Tennessee knows what comes next. She struggles but is too weak to resist as Sam and Victoria drag her to stand over the bucket of water. They hold her up.

"No, no, please. Don't do this."

"We have no choice, Tennie," Victoria's voice is trembling.

"No, I beg you," she pleads. "Please no. Please." Victoria is the very face of love, so how can this be happening?

Blood and water pour down her legs. Sam cuts the cord. Tennessee sobs and collapses onto the cot.

The perfect body is no bigger than Sam's hand. He gives it to Victoria. The baby's arm reaches up. Trembling, Victoria places the tip of her little finger in the palm of its hand. She realizes she is weeping, because all that is left is Tennessee's illness, Byron's condition, the scandal, the papers, suffering, regrets, and unspeakable shame. For a moment, the tiny fingers close around her pinky, then slowly let go.

"Oh God forgive me," Victoria whispers. "I baptize you in the name of the Lord." She places the infant under the water in the bucket. She holds him there until he is completely still. Softly, she adds, "Amen."

Sam wraps the body in an improvised shroud. Victoria bends over Tennessee and says, "It was a little boy. He is in heaven with the angels, dearest."

Tennessee murmurs, "I should see him." Sam places him on her chest. Tennessee pushes the shroud covering the baby away. She places one hand on the back of his head and strokes the tiny hands and feet with the other. They are like ice.

Sam whispers, "Eternal rest grant unto him, O Lord, and let perpetual light shine upon him. From the gates of Hell, deliver his soul, O Lord. May he rest in Peace. Amen."

Victoria murmurs, "O Lord, hear our prayer."

Sam prays with her in unison, "And let our cry come unto Thee."

Tennessee takes a deep breath. As she exhales, the tiny rib cage grows warm. She feels it expand and contract. Then, with a sigh, her child's spirit leaves his body and joins the others who've gone before him.

———

Sam gives Victoria a draught of morphine for her sister. Word is sent to their attorney that Tennessee is unwell, and Roxana is permitted to visit. Tennessee lies on the cot while her sister and mother kneel on the wet floor, praying feverishly.

Afterward, Victoria claims the cell was suddenly filled with light, and the voice of Jesus said, "Stay thy hand, my child. All these things are committed to my charge. In the fullness of time all hidden things shall be revealed, and you shall be justified where now you stand condemned. Wait!"

When asked, Tennessee says she must have been asleep at the time. She does not explain Sam's continued generosity with the morphine made her eyelids heavy nor that she cannot block what happened from her mind.

———

> "If a woman be delivered over a pail of water and the child dropped into the water, no one can say whether or not the child has been willfully destroyed."
>
> -From "Illegitimacy," by
> Tennessee Claflin Cook, 1890

———

"Gentlemen of the jury, have you reached a verdict?"

The foreman of the jury stands. "We have your honor." He looks at the defendants and then at the judge. "Not guilty."

There is a gasp, then cheering and thunderous applause. The judge pounds his gavel, and everyone ignores him. In the chaos, Tennessee realizes she is sobbing while Victoria hugs her and is sobbing, too, begging her forgiveness for all the times she had neglected her, crying she wanted to protect her from shame and from scandal...if she hadn't gone to get the Fowler's...indeed, if they hadn't gone back to the Tombs.

<hr/>

Docteur Hardy at l'Hôpital St. Louis is a leading authority on skin disease. He examines every crease and cranny of James Gordon Bennett's person, then has the younger man dress and join him in the adjoining office. "From all appearances, Monsieur, you are in excellent health. Is it possible the lady in question has been misdiagnosed?"

"I cannot answer for her. She hails from the middle part of our country, some parts of which are, uh, as yet, unsophisticated."

"Monsieur Bennett, without making a thorough examination of her myself, my interpretation of your health remains equivocal. We need both sides of the coin, Monsieur. However, for myself, I suspect she was misdiagnosed and that you are indeed at the peak of your physical powers. I might add Docteur Phillips was most prescient in supplying you with the sheaths. By all accounts, their efficacy is considered excellent."

After Jennie Jerome's wedding, Bennett stumbles home at four in the morning, naked as a blue jay, having raced his favorite horse through the Bois de Boulogne, leaving his clothes where he couldn't quite recall. The whole affair has given him a terrific headache. The only way to clear his head is to exile himself to the safety of *Dauntless*. But first he wants to contact Tennessee. She deserves to know. Better yet, he should arrange for her to see Dr. Hardy.

<hr/>

Tennessee crumples the unopened telegram in her hand. She has not told him nor is she about to do so. He behaved abominably and now that it is all over there is no point in revisiting the past. She knows that unless she is making headlines, he'll have little reason to contact her at this point. It has all been for naught. She lifts the burner on top of the stove and tosses the telegram inside.

TO WOMEN WHO HAVE AN
INTEREST IN HUMANITY

July 1874
East Tenth Street

FROM THE JOURNAL of Tennie C. Claflin:

Victoria now writes a great deal about Jesus' visit to the Tombs. Still, many subscriptions to the Weekly have been canceled. How ironic then that her bookings for lectures have increased tenfold. Which is bully for Dr. Treat, because like a bad penny, his pamphlet is sold everywhere she is booked. One can't help but wonder whether Dr. Treat does not enjoy the patronage of an enthusiastic printer. Someone from Brooklyn Plymouth Church or Hartford, Connecticut, perhaps in the person of Harriet Beecher Stowe? I wouldn't put it past her. But I do not have the will to raise this theory, particularly as the Colonel insists that we ignore the pamphlet, and not dignify it with a response. It is incomprehensible how he insists we soldier on as if we haven't been accused of the most salacious and wanton of promiscuities, and that my blood doesn't curdle when that wretched libel is sold outside every venue where Victoria is scheduled to speak.

The Claflins' new lodging is a ground-floor apartment on East Tenth Street. The kitchen and dining room look out onto a walled garden filled with roses, a shade tree, and a small shed in which one might keep some chickens or a goat.

Roxana removes the muslin strips from Tennessee's back and then reapplies the liniment. "You must have understanding for your poor sister, Tennie. She confuses every person's anguish with her own. It makes things very difficult for everyone, no?"

Tennessee eases herself into the copper tub. The door to the garden is open and she looks at the roses.

There is a knock at the front door on the street side, and Zula goes to answer it. The iceman tilts his hat. Zula runs back into the kitchen to fetch the tray they use for ice. When Roxana sees this, she comes out, saying, "No thank you, we haven't the funds for a second delivery."

"This is a gift, ma'am, courtesy of the *New York Herald*."

"The *New York Herald*!" Zula chirps. The man places the ice block in the tray Zula holds and Roxana watches him do the same again at the house next door.

When Tennessee emerges from her soak, Roxana says, "Why don't you make us some of that nice iced tea I like so well?"

"We finished the ice. We won't have more till Tuesday, Ma."

"Look in the ice chest."

Tennessee sees the five-pound block. "What's this?"

"From the *New York Herald*, Tennie."

"Oh. Well. I'll make you that tea, shall I?"

The next afternoon, the iceman knocks on the door, once again, courtesy of the *New York Herald*. Roxana watches to see where he makes his next stop. But he doesn't make another stop. Not the next day, or the one after that. But the ice keeps coming. Every afternoon. The following week, Zula hands Tennessee a note and waits for her to open it. The stationary is unmistakable. 425 Fifth Avenue.

> *Please see this learned man at your earliest opportunity.*
> *Docteur Alfred Hardy, Maladies de la Peau, Hopital St.*
> *Louis PARIS*

Lest you be tempted to put it off, enclosed are tickets (cour-
tesy of the Herald) for the venerable Claflin household. The
Lafayette sails August 8.- JGB.

August 1874
The Atlantic Ocean

From the journal of Tennie C. Claflin:

I wish I had not invited Victoria's latest conquest, a young man by the
name of Benjamin Tucker, to tag along on this voyage. But he speaks French
and Ma insisted it was the right thing to do. My father is not making the
journey with us, so our only chaperone is the Colonel, who is so preoccupied
with what he believes is our persecution by governmental forces, that I just
went along with it. On the second day of our crossing, I invited Benny to
play cards. He reacted with such a look of scandal that I couldn't resist invit-
ing him to share a bottle of whiskey the following night. This upset Victoria
no end, so last night, I then invited him to take a turn in the hay! Benny
is such a prude. I know I have done little but stoke the fires of my ruined
reputation. Ah well, a life of impropriety is my cross to bear. In a few days,
we will arrive at Brest, off the Breton coast, and from there it is but a cou-
ple days' train ride to Paris. Of course, the fare for the passage and this trip
are meant as a peace offering. After I see the doctor and perhaps even avail
myself of treatment, I will tell Bennett what happened. It wasn't his fault,
it just happened.

The doctor is very kind. He asks which medications she had been prescribed, and Tennessee discusses her mercury pills, the not infrequent
doses of Fowler's Solution, the occasional tincture of arsenic, the hashish,
and, most importantly, Roxana's squirrel fat and mugwort liniment.

"And still you have these infections, particularly on your mons, Mademoiselle. This is correct, no?"

Tennessee nods. The doctor examines the inside of her elbow where a breakout has healed, and on her side where another is beginning. "And the face?"

"Only once. My physician said it was impetigo."

"Mlle. Claflin, you have what is psoriasis of the skin. It is a lepra, no?"

Tennessee gasps. "I am a leper."

"No, no, this is an old word no longer used, to describe the nature of the—" He gently touches the lesion. "We now call this a plaque. And it is most painful, no?"

She nods. "Sometimes, sometimes I cannot get out of bed."

"Many people live with this condition. It appears it was an unhappy coincidence that your first outbreak was after relations with your husband. Perhaps brought on by some distress."

Roxana is in the waiting room on the other side of the door. Tennessee dresses and sits opposite the physician. "Doctor Hardy."

"Yes, Mlle. Claflin."

"There was a child. Would it have, would the child have been?" The doctor puts down his pen and looks at the beautiful young woman. He answers very gently.

"It would have been the same as any other child, Mlle. Claflin. Just the same."

Tennessee and Roxana walk down the boulevard in silence. Paris is Bennett's town, where he exiles himself when life in New York overwhelms him. At the steps of the hotel, Roxana says, "Forgive your sister, Tennie. She loves you as much as life itself."

That evening, Tennessee knocks on Victoria's door and lets herself in. Victoria is kneeling on the floor, praying, a rosary in her hands.

Tennessee says, "I saw the doctor. I do not have the French disease. What I have is something else. It is not contagious. He said that the baby…The doctor said the baby was the same. Most likely the same as any other."

Victoria whispers, "Your baby is in Heaven now."

Tennessee does not look away, but there is nothing else to say.

The next morning, she speaks with the concierge and writes a telegram to Bennett.

IT IS NOT AS I THOUGHT NOR IS IT CATCHING
BUT SOMETHING ALTOGETHER
DIFFERENT THANK HEAVEN

The concierge hands the telegram form over to the new office boy. When the boy sees that it is in English, he decides he'll get someone else to take care of it after lunch.

But during lunch, he enjoys a flirtation with the barkeeper's daughter and forgets about the telegram in his pocket until long after he's returned home. He looks in his pockets, but the form is gone. The boy shrugs, knowing if it's important, the guest will send another one.

When she returns to New York, Tennessee goes uptown to a newly opened Foundling Hospital on Sixty-Eighth Street. The infants there have been left by women who, for whatever reason, could not keep them. In the hospital's office, a nun shows Tennessee the ledger, inside of which are notes that had been pinned to the babies' garments.

"Look at these," she says. "They are the only hints we have of where the children come from." On each page, a note is pasted next to the date a child was received.

"Guard this little one and if things turn out as I hope I shall repay you for your trouble."

Tennessee turns the page.

"I am a poor woman and have been deceived under the promise of marriage. I am without means and without

relatives to nurse my baby. Therefore I beg you for God's sake to take my child and keep it. I remain your humble servant."

"Sometimes we think we don't have much to give," the nun in the nursery says, "but all they ask for is tenderness." She gives Tennessee the statistics. "For every legitimate birth, there are four born out of wedlock. Of those four, only one might live to see a year."

Tennessee plays with and bathes the young survivors and thinks about the ones who did not make it to the orphanage.

Before her visit ends, a little boy, he is no more than ten months old, reaches up and holds her face, as tiny children sometimes do. He gazes deeply at Tennessee and then places his head upon her shoulder. She breathes in the scent of his freshly washed neck. She closes her eyes and tries to stop seeing what happened at the Tombs.

Later she sits by the fire at Tenth Street and slowly rips the pages of her journals from their bindings and feeds them to the flames.

In the years before the War, Buck had owned a grist mill. It was powered by the creek next to their property, and Tennessee watched him disassemble the faulty blades which caught the water that drove the mechanism.

"I'm not an idea man," Buck would say. "But I figure things out. I think of possibilities, and with this here mill," Buck declared, "we will never starve."

But then the creek dried up, and a blight followed. She was seven years old and there were locusts everywhere. On the table, in the larder, on the backs of the chairs. *The Cultivator* magazine had prescribed kerosene as the only effective means to eradicate them. Tennessee had laughed, scooping them up in her hands, pushing them into her skirt, then running outside to set them free.

"Put them here, Tennie, put them here." Buck had stood near a small fire, shouting, "Lord God Almighty! Remove Your pestilential blight from this our dwelling!" He scattered kerosene, making the flames leap higher as the insects screamed and crackled.

"Don't stand so close. Step back, Tennessee." She watched Buck study a letter he took from his pocket, only to crumple the paper into a ball. Smiling at her, he tossed it into the fire.

"Always burn the correspondence, Tennie. Leave no tracks if you can help it. That way, you make your own bed, and not the one dictated to you by others. Now let's get those crickets."

"Pa," she asked, "don't Leviticus say, 'Even these of them ye may eat? The locust and the bald locust and the beetle,' sir, 'and the grasshopper after his kind?'"

"Yes, but when folks come for their readings, chirping bugs in their hair and hats don't make for good business."

"No, I guess it don't. Goodbye little critters. Crick-crick, crick!" She threw the last handful from her skirt into the flames. "Greet all children in heaven, now!"

The last of her journals burn until they are only glowing embers. She reaches for her writing tablet and writes "ILLEGITIMACY" across the top, but then crosses it out and thinks about *Uncle Tom's Cabin*. She had loved that book. How wise it had been. She writes a favorite observation from it onto her tablet:

> *Of course, in a novel, people's hearts break, and they die, and that is the end of it; and in a story, this is very convenient. But in real life we do not die when all that makes life bright dies to us.*

Would life have turned out differently had they never met nor offended Mrs. Stowe? She tears the sheet of paper from the tablet and throws it, like her journals, into the flames.

George Blood is five years younger than the Colonel. While everyone else was in France, George worked on the paper, played chess with the aged Buck, and cared for twenty-year-old Byron. The trip to Europe has done much to soothe the tensions created by Dr. Treat's pamphlet, but now that they have returned, George recommends Victoria resume touring as quickly as possible. To that end he books several speaking engagements out West.

By the time they leave for California, Tennessee knows she will not be hearing from James Gordon Bennett.

Following an exchange of telegrams, Dr. Hardy informs Bennett that Miss Claflin does not suffer from scars of Venus. Other than that, no further information is forthcoming. For his part, Bennett haunts the Central Park Zoo, not three blocks from the Foundling Hospital, staring at the lions' cages, wondering how on earth it went so wrong. He studies a pair of elephants and a rhinoceros. He looks at the monkeys and spends time with the seals. He sits opposite the bear.

Bennett watches the zookeepers do their rounds. They appear to have little interest in the creatures behind bars and he recalls Tennessee's roar. "Have you ever thought about that?" she had asked, dressed like a boy with her lavender gloves. "Well, I have, I can tell you, Bennett."

Delighted with the prank, the staff at the *Herald* are easily sworn to secrecy.

"Who, who," Bennett thinks, watching the issue go to press. "Miss Tennessee, this is for you."

A SHOCKING SABBATH CARNIVAL OF DEATH Savage Brutes at Large-Awful Combats between the Beasts and the Citizens - Bravery and Panic - How the Catastrophe Was Brought About - Proclamation by the Mayor - Gov. Dix Shoots the Bengal Tiger in the Street

Sales of the "Central Park Zoo Hoax" issue break newsstand records. Its audacity and genius is remarked upon for decades to come, long after the *New York Herald* ceases to exist. Indeed, the Central Park Zoo Hoax becomes one for the books.

But Tennessee's deafening silence forces Bennett to concede that she does not want to hear from him. So, he decides to give her back her space and just get on with it.

He does not know that Tennessee and Victoria are being inundated by Dr. Treat's pamphlet (now updated and revised) at every venue where Victoria is scheduled to speak. If he did, he might not have taken Tennessee's silence so much to heart. However, Bennett does not know. Like Colonel Blood, he mistakenly believes that nonsense is behind them.

Alas, Dr. Treat's pamphlet continues to smear their reputations, at what will be left of their very long lives.

SCARECROWS OF SEXUAL SLAVERY

July 1875

SUBJECTS OF ARTICLES, subjects of gossip, people one passes judgment upon, couples who seem ill-suited, girls who are plain, men who are weak—rarely do those who scrutinize others exercise the discernment of leaving well enough alone.

As a result of Victoria's exposing Theodore Tilton's unhappy domestic arrangement, Tilton sues Henry Ward Beecher for the illegal alienation of Mrs. Tilton's affection. Tilton's wife, Elizabeth had confessed to their affair, and then, at Beecher's insistence, retracted her confession. But at trial, she retracts her retraction of the confession, and then she retracts it again. This creates a havoc from which there is no recovering.

The case has raged on in court since January. It is considered the trial of the century.

When Victoria gives her testimony, she does so heavily veiled with what correspondence she still possesses in a Russian leather satchel.

"These are all I have left," she says, giving the letters to the judge. "I believe that both the defense and the prosecution helped themselves to whatever they could during my second incarceration. As you know, my offices were ransacked at that time."

Victoria Woodhull and Colonel Blood seek damages from the federal government for the illegal seizure and destruction of their property at their offices on Broad Street. They estimate the damages incurred at roughly half a million dollars but would be content to settle for twenty percent that amount. The government denies their request.

Tennessee takes the sleeper car to Toledo at the end of July. It arrives after eleven the next morning. It is noon before she finds a cab driver who will agree to take her to the edge of the city. They get to the house toward one. The driver does not want to wait, so she waves him off and approaches the steps. The door is ajar. She knocks before calling out, "Paschal? Hello?"

Inside, the hallway is dark. In a room off the parlor, a baby sits in his crib crying.

"Where's your mamma? Where's your papa, baby?" The room leads to a back porch. Tennessee hears the sound of a chair rocking. She walks past the crib to the porch. Paschal's wife Kate faces her, but stares unseeing, as if in a trance. The rocking chair moves back and forth, back and forth.

"Mrs. Randolph. I am Tennie C. Claflin."

The young woman stops rocking and looks up at her. "Is that a fact?"

Tennessee realizes Mrs. Randolph's face has the yellow markings of an old bruise. She dares not ask how it came to be.

"I've come to see your husband. Is Dr. Randolph expected soon?"

Mrs. Randolph shakes her head and closes her eyes. The baby's wails are intolerable. "Mrs. Randolph."

"He's dead. Paschal is dead." She opens her eyes and says, "You should go now. If people see you here, I am sure they'll think the worst. Of his being with you."

Words will not form themselves in Tennessee's mouth. "I…I am so sorry."

"He told me of his feelings for you. You were hardly a friend. If you'd been a true friend, you would have come in time. He would still be alive."

The baby will not stop screaming. Hands trembling, Tennessee removes all but two dollars from her purse. She kneels down and puts the money in Mrs. Randolph's lap. "To help with the funeral. I am so sorry."

———~~———

Outside, the heat from the sun is merciless. Tennessee walks back in the direction of the station. Arriving there, she makes enquiries for the next train east and buys the noon edition of the local paper. The clerk recommends she take a cup of tea in the station restaurant.

Tennessee is shown to a table. The tiles of the floor feel cool underfoot. She takes out the mirrored shard from her pocket and looks at the newspaper.

The headlines seem innocent enough. She opens the first page, and the sorrow of missing him and of realizing the truth of Kate Randolph's observation cause her to flush and sway in her chair. A waiter races over and asks, "Is everything all right, Miss?"

To which she can only nod and mutter, "Thank you, I am fine." Tennessee forces herself to read as the tears begin to fall on the page.

BY HIS OWN HAND
DEATH OF A WELL-KNOWN SPIRITUALISTIC AUTHOR BY SUICIDE-
DR. P.B. RANDOLPH TAKES HIS OWN LIFE THIS
MORNING AT A LITTLE AFTER EIGHT O'CLOCK

"Well, goodbye. In less than two hours I shall be a dead man. I'm going to shoot myself." Mrs. Worden told him that he wouldn't do a thing of that kind, but he replied: "Yes, I will... I want you two to witness the deed, and then you can testify. I leave all my property to my son. You will be witness to that, and testify that I said so, when they call upon you after I'm dead, and that won't be a long time, either." While making these remarks he was standing within fifteen feet of Mrs. Worden, who was so badly frightened at the way he was talking that she turned to go in the house. Just then she heard the report of a revolver, and turning she saw Randolph fall in his tracks...

It is most generally conceded that jealousy was the main cause. Randolph was part Spaniard and inherited all the suspicious distrusting qualities of the people of that nationality.

She knows he wasn't Spaniard. Why would he say so?

For some time, he has imagined that his wife has been untrue to him, and from brooding over his imagined injuries he became morose, overbearing, and tyrannical, and began to drink heavily. While in these fits he would treat his wife very badly and threatened several times to kill their little baby boy, which he claimed was not his; but when sober, he was generally a kind husband and father. For the past week he has been drinking worse than ever...Yesterday... his wife went to her mother's house...

This morning he arose and went to look for his wife, and not finding her became furious. Then he went out, took several drinks, and returned to Mrs. Worden's house where he committed the deed in the manner already described.

Dr. Paschal Beverly Randolph was 49 years old.

———

At the apartment on Tenth Street, Tennessee goes to her room and lies down. That disastrous night outside 425 Fifth Avenue she had scolded him, "How could you behave like that toward someone you want as patron?"

"That arrogant fool, so powerful with his silly-ass paper! The only reason he is with you, Tennie, is because he lusts after you and he is waiting for you to one day relent."

Tennessee had stopped at that point and declared, "I have relented. Besides, that's not true. He is my friend. And I lust after him, too."

"But I love you. I LOVE YOU. It does not matter what you say or do. I love you for everything that you are and even the things you are not."

He'd been so drunk, she had not bothered to respond, "But you are married."

"Evidently, you are too involved with your suffrage and crusades to comprehend this." Randolph added, "Ha!" then shook his head. "All we can do is try if we are to be happy in this world." And then he fell and broke his arm.

Tennessee stares at the ceiling in her room. She gets up and rummages through a box under the bed filled with old copies of the *Weekly*. There it is. They had run it not four weeks before the evening with Bennett. Sitting on the floor, she reads the poem.

LOVE

She said, "You offer me love- but what kind- ah, what kind?" And he answered, "Love, all truly human." – From "Zuleika," *A Tragedy,* by P. B. Randolph.

I will love thee as the spirits love,
Who, free of earth and heaven
Wreathe white and pale-blue flowers
For the brows of the forgiven;
And are dear to one another
For the blessings they bestow
On the weary and the wasted,
In our wilderness of woe;
By thy good name with the angels,
And the human heart's evangels,
Shall my love from holy silence to thee go.

June 1876

The Spiritualists have kept *Woodhull & Claflin's Weekly* afloat. But they dislike Victoria's evangelism. Now, with the Spiritualists gone, the *Weekly* is finished for good.

Liquidators auction what office equipment is still in the newspaper's possession. Miss Swindell moves to Connecticut. Pearl Andrews is long retired, and George Blood goes to Maine. As for the Colonel, both he and Victoria know their life together is over.

No amount of political enlightenment or progressive sentiment can repair the injury from his sleeping with Utica. Roxana was right after all. The words "Free Love" have left such a bitter taste in Victoria's mouth.

Colonel Blood is served his divorce papers. The charge is for adultery. But in truth, it is for not pursuing Dr. Treat. All might have played out differently had he challenged Treat to a duel. But Blood did not. By the time he brings libel charges against Treat, it is too late.

When Victoria and Tennessee accompany Buck and Zula to the Centennial Exposition in Philadelphia, Victoria asks Blood to please remove his belongings from their lodging before her return. Stoically, he nods and then bows. Straightening back up, he goes to kiss her on the cheek, but she shrinks away and rushes out of the room. All that remains of their union are documents to be signed and notarized by lawyers. As quickly and completely as she became the center of his world, so is he now banished from hers.

———

The displays at the Exposition are endless, and the different foods sublime. Following a leisurely lunch, they walk past the massive hand and torch of Liberty Enlightening the World to behold the Corliss steam engine, the largest of its kind anywhere on Earth.

Buck gives a low whistle. "Girls, girls. Would you look at that? Now this is what I call a machine! You could grind enough grain to feed these entire United States with a machine like that! You might also power a locomotive and have enough horsepower to fuel a ship besides. My, my."

On the other side of the engine, the engineer shows a client around the massive disk crank. The gentleman is head and shoulders above his companions, and the lady on his arm is dressed in elegant Parisian style. James Gordon Bennett's fiancée is reported to be somewhat younger than he. From Tennessee's perspective, she certainly looks so.

Tennessee turns to Victoria. "I'll join you at the ice stand, shall I?"

Victoria recognizes Bennett's group across the platform. She takes Buck by the arm and says, "Pa, let's stroll a little this way. Zula, keep up." Zula stops staring at the woman in the spectacular hat and joins her mother and grandfather.

Bennett sees them from the platform. He cannot explain to his entourage what his association with Mrs. Woodhull and Miss Claflin might be. It is simply too complex.

The engineer says, "The next model will boast at least 825 horsepower, Mr. Bennett."

"Hmm?" Bennett and Tennessee's eyes meet, then he loses her in the crowd. He says to the engineer, "Now, that's a speed worthy of discussion!"

His fiancée nudges him in the ribs. "Jimmy, are you going to show us the talking device?"

He decides to bring Caroline and her parents to the telephone display so he might break away for a few minutes. But by the time he does so, the Claflins are on the train back to New York.

Victoria and Tennessee are silent during the journey. However, Zula found the afternoon riveting and compares notes with Buck. They are agreed. The Corliss steam engine was astonishing to behold.

For all the faiths and philosophers there are in the world, few believe in an intervening god. Those claiming to be spiritualists, nine hundred and ninety-nine times out of a thousand, are frauds. Yet there is that rare case, that one thousandth person... Paschal Beverly Randolph's widow and son will flourish. He had mistreated that lady, but she will make a robust living from what is left of his work. For his friend, Tennessee Claflin, his chance to influence events on her behalf presents itself from the other side, where he is astonished to learn he wasn't a fraud after all. Indeed, as he so often said, we must try if we are to be happy in this world.

The spirits refer to this as influencing. The religious hope it's divine intervention.

Everyone else calls it magic.

THE CREATION OF SOCIETY

December 1876
Madison Square Park

AFTER ITS DEBUT in Philadelphia, the hand and torch sent by the French now has pride of place in the northern end of Madison Square Park. Tennessee studies the sculpture, lost as she often is these days, in deep thought. She knows the Commodore is fading and she sends loving ideas of music to some part of him that might still commune with the spirits. The air is bitter from the previous day's snowfall, and the late afternoon sun turns pink. It begins to flurry again, as the snowflakes dance upward rather than down. She crosses the park to begin the walk home.

"Tennessee." James Gordon Bennett has appeared from almost nowhere.

"Mr. Bennett. Where is your—? Where are the dogs?"

"I saw you and told Dixon to take them home. May I walk with you?"

"By all means." They continue in silence, peaceable. They go no more than a couple of blocks before reaching the black sled which waits at the corner.

Bennett says, "Have you ever been to Kip's Bay?"

"I don't think so. What is there?"

"It isn't far. It is the perfect place for you to see."

Wordlessly, they ride uptown, and make a right over to the river. The houses thin out, and a few cattle stand in shadow against a golden sky.

She wants to slip her hand into his, and suddenly, it is so. His grip is so warm, it feels as though they have never been apart.

The sled stops at what appears to be a steep incline. Bennett gets out and disappears over the edge. She gasps, and he reappears. "No worries, there's a ladder here. It's quite safe." He climbs down the ladder and she follows him. "It's not a distance at all."

The city seems far away as clasping each other's hand, they march along the shoreline until they come upon a cove, surrounded by trees and rocks. Bennett finds some twigs and builds a small fire.

The flurries continue and the sky turns a brilliant vermillion, something like the color of joy. Gradually, Tennessee realizes they are in an aviary of sorts. Several owls watch them, patiently waiting for the humans to leave that they might resume their New Year's meditation.

"I waited to hear from you after you went to France, Tennie."

"I sent you a telegram."

"No. No you didn't."

This takes a moment to sink in. How is it the spirits have neglected to mention that? She whispers, "I didn't hear from you either."

"It's the common wisdom: Entanglements with a woman of your ilk come fraught with..." He thinks about the opal and diamond ring he has given to Caroline May.

"Complications, is that what you're trying to say?"

He doesn't answer.

"Besides," she adds, "I had already lost the baby."

Bennett's heart stands utterly still. "What?"

"In the Tombs."

"What?"

It is an eternity before she trusts herself to respond. She whispers, "You're like Miss Tennessee, aren't you? Who, who?"

"Tennessee."

It is so important not to scream. He really has no idea. "From our stay on Thirty-Eighth Street." She cannot look at him. "I was so afraid,

Bennett. Those French letters. Perhaps we didn't use them properly. I thought I may have given you…and then it appeared there was…and I just couldn't. Now, I don't know when I might. Oh, my goodness." She loosens her beaver coat. "It is so warm."

It is too late for Bennett to smash every foolish reason he has lied to himself. Now, he is with pretty Caroline. But it is this woman sitting next to him. She is the one who knows him.

"Please tell me."

"Oh, Bennett. It was a boy." She realizes he is still holding her hand.

"My darling girl."

She sees his face is wet with tears. After a moment, she says, "So, it turns out I do not have the pox. It is lepra psoriasis, not to be confused with leprosy, nor syphilis. It is not infectious. It comes, and it goes. Jack did indeed give me an infection, but your doctor said it was likely bacterial and burned itself out. Jimmy, we had a little boy."

Where her face was once round and pink and laughing, there is a shadow and sadness. They sit silently as the sky fades to night and the stars begin coming out. Tennessee can see the moon will be full.

She stands up. "It's time to go, Bennett. I imagine you've engagements tonight."

He nods and scatters snow and sand on to the fire. When they return to the sled, Dixon is stamping his feet against the cold. Tennessee slides in first, and Bennett joins her, bundling the furs across their knees to keep them warm. She leans against him and he wraps her in his arms. Presently, they pull up to Tenth Street.

Bennett walks her to the door. "Good night, Tennessee."

"Goodbye, Bennett."

They kiss a deep soft moment lamenting everything they have lost and will not have again. She goes inside, and Bennett goes directly to his club. It is time to do some drinking.

January 1877
425 Fifth Avenue

Leonard Jerome pours him into his sled at dawn. Bennett crawls up the steps, unable to walk. His valet and the housekeeper put him to bed. At eleven the next day, when he is awake, he calls for champagne. There are three invites to get through before the May reception. He needs to pull himself together before he sees Caroline May. The Mays are a kind, well-connected family. He knows the trousseau has arrived from Paris. Caroline is not unlike Tennessee had been, without the other dimension of course. But sweet and lively. Very spirited.

The first stop is at the Belmont home, where Bennett catches up with friends from the yacht club. Mrs. Belmont serves a rather lethal punch, of which he has, perhaps, a glass too many.

Leonard Jerome meets him at Henry Clewes's house whereupon they head straight to the library for absinthe chasers with their demitasse. Most invigorating.

By the time James Gordon Bennett arrives at the Mays, the only way to find which door is the actual one is to employ his latest squint technique. It makes him appear as though he wears a monocle, but without the monocle.

There is a flight of stairs up to the reception rooms. The butler asks, "Are you all right, Mr. Bennett?"

In response, Bennett squints, unsure which is the actual butler.

The butler says, "May I take you to repose a moment, sir? Before going up?"

"Don't be ridiculous. I am a hundred percent!" he roars. "One hundred"— he starts to make his way up the stairs—"percent!"

At the top of the landing, Mrs. Morgan is with her sister, Miss Lawrence. Bennett waves in their direction. "Nice tits, girls! Keep up the good work!"

This so shocks Miss Lawrence that she bursts into tears.

Staggering into the reception, he surveys the room with his tightest squint. He sees his future in-laws, standing near his intended bride. Oh, God. isn't she lovely? Her mother is a tasty number too, really. Always good to see how the old nag ages, so the young filly can be vetted. As for that Mrs. Roxana Claflin…

Dr. May approaches him. "Jimmy, my boy. You look as though you've enjoyed rather too much cheer."

"No, no. Indeed, I am ready for more. All I need is a place to take a piss." There it was. Just like in the country. "Quelle bordelle, c'est quoi, ce machin, cette connerie!" He reaches for the mantel. Good thing it's nice and wide, so he won't make a mess. "Une minute, s'il vous plait." He opens his flies. Steady, aim. He lets it rip, just like a racehorse. "Ah. Happy New Year, everybody!"

There is a shout and much commotion. Bennett turns, member in hand, still pissing his mighty arc. He gets his future brother-in-law, Fred, on the trouser leg and boot. The next thing he knows, there are stars.

Leonard Jerome is a good friend. He sits quietly on a chair in the corner watching Bennett slowly open his eyes then quickly fill the chamber pot next to the bed.

Bennett croaks. "Was it that bad?"

"In my estimation? It was worse. Much, much worse."

"We're supposed to be doing nuptials within the fortnight."

"I imagine those plans have changed."

"Ah." Bennett puts a couple pillows behind his head. The dull ache after parting from Tennessee still smothers his chest. Damnit. "Just as well, really." It is just too awkward.

The housekeeper brings a steak for his eye. The dogs whine frantically, eager to get at it.

"No, little ones," Bennett groans. "If you keep squirming, I'm just going to puke."

Everyone at the Union Club has the decency to avoid any discussion about what transpired on New Year's Day. At least until Fredric May walks in. Seeing Bennett, he comes over to his chair. Bennett stands up.

The full extent of Fred May's rage catapults from his fist to Bennett's jaw. "Get outside. Sort this like a man, you swine."

Bennett reels backward from the blow then steadies himself. "Very well." He bows to his companions and pulls on his cuffs. Without speaking, they leave the room.

At the stairs, Fred grabs him by the scruff of his coat and throws him down to the landing. "You bastard! God damn you." He jumps on Bennett, punching him as hard as he might. They tumble down to the bottom of the stairs, burst the door open, and fall onto the pavement.

Bennett manages to pull Fred off him long enough to say, "Go on, Fred, just kill me. For Christ's sake."

Fred grabs Bennett by the head. "I will, so help me God. You humiliate my sister and shame my family. I will kill you!" He shoves Bennett's head to the ground.

Bennett realizes he is sobbing and laughing. "So, kill me! I won't ask your pardon. It's beyond pardoning, for God's sake, just do it, man!"

"You bastard, God damn you, I will!"

"Go on. Be a friend and just fucking kill me, won't you?"

Dixon and Fred May's driver separate the two men. It is agreed that a duel is in order. Fred's second will be in touch with the details. Dixon goes to help the limping Bennett into the sled. Bennett brushes him off and dabs at his mouth with his scarf. His blood has turned the snow to the blushing pink of a young girl's smile.

New York Herald, January 5, 1877
CORNELIUS VANDERBILT
Death of the Great Railroad King Yesterday Morning

SKETCH OF A BUSY LIFE How the Poor Boatman's Son Became
a Millionaire
Commodore Vanderbilt died yesterday morning at nine minutes to eleven
o'clock at his residence No. 10 Washington Place. Though well advanced in
years, he enjoyed comparative health and strength, far beyond the allotted
time of man...His extraordinary vitality was admitted, but the change for the
worse, though slowly and barely perceptible from day to day, was going on
steadily.

———

THE TRUE NORTHERNER, January 8, 1877

BENNETT REPORTED WOUNDED - NEW YORK- A report is current that
James Gordon Bennett and Frederick May fought a duel this morning near
Lake Champlain, Canada, and that Mr. Bennett was wounded.

NEW ORLEANS REPUBLICAN, January 8, 1877

SHOT IN THE BOWELS - NEW YORK -The following extra is issued here:
"It is reported in Wall Street that a private dispatch from Canada has been
received, announcing that a duel had been fought between Bennett and May
and that Bennett had been shot in the bowels."

THE MEMPHIS DAILY APPEAL, January 8, 1877

CONFLICTING RUMORS - NEW YORK, 3.15 p.m.-Rumor is many tongued
concerning the Bennett-May affair. One has it that Mr. Bennett was mortally
hurt, another that Mr. Bennett was only slightly wounded, and another that
Mr. Bennett was not injured at all. All attempts to authenticate any report have
proved futile, and the respective friends of Bennett and May claim to have no
positive information regarding the action of the principles.

THE SARATOGA TIMES, January 9, 1877

MAY DANGEROUSLY WOUNDED -BENNETT UNINJURED - PHILADELPHIA,
2.30 a.m. It is rumored around the city today that James Gordon Bennett and
Fred May had fought a duel, but the rumor did not state the place of meeting.
At the Union Club, when members were questioned, they said they had heard
the report, but could give no particulars, nor any reason why such rumors had
been started.

August 1877
10 Washington Square

The summer smell of New York is at its worst, with the manure and fuel and garbage in the streets. But the carriage's drapes are closed, and no one can see in. When the horses come to a stop, Tennessee pulls her black veil forward and descends. The Commodore's butler leads her up the marble stairs.

The years go by in such a flash, and one knows oneself as irrevocably changed, yet the Commodore's home has remained the same. She imagines her younger self, naked as a blue jay, save for her boots, approaching him and her life transformed forever.

She takes a deep breath and surveys the room. He is not there, although something of him lingers in the air. She imagines his spirit is most likely in the railroad car or, perhaps, at Saratoga.

William Vanderbilt clears his throat and says, "My sister is up in arms, as you might well imagine."

"I'm sure your father had his reasons."

"Her argument will be that your very presence proved his insanity, if not a rather pesky case of the pox."

The clock behind them strikes the quarter hour. She has never seen Cornelius much in William, but there he is. The shrewdness of the gaze.

"And you?" she asks.

"And me?"

"Would it have mattered, had you known, in the effort to further our acquaintance?"

He has noticed her jacket shines it is so worn. He wonders why she hasn't asked him for anything.

The painting Tennessee gave Cornelius leans against the wall, its back turned to face the room, lest it offend. She asks, "Mrs. Frank Vanderbilt does not object to my visiting?"

"On the contrary, but she is in Newport this month. So, the business at hand—"

"Billy, I shan't mince words. The Commodore invested $10,000 of my savings in '69, which I've yet to recoup."

Ah, he thinks, here we go. He raises his eyebrows and asked, "In '69?"

"Yes. Just after the *Icicle* race."

"But you have enjoyed extraordinarily robust returns Miss Claflin, have you not?"

"Indeed. However, that was a result of compounded interest, not the capital itself. Furthermore, after the summer of '71, I no longer drew upon the returns."

"I see."

William thinks the circles under her eyes are very dark. Her paleness resembles one of those Whistler studies in white. Something forlorn and otherworldly.

"Billy."

William meets her gaze.

"How do I make application for the return of my initial capital?"

"Miss Claflin, your initial capital will become a mere bagatelle in light of the arrangement I should like to propose to you. To you and Mrs. Woodhull, that is." He clasps his hands on the desk and leans forward. "What do you have in the way of letters?"

"I have none. Vicky has several. Mostly to do with bookkeeping. And your mother."

"My mother?"

"Cornelius was much concerned with the serenity of her spirit."

"My sister will make the claim that your services…"

"For your edification, Billy. It wasn't the pox. His trouble was with passing water. But you know that."

She can still look at a man in a way that no proper woman would ever dare. It is unnerving. He wants to aggress her and yet be held in her embrace. It is better he sort this business out as quickly as possible. He says, "Miss Claflin. Were you called upon to testify, the hearings would assume a character, which for my purposes, and undoubtedly, those of the Commodore's would not suit. Would not suit at all. Do you understand my meaning?"

"I do."

"Passage."

Tennessee remains still. William speaks again. "Passage to England."

"What should I do in England?"

"You would be, well, you should be..."

"I should be spirited away? Your siblings will receive a paltry fraction of your father's wealth and you maintain the lion's share?"

"I shall be very generous. To them and to you."

Tennessee does not answer.

He says, "You'll have the appropriate funds to set up your home and housekeeping for yourself and your sister and her children."

"And my parents?"

"Yes, and your parents."

"How much, William? How much do you estimate that should be, to set me up in England?"

It must be a number that guarantees she will never come back. Tennessee's gaze is unwavering. When she was his father's plaything, William wanted her for himself. Not only because she was his father's, but because she was vibrant and smiled in a way that acknowledged secrets one hid, even from one's self. Her lips are parted. He can't tell if she wants to speak or if he himself wants to kiss her.

"One hundred thousand will be in Lloyd's of London," William says. "It should set you up." But it is the Commodore who has spoken. Cornelius is there after all.

Softly, she repeats, "Yes. It should set me up."

Cornelius is there, in the chair by the window, his massive hands resting on his knees. Paschal stands behind him.

William says, "Do we have an understanding?"

Tennessee whispers, "Yes. Yes, you have an understanding." To which Paschal smiles broadly and then turns to look out the window.

William feels a strange movement of air behind him. "Miss Claflin, all we can do is try, if we are to be happy in this world." He swears he can smell his father's sandalwood soap. It is as if Cornelius were sitting there. Tennessee seems to shiver, and William realizes her eyes have filled with tears. Perhaps she's seen a ghost. It certainly feels as if there are spirits in the room with them. No wonder his father was a believer! William hands her an envelope, inside of which are several thousand dollars. "For incidentals. Until you reach London. Good day, Miss Claflin."

Staterooms in first class, steerage for two maids and a man servant for Byron. Tennessee remains in her cabin while everyone goes on deck as the steamer is towed out of the harbor. She removes her dress and slips on her Chinaman's robe. It is so hot. She can't seem to cool off. She thinks about melting ice on the back of her neck.

"You will do it," James Gordon Bennett had said. Then she told him that she loved him.

There is a knock on the door, and she calls out before opening it. "Yes?"

"Ice for Madame's cabin."

She opens the door, "Thank you."

A silver bucket, full of ice, the handles wrapped in tea towels. The steward bows to the man standing next to him. Bennett tips him and takes the bucket.

He looks as cool as the air that is rolling in from the sea. They are standing wonderfully close. She can almost feel his heartbeat.

He smiles at her. "Ah. Miss Claflin, I presume?"

THE END

AUTHOR'S NOTE
(INCLUDING PLOT SPOILERS AND
THE LIBERTIES TAKEN)

I WAS SITTING on a bus, reading Barbara Goldsmith's *Other Powers* when the extraordinary Claflin sisters came into my life. I have been in their thrall ever since. Tennessee and Victoria's political activism culminated with Victoria's candidacy for US President at a time when a woman could not vote nor hold elective office. That this pair of mavericks managed to charm and beguile and to fight, refusing to stay down when they were held down, was heroic. Which is not to say they weren't flawed. As spiritualists and healers, they were careful to cover their tracks, anticipating the day when they'd need to whitewash the evidence. Generous and charismatic one moment, filled with hubris the next, the official record on these two has been shrouded with inuendo and some accounts from their early days are so farfetched, one can only surmise what took place. Yet, for every ruse, there was an element of creative daring which had a quality that I recognized instantly. My mother, like Victoria and Tennessee was also a survivor and completely self invented.

There are different theories as to whether Victoria had an affair with Henry Ward Beecher. There is no evidence that Utica had an affair with Colonel Blood or Canning Woodhull. Any evidence that James Gordon Bennett and Tennessee were lovers has yet to come to light, but he did live just a few doors down on Thirty Eighth street. Two blocks further west, was Dr. Taylor's Swedish Movement Cure, where Harriet Beecher Stowe was both a client and enthusiastic participant in the seances held there.

In 1877, following his duel with Fredric May, Bennett exiled himself, first to Great Britain, then to France, only sporadically returning to America thereafter. Tennessee and Victoria left the United States that same year.

For the purposes of narrative, the masked Ball rape was conflated and simplified to feature only one girl as victim at the event itself. Seventeen years later, Luther Challis died in Kansas, alone and penniless.

Illustrations:

Looking South on Fifth Avenue from Brick Presbyterian Church, *Harper's Weekly* 1873
Tennie C. Claflin *William R. Howell Studio*, circa 1868
Mesmerism on Wall Street, *Punchinello*, April 1870
The *New York Evening Telegraph*, February 1870
Tennessee Claflin Alberti Lowe Collection, circa 1873
Tennie C. Claflin *Mathew Brady Studios,* Miriam and Ira D. Wallach Division of Art, Prints and Photographs: Print Collection, The New York Public Library circa 1874

Acknowledgements

To those who wore several hats, doing the heavy lifting, hand holding, proof reading, beta reading, and pooling funds through generous donations, thank you so very much.

Frederic Bender, David Brune, Julie Dvorak, Pamela Forbes, Amanda Garcia, Rebecca Guenther, Tom and Kristina Hayes, Phyllis Johnson, Floortje Jongkoen, Julie Laken Harnisher, Ragna Arny Larusdottir, Amy Lederman, Eva Lesko Natiello, Debra MacFarlane, Lisa Mandelblatt, Hayes McNeill, Fred and Alice Miller, Terry O'Brien, Charles Pringle,

Sue Ross, Jacqueline Roussety, Mark Strausman, Katya Thomas and Sarah Watson. Your generosity made this book possible. Thank you.

Judy Kessler heroically supported my efforts to improve the material. With the tactful discretion which is the mark of the very best, Nikki-Lee Birdsey, Nicole Bokat, Lillian Duggan, Karen Moore, Susan Squire, and Ann Leslie Tuttle helped me to do so.

When I first embarked on this journey, Gail Godwin challenged me with patience and love, gracefully enduring read after read of a manuscript that lurched back and forth, morphing from one thing to another. Thank you, Gail, for giving me the chops to believe in myself and to stick with it.

The inclusive, all 'round good vibes of the New Providence Writers Group helped keep this project alive. Thank you and I'll see you on Sunday.

Further reading about the Claflins and their world

Applegate, Debby. *The Most Famous Man in America: The Biography of Henry Ward Beecher.* New York: Doubleday, 2006

Braude, Ann. *Radical Spirits: Spiritualism and Women's Rights in Nineteenth Century America.* Bloomington, IN: Indiana University Press, 1989

Brands, H.W. *The Murder of Jim Fisk for the Love of Josie Mansfield.* New York: Anchor Books, 2011

Cook, Tennessee Claflin. *Constitutional Equality, A Right of Woman.* New York: Woodhull, Claflin & Co. 1871

—*The Life-History.* A prospectus for Lady Cook's memoirs (self-published) c. 1912

—*Lady Cook's Talks and Essays, Vol I - IV.* London: The Roxburghe Press, 1897

—*Illegitimacy.* London: London & County Printing Works, 1890

Cooper, George. *Lost Love, A true story of Passion, Murder, and Justice in Old New York.* New York: Pantheon Books, 1994

Deveney, John Patrick. *Paschal Beverly Randolph: A nineteenth Century Black American Spiritualist, Rosicrucian and Sex Magician.* Albany, NY: State University of New York Press, 1997

Frisken, Amanda. *Victoria Woodhull's Sexual Revolution: Political Theater and the Popular Press in Nineteenth-Century America.* Philadelphia: University of Pennsylvania Press, 2004

Gabriel, Mary. *Notorious Victoria: The Life of Victoria Woodhull, Uncensored.* Chapel Hill: Algonquin Books, 1998

Goldsmith, Barbara. *Other Powers: The Age of Suffrage, Spiritualism and the Scandalous Victoria Woodhull.* New York: Alfred A. Knopf, 1998

Gordon, John Steele. *The Scarlet Woman of Wall Street: Jay Gould, Jim Fisk, Cornelius Vanderbilt, the Erie Railway Wars and the birth of Wall Street.* New York: Weidenfeld & Nicholson, 1988

Hayden, Deborah. *POX: Genius, Madness and the History of Syphilis.* New York: Basic Books, 2003

Hedrick, Joan D. *Harriet Beecher Stowe, A Life.* New York: Oxford University Press, 1995

Jefferson, Sam. *Gordon Bennett and the First Yacht Race across the Atlantic.* London: Bloomsbury, 2016

MacPherson, Myra. *The Scarlet Sisters: Sex, Suffrage and Scandal in the Gilded Age.* New York: Twelve, Hachette Book Group, 2014

Marberry, M.M. *Vicky, A Biography of Victoria Woodhull.* New York: Funk & Wagnalls, 1967

Messer-Krus, Timothy. *The Yankee International. Marxism and The American Reform Tradition.* Chapel Hill: University of North Carolina Press, 1998

Murphy, Cait. *Scoundrels in Law: The trials of Howe & Hummel, Lawyers to the Gangsters, Cops, Starlets and Rakes who made the Gilded Age.* New York: Harper Collins, 2010

Nevins, Allan & Thomas, Milton Halsley, ed. *The Diary of George Templeton Strong: The Post War Years: 1865-1875.* New York: Macmillan, 1952

Quétel, Claude. *History of Syphilis*. Baltimore: Johns Hopkins University Press, 1990

Rovere, Richard H. *Howe & Hummel, Their True and Scandalous History*. New York: Farrar Strauss & Giroux, 1947

Sachs, Emanie. *The Terrible Siren*. New York: Harper & Brothers, 1928

Seitz, Don Carlos. *The James Gordon Bennetts Father and Son, Proprietors of the New York Herald*. Indianapolis: The Bobs-Merrill Company, 1928

Sherr, Lynn. *Failure is Impossible, Susan B. Anthony in Her Own Words*. New York: Random House, 1995

Stern, Madeleine B. *The Pantarch, A Biography of Stephen Pearl Andrews*. Austin: University of Texas Press, 1968

Stiles, TJ. *The First Tycoon: The Epic Life of Cornelius Vanderbilt*. New York: Alfred A. Knopf, 2009

Underhill, Lois Beachy. *The Woman who ran for President: The Many Lives of Victoria Woodhull*. New York: Penguin, 1995

White, Barbara A. *The Beecher Sisters*. New Haven: Yale University Press, 2003

Woodhull, Victoria & Claflin, Tennessee. *The Human Body, The Temple of God*. (self-published) London: 1890

Woodhull, Victoria. *Victoria Woodhull, Lady Eugenist*. Edited by Michael Perry. Seattle: Inkling Books, 2005

—*Selected Writings of Victoria Woodhull*. Edited by Cari M. Carpenter. Lincoln: University of Nebraska Press, 2010

—*The Victoria Woodhull Reader*. Edited by Madeleine B. Stern. Weston, MA: M& S Books, 1974

Websites:

www.chroniclingamerica.loc.gov Library of Congress Historic American Newspapers www.woodhullrising.org The Robbins Hunter Museum in Ohio is dedicated to "inspire interest in Victoria Woodhull and her place in history"

www.iapsop.com the International Association for the Preservation of Spiritualist and Occult Periodicals

www.victoria-woodhull.com historical research and analysis provided by a descendant of Colonel Blood's extended family

ehbritten.blogspot.com Chasing Down Emma – Resolving the contradictions of, and filling in the gaps in, the life, work and world of (spiritualist) Emma Hardinge Britten

FOR BOOK GROUP DISCUSSIONS

1. Free Love and the complications that ensue….

   Victoria believed that Free Love was a way of saying that sexual rights are human rights. However, the term was used to encompass everything from communal marriage to a woman's right to divorce-and her right to refuse sexual congress in the marriage bed (which was also Victoria's definition of free love).

   But because a woman was considered (or more bluntly put, monetized as) her husband's property, *she had no rights because she was his property.*

   However Victoria's discussion of sex and sexuality was so charged (on page 203) "Yes I am a Free Lover, I have an inalienable, constitutional and natural right to love whom I may…and to change that love every day, and neither you, nor any law you can frame have any right to interfere." That the women's movement sidestepped sexual rights altogether.

   Why do you suppose that they decided to only pursue suffrage and chose not to address this issue?

2. Which brings us to Susan B. Anthony. Were her actions in minimizing Victoria Woodhull's presence in the movement justifiable? How much do you think this exclusion of sexual rights contributed to our continued dis-comfort with our own sexuality and role in public life? Do you believe that Americans can separate a woman's sexuality from her ability to perform in the public arena?

3. How has the #MeToo movement colored your reading of the book?

4. Do you believe Hillary Clinton's campaign was negatively impacted by her association with Bill, vis a vis his marital indiscretions? How much does attractiveness and sexual charisma come into play when considering a candidate?

5. No one knows whether Henry Ward Beecher had an affair with Victoria or not. One of her biographers, Lois Beachy Underhill, believes that he did, which I used to inform part of the urgency with which Victoria ventilates his hypocrisy. There is an element of blind rage in Victoria's actions from that time, and it is difficult to empathize with her disregard for Mrs. Tilton's feelings-after all, it was Mrs. Tilton's life that was ruined. Do you believe it is ever worth compromising one's own integrity when fighting for the greater good?

6. Victoria underwent a profound religious conversion during the three nights' incarceration at the Tombs while the libel trial was conducted. Afterward, she claimed that Jesus came to her in a vision. When asked about this, Tennessee demurred from elaborating further. What I attempted to do here was to create a situation that was so appalling, so unthinkable, that someone would turn to faith for absolution. Do you believe that such religious conversions actually happen? Or are they a knee jerk response made when one's circumstances or actions are untenable?

7. What percentage of the population (at the time) do you think believed that Spiritualism was a legitimate practice? What percentage of the population do you think still believe it? Why?

8. Tennessee's willingness to use her 'gifts' is not unlike that of a trained monkey. Yet there is no doubt that she is a seasoned pro and is perfectly comfortable 'faking it' when necessary. Does that make her a cynic, or is she still capable of idealism?

9. Why does PB Randolph never make a romantic overture towards Tennessee, at least not until it's too late? Does he have more in common with James Gordon Bennett than what first meets the eye?

10. Tennessee's romance with Bennett is fraught with challenges. Is that because he is a misogynist, or just jealous? Is he a snob or just ridiculously wealthy? Will his alcoholism prevent him from seeing the forest for the trees? Does he have a chance at redemption? And what about their friendship?

From *A Well-Dressed Lie* – the Sequel to *Naked Truth*

August, 1877
SS Lafayette, New York Harbor.

THE CRY FOR All Ashore is the moment to escape. Slipping past my mother, my sister and her children, past the ship's reporters and countless throngs waving farewell. Farewell, farewell, bon voyage!

At last, I am alone in my cabin. It is so, so hot. I open the porthole and peel off my travelling clothes. A plaque has begun along the inside of my elbow. Rummaging through the smaller trunk, the liniment and muslin are easily found. Within moments, the ointment soothes the mad itch, and I wrap the muslin over it, to shield it from it from any clothing. Slowly, I take in my surroundings. It is almost impossible not to laugh. William Vanderbilt's subsidy has afforded us every comfort indeed. First class staterooms in addition to two rooms for the servants. My ceiling is graced with plaster ornaments around the canopy of the bed, and the sink has brass taps with painted winding flowers up its side. There are two gilt mirrors and an armoire of crotch mahogany with inlaid carvings, next to a divan where I might recline should I weary of doing so on the bed.

Someone knocks on the door and I shout, "No, thank you!"

The knock continues, insistent until a steward's voice says, "Ice for madame!"

Ice to cool the water pitcher and to wrap inside a cloth and place on the back of my neck. My Chinese dragon robe is in the other trunk. After a moment, I slip it on and open the door.

Beside the steward is James Gordon Bennett. The steward hands him the ice bucket. Bennett says to me, "Miss Claflin, I presume?"

The thought of snatching the bucket and slamming the door in James Gordon Bennett's face does cross my mind, but I do not do this. Instead I murmur, "How kind. Thank you."

Swirling emotions and possibilities. Bennett comes in and closes the door behind him. The sensation that our hearts are beating in tandem is in truth the echo of my pulse moving through my body, as he takes the tea towel from one of the ice bucket's handles. He wraps some ice inside it, then whispers, "You will do it."

Slowly, he places the cloth on the back of my neck as the memory of his touch competes with the fierceness of our crushed embrace.

There is no excuse nor apology needed. His clothes and my robe are soon crumpled under foot, and the bedlinens are rendered an impossible mess. Time and tobacco, whiskey and the shadows of his tenderness envelop me and there are only the folds of his freckled body surrounding mine. My pulse and his heartbeat do indeed move together, and it seems that we are barely breathing as I feel him beginning to come while his fingers ensure that I do as well.

I slowly become aware of another knock at the door. My shout is muffled against his shoulder, "Go away, please. I'm sleeping!"

When we begin to revisit one another's body, I am longing for the time before, yet grateful for the time present, already regretful in the face of what's to come. The dusk gives way to night. Lights along the coast seem like low slung stars as the ship leaves Long Island Sound. It's somewhat overcast, and turbulent weather is expected in the morning.

"Tennie."

"Hmm." Our faces are obscured in the dimming light.

"Seeing how we left things," he moves a lock of my hair and tucks it behind my ear. "Seeing how we left things," he begins again.

"Do you mean how you left things with Miss May?"

"Yes, yes I do, and also-"

"How I left things with Billy Vanderbilt?"

"Yes, that too." He is silent for a moment and then says, "It might suit us better, were we to keep a low profile during the crossing."

"Yes, it might."

He turns up the lamp next to the bed and lies back down. I study the elaborate pleats inside the bed's canopy then lean on my elbows to survey the wreckage. Bennett's clothes are strewn across the floor, my robe is in a heap by the door. His straw boater is on the writing table and his walking stick leans against the divan. The ice bucket on the sideboard is surrounded by a polite small puddle on the marble, no doubt deliciously cool from having been chilled.

He says, "I don't enjoy the press knowing my whereabouts." To which I remain silent, so he adds, somewhat uselessly, "such as it is."

I touch the space below his ear where the sun left a mark around his collar. I trace it with my finger, "Indeed, it can put one at a disadvantage."

"Would you mind very much were I to remain in my stateroom for the most part?" He asks.

"Would you mind very much were I to take my meals in the dining room?" I reply.

He chuckles, "Not at all. Then we could seem beyond reproach and need not acknowledge or even know that we're both on board."

Ah Bennett, always one for subterfuge! Instead I say, "It's a far cry from making news and being the news at the same time, isn't it?"

"Well said." He smiles sadly and then dangles his long legs over the side of the bed. Remaining naked, I turn away as he begins the elaborate business of dressing. So that is that. We shan't be together in public, as we are both magnets in our own hellish scandals and it would be ridiculous for us to share either debacle.

Fully dressed, he stretches out against me and we exchange our hollow promises.

That evening, I am seated next to my puzzled mother in the dining room. And of course, there is Bennett, at a table full of swells, having obviously forgotten if not neglected our previous arrangement. We barely acknowledge one another, with only the slightest nod of recognition. Any association that must be kept under wraps is one that is not worth having, and I offer my best smile to the charming Spaniard who introduces himself and sits on the other side of me. Not long thereafter, another gentleman, an Englishman, a Mr. Cook, who's a good twenty years older than myself is seated to the right of my sister.

The Spaniard asks if my sister, Victoria and I won't join them for cards, which I know Bennett will not be playing. His intemperance has never served him well when the bidding goes to a certain level. A few of William Vanderbilt's thousands are still in that envelope inside my room, and it would be such a pity were I not to try and augment their quantity. Chance and money now bathe this crossing with possibility. I care not whether Bennett is on this trip or no. Whether we reconcile or not. Apart from the afternoon's dalliance I learned to live without him years ago. I sense Mr. Cook's admiring appraisal and look up from my cards. Should I wink? Better not, and I discard instead.

TO BE CONTINUED...

Made in the USA
Monee, IL
08 March 2020

22702551R00187